DUSTY ZEBRA

AND OTHER STORIES

The Complete Short Fiction of Clifford D. Simak, Volume Eleven

Introduction by David W. Wixon

OPEN ROAD
INTEGRATED MEDIA
NEW YORK

ISBN: 978-1-5040-6905-2

Published in 2021 by Open Road Integrated Media, Inc.
180 Maiden Lane
New York, NY 10038
www.openroadmedia.com

DUSTY ZEBRA

CONTENTS

CLIFFORD D. SIMAK: OPINIONS OF A RETICENT AUTHOR

"Destiny, the way you made your life, the way you shaped your living . . . the way it was meant to be, that way that it would be if you listened to the still, small voice that talked to you at the many turning points and crossroads."

—*Clifford D. Simak, in* Time and Again

Clifford D. Simak fell in love with science fiction when he was very young—and when the field itself was very young. Science fiction magazines were a new thing, and they were desperate for material. It did not take a great deal of ability to become a science fiction writer in those days, Cliff would later say—there just was very little competition. That would change quickly, of course, as the new writers learned their craft by doing.

That early science fiction, Cliff would one day tell interviewer Darrell Schweitzer, "was something new, and it was wonderful. It was not well written, but we didn't know it at the time. I realized years later that it was badly written.

But becoming better at his craft was important to Cliff Simak, and he would become known as a true craftsman. As such, he would occasionally comment on his past work (not often; for him a work, once finished, was a done thing, not to be tampered with or second-guessed).

"Madness from Mars" (1938) and "Sunspot Purge" (1940), for instance, were two stories he would later regret in public. In later years he would say that they were "truly horrible examples of an author's fumbling agony in the process of finding himself. . . . It is possible the discerning reader may discover in them some of the seeds of later writing, but I cringe at their being read." (Note: This editor and reader found something good in both.)

What other stories was Cliff particularly proud of? Or not? (Check the guide at the very end of this article to find out which collection contains each story.)

Cliff would later tell a bibliographer that he "was elated with" "Auk House" and "The Marathon Photograph," but he did not really explain his reasons for that feeling. Having worked out a story he initially called the "stamp story," Cliff would later note in a journal that it ("Leg. Forst.") turned out to be "a better story than I thought it was."

He confided in his journal that a story called "Realtor" (which would become "Carbon Copy") "writes smoothly and easily." A story that first appeared in Cliff's journal as "Rats in the Walls" turned out to be "The Big Front Yard," which he would describe as "perhaps the best example of" a first-contact story "as I have done."

On the other hand, Cliff would describe "Good Night, Mr. James" as "so vicious that it is the only one of my stories adapted to television" (I read that as a pretty vicious comment about television, too.) "It is so unlike anything I have ever written," he continued, "that at times I find myself wondering how I came to do it."

But "The Sitters," Cliff later said, was "the most tender story I have ever written." It had, he said, "that quality of compassion and human need that I have often attempted but never made come off so well." He also felt that he did a very good job with "The Thing in the Stone"; "The Ghost of a Model T," which he felt was closer to the spirit of the early 1920s "than all the books that have been devoted to it"; and "The Autumn Land." (The latter story he described as "one of the few stories I wrote on order"—Cliff was to be Guest of Honor at the 1971 World Science Fiction Convention, and the people at the Magazine of Fantasy and Science Fiction had asked him for a story they could publish in conjunction with that appearance. Cliff would later write, "No writer, of course, is ever completely satisfied with what he writes. He sees failures in it and often wishes he might have done it somewhat differently. But this, in my case, is less true of 'Autumn Land' than of any other title I've written.")

Cliff Simak considered his first novel, The Cosmic Engineers, to be a failure. He had never, at that point, written at novel length, but John W. Campbell Jr., the editor of Astounding Stories, asked him to do a story that could be serialized, and Cliff obliged.

Cliff would later tell Sam Moskowitz that he had hoped to blend some of the "grassroots" feel of ordinary people (a technique he had begun with "Rule 18" a couple of years earlier) into the book, but found that "sometimes you had to be grandiose in spite of yourself." (I will note that while this makes it sound as if the perceived failure was partially a matter of technique, it was really the case that Cliff did not meet his own expectations—he was still learning how to be the writer he wanted to be.)

Some years later a new novel presented Cliff with a bit of a quandary: Galaxy had purchased Destiny Doll with the intention of publishing it as a serial in its new magazine, Worlds of Fantasy, which was to be edited by Lester del Rey. But del Rey soon realized that the new magazine was not going to survive in the marketplace long enough to allow publication of all of Destiny Doll, and so he asked Cliff to condense it to fit into a single issue.

"So I sat for a long time," Cliff would later say, "thinking whether or not I should cut that much or give him back the money he had paid for it. I needed the money so I cut it in half and ruined it absolutely." (Cliff would find it ironic that the cut version, which appeared in what was indeed the last issue of the magazine under the title "Reality Doll," would go on to be nominated for a Nebula Award.)

The novel Out of Their Minds, Cliff would later say, "probably has the best critical potential of anything I've written," that he "got such a kick out of writing Goblin Reservation," and that Mastodonia was "plain fun to write."

But A Choice of Gods presented an entirely different situation. "At the time I wrote it," he would later say, "I wrote with hunched shoulders: I knew there was no plot line; the tale didn't have a hero; it didn't have a villain; and there was no action. . . . But it did have something to say. My agent was appalled."

But then the publisher gave Cliff "the biggest advance they had ever given me on a story."

Finally, I'd like to tell you the story Cliff told me, one day when I tried to explain to him how much his novel Way Station had meant to me when I read it as a teen.

At the time, he explained to me, the drivers at his newspaper had gone out on strike, and his guild had decided to honor the picket line. It was going to be a long strike, Cliff knew, and he only had a thousand dollars in the bank (money went a lot farther in the early 1960s, of course, but he had a family to support.)

He had been about to go out looking for a job, he told me, when he abruptly realized, late one night, that he already had a job: he had a novel already started, with about 40 pages written.

So the next morning he began a regimen of sitting down to write at 8 am, taking off an hour at noon, and then working the rest of the day.

He hated it. Writing, for Cliff Simak, did not work that way. But he was nothing if not disciplined.

He finished the book, sent it to his agent, and received, a bit later and while the strike was still going on, a check for $2500. And he won a Hugo Award for the book.

David W. Wixon

DUSTY ZEBRA

For all the mentions over the years of critical commentary of Clifford D. Simak's many writings in so-called "pastoral" settings, those stories are perhaps made all the more effective—in whatever vision they might seek to portray—when compared to those the author put into more usual urban and suburban settings. This story, which was purchased by Horace Gold, less than three weeks after Cliff mailed it in, for $320, was originally published in the September 1954 issue of Galaxy Science Fiction. It's about the most basic of human economic activities.

"Good business sense," as Joe Adams saw it; but his wife said, "What have you been up to?"

—dww

If you're human, you can't keep a thing around the house. You're always losing things and never finding them and you go charging through the place, yelling, cross-examining, blaming.

That's the way it is in all families.

Just one warning—don't try to figure out where all those things have gone or who might have taken them. If you have any notion of investigating, forget it. You'll be happier!

I'll tell you how it was with me.

I'd bought the sheet of stamps on my way home from the office so I could mail out the checks for the monthly bills. But I'd just sat down to write the checks when Marge and Lewis Shaw dropped over. I don't care much for Lewis and he barely tolerates me. But Marge and Helen are good friends, and they got to talking, and the Shaws stayed all evening.

Lewis told me about the work he was doing at his research laboratory out at the edge of town. I tried to switch him off to something else, but he kept right on. I suppose he's so interested in his work that he figures everyone else must be. But I don't know a thing about electronics and I can't tell a microgauge from a microscope.

It was a fairly dismal evening and the worst of it was that I couldn't say so. Helen would have jumped all over me for being anti-social.

So, the next evening after dinner, I went into the den to write the checks and, of course, the stamps were gone.

I had left the sheet on top of the desk and now the desk was bare except for one of the Bildo-Blocks that young Bill had outgrown several years before, but which still turn up every now and then in the most unlikely places.

I looked around the room. Just in case they might have blown off the desk, I got down on my hands and knees and searched under everything. There was no sign of the stamps.

I went into the living room, where Helen was curled up in a chair, watching television.

"I haven't seen them, Joe," she said. "They must be where you left them."

It was exactly the kind of answer I should have expected.

"Bill might know," I said.

"He's scarcely been in the house all day. When he does show up, you've got to speak to him."

"What's the matter now?"

"It's this trading business. He traded off that new belt we got him for a pair of spurs."

"I can't see anything wrong in that. When I was a kid . . ."

"It's not just the belt," she said. "He's traded everything. And the worst of it is that he always seems to get the best of it."

"The kid's smart."

"If you take that attitude, Joe . . ."

"It's not my attitude," I said. "It's the attitude of the whole business world. When Bill grows up . . ."

"When he grows up, he'll be in prison. Why, the way he trades, you'd swear he was training to be a con man!"

"All right, I'll talk to him."

I went back into the den because the atmosphere wasn't exactly as friendly as it might have been and, anyhow, I had to send out those checks, stamps or no stamps.

I got the pile of bills and the checkbook and the fountain pen out of the drawer. I reached out and picked up the Bildo-Block to put it to one side, so I'd have a good, clear space to work on. But the moment I picked it up, I knew that this thing was no Bildo-Block.

It was the right size and weight and was black and felt like plastic, except that it was slicker than any plastic I had ever felt. It felt as if it had oil on it, only it didn't.

I set it down in front of me and pulled the desk lamp closer. But there wasn't much to see. It still looked like one of the Bildo-Blocks.

Turning it around, I tried to make out what it was. On the second turn, I saw the faint oblong depression along one side of it—a very shallow depression, almost like a scratch.

I looked at it a little closer and could see that the depression was machined and that within it was a faint red line. I could have sworn the red line flickered just a little. I held it there, studying it, and could detect no further flicker. Either the red had faded or I had been seeing things to start with, for after a few seconds I couldn't be sure there was any line at all.

I figured it must have been something Bill had picked up or traded for. The kid is more than half pack-rat, but there's nothing wrong with that, nor with the trading, either, for all that Helen says. It's just the first signs of good business sense.

I put the block over to one side of the desk and went on with the checks. The next day, during lunch hour, I bought some more stamps so I could mail them. And off and on, all day, I wondered what could have happened to that sheet of stamps.

I didn't think at all about the block that had the oily feel. Possibly I would have forgotten it entirely, except that when I got home, the fountain pen was missing.

I went into the den to get the pen and there the pen was, lying on top of the desk where I'd left it the night before. Not that I remembered leaving it there. But when I saw it there, I remembered having forgotten to put it back into the drawer.

I picked it up. It wasn't any pen. It felt like a cylinder of cork, but much too heavy to be any kind of cork. Except that it was heavier and smaller, it felt something—somehow—like a fly rod.

Thinking of how a fly rod felt, I gave my hand a twitch, the way you do to cast a line, and suddenly it seemed to be, in fact, a fly rod. It apparently had been telescoped and now it came untelescoped and lengthened out into what might have been a rod. But the funny thing about it was that it went out only about four feet and then disappeared into thin air.

Instinctively, I brought it up and back to free the tip from wherever it might be. I felt the slack take up against a sudden weight and I knew I had something on the other end of it. Just like a fish feels, only it wasn't fighting.

Then, as quickly as it happened, it unhappened. I felt the tension snap off and the weight at the other end was gone and the rod had telescoped again and I held in my hand the thing that looked like a fountain pen.

* * *

I laid it down carefully on the desk, being very certain to make no more casting motions, and it wasn't until then that I saw my hand was shaking.

I sat down, goggling at the thing that looked like the missing fountain pen and the other thing that looked like a Bildo-Block.

And it was then, while I was looking at the two of them, that I saw, out of the corner of my eye, the little white dot in the center of the desk.

It was on the exact spot where the bogus pen had lain and more than likely, I imagined, the exact spot where I'd found the Bildo-Block the night before. It was about a quarter of an inch in diameter and it looked like ivory.

I put out my thumb and rubbed it vigorously, but the dot would not rub off. I closed my eyes so the dot would have a chance to go away, and then opened them again, real quick, to surprise it if it hadn't. It still was there.

I bent over the desk to examine it. I could see it was inlaid in the wood, and an excellent job of inlaying, too. I couldn't find even the faintest line of division between the wood and the dot.

It hadn't been there before; I was sure of that. If it had been, I would have noticed it. What's more, Helen would have noticed it, for she's hell on dirt and forever after things with a dusting cloth. And to cinch the fact that it had not been there before, no one I've ever heard of sold desks with single inlaid ivory dots.

And no one sold a thing that looked like a fountain pen but could become a fly rod, the business end of which disappeared and hooked a thing you couldn't even see—and which, the next time, might bring in whatever it had caught instead of losing it.

Helen called to me from the living room. "Joe."

"Yeah. What is it?"

"Did you talk to Bill?"

"Bill? About what?"

"About the trading."

"No. I guess I forgot."

"Well, you'll have to. He's at it again. He traded Jimmy out of that new bicycle. Gave him a lot of junk. I made him give back the bicycle."

"I'll have a talk with him," I promised again.

But I'm afraid I wasn't paying as close attention to the ethics of the situation as I should have been.

You couldn't keep a thing around the house. You were always losing this or that. You knew just where you'd put it and you were sure it was there and then, when you went to look for it, it had disappeared.

It was happening everywhere—things being lost and never turning up.

But other things weren't left in their places—at least not that you heard about.

Although maybe there had been times when things had been left that a man might pick up and examine and not know what they were and puzzle over, then toss in a corner somewhere and forget.

Maybe, I thought, the junkyards of the world were loaded with outlandish blocks and crazy fishing rods.

I got up and went into the living room, where Helen had turned on the television set.

She must have seen that something had me upset, because she asked, "What's the matter now?"

"I can't find the fountain pen."

She laughed at me. "Honestly, Joe, you're the limit. You're always losing things."

That night, I lay awake after Helen went to sleep and all I could think about was the dot upon the desk. A dot, perhaps, that said: Put it right here, pardner, and we will make a swap.

And, thinking of it, I wondered what would happen if someone moved the desk.

I lay there for a long time, trying not to worry, trying to tell myself it didn't matter, that I was insane to think what I was thinking.

But I couldn't get it out of my mind.

So I finally got up and sneaked out of the bedroom and, feeling like a thief in my own house, headed for the den.

I closed the door, turned on the desk lamp and took a quick look to see if the dot was still there.

It was.

I opened the desk drawer and hunted for a pencil and couldn't find one, but I finally found one of Bill's crayons. I got down on my knees and carefully marked the floor around the desk legs, so that, if the desk were moved, I could put it back again.

Then, pretending I had no particular purpose for doing it, I laid the crayon precisely on the dot.

In the morning, I sneaked a look into the den and the crayon was still there. I went to work a little easier in my mind, for by then I'd managed to convince myself that it was all imagination.

But that evening, after dinner, I went back into the den and the crayon was gone.

In its place was a triangular contraption with what appeared to be lenses set in each angle, and with a framework of some sort of metal, holding in place what apparently was a suction cup in the center of the triangle.

While I was looking at it, Helen came to the door. "Marge and I are going to see a movie," she said. "Why don't you go over and have a beer with Lewis?"

"With that stuffed shirt?"

"What's the matter with Lewis?"

"Nothing, I guess." I didn't feel up to a family row right then.

"What's that you've got?" she asked.

"I don't know. Just something I found."

"Well, don't you start bringing home all sorts of junk, the way Bill does. One of you is enough to clutter up the house."

I sat there, looking at the triangle, and the only thing I could figure out was that it might be a pair of glasses. The suction cup in the center might hold it on the wearer's face and, while that might seem a funny way to wear a pair of glasses, it made sense when you thought about it. But if that were true, it meant that the wearer had three eyes, set in a triangle in his face.

I sat around for quite a while after Helen left, doing a lot of thinking. And what I was thinking was that even if I didn't care too much about Lewis, he was the only man I knew who might be able to help me out.

So I put the bogus fountain pen and the three-eyed glasses in the drawer and put the counterfeit Bildo-Block in my pocket and went across the street.

Lewis had a bunch of blueprints spread out on the kitchen table, and he started to explain them to me. I did the best I could to act as if I understood them. Actually, I didn't know head nor tail of it.

Finally, I was able to get a word in edgewise and I pulled the block out of my pocket and put it on the table.

"What is that?" I asked.

I expected him to say right off it was just a child's block. But he didn't. There must have been something about it to tip him off that it wasn't just a simple block. That comes, of course, of having a technical education.

Lewis picked the block up and turned it around in his fingers. "What's it made of?" he asked me, sounding excited.

I shook my head. "I don't know what it is or what it's made of or anything about it. I just found it."

"This is something I've never seen before." Then he spotted the depression in one side of it and I could see I had him hooked. "Let me take it down to the shop. We'll see what we can learn."

I knew what he was after, of course. If the block was something new, he wanted a chance to go over it—but that didn't bother me any. I had a hunch he wouldn't find out too much about it.

We had a couple more beers and I went home. I hunted up an old pair of spectacles and put them on the desk right over the dot.

I was listening to the news when Helen came in. She said she was glad I'd spent the evening with Lewis, that I should try to get to know him better and that, once I got to know him better, I might like him. She said, since she and Marge were such good friends, it was a shame Lewis and I didn't hit it off.

"Maybe we will," I said and let it go at that.

The next afternoon, Lewis called me at the office.

"Where'd you get that thing?" he asked.

"Found it," I said.

"Have any idea what it is?"

"Nope," I told him cheerfully. "That's why I gave it to you."

"It's powered in some way and it's meant to measure something. That depression in the side must be a gauge. Color seems to be used as an indicator. At any rate, the color line in the depression keeps changing all the time. Not much, but enough so you can say there's some change."

"Next thing is to find out what it's measuring."

"Joe, do you know where you can get another of them?"

"No, I don't."

"It's this way," he said. "We'd like to get into this one, to see what makes it tick, but we can't find any way to open it. We could break into it, probably, but we're afraid to do that. We might damage it. Or it might explode. If we had another . . ."

"Sorry, Lewis. I don't know where to get another."

He had to let it go at that.

I went home that evening grinning to myself, thinking about Lewis. The guy was fit to be tied. He wouldn't sleep until he found out what the thing was, now that he'd started on it. It probably would keep him out of my hair for a week or so.

I went into the den. The glasses still were on the desk. I stood there for a moment, looking at them, wondering what was wrong. Then I saw that the lenses had a pinkish shade.

I picked them up, noticing that the lenses had been replaced by the kind in the triangular pair I had found there the night before.

Just then, Helen came into the room and I could tell, even before she spoke, that she had been waiting for me.

"Joe Adams," she demanded, "what have you been up to?"

"Not a thing," I told her.

"Marge says you got Lewis all upset."

"It doesn't take a lot to upset him."

"There's something going on," she insisted, "and I want to know what it is."

I knew I was licked. "I've been trading."

"Trading! After all I've said about Bill!"

"But this is different."

"Trading is trading," she said flatly.

Bill came in the front door, but he must have heard his mother say "trading," for he ducked out again. I yelled for him to come back.

"I want both of you to sit down and listen to me," I said. "You can ask questions and offer suggestions and give me hell after I'm through."

So we sat down, all three of us, and had a family powwow.

It took quite a bit to make Helen believe what I had to tell, but I pointed out the dot in the desk and showed them the triangular glasses and the pair of glasses that had been refitted with the pink lenses and sent back to me. By that time, she was ready to admit there was something going on. Even so, she was fairly well burned up at me for marking up the floor around the desk legs.

I didn't show either her or Bill the pen that was a fishing rod, for I was scared of that. Flourish it around a bit and there was no telling what would happen.

Bill was interested and excited, of course. This was trading, which was right down his alley.

I cautioned both of them not to say a word about it. Bill wouldn't, for he was hell on secrets and special codes. But bright and early in the morning, Helen would probably swear Marge to secrecy, then tell her all about it and there wasn't a thing that I could do or say to stop her.

Bill wanted to put the pink-lensed spectacles on right away, to see how they were different from any other kind. I wouldn't let him. I wanted to put those specs on myself, but I was afraid to, if you want to know the truth.

When Helen went out to the kitchen to get dinner, Bill and I held a strategy session. For a ten-year-old, Bill had a lot of good ideas. We agreed that we ought to get some system into the trading, because, as Bill pointed out, the idea of swapping sight unseen was a risky sort of business. A fellow ought to have some say in what he was getting in return.

But to arrive at an understanding with whoever we were trading with meant that we'd have to set up some sort of communication system. And how do you communicate with someone you don't know the first thing about, except that perhaps it has three eyes?

Then Bill hit upon what seemed a right idea. What we needed, he said, was a catalogue. If you were going to trade with someone, the logical first step would be to let them know what you had to trade.

To be worth anything in such a circumstance, it would have to be an illustrated catalogue. And even then it might be worthless, for how could we be sure that the Trader on the other side of the desk would know what a picture was? Maybe he'd never seen a picture before. Maybe he saw differently—not so much physically, although that was possible, too, but from a different viewpoint and with totally alien concepts.

But it was the only thing we had to go on, so we settled down to work up a catalogue. Bill thought we should draw one, but neither of us was any good at drawing. I suggested illustrations from magazines. But that wasn't too hot an idea, either, for pictures of items in the magazine ads are usually all prettied up, designed to catch the eye.

Then Bill had a top-notch idea. "You know that kid dictionary Aunt Ethel gave me? Why don't we send that to them? It's got a lot of pictures and not much reading in it, and that's important. The reading might confuse them."

So we went into his room and started looking through all the junk he had, searching for the dictionary. But we ran across one of the old ABC books he'd had when he was just a toddler and decided it was even better than the dictionary. It had good clear pictures and almost no reading at all. You know the kind of book I mean—A for apple, B for ball and so forth.

We took the book into the den and put it on the desk, centering it on the dot, then went out to dinner.

In the morning, the book had disappeared and that was a little odd. Up until then, nothing had disappeared from the desk until later in the day.

Early that afternoon, Lewis called me up. "I'm coming down to see you, Joe. Is there a bar handy where the two of us can be alone?"

I told him there was one only a block from me and said I'd meet him there.

I got a few things cleared away, then left the office, figuring I'd go over to the bar and have a quick one before Lewis showed up.

I don't know how he did it, but he was there ahead of me, back in a corner booth. He must have broken every traffic regulation on the books.

He had a couple of drinks waiting for us and was all huddled over, like a conspirator. He was a bit out of breath, as he had every right to be.

"Marge told me," he said.

"I suspected she would."

"There could be a mint in it, Joe!"

"That's what I thought, too. That's why I'm willing to give you ten per cent . . ."

"Now look here," squawked Lewis. "You can't pull a deal like that. I wouldn't touch it for less than fifty."

"I'm letting you in on it," I said, "because you're a neighbor. I don't know beans about this technical business. I'm getting stuff I don't understand and I need some help to find out what it is, but I can always go to someone else . . ."

It took us three drinks to get the details settled—thirty-five per cent for him, sixty-five for me.

"Now that that's settled," I said, "suppose you tell me what you found."

"Found?"

"That block I gave you. You wouldn't have torn down here and had the drinks all set up and waiting if you hadn't found something."

"Well, as a matter of fact . . ."

"Now just a minute," I warned him. "We're going to put this in the contract—any failure to provide full and complete analysis . . ."

"What contract?"

"We're going to have a contract drawn up, so either of us can sue the other within an inch of his life for breaking it."

Which is a hell of a way to start out a business venture, but it's the only way to handle a slippery little skate like Lewis.

So he told me what he'd found. "It's an emotions gauge. That's awkward terminology, I know, but it's the best I can think of."

"What does it do?"

"It tells how happy you are or how sad or how much you hate someone."

"Oh, great," I said, disappointed. "What good is a thing like that? I don't need a gauge to tell me if I'm sore or glad or anything."

He waxed practically eloquent. "Don't you see what an instrument like that would mean to psychiatrists? It would tell more about patients than they'd ever be willing to tell about themselves. It could be used in mental institutions and it might be important in gauging reactions for the entertainment business, politics, law-enforcement and Lord knows what else."

"No kidding! Then let's start marketing!"

"The only thing is . . ."

"Yes?"

"We can't manufacture them," he said frustratedly. "We haven't got the materials and we don't know how they're made. You'll have to trade for them."

"I can't. Not right away, that is. First I've got to be able to make the Traders understand what I want, and then I'll have to find out what they're willing to trade them for."

"You have some other stuff?"

"A few things."

"You better turn them over to me."

"Some that could be dangerous. Anyhow, it all belongs to me. I'll give you what I want, when I want and . . ."

We were off again.

We finally wound up by adjourning to an attorney's office. We wrote up a contract that is probably one of the legal curiosities of all time.

I'm convinced the attorney thought, and still thinks, both of us are crazy, but that's the least of my worries now.

The contract said I was to turn over to Lewis, for his determination of its technical and merchandisable nature, at least 90 per cent of certain items, the source of which I alone controlled, and with the further understanding that said source was to remain at all times under my exclusive control. The other 10 per cent might, without prejudice, be withheld from his examination, with the party of the first part having sole authority to make determination of which items should constitute the withheld 10 per cent.

Upon the 90 per cent of the items supplied him, the party of the second part was to make a detailed analysis, in writing, accompanied by such explanatory material as was necessary to the complete understanding of the party of the first part, within no more than three months after receipt, at the end of which time the items reverted solely to the ownership of the party of the first part. Except that such period of examination and determination might be extended, under a mutual agreement made in writing, for any stated time.

Under no circumstances should the party of the second part conceal from the party of the first part any findings he might have made upon any of the items covered by the agreement, and that such concealment, should it occur, should be considered sufficient cause for action for the recovery of damages. That under certain conditions where some of the items might be found to be manufacturable, they could be manufactured under the terms of clauses A, B and C, section XII of this agreement.

Provisions for a sales organization to market any of said items shall be set up and made a part of this agreement. That any proceeds from such sales shall be divided as follows: 65 per cent to the party of the first part (me, in case you've gotten lost, which is understandable), and 35 per cent to the party of the second part (Lewis); costs to be apportioned accordingly.

There were a lot more details, of course, but that gives you an idea.

We got home from the attorney's office, without either of us knifing the other, and found Marge over at my place. Lewis went in with me to have a look at the desk.

Apparently the Trader had received the ABC book all right and had been able to understand why it was sent, for there, lying on the desk, was a picture cut out of the book. Well, not cut out, exactly—it looked more as though it had been burned out.

The picture on the desk was Z for zebra.

Lewis stared worriedly at it. "Now we're really in a fix."

"Yeah," I admitted. "I don't know what the market price is, but they can't be cheap."

"Figure it out—expedition, safari, cages, ship, rail, fodder, keeper. You think we can switch him to something else?"

"I don't see how. He's put in his order."

Bill came wandering in and wanted to know what was up. When I glumly told him, he said cheerfully, "Aw, that's the whole trick in trading, Pop. If you got a bum jackknife you want to trade, you unload it on somebody who doesn't know what a good knife is like."

Lewis didn't get it, but I did. "That's right! He doesn't know a zebra is an animal, or, if he does, how big it is!"

"Sure," Bill said confidently. "All he saw was a picture."

It was five o'clock then, but the three of us went uptown and shopped. Bill found a cheap bracelet charm about the size of the drawing in the book. When it comes to junk like that, my kid knows just where it's sold and how much it costs. I considered making him a junior partner in charge of such emergencies, with about 10 per cent share or so—out of Lewis's 35 per cent, of course—but I was sure Lewis wouldn't hold still for that. I decided instead to give Bill a dollar a week allowance, said compensation to commence immediately upon our showing a profit.

Well, we had Z for zebra—provided the Trader was satisfied with a little piece of costume jewelry. It was lucky, I thought, that it hadn't been Z for zephyr.

The rest of the alphabet was easy, yet I couldn't help but kick myself over all the time we were wasting. Of all the unworthy catalogues we might have sent, that ABC book was the worst. But until the Trader had run through the whole list, I was afraid to send another for fear of confusing him.

So I sent him an apple and a ball and a small doll for a girl and a toy cat and toy dog, and so on, and then I lay awake nights wondering what the Trader would make of them. I could picture him trying to learn the use of a rubber doll or cat.

I'd given Lewis the two pairs of glasses, but had held back the fountain-pen fishing rod, for I was still scared of that one. He had turned over the emotion gauge to a psychiatrist to try out in his practice as a sort of field test.

Marge and Helen, knowing that Lewis and I had entered into some kind of partnership, were practically inseparable now. Helen kept telling me how glad she was that I had finally recognized what a sterling fellow Lewis was. I suppose Lewis heard the same thing about me from Marge.

Bill went around practically busting to do some bragging. But Bill is a great little businessman and he kept his mouth shut. I had told him about the allowance, of course.

Lewis was all for trying to ask the Trader for a few more of the emotion gauges. He had a draftsman at the plant draw up a picture of the gauge and he wanted me to send it through to indicate that we were interested in it.

But I told him not to try to rush things. While the emotion gauge might be a good deal, we should sample what the Trader had to offer before we made up our minds.

The Trader, apparently certain now that someone was cooperating with him, had dropped his once-a-day trade schedule and was open for business around the clock. After he had run through the list in the ABC book, he sent back a couple of blank pages from the book with very crude drawings on them—drawings that looked as if they had been made with crumbly charcoal. Lewis drew a series of pictures, showing how a pencil worked, and we sent the Trader a ream of paper and a gross of sharpened pencils, then sat back to wait.

We waited a week and were getting sort of edgy, when back came the entire ream of paper, with each sheet covered on both sides with all kinds of drawings. So we sent him a mail-order catalogue, figuring that would hold him for a while, and settled down to try to puzzle out the drawings he had made.

There wasn't a single thing that made any sense at all—not even to Lewis. He'd study some of the drawings, then pace up and down the room, pulling his hair and twitching his ears.

Then he'd study the drawings some more.

To me, it all looked plain Rube Goldbergish.

Finally, we figured we might as well forget about the catalogue idea, for the time being at least, and we started feeding all sorts of stuff through the desk—scissors, dishes, shoes, jackknives, mucilage, cigars, paper clips, erasers, spoons—almost anything that was handy. It wasn't the scientific way, I know, but we didn't have the time to get very methodical about it and, until we had a chance to work out a more sensible program, we figured we might as well try the shotgun method.

And the Trader started shooting things back at us. We'd sit for hours and feed stuff through to him and then he'd shoot stuff back at us and we had the damnedest pile of junk heaped all over the place you ever laid eyes on.

We rigged up a movie camera and took a lot of film of the spot on the desk where the exchange was going on. We spent a lot of time viewing that film, slowing it down and even stopping it, but it didn't tell us anything at all. When the stuff disappeared or appeared, it just disappeared or appeared. One frame it would be there, the next frame it would be gone.

Lewis cancelled all his other work and used the lab for nothing but trying to puzzle out the gadgets that we got. Most of them we couldn't crack at all. I imagine they were useful in some way, but we never managed to learn how.

There was the perfume bottle, for example. That is what we called it, anyhow. But there was a suspicion in our minds that the perfume was simply a secondary effect, that the so-called bottle was designed for some other purpose entirely.

Lewis and his boys were studying it down at the lab, trying to make out some rhyme or reason for it, and somehow they turned it on. They worked for three days, the last two in gas masks, trying to turn it off again. When the smell got so bad that people began calling the police, we took the contraption out into the country and buried it. Within a few days, all the vegetation in the area was dead. All the rest of the summer, the boys from the agricultural department at the university ran around, practically frothing at the mouth, trying to find the cause.

There was the thing that might have been a clock of some sort, although it might just as easily have been something else. If it was a clock, the Trader had a time system that would drive you nuts, for it would measure the minutes or hours or whatever they were like lightning for a while, then barely move for an entire day.

And there was the one you'd point at something and press a certain spot on it—not a button or a knob or anything as crass and mechanical as that, just a certain spot—and there'd be just a big blank spot in the landscape. But when you stopped pressing, the landscape would come back again, unchanged. We filed it away in the darkest corner of the laboratory safe, with a big red tag on it marked: Dangerous! Don't Monkey with This!

But most of the items we just drew blanks on. And it kept coming all the time. I piled the garage full of it and started dumping it in the basement. Some of it I was scared of and hauled out to the dump.

In the meantime, Lewis was having trouble with the emotion gauge. "It works," he said. "The psychiatrist I gave it to to try out is enthusiastic about it. But it seems almost impossible to get it on the market."

"If it works," I objected, handing him a can of beer, "it ought to sell."

"In any other field, it might, but you don't handle merchandise that way in the medical field. Before you can put something on the market, you have to have it nailed down with blueprints and theory and field tests and such. And we can't. We don't know how it works. We don't know why it works. Until we do, no reputable medical supply house will take it on, no approved medical journal will advertise it, no practitioner will use it."

"Then I guess it's out." I felt fairly blue about it, because it was the only thing we had that we knew how to use.

Lewis nodded and drank his beer and was glummer than ever.

Looking back on it, it's funny how we found the gadget that made us all the money. Actually, it wasn't Lewis but Helen who found it.

Helen is a good housewife. She's always going after things with the vacuum and the dustcloth and she washes the woodwork so often and so furiously that we have to paint it every year.

One night, we were sitting in the living room, watching television.

"Joe," she asked me, "did you dust the den?"

"Dust the den? What would I want to do that for?"

"Well, someone did. Maybe it was Bill."

"Bill wouldn't be caught dead with a dustcloth in his mitt."

"I can't understand it, Joe," she said. "I went in there to dust it and it was absolutely clean. Everything just shone."

Sgt. Friday was trying to get the facts out of someone and his sidekick was complaining about some relatives that had come to visit and I didn't pay much attention at the time.

But the next day, I got to thinking about it and I couldn't get it off my mind. I certainly hadn't dusted the den and it was a cinch Bill hadn't, yet someone had if Helen was ready to admit it was clean.

So, that evening, I went out into the street with a pail and shoveled up a pailful of dirt and brought it in the house.

Helen caught me as I was coming in the door. "What do you think you're doing with that?"

"Experimenting," I told her.

"Do it in the garage."

"It isn't possible," I argued. "I have to find out who's been dusting the den."

I knew that, if my hunch failed, I'd have a lot to answer for when she followed me and stood in the doorway, ready to pounce.

There was a bunch of junk from the Trader standing on the desk and a lot more of it in one corner. I cleared off the desk and that was when Bill came in.

"What you doing, Dad?" he asked.

"Your father's gone insane," Helen explained quietly.

They stood there, watching me, while I took a handful of dirt and sprinkled it on the desk top.

It stayed there for just an instant—and then it was gone. The top of the desk was spotless.

"Bill," I said, "take one of those gadgets out to the garage."

"Which one?"

"It doesn't matter."

So he took one and I spread another handful of dirt and, in a second, it was gone. Bill was back by that time and I sent him out with another gadget.

We kept on like that for quite a while and Bill was beginning to get disgusted with me. But finally I sprinkled the dirt and it stayed.

"Bill," I said, "you remember the last thing you took out?"

"Sure."

"Well, go out and bring it back again."

He got it and, as soon as he reached the door of the den, the dirt disappeared.

"Well, that's it," I said.

"That's what?" asked Helen.

I pointed to the contraption Bill had in his hand. "That. Throw away your vacuum cleaner. Burn up the dustcloth. Heave out the mop. Just have one of those in the house and . . ."

She threw herself into my arms.

"Oh, Joe!"

We danced a jig, the two of us.

Then I sat around for a while, kicking myself for tying up with Lewis, wondering if maybe there wasn't some way I could break the contract now that I had found something without any help from him. But I remembered all those clauses we had written in. It wouldn't have been any use, anyhow, for Helen was already across the street, telling Marge about it.

So I phoned Lewis at the lab and he came tearing over.

We ran field tests.

The living room was spotless from Bill just having walked through it, carrying the gadget, and the garage, where he had taken it momentarily, was spick and span. While we didn't check it, I imagine that an area paralleling the path he had taken from the front door to the garage was the only place outdoors that didn't have a speck of dust upon it.

We took the gadget down in the basement and cleaned that up. We sneaked over to a neighbor's back yard, where we knew there was a lot of cement dust, held the gadget over it and in an instant there wasn't any cement dust. There were just a few pebbles left and the pebbles, I suppose, you couldn't rightly classify as dust.

We didn't need to know any more.

Back at the house, I broke open a bottle of Scotch I'd been saving, while Lewis sat down at the kitchen table and drew a sketch of the gadget.

We had a drink, then went into the den and put the drawing on the desk. The drawing disappeared and we waited. In a few minutes, another one of the gadgets appeared. We waited for a while and nothing happened.

"We've got to let him know we want a lot of them," I said.

"There's no way we can," said Lewis. "We don't know his mathematical symbols, he doesn't know ours, and there's no surefire way to teach him. He doesn't know a single word of our language and we don't know a word of his."

We went back to the kitchen and had another drink.

Lewis sat down and drew a row of the gadgets across a sheet of paper, then sketched in representations of others behind them so that, when you looked at it, you could see that there were hundreds of them.

We sent that through.

Fourteen gadgets came back—the exact number Lewis had sketched in the first row.

Apparently the Trader had no idea of perspective. The lines that Lewis had drawn to represent the other gadgets behind the first row didn't mean a thing to him.

We went back to the kitchen and had a few more drinks.

"We'll need thousands of the things," said Lewis, holding his head in his hands. "I can't sit here day and night, drawing them."

"You may have to do that," I said, enjoying myself.

"There must be another way."

"Why not draw a bunch of them, then mimeograph the drawing?" I suggested. "We could send the mimeographed sheets through to him in bundles."

I hated to say it, because I was still enamored of the idea of sticking Lewis somewhere off in a corner, sentenced to a lifetime of drawing the same thing over and over.

"That might work," said Lewis, brightening annoyingly. "It's just simple enough . . ."

"Practical is the word," I snapped. "If it were simple, you'd have thought of it."

"I leave things like that to detail men."

"You'd better!"

It took a while and a whole bottle before we calmed down.

Next day, we bought a mimeograph machine and Lewis drew a stencil with twenty-five of the gadgets on it. We ran through a hundred sheets and sent them through the desk.

It worked—we were busy for several hours, getting those gadgets out of the way as they poured through to us.

I'm afraid we never stopped to think about what the Trader might want in return for the dust-collectors. We were so excited that we forgot, for the moment, that this was a commercial proposition and not just something gratis.

But the next afternoon, back came the mimeographed sheets we'd sent through and, on the reverse side of each of them, the Trader had drawn twenty-five representations of the zebra on the bracelet charm.

And there we were, faced with the necessity of getting together, pronto, twenty-five hundred of those silly zebras.

I tore down to the store where I'd gotten the bracelet, but all they had in stock were two dozen of the things. They said they didn't think they could order any more. The number, they said, had been discontinued.

The name of the company that made them was stamped on the inside of the bracelet and, as soon as I got home, I put in a long distance call.

I finally got hold of the production manager. "You know those bracelets you put out?"

"We put out millions of 'em. Which one are you talking about?"

"The one with the zebra on it."

He thought a moment. "Yeah, we did. Quite a while ago. We don't make them any more. In this business . . ."

"I need at least twenty-five hundred of them."

"Twenty-five hundred bracelets?"

"No, just the zebras."

"Look, is this a gag?"

"It's no gag, mister," I said. "I need those zebras. I'm willing to pay for them."

"We haven't any in stock."

"Couldn't you make them?"

"Not just twenty-five hundred of them. Wouldn't be worth it to put through a special order for so few. If it was fifty thousand, say, we might consider it."

"All right, then," I said. "How much for fifty thousand?"

He named a price and we haggled some, but I was in no position to do much bargaining. We finally agreed on a price I knew was way too high, considering the fact that the entire bracelet, with the zebra and a lot of other junk, had only retailed at 39 cents.

"And hold the order open," I told him. "We might want more of them."

"Okay," he said. "Just one thing—would you mind telling me what you want with fifty thousand zebras?"

"Yes, I would," I said and hung up.

I suppose he thought I was off my rocker, but who cared what he thought?

It took ten days to get that shipment of fifty thousand zebras and I sweated out every minute of it. Then there was the job of getting them under cover when it came and, in case you don't know, fifty thousand zebras, even when they're only bracelet charms, take up room.

But first I took out twenty-five hundred and sent them through the desk.

For the ten days since we'd gotten the dust-collectors, we'd sent nothing through and there had been no sign from the Trader that he might be getting impatient. I wouldn't have blamed him a bit if he'd done something, like sending through his equivalent of a bomb, to express his dissatisfaction at our slow delivery. I've often wondered what he thought of the long delay—if he hadn't suspected we were reneging on the bargain.

All this time, I had been smoking too much and gnawing my fingernails and I'd figured that Lewis was just as busy seeing what could be done about marketing the dusters.

But when I mentioned it to him, he just looked blank. "You know, Joe, I've been doing a lot of worrying."

"We haven't a thing to worry about now," I said, "except getting these things sold."

"But the dust must go somewhere," he fretted.

"The dust?"

"Sure, the dust these things collect. Remember we picked up an entire pile of cement dust? What I want to know is where it all went. The gadget itself isn't big enough to hold it. It isn't big enough to hold even a week's collection of dust from the average house. That's what worries me—where does it go?"

"I don't care where. It goes, doesn't it?"

"That's the pragmatic view," he said scornfully.

It turned out that Lewis hadn't done a thing about marketing, so I got busy.

But I ran into the same trouble we'd had trying to sell the emotion gauge.

The dust collector wasn't patented and it didn't have a brand name. There was no fancy label stuck on it and it didn't bear a manufacturer's imprint. And when anybody asked me how it worked, I couldn't answer.

One wholesaler did make me a ridiculous offer. I laughed in his face and walked out.

That night, Lewis and I sat around the kitchen table, drinking beer, and neither of us too happy. I could see a lot of trouble ahead in getting the gadgets sold. Lewis, it seemed, was still worrying about what happened to the dust.

He had taken one of the dust-collectors apart and the only thing he could find out about it was that there was some feeble force-field operating inside of it—feeble yet strong enough to play hell with the electrical circuits and fancy metering machinery he has at the lab. As soon as he found out what was happening, he slapped the cover back on as quick as he could and then everything was all right. The cover was a shield against the force-field.

"That dust must be getting thrown into another dimension," he told me, looking like a hound dog that had lost a coon track.

"Maybe not. It could be winding up in one of those dust clouds way out in space."

He shook his head.

"You can't tell me," I said, "that the Trader is crazy enough to sell us a gadget that will throw dust back into his face."

"You miss the point entirely. The Trader is operating from another dimension. He must be. And if there are two dimensions, his and ours, there may be others. The Trader must have used these dust-collectors himself—not for the same purpose we intend, perhaps, but they get rid of something that he doesn't want around. So, necessarily, they'd have to be rigged to get rid of it in a dimension other than his."

We sat there drinking beer and I started turning over that business about different dimensions in my head. I couldn't grasp the concept. Maybe Lewis was right about me being a pragmatist. If you can't see it or touch it or even guess what it would be like, how can you believe there might be another dimension? I couldn't.

So I started to talk about marketing the dust collector and before Lewis went home that night, we'd decided that the only thing left to do was sell it door to door. We even agreed to charge $12.50 for it. The zebras figured out to four cents each and we would pay our salesmen ten per cent commission, which would leave us a profit of $11.21 apiece.

I put an ad in the paper for salesmen and the next day we had several applicants. We started them out on a trial run.

Those gadgets sold like hotcakes and we knew we were in!

I quit my job and settled down to handling the sales end, while Lewis went back to the lab and started going through the pile of junk we had gotten from the Trader.

There are a lot of headaches running a sales campaign. You have to map out territories for your salesmen, get clearance from Better Business Bureaus, bail out your men if they're thrown in the clink for running afoul of some obscure village ordinance. There are more worrisome angles to it than you can ever imagine.

But in a couple of months' time, things were running pretty smoothly. We had the state well covered and were branching out into others. I had ordered another fifty thousand zebras and told them to expect re-orders—and the desk top was a busy place. It got to a point, finally, where I had to hire three men full time, paying them plenty not to talk, to man that desk top 24 hours a day. We'd send through zebras for eight hours, then take away dust gadgets for eight hours, then feed through zebras for another eight.

If the Trader had any qualms about what was happening, he gave no sign of it. He seemed perfectly happy to send us dust collectors so long as we sent him zebras.

The neighbors were curious and somewhat upset at first, but finally they got used to it. If I could have moved to some other location, I would have, for the house was more an office than a home and we had practically no family life at all. But if we wanted to stay in business, we had to stay right where we were because it was the only place we had contact with the Trader.

The money kept rolling in and I turned the management of it over to Helen and Marge. The income tax boys gave us a rough time when we didn't show any manufacturing expenses, but since we weren't inclined to argue over what we had to pay, they couldn't do anything about it.

Lewis was wearing himself down to a nubbin at the lab, but he wasn't finding anything that we could use.

But he still did some worrying now and then about where all that dust was going. And he was right, probably for the first time in his life.

* * *

One afternoon, a couple of years after we'd started selling the dust collectors, I had been uptown to attend to some banking difficulties that Helen and Marge had gotten all bollixed up. I'd no more than pulled into the driveway when Helen came busting out of the house. She was covered with dust, her face streaked with it, and she was the maddest-looking woman I have ever seen.

"You've got to do something about it, Joe!" she shrieked.

"About what?"

"The dust! It's pouring into the house!"

"Where is it pouring from?"

"From everywhere!"

I could see she'd opened all the windows and there was dust pouring out of them, almost like a smoke cloud. I got out of the car and took a quick look up and down the street. Every house in the block had its windows open and there was dust coming out of all of them and the neighborhood was boiling with angry, screaming women.

"Where's Bill?" I asked.

"Out back."

I ran around the house and called him and he came running.

Marge had come across the street and, if anything, she was about six degrees sorer about all the dust than Helen was.

"Get in the car," I said.

"Where are we going?" Marge demanded.

"Out to pick up Lewis."

I must have sounded like nothing to trifle with, for they piled in and I got out of there as fast as the car would take us.

The homes and factories and stores that had bought the gadget were gushing so much dust, visibility wouldn't be worth a damn before long.

I had to wade through about two feet of dust on the laboratory floor to get to Lewis's office and hold a handkerchief over my nose to keep from suffocating.

* * *

Inside the car, we got our faces wiped off and most of the dust hacked out of our throats. I could see then that Lewis was about three shades paler than usual, although, to tell the truth, he always was a pasty-looking creature.

"It's the creatures from that third dimension," he said anxiously. "The place where we were sending all the dust. They got sick and tired of having it pour in on them and they got it figured out and now they're firing the dust right back at us."

"Now calm down. We're just jumping to the conclusion that this was caused by our gadget."

"I checked, Joe. It was. The dust is coming out in jets from every single place where we sent it through. No place else."

"Then all we have to do is fire it back at them."

He shook his head. "Not a chance. The gadget works one way now—from them to us." He coughed and looked wildly at me. "Think of it! A couple of million of those gadgets, picking up dust from a couple of million homes, stores and factories—some of them operating for two whole years! Joe, what are we going to do?"

"We're going to hole up somewhere till this—well, blows over."

Being of a nasty legal turn of mind, he probably foresaw even then the countless lawsuits that would avalanche on us. Personally, I was more scared of being mobbed by angry women.

But that's all past history. We hid out till people had quieted down and then began trying to settle the suits out of court. We had a lot of money and were able to pay off most of them. The judgements against us still outstanding don't amount to more than a few hundred thousand. We could wipe that out pretty quickly if we'd just hit on something else as profitable as the cleaning gadget.

Lewis is working hard at it, but he isn't having any luck. And the Trader is gone now. As soon as we dared come home, I went into the house and had a look at the desk. The inlaid dot was gone. I tried putting something where it had been, but nothing happened.

What scared the Trader off? I'd give a lot to know. Meanwhile, there are some commercial prospects.

The rose-tinted glasses, for instance, that we call the Happiness Lenses. Put them on and you're happy as a clam. Almost every person on the face of the Earth would like a pair of them, so they could forget their troubles for a while. They would probably play hob with the liquor business.

The trouble is that we don't know how to make them and, now that the Trader's gone, we can't swap for them.

But there's one thing that keeps worrying me. I know I shouldn't let it bother me, but I can't keep it out of mind.

Just what did the Trader do with those couple of million zebras we sent him?

HOBBIES

"Hobbies" is the sixth of the tales that, originally published as short stories in magazines, would later be woven into one of the most iconic books in the science fiction field: City. Written in early 1946 and published in the November 1946 issue of Astounding Science Fiction, "Hobbies," like the "City" stories that appeared before it, strongly reflects the world war that horrified, and disillusioned, so many.

By the time this story begins, the Dogs, who have been given powers of speech and the guidance of robot aides, have largely been abandoned by the humans they so loved—until another Webster shows up.

—dww

The rabbit ducked around a bush and the little black dog zipped after him, then dug in his heels and skidded. In the pathway stood a wolf, the rabbit's twitching, bloody body hanging from his jaws.

Ebenezer stood very still and panted, red rag of a tongue lolling out, a little faint and sick at the sight before him.

It had been such a nice rabbit!

Feet pattered on the trail behind him and Shadow whizzed around the bush, slid to a stop alongside Ebenezer.

The wolf flicked his glare from the dog to the pint-size robot, then back to the dog again. The yellow light of wildness slowly faded from his eyes.

"You shouldn't have done that, Wolf," said Ebenezer, softly. "The rabbit knew I wouldn't hurt him and it was all in fun. But he ran straight into you and you snapped him up."

"There's no use talking to him," Shadow hissed out of the corner of his mouth. "He doesn't know a word you're saying. Next thing you know, he'll be gulping you."

"Not with you around, he won't," said Ebenezer. "And, anyhow, he knows me. He remembers last winter. He was one of the pack we fed."

The wolf paced forward slowly, step by cautious step, until less than two feet separated him from the little dog. Then, very slowly, very carefully, he laid the rabbit on the ground, nudged it forward with his nose.

Shadow made a tiny sound that was almost a gasp. "He's giving it to you!"

"I know," said Ebenezer calmly. "I told you he remembered. He's the one that had a frozen ear and Jenkins fixed it up."

The dog advanced a step, tail wagging, nose outstretched. The wolf stiffened momentarily, then lowered his ugly head and sniffed. For a second the two noses almost rubbed together, then the wolf stepped back.

"Let's get out of here," urged Shadow. "You high-tail it down the trail and I'll bring up the rear. If he tries anything—"

"He won't try anything," snapped Ebenezer. "He's a friend of ours. It's not his fault about the rabbit. He doesn't understand. It's the way he lives. To him a rabbit is just a piece of meat."

Even, he thought, as it once was for us. As it was for us before the first dog came to sit with a man before a cave-mouth fire—and for a long time after that. Even now a rabbit sometime—

Moving slowly, almost apologetically, the wolf reached forward, gathered up the rabbit in his gaping jaws. His tail moved—not quite a wag, but almost.

"You see!" cried Ebenezer and the wolf was gone. His feet

moved and there was a blur of gray fading through the trees—a shadow drifting in the forest.

"He took it back," fumed Shadow. "Why, the dirty—"

"But he gave it to me," said Ebenezer, triumphantly. "Only he was so hungry he couldn't make it stick. He did something a wolf has never done before. For a moment he was more than an animal."

"Indian giver," snapped Shadow.

Ebenezer shook his head. "He was ashamed when he took it back. You saw him wag his tail. That was explaining to me—explaining he was hungry and he needed it. Worse than I needed it."

The dog stared down the green aisles of the fairy forest, smelled the scent of decaying leaves, the heady perfume of hepaticas and bloodroot and spidery windflower, the quick, sharp odor of the new leaf, of the woods in early spring.

"Maybe some day—" he said.

"Yeah, I know," said Shadow. "Maybe some day the wolves will be civilized, too. And the rabbits and squirrels and all the other wild things. The way you dogs go mooning around—"

"It isn't mooning," Ebenezer told him. "Dreaming, maybe. Men used to dream. They used to sit around and think up things. That's how we happened. A man named Webster thought us up. He messed around with us. He fixed up our throats so we could talk. He rigged up contact lenses so that we could read. He—"

"A lot of good it did men for all their dreaming," said Shadow, peevishly.

And that, thought Ebenezer, was the solemn truth. Not many men left now. Just the mutants squatting in their towers and doing God knows what and the little colony of real men still living in Geneva. The others, long ago, had gone to Jupiter. Had gone to Jupiter and changed themselves into things that were not human.

Slowly, tail drooping, Ebenezer swung around, clumped slowly up the path.

Too bad about the rabbit, he thought. It had been such a nice rabbit. It had run so well. And it really wasn't scared. He had chased it lots of times and it knew he wouldn't catch it.

But even at that, Ebenezer couldn't bring himself to blame the wolf. To a wolf a rabbit wasn't just something that was fun to chase. For the wolf had no herds for meat and milk, no fields of grain for meal to make dog biscuits.

"What I ought to do," grumbled the remorseless Shadow, treading at his heels, "is tell Jenkins that you ran out. You know that you should be listening."

Ebenezer did not answer, kept on trudging up the trail. For what Shadow said was true. Instead of rabbit-chasing, he should have been sitting up at Webster House listening—listening for the things that came to one—sounds and scents and awareness of something that was near. Like listening on one side of a wall to the things that were happening on the other, only they were faint and sometimes far away and hard to catch. Even harder, most times, to understand.

It's the animal in me, thought Ebenezer. *The old flea-scratching, bone-chewing, gopher-digging dog that will not let me be—that sends me sneaking out to chase a rabbit when I should be listening, out prowling the forest when I should be reading the old books from the shelves that line the study wall.*

Too fast, he told himself. *We came up too fast. Had to come up too fast.*

It took Man thousands of years to turn his grunts into the rudiments of speech. Thousands of years to discover fire and thousands more of years to invent the bow and arrow—thousands of years to learn to till the soil and harvest food, thousands of years to forsake the cave for a house he built himself.

But in a little more than a thousand years from the day we learned to talk we were on our own—our own, that is, except for Jenkins.

The forest thinned out into gnarled, scattered oaks that

straggled up the hill, like hobbling old men who had wandered off the path.

The house stood on the hilltop, a huddled structure that had taken root and crouched close against the earth. So old that it was the color of the things around it, of grass and flowers and trees, of sky and wind and weather. A house built by men who loved it and the surrounding acres even as the dogs now loved them. Built and lived in and died in by a legendary family that had left a meteoric trail across centuries of time. Men who lent their shadows to the stories that were told around the blazing fireplace of stormy nights when the wind sucked along the eaves. Stories of Bruce Webster and the first dog, Nathaniel; of a man named Grant who had given Nathaniel a word to pass along; of another man who had tried to reach the stars and of the old man who had sat waiting for him in the wheelchair on the lawn. And other stories of the ogre mutants the dogs had watched for years.

And now the men had gone and the family was a name and the dogs carried on as Grant had told Nathaniel that far-gone day they must.

As if you were men, as if the dog were man. Those were the words that had been handed down for ten full centuries—and at last the time had come.

The dogs had come home when the men had gone, come from the far corners of the earth back to the place where the first dog had spoken the first word, where the first dog had read the first line of print—back to Webster House where a man, long ago, had dreamed of a dual civilization, of man and dog going down the ages, hand in paw.

"We've done the best we could," said Ebenezer, almost as if he were speaking to someone. "We still are doing it."

From the other side of the hill came the tinkle of a cow bell, a burst of frantic barking. The pups were bringing in the cows for the evening milking.

* * *

The dust of centuries lay within the vault, a gray, powdery dust that was not an alien thing, but a part of the place itself—the part that had died in the passing of the years.

Jon Webster smelled the acrid scent of the dust cutting through the mustiness of the room, heard the silence humming like a song within his head. One dim radium bulb glowed above the panel with its switch and wheel and half a dozen dials.

Fearful of disturbing the sleeping silence, Webster moved forward quietly, half awed by the weight of time that seemed to press down from the ceiling. He reached out a finger and touched the open switch, as if he had expected it might not be there, as if he must feel the pressure of it against his fingertip to know that it was there.

And it was there. It and the wheel and dials, with the single light above them. And that was all. There was nothing else. In all that small, bare vault there was nothing else.

Exactly as the old map had said that it would be.

Jon Webster shook his head, thinking: I might have known that it would have been. The map was right. The map remembered. We were the ones that had forgotten—forgotten or never known or never cared. And he knew that more than likely it was the last that would be right. Never cared.

Although it was probable that very few had ever known about this vault. Had never known because it was best that only few should know. That it never had been used was no factor in its secrecy. There might have been a day—

He stared at the panel, wondering. Slowly his hand reached out again and then he jerked it back. Better not, he told himself, better not. For the map had given no clue to the purpose of the vault, to the mechanics of the switch.

"Defense," the map had said, and that was all.

Defense! Of course, there would have been defense back in that day of a thousand years ago. A defense that never had been needed, but a defense that had to be there, a defense against the emergency of uncertainty. For the brotherhood of peoples even then was a shaky thing that a single word or act might have thrown out of kilter. Even after ten centuries of peace, the memory of war would have been a living thing—an ever-present possibility in the mind of the World Committee, something to be circumvented, something to be ready for.

Webster stood stiff and straight, listening to the pulse of history beating in the room. History that had run its course and ended. History that had come to a dead end—a stream that suddenly had flowed into the backwater of a few hundred futile human lives and now was a stagnant pool unrelieved by the eddying of human struggle and achievement.

He reached out a hand, put it flat against the masonry, felt the slimy cold, the rough crawl of dust beneath his palm.

The foundation of empire, he thought. The subcellar of empire. The nethermost stone of the towering structure that soared in proud strength on the surface far above—a great building that in olden times had hummed with the business of a solar system, an empire not in the sense of conquest but an empire of orderly human relations based on mutual respect and tolerant understanding.

A seat of human government lent an easy confidence by the psychological fact of an adequate and foolproof defense. For it would have been both adequate and foolproof, it would have had to be. The men of that day took no chances, overlooked no bets. They had come up through the hard school and they knew their way around.

Slowly, Webster swung about, stared at the trail his feet had left across the dust. Silently, stepping carefully, following the trail he'd made, he left the vault, closed the massive door behind him and spun the lock that held its secret fast.

Climbing the tunneled stairs, he thought: *Now I can write my history. My notes are almost complete and I know how it should go. It will be brilliant and exhaustive and it might be interesting if anyone should read it.*

But he knew that no one would. No one would take the time or care.

For a long moment, Webster stood on the broad marble steps before his house, looking down the street. A pretty street, he told himself, the prettiest street in all Geneva, with its boulevard of trees, its carefully tended flower beds, the walks that glistened with the scrub and polish of ever-working robots.

No one moved along the street and it wasn't strange. The robots had finished their work early in the day and there were few people.

From some high treetop a bird sang and the song was one with the sun and flowers, a gladsome song that strained at the bursting throat, a song that tripped and skipped with boundless joy.

A neat street drowsing in the sun and a great, proud city that had lost its purpose. A street that should be filled with laughing children and strolling lovers and old men resting in the sun. And a city, the last city on Earth, the only city on Earth, that should be filled with noise and business.

A bird sang and a man stood on the steps and looked and the tulips nodded blissfully in the tiny fragrant breeze that wafted down the street.

Webster turned to the door, fumbled it open, walked across the threshold.

The room was hushed and solemn, cathedral-like with its stained glass windows and soft carpeting. Old wood glowed with the patina of age and silver and brass winked briefly in the light that fell from the slender windows. Over the fireplace hung a massive canvas, done in subdued coloring—a house upon a hill, a house that had grown roots and clung against the land with a jealous grip. Smoke came from the chimney, a wind-whipped, tenuous smoke that smudged across a storm-gray sky.

Webster walked across the room and there was no sound of walking. *The rugs,* he thought, *the rugs protect the quietness of the place. Randall wanted to do this one over, too, but I wouldn't let him touch it and I'm glad I didn't. A man must keep something that is old, something he can cling to, something that is a heritage and a legacy and promise.*

He reached his desk, thumbed a tumbler and the light came on above it. Slowly, he let himself into a chair, reached out for the portfolio of notes. He flipped the cover open and stared at the title page: *"A study of the Functional Development of the City of Geneva."*

A brave title. Dignified and erudite. And a lot of work. Twenty years of work. Twenty years of digging among old dusty records, twenty years of reading and comparing, of evaluating the weight and words of those who had gone before, sifting and rejecting and working out the facts, tracing the trend not only of the city but of men. No hero worship, no legends, but facts. And facts are hard to come by.

Something rustled. No footstep, but a rustle, a sense that someone was near. Webster twisted in his chair. A robot stood just outside the circle of the desk light.

"Beg pardon, sir," the robot said, "but I was supposed to tell you. Miss Sara is waiting in the Seashore."

Webster started slightly. "Miss Sara, eh? It's been a long time since she's been here."

"Yes, sir," said the robot. "It seemed almost like old times, sir, when she walked in the door."

"Thank you, Roscoe, for telling me," said Webster. "I'll go right out. You will bring some drinks."

"She brought her own drinks, sir," said Roscoe. "Something that Mr. Ballentree fixed up."

"Ballentree!" exclaimed Webster. "I hope it isn't poison."

"I've been observing her," Roscoe told him, "and she's been drinking it and she's still all right."

Webster rose from his chair, crossed the room and went down the hall. He pushed open the door and the sound of the surf came to him. He blinked in the light that shone on the hot sand beach, stretching like a straight white line to either horizon. Before him the ocean was a sun-washed blue tipped with the white of foaming waves.

Sand gritted underneath his feet as he walked forward, eyes adjusting themselves to the blaze of sunlight.

Sara, he saw, was sitting in one of the bright canvas chairs underneath the palm trees and beside the chair was a pastel, very ladylike jug.

The air had a tang of salt and the wind off the water was cool in the sun-warm air.

The woman heard him and stood up and waited for him, with her hands outstretched. He hurried forward, clasped the outstretched hands and looked at her.

"Not a minute older," he said. "As pretty as the day I saw you first."

She smiled at him, eyes very bright. "And you, Jon. A little gray around the temples. A little handsomer. That is all."

He laughed. "I'm almost sixty, Sara. Middle age is creeping up."

"I brought something," said Sara. "One of Ballentree's latest masterpieces. It will cut your age in half."

He grunted. "Wonder Ballentree hasn't killed off half Geneva, the drinks that he cooks up."

"This one is really good."

It was. It went down smooth and it had a strange, half metallic, half ecstatic taste.

Webster pulled another chair close to Sara's, sat down and looked at her.

"You have such a nice place here," said Sara. "Randall did it, didn't he?"

Webster nodded. "He had more fun than a circus, I had to beat him off with a club. And those robots of his! They're crazier than he is."

"But he does wonderful things. He did a Martian room for Quentin and it's simply *unworldly.*"

"I know," said Webster. "Was set on a deep-space one for here. Said it would be just the place to sit and think. Got sore at me when I wouldn't let him do it."

He rubbed the back of his left hand with his right thumb, staring off at the blue haze above the ocean. Sara leaned forward, pulled his thumb away.

"You still have the warts," she said.

He grinned. "Yes. Could have had them taken off, but never got around to it. Too busy, I guess. Part of me by now."

She released the thumb and he went back to rubbing the warts absent-mindedly.

"You've been busy," she said. "Haven't seen you around much. How is the book coming?"

"Ready to write," said Webster. "Outlining it by chapters now. Checked on the last thing today. Have to make sure, you know. Place way down under the old Solar Administration Building. Some sort of a defense set-up. Control room. You push a lever and—"

"And what?"

"I don't know," said Webster. "Something effective, I suppose. Should try to find out, but can't find the heart to do it. Been digging around in too much dust these last twenty years to face any more."

"You sound discouraged, Jon. Tired. You shouldn't get tired. There's no reason for it. You should get around. Have another drink?"

He shook his head. "No, Sara, thanks. Not in the mood, I guess. I'm afraid, Sara—afraid."

"Afraid?"

"This room," said Webster. "Illusion. Mirrors that give an illusion of distance. Fans that blow the air through a salt spray, pumps that stir up the waves. A synthetic sun. And if I don't like the sun, all I have to do is snap a switch and I have a moon."

"Illusion," said Sara.

"That's it," said Webster. "That is all we have. No real work, no real job. Nothing that we're working for, no place we're going. I've worked for twenty years and I'll write a book and not a soul will read it. All they'd have to do would be spend the time to read it, but they won't take the time. They won't care. All they'd have to do would be come and ask me for a copy—and if they didn't want to do that I'd be so glad someone was going to read it that I'd take it to them. But no one will. It will go on the shelves with all the other books that have been written. And what do I get out of it? Wait . . . I'll tell you. Twenty years of work, twenty years of fooling myself, twenty years of sanity."

"I know," said Sara, softly. "I know, Jon. The last three paintings—"

He looked up quickly. "But, Sara—"

She shook her head. "No, Jon. No one wanted them. They're out of style. Naturalistic stuff is passé. Impressionalism now. Daubs—"

"We are too rich," said Webster. "We have too much. Everything was left for us—everything and nothing. When Mankind went out to Jupiter the few that were left behind inherited the Earth and it was too big for them. They couldn't handle it. They couldn't manage it. They thought they owned it, but they were the ones that were owned. Owned and dominated and awed by the things that had gone before."

She reached out a hand and touched his arm.

"Poor Jon," she said.

"We can't flinch away from it," he said. "Some day some of us must face the truth, must start over again—from scratch."

"I—"

"Yes, what is it, Sara?"

"I came here to say good-by."

"Good-by?"

"I'm going to take the Sleep."

He came to his feet, swiftly, horrified. "No, Sara!"

She laughed and the laugh was strained. "Why don't you come with me, Jon. A few hundred years. Maybe it will all be different when we awake."

"Just because no one wants your canvases. Just because—"

"Because of what you said just a while ago. Illusion, Jon. I knew it, felt it, but I couldn't think it out."

"But the Sleep is illusion, too."

"I know. But you don't know it's illusion. You think it's real. You have no inhibitions and you have no fears except the fears that are planned deliberately. It's natural, Jon—more natural than life. I went up to the Temple and it was all explained to me."

"And when you awake?"

"You're adjusted. Adjusted to whatever life is like in whatever era you awake. Almost as if you belonged, even from the first. And it might be better. Who knows? It might be better."

"It won't be," Jon told her, grimly. "Until, or unless, someone does something about it. And a people that run to the Sleep to hide are not going to bestir themselves."

She shrank back in the chair and suddenly he felt ashamed.

"I'm sorry, Sara. I didn't mean you. Nor any one person. Just the lot of us."

The palms whispered harshly, fronds rasping. Little pools of water, left by the surging tide, sparkled in the sun.

"I won't try to dissuade you," Webster said. "You've thought it out, you know what it is you want."

It hadn't always been like that with the human race, he thought. *There would have been a day, a thousand years ago, when a man would have argued about a thing like this. But Juwainism had ended all the petty quarrels. Juwainism had ended a lot of things.*

"I've always thought," Sara told him, softly, "if we could have stayed together—"

He made a gesture of impatience. "It's just another thing we've lost, another thing that the human race let loose. Come to think it over, we lost a lot of things. Family ties and business, work and purpose."

He turned to face her squarely. "If you want to come back, Sara—"

She shook her head. "It wouldn't work, Jon. It's been too many years."

He nodded. There was no use denying it.

She rose and held out her hand. "If you ever decide to take the Sleep, find out my date. I'll have them reserve a place right next to me."

"I don't think I ever shall," he told her.

"All right, then. Good-bye, Jon."

"Wait a second, Sara. You haven't said a word about our son. I used to see him often, but—"

She laughed brightly. "Tom's almost a grown man now, Jon. And it's the strangest thing. He—"

"I haven't seen him for so long," Webster said again.

"No wonder. He's scarcely in the city. It's his hobby. Something he inherited from you, I guess. Pioneering in a way. I don't know what else you'd call it."

"You mean some new research. Something unusual."

"Unusual, yes, but not research. Just goes out in the woods and lives by himself. He and a few of his friends. A bag of salt, a bow and arrows—yes, it's queer," Sara admitted, "but he has a lot of fun. Claims he's learning something. And he does look healthy. Like a wolf. Strong and lean and a look about his eyes."

She swung around and moved away.

"I'll see you to the door," said Webster.

She shook her head. "No. I'd rather that you wouldn't."

"You're forgetting the jug."

"You keep it, Jon. I won't need it where I'm going."

Webster put on the plastic "thinking cap," snapped the button of the writer on his desk.

Chapter Twenty-six, he thought and the writer clicked and chuckled and wrote "Chapter XXVI."

For a moment Webster held his mind clear, assembling his data, arranging his outline, then he began again. The writer clicked and gurgled, hummed into steady work:

The machines ran on, tended by the robots as they had been before, producing all the things they had produced before.

And the robots worked as they knew it was their right to work, their right and duty, doing the things they had been made to do.

The machines went on and the robots went on, producing wealth as if there were men to use it, just as if there were millions of men instead of a bare five thousand.

And the five thousand who had stayed behind or who had been left behind suddenly found themselves the masters of a world that had been geared to the millions, found themselves possessed of the wealth and services that only months before had been the wealth and services that had been due the millions.

There was no government, but there was no need of government, for all the crimes and abuses that government had held in check were as effectively held in check by the sudden wealth the five thousand had inherited. No man will steal when he can pick up what he wants without the bother of thievery. No man will contest with his neighbor over real estate when the entire world is real estate for the simple taking. Property rights almost overnight became a phrase that had no meaning in a world where there was more than enough for all.

Crimes of violence long before had been virtually eliminated from human society and with the economic pressure eased to a point where property rights ceased to be a point of friction, there was no need of government. No need, in fact, of many of the encumbrances of custom and convenience which man had carried forward from the beginnings of commerce. There was no need of currency, for exchange had no meaning in a world where to get a thing one need but ask for it or take it.

Relieved of economic pressure, the social pressures lessened, too. A man no longer found it necessary to conform to the standards and the acts of custom which had played so large a part in the post-Jovian world as an indication of commercial character.

Religion, which had been losing ground for centuries, entirely disappeared. The family unit, held together by tradition and by the economic necessity of a provider and protector, fell apart. Men and women lived together as they wished, parted when they wished. For there was no economic reason, no social reason why they shouldn't.

Webster cleared his mind and the machine purred softly at him. He put up his hands, took off the cap, reread the last paragraph of the outline.

There, he thought, there is the root of it. *If the families had stayed together. If Sara and I had stayed together.*

He rubbed the warts on the back of his hand, wondering:

Wonder if Tom goes by my name or hers. Usually they take their mother's name. I know I did at first until my mother asked me to change it. Said it would please my father and she didn't mind. Said he was proud of the name he bore and I was his only child. And she had others.

If only we had stayed together. Then there'd be something worth living for. If we'd stayed together, Sara wouldn't be taking the Sleep, wouldn't be lying in a tank of fluid in suspended animation with the "dream cap" on her head.

Wonder what kind of dream she chose—what kind of synthetic life she picked out to live. I wanted to ask her, but I didn't dare. It's not the kind of thing, after all, that one can ask.

He reached out and picked up the cap again, put it on his head, marshaled his thoughts anew. The writer clicked into sudden life:

Man was bewildered. But not for long. Man tried. But not for long.

For the five thousand could not carry on the work of the millions who had gone to Jupiter to enter upon a better life in alien bodies.

The five thousand did not have the skill, nor the dreams, nor the incentive.

And there were the psychological factors. The psychological factor of tradition which bore like a weight upon the minds of the men who had been left behind. The psychological factor of Juwainism which forced men to be honest with themselves and others, which forced men to perceive at last the hopelessness of the things they sought to do. Juwainism left no room for false courage. And false, foolhardy courage that didn't know what it was going up against was the one thing the five thousand needed most.

What they did suffered by comparison with what had been done before and at last they came to know that the human dream of millions was too vast a thing for five thousand to attempt.

Life was good. Why worry? There was food and clothes and shelter, human companionship and luxury and entertainment—there was everything that one could ever wish.

Man gave up trying. Man enjoyed himself. Human achievement became a zero factor and human life a senseless paradise.

Webster took off the cap again, reached out and clicked off the writer.

If someone would only read it once I get it done, he thought. If someone would read and understand. If someone could realize where human life is going.

I could tell them, of course. I could go out and buttonhole them one by one and hold them fast until I told them what I thought. And they would understand, for Juwainism would make them understand. But they wouldn't pay attention. They'd tuck it all away in the backs of their brains somewhere for future reference and they'd never have the time or take the trouble to drag it out again.

They'd go on doing the foolish things they're doing, following the footless hobbies they have taken up in lieu of work. Randall with his crew of zany robots going around begging to be allowed to re-design his neighbors' homes. Ballentree spending hours on end figuring out new alcoholic mixtures. Yes, and Jon Webster wasting twenty years digging into the history of a single city.

A door creaked faintly and Webster swung around. The robot catfooted into the room.

"Yes, what is it, Roscoe?"

The robot halted, a dim figure in the half-light of the dusk-filled room.

"It's time for dinner, sir. I came to see—"

"Whatever you can think up," said Webster. "And, Roscoe, you can lay the fire."

"The fire is laid, sir."

Roscoe stalked across the room, bent above the fireplace. Flame flickered in his hand and the kindling caught.

Webster, slouched in his chair staring at the flames crawling up the wood, heard the first, faint hiss and crackle of the wood, the suction mumble at the fireplace throat.

"It's pretty, sir," said Roscoe.

"You like it, too?"

"Indeed I do."

"Ancestral memories," said Webster, soberly. "Remembrance of the forge that made you."

"You think so, sir?" asked Roscoe.

"No, Roscoe, I was joking. Anachronisms, that's what you and I are. Not many people have fires these days. No need for them. But there's something about them, something that is clean and comforting."

He stared at the canvas above the mantelpiece, lighted now by the flare of burning wood. Roscoe saw his stare.

"Too bad about Miss Sara, sir."

Webster shook his head. "No, Roscoe, it was something that she wanted. Like turning off one life and starting on another. She will lie up there in the Temple, asleep for years, and she will live another life. And this one, Roscoe, will be a happy life. For she would have it planned that way."

His mind went back to other days in this very room.

"She painted that picture, Roscoe," he said. "Spent a long time at it, being very careful to catch the thing she wanted to express. She used to laugh at me and tell me I was in the painting, too."

"I don't see you, sir," said Roscoe.

"No. I'm not. And yet, perhaps, I am. Or part of me. Part of what and where I came from. That house in the painting, Roscoe, is the Webster House in North America. And I am a Webster. But a long ways from the house—a long ways from the men who built that house."

"North America's not so far, sir."

"No," Webster told him. "Not so far in distance. But far in other ways."

He felt the warmth of the fire steal across the room and touch him.

Far. Too far—and in the wrong direction.

The robot moved softly, feet padding on the rug, leaving the room.

She worked a long time, being very careful to catch the thing she wanted to express.

And what was that thing? He had never asked her and she had never told him. He had always thought, he remembered, that it probably had been the way the smoke streamed, wind-whipped across the sky, the way the house crouched against the ground, blending in with the trees and grass, huddled against the storm that walked above the land.

But it may have been something else. Some symbolism. Something that made the house synonymous with the kind of men who built it.

He got up and walked closer, stood before the fire with head tilted back. The brush strokes were there and the painting looked less a painting than when viewed from the proper distance. A thing of technique, now. The basic strokes and shadings the brushes had achieved to create illusion.

Security. Security by the way the house stood foursquare and solid. Tenacity by the way it was a part of the land itself. Sternness, stubbornness and a certain bleakness of the spirit.

She had sat for days on end with the visor beamed on the house, sketching carefully, painting slowly, often sitting and watching and doing nothing at all. There had been dogs, she said, and robots, but she had not put them in, because all she wanted was the house. One of the few houses left standing in the open country. Through centuries of neglect, the others had fallen in, had given the land back to the wilderness.

But there were dogs and robots in this one. One big robot, she had said, and a lot of little ones.

Webster had paid no attention—he had been too busy.

He swung around, went back to the desk again.

Queer thing, once you came to think of it. Robots and dogs living together. A Webster once had messed around with dogs, trying to put them on the road to a culture of their own, trying to develop a dual civilization of man and dog.

Bits of remembrance came to him—tiny fragments, half recalled, of the legends that had come down the years about the Webster House. There had been a robot named Jenkins who had served the family from the very first. There had been an old man sitting in a wheel chair on the front lawn, staring at the stars and waiting for a son who never came. And a curse had hung above the house, the curse of having lost to the world the philosophy of Juwain.

The visor was in one corner of the room, an almost forgotten piece of furniture, something that was scarcely used. There was no need to use it. All the world was here in the city of Geneva.

Webster rose, moved toward it, stopped and thought. The dial settings were listed in the log book, but where was the log book? More than likely somewhere in his desk.

He went back to the desk, started going through the drawers.

Excited now, he pawed furiously, like a terrier digging for a bone.

Jenkins, the ancient robot, scrubbed his metallic chin with metallic fingers. It was a thing he did when he was deep in thought, a meaningless, irritating gesture he had picked up from long association with the human race.

His eyes went back to the little dog sitting on the floor beside him.

"So the wolf was friendly," said Jenkins. "Offered you the rabbit."

Ebenezer jigged excitedly upon his bottom. "He was one of them we fed last winter. The pack that came up to the house and we tried to tame them."

"Would you know the wolf again?"

Ebenezer nodded. "I got his scent," he said. "I'd remember him."

Shadow shuffled his feet against the floor. "Look, Jenkins, ain't you going to smack him one? He should have been listening and he ran away. He had no business chasing rabbits—"

Jenkins spoke sternly. "You're the one that should get the smacking, Shadow. For your attitude. You are assigned to Ebenezer, you should be part of him. You aren't an individual. You're just Ebenezer's hands. If he had hands, he'd have no need of you. You aren't his mentor nor his conscience. Just his hands. Remember that."

Shadow shuffled his feet rebelliously. "I'll run away," he said.

"Join the wild robots, I suppose," said Jenkins.

Shadow nodded. "They'd be glad to have me. They're doing things. They need all the help that they can get."

"They'd bust you up for scrap," Jenkins told him sourly. "You have no training, no abilities that would make you one of them."

He turned to Ebenezer. "We have other robots."

Ebenezer shook his head. "Shadow is all right. I can handle him. We know one another. He keeps me from getting lazy, keeps me on my toes."

"That's fine," said Jenkins. "You two run along. And if you ever happen to be out chasing rabbits, Ebenezer, and run onto this wolf again, try to cultivate him."

The rays of the westering sun were streaming through the windows, touching the age-old room with the warmth of a late spring evening.

Jenkins sat quietly in the chair, listening to the sounds that came from outside—the tinkle of cowbells, the yapping of the puppies, the ringing thud of an axe splitting fireplace logs.

Poor little fellow, thought Jenkins. *Sneaking out to chase a rabbit when he should have been listening. Too far—too fast. Have to watch that. Have to keep them from breaking down. Come fall and we'll knock off work for a week or two and have some coon hunts. Do them a world of good.*

Although there'd come a day when there'd be no coon hunts, no rabbit chasing—the day when the dogs finally had tamed everything, when all the wild things would be thinking, talking, working beings. A wild dream and a far one—*but,* thought Jenkins, *no wilder and no farther than some of the dreams of man.*

Maybe even better than the dreams of man, for they held none of the ruthlessness that the human race had planned, aimed at none of the mechanistic brutality the human race spawned. A new civilization, a new culture, a new way of thought. Mystic, perhaps, and visionary, but so had man been visionary. Probing into mysteries that man had brushed by as unworthy of his time, as mere superstition that could have no scientific basis.

Things that go bump in the night. Things that prowl around a house and the dogs get up and growl and there are no tracks in the snow. Dogs howling when someone dies.

The dogs knew. The dogs had known long before they had been given tongues to talk, contact lenses to read. They had not come along the road as far as men—they were not cynical and skeptic. They believed the things they heard and sensed. They did not invent superstition as a form of wishful thinking, as a shield against the things unseen.

Jenkins turned back to the desk again, picked up the pen, bent above the notebook in front of him. The pen screeched as he pushed it along.

Ebenezer reports friendliness in wolf. Recommend council detach Ebenezer from listening and assign him to contact the wolf.

Wolves, mused Jenkins, would be good friends to have. They'd make splendid scouts. Better than the dogs. Tougher, faster, sneaky. They could watch the wild robots across the river and relieve the dogs. Could keep an eye on the mutant castles.

Jenkins shook his head. Couldn't trust anyone these days. The robots seemed to be all right. Were friendly, dropped in at times, helped out now and then. Real neighborly, in fact. But you never knew. And they were building machines.

The mutants never bothered anyone, were scarcely seen, in fact. But they had to be watched, too. Never knew what devilment they might be up to. Remember what they'd done to man. That dirty trick with Juwainism, handing it over at a time when it would doom the race.

Men. They were gods to us and now they're gone. Left us on our own. A few in Geneva, of course, but they can't be bothered, have no interest in us.

He sat in the twilight, thinking of the whiskies he had carried, of the errands he had run, of the days when Websters had lived and died within these walls.

And now—father-confessor to the dogs. Cute little devils and bright and smart—and trying hard.

A bell buzzed softly and Jenkins jerked upright in his seat. It buzzed again and a green light winked on the televisor. Jenkins came to his feet, stood unbelieving, staring at the winking light.

Someone calling!

Someone calling after almost a thousand years!

He staggered forward, dropped into the chair, reached out with fumbling fingers to the toggle, tripped it over.

The wall before him melted away and he sat facing a man across a desk. Behind the man the flames of a fireplace lighted up a room with high, stained-glass windows.

"You're Jenkins," said the man and there was something in his face that jerked a cry from Jenkins.

"You . . . you—"

"I'm Jon Webster," said the man.

Jenkins pressed his hands flat against the top of the televisor, sat straight and stiff, afraid of the unrobotlike emotions that welled within his metal being.

"I would have known you anywhere," said Jenkins. "You have the look of them. I should recognize one of you. I worked for you long enough. Carried drinks and . . . and—"

"Yes, I know," said Webster. "Your name has come down with us. We remembered you."

"You are in Geneva, Jon?" And then Jenkins remembered. "I meant, sir."

"No need of it," said Webster. "I'd rather have it Jon. And, yes, I'm in Geneva. But I'd like to see, you. I wonder if I might."

"You mean come out here?"

Webster nodded.

"But the place is overrun with dogs, sir."

Webster grinned. "The talking dogs?" he asked.

"Yes," said Jenkins. "and they'll be glad to see you. They know all about the family. They sit around at night and talk themselves to sleep with stories from the old days and . . . and—"

"What is it, Jenkins?"

"I'll be glad to see you, too. It has been so lonesome!"

* * *

God had come.

Ebenezer shivered at the thought, crouching in the dark. *If Jenkins knew I was here, he thought, he'd whale my hide for fair. Jenkins said we were to leave him alone, for a while, at least.*

Ebenezer crept forward on fur-soft pads, sniffed at the study door. And the door was open—open by the barest crack!

He crouched on his belly, listening, and there was not a thing to hear. Just a scent, an unfamiliar, tangy scent that made the hair crawl along his back in swift, almost unbearable ecstasy.

He glanced quickly over his shoulder, but there was no movement. Jenkins was out in the dining room, telling the dogs how they must behave, and Shadow was off somewhere tending to some robot business.

Softly, carefully, Ebenezer pushed at the door with his nose and the door swung wider. Another push and it was half open.

The man sat in front of the fireplace, in the easy-chair, long legs crossed, hands clasped across his stomach.

Ebenezer crouched tighter against the floor, a low involuntary whimper in his throat.

At the sound Jon Webster jerked erect.

"Who's there?" he asked.

Ebenezer froze against the floor, felt the pumping of his heart jerking at his body.

"Who's there?" Webster asked once more, and then he saw the dog.

His voice was softer when he spoke again. "Come in, feller. Come on in."

Ebenezer did not stir.

Webster snapped his fingers at him. "I won't hurt you. Come on in. Where are all the others?"

Ebenezer tried to rise, tried to crawl along the floor, but his bones were rubber and his blood was water. And the man was striding toward him, coming in long strides across the floor.

He saw the man bending over him, felt strong hands beneath his body, knew that he was being lifted up. And the scent that he had smelled at the open door—the overpowering god-scent—was strong within his nostrils.

The hands held him tight against the strange fabric the man wore instead of fur and a voice crooned at him—not words, but comforting.

"So you came to see me," said Jon Webster. "You sneaked away and you came to see me."

Ebenezer nodded weakly. "You aren't angry, are you? You aren't going to tell Jenkins?"

Webster shook his head. "No, I won't tell Jenkins."

He sat down and Ebenezer sat in his lap, staring at his face—a strong, lined face with the lines deepened by the flare of the flames within the fireplace.

Webster's hand came up and stroked Ebenezer's head and Ebenezer whimpered with doggish happiness.

"It's like coming home," said Webster, and he wasn't talking to the dog. "It's like you've been away for a long, long time and then you come home again. And it's so long you don't recognize the place. Don't know the furniture, don't recognize the floor plan. But you know by the feel of it that it's an old familiar place and you are glad you came."

"I like it here," said. Ebenezer and he meant Webster's lap, but the man misunderstood.

"Of course, you do," he said. "It's your home as well as mine. More your home, in fact, for you stayed here and took care of it while I forgot about it."

He patted Ebenezer's head and pulled Ebenezer's ears.

"What's your name?" he asked.

"Ebenezer."

"And what do you do, Ebenezer?"

"I listen."

"You listen?"

"Sure, that's my job. I listen for the cobblies."

"And you hear the cobblies?"

"Sometimes. I'm not very good at it. I think about chasing rabbits and I don't pay attention."

"What do cobblies sound like?"

"Different things. Sometimes they walk and other times they just go bump. And once in a while they talk. Although oftener, they think."

"Look here, Ebenezer, I don't seem to place these cobblies."

"They aren't any place," said Ebenezer. "Not on this earth, at least."

"I don't understand."

"Like there was a big house," said Ebenezer. "A big house with lots of rooms. And doors between the rooms. And if you're in one room, you can hear whoever's in the other rooms, but you can't get to them."

"Sure you can," said Webster. "All you have to do is go through the door."

"But you can't open the door," said Ebenezer. "You don't even know about the door. You think this one room you're in is the only room in all the house. Even if you did know about the door you couldn't open it."

"You're talking about dimensions."

Ebenezer wrinkled his forehead in worried thought. "I don't know that word you said, dimensions. What I told you was the way Jenkins told it to us. He said it wasn't really a house and it wasn't really rooms and the things we heard probably weren't like us."

Webster nodded to himself. That was the way one would have to do. Have to take it easy. Take it slow. Don't confuse them with big names. Let them get the idea first and then bring in the more exact and scientific terminology. And more than likely it would be a manufactured terminology. Already there was a coined word—

Cobblies—the things behind the wall, the things that one hears and cannot identify—the dwellers in the next room.

Cobblies.

The cobblies will get you if you don't watch out.

That would be the human way. Can't understand a thing. Can't see it. Can't test it. Can't analyze it. O.K., it isn't there. It doesn't exist. It's a ghost, a goblin, a cobbly.

The cobblies will get you—

It's simpler that way, more comfortable. Scared? Sure, but you forget it in the light. And it doesn't plague you, haunt you. Think hard enough and you wish it away. Make it a ghost or goblin and you can laugh at it—in the daylight.

A hot, wet tongue rasped across his chin and Ebenezer wriggled with delight.

"I like you," said Ebenezer. "Jenkins never held me this way. No one's ever held me this way."

"Jenkins is busy," said Webster.

"He sure is," agreed Ebenezer. "He writes things down in a book. Things that us dogs hear when we are listening and things that we should do."

"You've heard about the Websters?" asked the man.

"Sure. We know all about them. You're a Webster. We didn't think there were any more of them."

"Yes, there is," said Webster. "There's been one here all the time. Jenkins is a Webster."

"He never told us that."

"He wouldn't."

The fire had died down and the room had darkened. The sputtering flames chased feeble flickers across the walls and floor.

And something else. Faint rustlings, faint whisperings, as if the very walls were talking. An old house with long memories and a lot of living tucked within its structure. Two thousand years of living. Built to last and it had lasted. Built to be a home and it still was a home—a solid place that put its arms around one and held one close and warm, claimed one for its own.

Footsteps walked across his brain—footsteps from the long ago, footsteps that had been silenced to the final echo centuries before. The walking of the Websters. Of the ones that went before me, the ones that Jenkins waited on from their day of birth to the hour of death.

History. Here is history. History stirring in the drapes and creeping on the floor, sitting in the corners, watching from the wall. Living history that a man can feel in the bones of him and against his shoulder blades—the impact of the long dead eyes that come back from the night.

Another Webster, eh! Doesn't look like much. Worthless. The breed's played out. Not like we were in our day. Just about the last of them.

Jon Webster stirred. "No, not the last of them," he said. "I have a son."

Well, it doesn't make much difference. He says he has a son. But he can't amount to much—

Webster started from the chair, Ebenezer slipping from his lap.

"That's not true," cried Webster. "My son—"

And then sat down again.

His son out in the woods with bow and arrows, playing a game, having fun.

A hobby, Sara had said before she climbed the hill to take a hundred years of dreams.

A hobby. Not a business. Not a way of life. Not necessity.

A hobby.

An artificial thing. A thing that had no beginning and no end. A thing a man could drop at any minute and no one would ever notice.

Like cooking up recipes for different kinds of drinks.

Like painting pictures no one wanted.

Like going around with a crew of crazy robots begging people to let you redecorate their homes.

Like writing history no one cares about.

Like playing Indian or caveman or pioneer with bow and arrows.

Like thinking up centuries-long dreams for men and women who are tired of life and yearn for fantasy.

The man sat in the chair, staring at the nothingness that spread before his eyes, the dread and awful nothingness that became tomorrow and tomorrow.

Absent-mindedly his hands came together and the right thumb stroked the back of the left hand.

Ebenezer crept forward through the fire-flared darkness, put his front paws on the man's knee and looked into his face.

"Hurt your hand?" he asked.

"Eh?"

"Hurt your hand? You're rubbing it."

Webster laughed shortly. "No, just warts." He showed them to the dog.

"Gee, warts!" said Ebenezer. "You don't want them, do you?"

"No," Webster hesitated. "No, I guess I don't. Never got around to having them taken off."

Ebenezer dropped his nose and nuzzled the back of Webster's hand.

"There you are," he announced triumphantly.

"There I'm what?"

"Look at the warts," invited Ebenezer.

A log fell in the fire and Webster lifted his hand, looked at it in the flare of light.

The warts were gone. The skin was smooth and clean.

Jenkins stood in the darkness and listened to the silence, the soft sleeping silence that left the house to shadows, to the half-forgotten footsteps, the phrase spoken long ago, the tongues that murmured in the walls and rustled in the drapes.

By a single thought the night could have been as day, a simple adjustment in his lenses would have done the trick, but the ancient robot left his sight unchanged. For this was the way he liked it, this was the hour of meditation, the treasured time when the present sloughed away and the past came back and lived.

The others slept, but Jenkins did not sleep. For robots never sleep. Two thousand years of consciousness, twenty centuries of full time unbroken by a single moment of unawareness.

A long time, thought Jenkins. *A long time, even for a robot. For even before man had gone to Jupiter most of the older robots had been deactivated, had been sent to their death in favor of the newer models. The newer models that looked more like men, that were smoother and more sightly, with better speech and quicker responses within their metal brains.*

But Jenkins had stayed on because he was an old and faithful servant, because Webster House would not have been home without him.

"They loved me," said Jenkins to himself. And the three words held deep comfort—comfort in a world where there was little comfort, a world where a servant had become a leader and longed to be a servant once again.

He stood at the window and stared out across the patio to the night-dark clumps of oaks that staggered down the hill. Darkness. No light anywhere. There had been a time when there had been lights. Windows that shone like friendly beams in the vast land that lay across the river.

But man had gone and there were no lights. The robots needed no lights, for they could see in darkness, even as Jenkins could have seen, had he but chosen to do so. And the castles of the mutants were as dark by night as they were fearsome by day.

Now man had come again, one man. Had come, but he probably wouldn't stay. He'd sleep for a few nights in the great master bedroom on the second floor, then go back to Geneva. He'd walk the old forgotten acres and stare across the river and rummage through the books that lined the study wall, then he would up and leave.

Jenkins swung around. *Ought to see how he is,* he thought. *Ought to find if he needs anything. Maybe take him up a drink, although I'm afraid the whisky is all spoiled. A thousand years is a long time for a bottle of good whisky.*

He moved across the room and a warm peace came upon him, the close and intimate peacefulness of the old days when he had trotted, happy as a terrier, on his many errands.

He hummed a snatch of tune in minor key as he headed for the stairway′.

He'd just look in and if Jon Webster were asleep, he'd leave, but if he wasn't, he'd say: "Are you comfortable, sir? Is there anything you wish? A hot toddy, perhaps?"

And he took two stairs at the time.

For he was doing for a Webster once again.

Jon Webster lay propped in bed, with the pillows piled behind him. The bed was hard and uncomfortable and the room was close and stuffy—not like his own bedroom back in Geneva, where one lay on the grassy bank of a murmuring stream and stared at the artificial stars that glittered in an artificial sky. And smelled the artificial scent of artificial lilacs that would go on blooming longer than a man would live. No murmur of a hidden waterfall, no flickering of captive fireflies—but a bed and room that were functional.

Webster spread his hands flat on his blanket-covered thighs and flexed his fingers, thinking.

Ebenezer had merely touched the warts and the warts were gone. And it had been no happenstance—it had been intentional. It had been no miracle, but a conscious power. For miracles sometimes fail to happen, and Ebenezer had been sure.

A power, perhaps, that had been gathered from the room

beyond, a power that had been stolen from the cobblies Ebenezer listened to.

A laying-on of hands, a power of healing that involved no drugs, no surgery, but just a certain knowledge, a very special knowledge.

In the old dark ages, certain men had claimed the power to make warts disappear, had bought them for a penny, or had traded them for something or had performed other mumbo-jumbo—and in due time, sometimes, the warts would disappear.

Had these queer men listened to the cobblies, too?

The door creaked just a little and Webster straightened suddenly.

A voice came out of the darkness: "Are you comfortable, sir? Is there anything you wish?"

"Jenkins?" asked Webster.

"Yes, sir," said Jenkins.

The dark form padded softly through the door.

"Yes, there's something I want," said Webster. "I want to talk to you."

He stared at the dark, metallic figure that stood beside the bed.

"About the dogs," said Webster.

"They try so hard," said Jenkins. "And it's hard for them. For they have no one, you see. Not a single soul."

"They have you."

Jenkins shook his head. "But I'm not enough, you see. I'm just . . . well, just a sort of mentor. It is men they want. The need of men is ingrown in them. For thousands of years it has been man and dog. Man and dog, hunting together. Man and dog, watching the herds together. Man and dog, fighting their enemies together. The dog watching while the man slept and the man dividing the last bit of food, going hungry himself so that his dog might eat."

Webster nodded. "Yes, I suppose that is the way it is."

"They talk about men every night," said Jenkins, "before they go to bed. They sit around together and one of the old ones tells one of the stories that have been handed down and they sit and wonder, sit and hope."

"But where are they going? What are they trying to do? Have they got a plan?"

"I can detect one," said Jenkins. "Just a faint glimmer of what may happen. They are psychic, you see. Always have been. They have no mechanical sense, which is understandable, for they have no hands. Where man would follow metal, the dogs will follow ghosts."

"Ghosts?"

"The things you men call ghosts. But they aren't ghosts. I'm sure of that. They're something in the next room. Some other form of life on another plane."

"You mean there may be many planes of life coexisting simultaneously upon Earth?"

Jenkins nodded. "I'm beginning to believe so, sir. I have a notebook full of things the dogs have heard and seen and now, after all these many years, they begin to make a pattern."

He hurried on. "I may be mistaken, sir. You understand I have no training. I was just a servant in the old days, sir. I tried to pick up things after . . . after Jupiter, but it was hard for me. Another robot helped me make the first little robots for the dogs and now the little ones produce their own kind in the workshop when there is need of more."

"But the dogs—they just sit and listen."

"Oh, no, sir, they do many other things. They try to make friends with the animals and they watch the wild robots and the mutants—"

"These wild robots? There are many of them?"

Jenkins nodded. "Many, sir. Scattered all over the world in little camps. The ones that were left behind, sir. The ones man had no further use for when he went to Jupiter. They have banded together and they work—"

"Work. What at?"

"I don't know, sir. Building machines, mostly. Mechanical,

you know. I wonder what they'll do with all the machines they have. What they plan to use them for."

"So do I," said Webster.

And he stared into the darkness and wondered—wondered how man, cooped up in Geneva, should have lost touch with the world. How man should not have known about what the dogs were doing, about the little camps of busy robots, about the castles of the feared and hated mutants.

We lost touch, Webster thought. *We locked the world outside. We created ourselves a little niche and we huddled in it—in the last city in the world. And we didn't know what was happening outside the city—we could have known, we should have known, but we didn't care.*

It's time, he thought, *that we took a hand again.*

We were lost and awed and at first we tried, but finally we just threw in the hand.

For the first time the few that were left realized the greatness of the race, saw for the first time the mighty works the hand of man had reared. And they tried to keep it going and they couldn't do it. And they rationalized—as man rationalizes almost everything. Fooling himself that there really are no ghosts, calling things that go bumping in the night the first suave, sleek word of explanation that comes into his mind.

We couldn't keep it going and so we rationalized, we took refuge in a screen of words and Juwainism helped us do it. We came close to ancestor worship. We sought to glorify the race of man. We couldn't carry on the work of man and so we tried to glorify it, attempted to enthrone the men who had. As we attempt to glorify and enthrone all good things that die.

We became a race of historians and we dug with grubby fingers in the ruins of the race, clutching each irrelevant little fact to our breast as if it were a priceless gem. And that was the first phase, the hobby that bore us up when we knew ourselves for what we really were—the dregs in the tilted cup of humanity.

But we got over it. Oh, sure, we got over it. In about one generation. Man is an adaptable creature—he can survive anything. So we couldn't build great spaceships. So we couldn't reach the stars. So we couldn't puzzle out the secret of life. So what?

We were the inheritors, we had been left the legacy, we were better off than any race had ever been or could hope to be again. And so we rationalized once more and we forgot about the glory of the race, for while it was a shining thing, it was a toilsome and humiliating concept.

"Jenkins," said Webster, soberly, "we've wasted ten whole centuries."

"Not wasted, sir," said Jenkins. "Just resting, perhaps. But now, maybe, you can come out again. Come back to us."

"You want us?"

"The dogs need you," Jenkins told him. "And the robots, too. For both of them were never anything other than the servants of man. They are lost without you. The dogs are building a civilization, but it is building slowly."

"Perhaps a better civilization than we built ourselves," said Webster. "Perhaps a more successful one. For ours was not successful, Jenkins."

"A kinder one," Jenkins admitted, "but not too practical. A civilization based on the brotherhood of animals—on the psychic understanding and perhaps eventual communication and intercourse with interlocking worlds. A civilization of the mind and of understanding, but not too positive. No actual goals, limited mechanics—just a groping after truth, and the groping is in a direction that man passed by without a second glance."

"And you think that man could help?"

"Man could give leadership," said Jenkins.

"The right kind of leadership?"

"That is hard to answer."

Webster lay in the darkness, rubbed his suddenly sweating hands along the blankets that covered his body.

"Tell me the truth," he said and his words were grim. "Man could give leadership, you say. But man also could take over once again. Could discard the things the dogs are doing as impractical. Could round the robots up and use their mechanical ability in the old, old pattern. Both the dogs and robots would knuckle down to man."

"Of course," said Jenkins. "For they were servants once. But man is wise—man knows best."

"Thank you, Jenkins," said Webster. "Thank you very much."

He stared into the darkness and the truth was written there.

His track still lay across the floor and the smell of dust was a sharpness in the air. The radium bulb glowed above the panel and the switch and wheel and dials were waiting, waiting against the day when there would be need of them.

Webster stood in the doorway, smelled the dampness of the stone through the dusty bitterness.

Defense, he thought, staring at the switch. *Defense—a thing to keep one out, a device to seal off a place against all the real or imagined weapons that a hypothetical enemy might bring to bear.*

And undoubtedly the same defense that would keep an enemy out would keep the defended in. Not necessarily, of course, but—

He strode across the room and stood before the switch and his hand went out and grasped it, moved it slowly and knew that it would work.

Then his arm moved quickly and the switch shot home. From far below came a low, soft hissing as machines went into action. The dial needles flickered and stood out from the pins.

Webster touched the wheel with hesitant fingertips, stirred it on its shaft and the needles flickered again and crawled across the glass. With a swift, sure hand, Webster spun the wheel and the needles slammed against the farther pins.

He turned abruptly on his heel, marched out of the vault, closed the door behind him, climbed the crumbling steps.

Now if it only works, he thought. *If it only works.* His feet quickened on the steps and the blood hammered in his head.

If it only works!

He remembered the hum of machines far below as he had slammed the switch. That meant that the defense mechanism—or at least part of it—still worked.

But even if it worked, would it do the trick? What if it kept the enemy out, but failed to keep men in?

What if—

When he reached the street, he saw that the sky had changed. A gray, metallic overcast had blotted out the sun and the city lay in twilight, only half relieved by the automatic street lights. A faint breeze wafted at his cheek.

The crinkly gray ash of the burned notes and the map that he had found still lay in the fireplace and Webster strode across the room, seized the poker, stirred the ashes viciously until there was no hint of what they once had been.

Gone, he thought. The last clue gone. Without the map, without the knowledge of the city that it had taken him twenty years to ferret out, no one would ever find that hidden room with the switch and wheel and dials beneath the single lamp.

No one would know exactly what had happened. And even if one guessed, there'd be no way to make sure. And even if one were sure, there'd be nothing that could be done about it.

A thousand years before it would not have been that way. For in that day man, given the faintest hint, would have puzzled out any given problem.

But man had changed. He had lost the old knowledge and old skills. His mind had become a flaccid thing. He lived from one day to the next without any shining goal. But he still kept the old vices—the vices that had become virtues from his own viewpoint and raised him by his own bootstraps. He kept the unwavering belief that his was the only kind, the only life that mattered—the smug egoism that made him the self-appointed lord of all creation.

Running feet went past the house on the street outside and Webster swung away from the fireplace, faced the blind panes of the high and narrow windows.

I got them stirred up, he thought. *Got them running now. Excited. Wondering what it's all about. For centuries they haven't stirred outside the city, but now that they can't get out—they' re foaming at the mouth to do it.*

His smile widened.

Maybe they'll be so stirred up, they'll do something about it. Rats in a trap will do some funny things—if they don't go crazy first.

And if they do get out—well, it's their right to do so. If they do get out, they've earned their right to take over once again.

He crossed the room, stood in the doorway for a moment, staring at the painting that hung above the mantel. Awkwardly, he raised his hand to it, a fumbling salute, a haggard goodbye. Then he let himself out into the street and climbed the hill—the route that Sara had walked only days before. The Temple robots were kind and considerate, soft-footed and dignified. They took him to the place where Sara lay and showed him the next compartment that she had reserved for him.

"You will want to choose a dream," said the spokesman of the robots. "We can show you many samples. We can blend them to your taste. We can—"

"Thank you," said Webster. "I do not want a dream." The robot nodded, understanding. "I see, sir. You only want to wait, to pass away the time."

"Yes," said Webster. "I guess you'd call it that."

"For about how long?"

"How long?"

"Yes. How long do you want to wait?"

"Oh, I see," said Webster. "How about forever?"

"Forever!"

"Forever is the word, I think," said Webster. "I might have said eternity, but it doesn't make much difference. There is no use of quibbling over two words that mean about the same."

"Yes, sir," said the robot.

No use of quibbling. No, of course, there wasn't. For he couldn't take the chance. He could have said a thousand years, but then he might have relented and gone down and flipped the switch.

And that was the one thing that must not happen. The dogs had to have their chance. Had to be left unhampered to try for success where the human race had failed. And so long as there was a human element they would not have that chance. For man would take over, would step in and spoil things, would laugh at the cobblies that talked behind a wall, would object to the taming and civilizing of the wild things of the earth.

A new pattern—a new way of thought and life—a new approach to the age-old social problem. And it must not be tainted by the stale breath of man's thinking.

The dogs would sit around at night when the work was done and they would talk of man. They would spin the old, old story and tell the old, old tales and man would be a god.

And it was better that way.

For a god can do no wrong.

GUNS ON GUADALCANAL

Of the five stories of World War II air combat that Clifford D. Simak wrote during the war era, this was the fourth—and the first to be written after the United States entered that war. And whereas the earlier ones all took place in the European theater, this one, as well as the one that followed, featured Americans in action against the Japanese. This story was sent to American Eagle in October 1942 (following a hiatus caused at least in part by Cliff's short-lived job with an American intelligence organization), but it would first appear in a magazine called Air War, in fall 1943.

The issue had a ten-cent cover price, and it was a good deal thinner than most pulp magazines, most likely the result of wartime paper shortages, but the issue carried reassuring notices that although changes in the customary typography and layout made the magazine look smaller, it had the normal content.

—dww

Mason saw the Zeroes first and spoke to Foster through the phones.

"Three rat cages high up, Steve. Getting ready to gang us."

The pilot craned his neck and looked, finally spotted the dots far overhead.

"O.K.," he said. "Let them think we haven't seen them. They'll come sliding in for a kill. We'll nail them then."

Mason hunkered down behind his gun and waited, watching the planes with eyes narrowed against the setting sun. Up ahead, Foster drove the throbbing Avenger along its serene way. Off to the right was the shoreline of Guadalcanal, a mass of jungle green, with a strip of white sand between the green and the darkening blue of the ocean.

"The Old Man has the right hunch, all right," Foster said quietly. "Those yellow rats have a hidden base somewhere on the island. Otherwise those planes of theirs couldn't make such quick appearances and then disappear as completely as they do. Those babies up there probably are from that very field."

Mason wasn't too interested in conversation. The Zeroes were edging in closer.

One of them slid off in a knifelike power dive.

"Here they come," yelped Mason, getting braced.

For what seemed an eternity, Foster held the Avenger on course. The second Zero was diving now and the third was wheeling over. Mason huddled grimly, waiting. He knew the Avenger wouldn't keep sailing along like this until Jap slugs reached out for it.

Any minute now . . .

Suddenly the Avenger came to life, snapped skyward, stood on its tail and climbed, the Wright Cyclone shrieking a challenge to the diving enemy.

The leading Zero twisted desperately to follow the American plane, skidding a sharp angle that almost tore it apart. Calmly Mason lined his sights with the pool of light that was the Jap's propeller as the plane came about, pressed the trips.

Fifty calibre slugs slammed into that pool of whirling steel and the Zero came unstuck.

The wash of light disappeared in an explosion of shattered metal. Long strips peeled off the cowling and the plexiglass that housed the pilot disappeared in shreds of flying debris that glinted in the sun.

For a split second something was punching holes along the Avenger's left wing as the second Zero flashed past, guns still smoking.

Then the wing guns of the Grumman opened up and Mason flipped his turret around.

The Avenger still was climbing and the wing guns were stabbing out at the third Jap, storming straight down upon them.

The red mouths of the Zero's guns flickered at them wickedly and the Avenger shuddered slightly as bullets struck home.

Ducking, Mason got behind his sights and swung his guns to bear, but even as he did, there was a thudding wham, the Grumman bucked to the recoil of the cannon in its nose and then rolled over, tumbling out of the Zero's way.

The Jap ship shook for a moment in the sky, seemed to stall in its downward dive, then slowly fell apart. One wing came off and tumbled seaward. The plane sideslipped and started screaming down, whirling and twisting, heaving wreckage as it fell, part of the second wing, the tail assembly, the motor, wrenched from the mountings, falling free.

But Mason did not watch it. There was other business at hand.

"Where is the other one?" he yelled at Foster.

Apparently Foster didn't know, for there was no answer.

There was not long to wonder.

Mason straightened up to sweep the sky and a moment later a hurricane of slashing, ripping steel caught the American ship—just a brief two second burst, but one that slivered chunks of metal off the wings, that shattered the plexiglass, that punched the tail full of gaping holes.

The Jap had attacked from below, even now was swinging up on the side of them, motor full out to make his getaway.

Mason whipped the guns around, got set as the Jap climbed into view. It was sheer luck, of course, that the Zero happened to climb straight into his sights.

Mason took advantage of that luck. He pressed the trips and kept them down.

The 50 calibres raked the rat cage from prop to tail, chewed it into a sieve-like hulk.

It went on climbing for a moment, faltered, wobbled for a second, then slid in a long slanting dive down toward the water.

Mason rubbed his hands gleefully.

"Well, that's that," he announced, but even before the words were out of his mouth he knew something was wrong. Something wrong with the throbbing of the Cyclone. As if the motor had the hiccoughs.

"Steve," he yelled. "Steve! Are you all right?"

"I'm all right," said Foster, "but the motor isn't. Acts like it can't get gas."

"Feed-line," suggested Mason.

"Yeah," agreed Foster. "That last monkey must have messed us up a bit."

"Nothing," said Mason, "like we messed him up."

Foster was craning his head over the side, trying to figure something out. The motor was choking and gasping.

"How does that beach down there look to you?" asked Foster.

Mason studied it carefully. "Ought to get her down. Might smack into a boulder or a hole or something. Never can tell."

"There's nothing else we can do," said Foster. "Hang onto your hat and cross your fingers. Here we go."

The motor gasped one last time and stopped, the prop circling idly, then hanging dead. The silence was terrifying. Wind whistled eerily along the ship's metal skin and they were going fast.

Mason, fascinated, watched and tried to relax. Mentally he made bets with himself whether they would make it.

The sea was coming up at them. The beach was off to the right. They would never make it . . .

* * *

And then they were above the beach, Foster fighting to keep the ship level. The Avenger struck the sand with a force that jarred Mason's teeth, leaped and struck again, threatening to nose over, then was rolling free, gliding to a stop.

Foster stood up, took off his helmet, wiped his brow with the back of his hand. He looked at Mason and grinned. "What are we going to do now?" asked the gunner.

"Take a look. Maybe we can patch her up."

It was the feed-line, all right. Sliced in two and not too hard to patch, but that wasn't all.

Foster, stepping back in the ship, switched on the ignition, stared at the gauges for a while and then snapped it off again.

"What's wrong now?" demanded Mason.

"The gas," said the pilot. "We lost practically all of it."

He snapped the ignition on again. The needle on the fuel gauge barely quivered.

"About two cups full," moaned Foster.

"We can call the base," said Mason. "One of the boys will be down in half an hour with enough to get us home."

"Not with this radio." Foster snapped the switch. There was no hum.

Mason groaned.

"We might just as well start matching now," he said, "to see which one of us hikes back to let them know the fix we're in."

Foster stared up and down the beach.

"Yeah, I guess you're right at that, Hank. We'll have to be careful, though. Sun'll be down in a while and one of us can start. Have to stick to the shadows as much as we can. Some Jap patrols are apt to be gum-shoeing around."

Feet crunched on the sand and Mason leaped from the wing, gun half out of his holster.

It wasn't a Jap, however. It was a native.

The man, apparently, had slipped from the jungle without them noticing him.

He stared at Mason for a moment, then stabbed a thumb at his own naked chest.

"Me N'Goni," he announced. "Me mission boy."

Mason grinned. "Me Hank," he said. "Him Steve. Americans."

N'Goni gestured at the Avenger. "Machine that fly, him haywire?"

"No gas," Mason explained. "You know him, gas?"

"Know him," declared the native. "Water make machine go put-put."

"Know where we can get any?" demanded Foster, impatient at the pidgin conversation.

N'Goni considered. "Jap maybe have him."

"Jap!" yelled Foster.

"Jap here," N'Goni told him. "In the hills. Not far."

"Sure, I know all that," said Foster. "Patrols sneaking around."

N'Goni shook his head. "Many Japs. Machine that fly. Gas."

The two Yanks looked at one another. N'Goni scraped his feet in the sand.

"The Old Man was right," said Foster. "Those dirty rats do have a field right on this island. Maybe more than one. Sending in supplies and reinforcements at night, trying to build them up."

He whirled on the native. "Can you show us where?" he demanded.

N'Goni grinned viciously. "Make go *bang boom?"* he asked.

"You're darn right we'll make them go *bang boom,"* promised Foster.

"Me show," said the native, apparently satisfied.

He started off up the beach, but they called him back.

"Not yet," explained Mason. "Go big American village first time. Tell big chief. Many machine that fly come. Bigger *bang boom."*

N'Goni's grin widened. "Me show big American village," he offered.

"Gee," said Foster, "that guy knows everything."

"Mission boy," N'Goni explained patiently.

"All right," said Mason. "You show short way. We know long way."

"Short way," agreed N'Goni.

Mason turned to Foster, waiting for his decision. Foster wrinkled his brow.

"By rights," he said, "we both should go. Blow up the ship before we leave."

"Blow up the ship!" yelled Mason. "Steve, you ain't in your right mind. That ship's all right."

"We can't allow the Japs to get hold of one," snapped Foster. "You know that as well as I do. It's too new a job. Once those monkeys got their claws on one, they'd be making them."

"One of us could stay and guard it while the other went," argued Mason. "The Japs would never know it was here. You just can't blow up a perfectly good ship. Cripes, those bombs might make a bunch of Japs say uncle."

In the end Mason won. They flipped to see who'd go and the coin turned heads for Foster.

Mason, sitting in the sand, leaned back against a palm and watched the ocean.

For a change, it wasn't raining and a brilliant tropical moon made the beach almost as light as day.

The Avenger was hidden in a coconut grove, where Foster had taxied it before he left and everything was peaceful. Too peaceful, Mason thought, leaving against the palm, trying to keep his eyes open. Waves charged upon the beach and foamed in silver spray. The wind sang in the palms and back in the jungle a monkey scolded.

Mason dozed, jerked himself awake guiltily. It was his job to watch the plane. He couldn't sleep.

The monkey was chattering again, down the beach somewhere. A muted chatter that Mason suddenly realized was no monkey chatter at all.

He sat bolt upright and listened intently. A breeze swept the sound away for a moment and then it came back again.

The gunner got to his feet, slid back into the shadows, still listening intently. He was sure he couldn't be mistaken. There were men down on that beach.

Moving swiftly, but keeping in the shadows, he hurried toward the sounds.

Rounding a rocky point that thrust out into the water, he saw the beach alive with men, small men who scurried about and carried rifles on their back. Off shore stood a ship and beyond it a couple of more ships, riding without lights, like gray ghosts in the moonlight. Boats were coming in through the surf and the men were busy unloading small steel drums.

Lying flat among the rocks, Mason watched eagerly. There was gasoline in those drums, he knew. Gasoline for the few planes the Japs were operating out of their hidden base up in the hills.

And, Lord, what beautiful targets they were, working away in the moonlight. Just about the right range, too.

Common sense tried to reason with him. "You haven't got a chance," he said. "You're just one man against them all."

"But," Hank told Common Sense, "think of the fun it'd be. Boy, could I scatter those babies!"

A truck rumbled out of the jungle, backed up to the pile of drums.

Stealthily, Mason crept from the rocks, slipped into the shadows and ran. Back at the plane, he dismounted the gun in the turret, looped his shoulders with belts of ammo and staggered at a bent-kneed gallop down the beach again.

The Japs still were there. The last of the drums were being rolled up on the truck and the little brown men, chattering like apes, were clustered around the machine. The boats had left the shore, were going back to the ship.

Softly, gingerly, Mason swung the gun off his shoulder, rested it on top of a flat rock. Carefully he laid out the ammo belts.

Waiting for a second to catch his breath, he slid behind the gun, trained it carefully. Slowly his finger squeezed the trip and suddenly the gun was jabbering.

Tracers ripped across the sand and tore into the soldiers standing at the tail of the truck. The group seemed to explode into dozens of screaming men. Others did not run, but lay still where the gun had chopped them down.

Coldly, precisely, Mason picked off the running groups. A rifle cracked and a bullet clicked against a rock nearby and went whining into space. Another rifle spat out of the shadows and Mason heard the bullet drone overhead.

The men had disappeared. More rifles were beginning to talk, bullets *spatted* close. The ammo belt ran clear. Mason jerked up another, slammed it home, pointed the gun at the loaded truck and let drive. He heard the 50 calibres spanging into the drums and suddenly the truck exploded in a gush of blue and yellow flame that paled out the moonlight and lighted beach and jungle with a garish glow.

More men were running now and Mason picked them off. Several had leaped from under the truck when the first bullets drove into the drums, but the sheet of flame had reached out, caught them before they could get away.

The burning gasoline snaked steadily into the sky now, lighting every boulder and tree upon the beach. But the Japs had disappeared.

With the last of his belt, Mason sprayed the beach, then leaped from the rocks and turned to run. But as he wheeled about he almost collided with three charging Japs. With a shout, he heaved the empty gun at the first one. It caught the little yellow man full in the stomach and bowled him over.

The second Jap was bearing down, however, bayonet gleaming.

Snatching free his .45, Mason shot from the hip and brought him down. The third man halted momentarily, lifting his rifle. The pistol barked angrily and the Jap collapsed, clutching his stomach, making choking noises.

Mason ran, ran with all the power that drove his legs, diving for the shadows. And as he reached them, a figure rose from behind a boulder, smashed a rifle butt down upon his head.

"This way," said N'Goni. "Leave ocean now. Take to hills."

Foster nodded wearily. "How much farther?" he asked.

"Not so much," the native said, and Foster suspected he was lying.

"Let's rest a minute," the pilot suggested.

N'Goni squatted on the sand and Foster sat down.

"Guns," N'Goni said calmly.

"What do you mean? Guns?"

"Guns," insisted the native, sweeping a hand the way they had come.

Foster tried to still the roaring in his head, strained his ears.

But it was several seconds before he heard the far-off chatter of a machine gun and the less frequent popping of rifles.

Walking softly, still straining his ears, he stared back down the beach. The faint chatter of the guns was muffled by a thudding roar and the distant sky was lighted with a sudden puff of brilliance.

"They found Hank!" Foster yelled at N'Goni. "They found him and he blew up the ship."

He was running and marveled that he had it in him.

"N'Goni," he yelled, but there was no answer. Stopping, he looked back. The native had disappeared.

The guns were still going, but he lost the sound of them as he resumed his run. The run dwindled to a trot, the trot to a determined slog. When next he stopped to listen, there were no guns, although a flickering brilliance still glowed ahead.

"They got him," he told himself. "They got Hank!"

And the thought became a drum that beat through his brain, a marching song that kept his feet moving down the sand.

He cursed himself that he had left Hank behind. He should have insisted on the gunner coming with him. They should have destroyed the ship in the first place. That really was what they were supposed to do.

It was near dawn as he drew near the point where they had left the Avenger and from there on he moved cautiously. The moon had sunk several hours before, but the beach still was lighted by the wash of stars that spangled the tropic sky.

The Avenger, he saw with a start, still was there, half hidden in the clump of palms. The explosion, then, hadn't been the ship, but something else.

Hope welled within him as he lay stretched flat in a jungle thicket and watched. Hank might still be there, out there watching the plane. The explosion might have been something else, maybe miles away. It would have been hard to estimate distances out there on the beach last night.

A figure moved near the plane and Foster caught his breath, half raised himself, a shout welling in his throat. But the shout died and he hugged the earth again. The figure wore a battle helmet and carried a rifle on its shoulder.

In the half light of the waning stars, he saw the first figure meet a second one, saw the two wheel about and continue their patrol. There was no question now. The Japanese had found the ship and were guarding it.

That meant that Hank was dead.

Tired, baffled rage shook Foster as he lay there, watching. Finally he moved, crawling and running at a crouch, stalking. One fact drummed in his brain. The Japs must never keep that ship!

* * *

He reached the palm thicket, slid belly-flat through the scanty undergrowth, stopping and lying like one dead when the Jap sentry was in sight, moving swiftly, but cautiously when the opportunity presented itself.

Crouching in a thicket, he waited. One of the Japs was coming. Foster listened to the steady tramp, the methodical drill-field tread. The Jap was opposite him now, was moving on.

The American pilot was a silent wraith that rose out of the bushes almost at the Jap's side, the hands that moved to the Jap's throat were death itself.

The guard opened his mouth to cry out, but the sound died in his throat and he was lifted from his feet and iron-like fingers bit into his neck. He dropped his rifle and it thudded on the damp ground, but that was the only sound. He kicked his feet and thrashed his arms, but the fingers did not relax. When Foster laid him down, the Jap was dead.

Back in his bushes, Foster waited.

The second guard ended his beat, stopped uncertainly when he did not meet the first one. Half turning to resume his march, he hesitated, moved softly, almost like a cat, down the side of the ship where his missing companion should have been.

Rigid, Foster kept his eyes on him, saw him stop when he sighted the limp figure on the ground.

For a long time the Jap stood there, staring, rifle at the ready, occasionally glancing about, sharp, quick glances as if he might surprise someone.

He came closer, thought better of it. Plainly he was afraid of a trap, afraid that what had struck down his companion might strike him down as well.

Foster could have shot him as he stood there, but that would have meant the sound of a shot; would have aroused any enemy within earshot.

Quickly, as if he made a swift decision, the Jap turned about and started to run. Foster rose silently, gripping his revolver by its barrel. He threw it with all his might and it glittered in the fading starlight as it tumbled toward the Jap, twirling end over end. It caught the little man in the small of the back, knocked him sprawling.

With a rush, Foster was on him, pinning him to earth, crushing his face to the ground to prevent an outcry. But the man twisted under him like a greased eel and thick-fingered hands clawed at the American.

Foster chopped at the man's chin with an awkward right, for there was no room to swing. The Jap's fingers found the pilot's throat, failed to get a grip, clawed viciously at his face, leaving painful gashes on the cheek.

A knee came up viciously, slugged into Foster's stomach, knocking the wind half from him.

In a blind haze of rage, the American reached the Jap's throat with one hand, dragged him forward. His other clutching hand closed on a leg. Slowly, fighting with all this strength, Foster rose to his knees, struggled to his feet, lifted the squirming Jap above his head. Lifted him and threw him, with all his strength, against the Avenger's metal side.

The Jap screamed shortly before he crashed against the plane, before he flopped into a grotesque rag-doll bundle, head twisted at an angle that said his neck was broken.

Foster leaned weakly against the ship, stared dully out to sea, where the first pale streamers of the sun were lighting a new day.

Minutes later, he walked over to pick up his revolver. Then he dragged the two dead Japs into the brush and staggered down the beach.

There, behind a spur of rock, he found the machine gun from the Avenger and on the rock a belt of ammo and many empty cases.

On the beach beyond was the burned skeleton of a truck and

bursted steel drums. There also were dark spots in the sand . . . spots where men had died.

Legs braced wide, his body drooping with the punishment it had taken, Foster stared at the tracks of the truck leading out of the jungle, shifted his gaze to the climbing jungle, black and green with the coming dawn.

Up there somewhere was the Jap air base. Up there was a job to do.

And there was the Avenger to be destroyed and bombs that could be used.

Another thing, too. Hank was dead. That called for some sort of fitting gesture, some sort of rough tribute.

Steve Foster stood, stiff-legged, and stared at the hills.

But Hank Mason wasn't dead.

He sat on the edge of a bed fashioned of poles and held his head in his hands. His head ached. No wonder, he thought, after the clout he'd got with that rifle butt.

The jungle bowl in which lay the Jap base swam with sullen heat.

A Japanese guard lounged against the hut's door and looking past him Mason could see the air field, small but good enough for small planes and pilots that didn't care whether they lived or died. Taking off and landing would be tricky in such a place, but it had the advantage of being well hidden, hard to find. The only way it could be spotted, Mason knew, was by a plane flying directly over it.

Great drums of fuel were stacked along the field and a line of planes rested under a flimsy camouflage. A group of natives were toiling on the field, wrestling stones and stumps, while Jap guards kept close watch, shrilling sharp words at any who might lag.

Mason took his left hand down from his head and looked at his wrist watch. It was almost 10 o'clock. By this time Foster and his native guide would have reached the American base. Soon a plane or two would be roaring out to rescue the stranded Avenger.

If there was only some way to let them know. N'Goni, of course, would have told them of the Jap base, but there was the problem of finding it. Unless a plane flew directly overhead, it would be hard to spot.

If there were only some way—

His eyes narrowed as he stared at the fuel drums. There might be a way, after all. If only he just knew when those planes would be around.

He shifted his gaze to the guard. The fellow watched him closely with shiny black eyes. Something was sticking out of the man's pocket . . . a long handle and a bulge in the pocket. Mason gulped. Unless he was mistaken, it was a hand grenade, one of those potato-masher affairs.

"American feel so bad," suggested the guard, hopefully.

"Shut up," snarled Mason.

The Jap's face darkened and his eyes grew brighter, if that were possible.

"You no talk to me like that," he said. "Me good as you are. Better maybe."

"Like heck, you say," said Mason.

The guard jerked his gun down toward Mason.

"Me tickle you up a bit, maybe. Talk different, then."

Mason stared at the bayonet. "You keep that thing out of my reach, Joe," he warned, "or I'll take it away from you and slit your gizzard with it."

"Commander see you in little while. Talk with you. Then we take you out, kill you." The Jap squinted his eyes to see how Mason took it.

"You scummy little buzzards get a big kick out of killing people, don't you?" said Mason.

"You talk too much," hissed the Jap.

"Sez you!" said Mason.

The guard stepped inside the hut, moved closer, bayonetted rifle held stiffly in front of him.

"Me mess you up a bit," he decided.

"The commander won't like that," Mason warned.

"Commander won't care. Just so not too much."

He advanced with mincing steps, pushing the pointed steel closer and closer. Mason watched it idly, but the blood was pounding in his throat. This baiting of the guard was taking a chance, an awful chance.

The Jap danced nearer, eyes sparkling.

The bayonet was no more than six inches away when Mason moved . . . moved like an unwinding coil spring. With a single motion he slapped the bayonet aside, rose to his feet and hit the Jap with his fist. The swing was a round-house blow, coming almost from the floor. It caught the Jap on the chin even before he could look surprised, lifted him off the floor, slammed him against the wall.

Glassy-eyed, the man sagged to the floor.

Grunting in satisfaction, Mason picked up the fallen rifle, used the bayonet, then bent above the erstwhile guard and took the long-handled thing from his pocket. It was a grenade, all right.

Clutching it in his hand, he walked to the door of the hut, stuck out his head, glanced cautiously up and down. There seemed to be Japs everywhere, but none of them were looking in his direction.

There was, he decided, only one way to do it. If he ran, they'd notice him, be on him in a minute, sure he was making a break. But if he walked he might not attract attention. They might be puzzled, but they might think it was all right, give him the time he needed.

Regretfully, he leaned the rifle against the wall, slipped the grenade in his belt and sauntered out into the open.

Walking slowly, he had gone a hundred feet when someone yelled at him. Stifling a desire to run, he kept on unhurriedly. The yell was not repeated.

Another hundred feet. Those fuel barrels were nearer now, much nearer. Just a few more steps and in a pinch he could reach them.

Another shout. A chorus of shouts and the patter of running feet.

Mason jerked the grenade from his belt, snapped out the pin and heaved. Then he ducked and ran. Rifles cracked and chugging things kicked up dust at his feet and in front of him.

He doubled behind a hut, ran full tilt into a startled soldier. From the field came the roar of the grenade, the gushy sigh of rushing flame.

The impact had knocked the soldier off his balance and, as he staggered, Mason reached out and snatched away his rifle.

A rocky hillside lay just ahead. He sprinted for it. Something tugged at his side and a sharp jab of pain went through him.

Behind him an oil drum exploded with a hollow boom. He snatched a quick glance over his shoulder. Black smoke was mushrooming far above the field.

Also, and more important, at least a dozen Japs were on his heels.

He swung around and snapped the rifle up. The mechanism was unfamiliar, but he got in two shots. Both counted. Then he was running again, stumbling as something smacked into his shoulder.

A roaring filled his head and he went down on hands and knees. This was the end, he knew. They'd get him now. He'd be cold meat for the Japs and no mistake.

But the roaring wasn't all in his head. There was another roar. The throaty roar of a motor sweeping down into the bowl. And then another sound. The chattering of guns, a wicked, vicious sound, a snarling crescendo that seemed to sweep down upon him, then snapped off.

He flopped over and sat down, stared into the sky.

Climbing over the field was a ship—a ship he'd know anywhere. The Avenger he'd left back on the beach!

The camp was in pandemonium. Shrieking Japs were running. In front of him lay five of them, where they had been mowed down by the strafing guns. "Steve," he yelled. "Give it to 'em, Steve!"

As if in answer, a black object leaped from the belly of the plane and streaked earthward. Earth and dust billowed up in a flash of fire and rolling smoke. Another bomb was falling and again the hills echoed with the thud of a five-hundred-pounder.

The camouflaged planes were gone, fire licking through them.

Painfully, hopefully, Mason got back on his hands and knees and crawled. Maybe if he got up that hillside when nobody was noticing him, he might have a chance.

Another bomb shook the earth and Mason counted: "Three." There was one left.

The explosion came. That was all there was.

An anti-aircraft cut loose and the Avenger howled in answer, howled, then stuttered with fiendish gunbursts.

Feet pattered behind Mason and someone bent to lift him.

"Me carry," said N'Goni.

"N'Goni," yelled Mason. "What are you doing here?"

But he didn't wait for the answer, for, even as he spoke, a sound came that chilled his heart. The coughing of the Avenger's motor.

Then he remembered. There had been only a little gas. Now that was used up. The ship would fall.

He struggled to his feet and watched, with a dull ache in his heart. The Grumman, prop barely turning over, was wheeling toward the very hillside where he stood. Plunging at them, faster and faster.

"Is that Steve?" shouted Mason at N'Goni. "Is that Steve in there?"

"Maybe," said N'Goni. "Him go back. Hear guns. So him go."

So Steve had come back. Had heard guns and had come back. Figuring he'd keep his gunner out of trouble, get him out of a mess.

The Avenger lifted its nose slightly as it hit the up-currents of the hillside, seemed for a moment almost to stall and then crashed no more than a hundred yards above them.

N'Goni was loping up the hill, eating up the distance, while Mason limped behind.

Down below the Jap base was ablaze, thick columns of smoke standing in the air. The parked planes were burning, gas dumps were belching thick black clouds.

A new sound stopped Mason in his tracks. The distant hum of many motors. A hum that grew until it was a roar and then a shriek.

Streaming over the lip of the bowl was a formation of American bombers, bombers that howled down upon the Japs with blazing guns and a roar of bombs. Blindly Mason stumbled up the hillside.

N'Goni was helping Foster out of the Avenger and, through the blood that streamed from a cut across his forehead, the pilot grinned at Mason.

"You O.K.?" gasped Mason.

"Right as rain," said Foster.

"But N'Goni, how did the Americans know? You couldn't have gotten there and got back this soon."

"Me send brother," N'Goni explained. "Remember got to work for Jap. No work, Jap mad. Kill family, maybe. So send brother. Tell him what to say."

"So that's why you ran out on me," said Foster.

N'Goni grinned. "Me remember quick. Mad Jap, bad Jap."

"They aren't mad now," said Foster. "They're just plain scared to death."

The base was a froth of smoke and flame and bellowing motors as the Yank planes crossed and criss-crossed it, sowing destruction. With guns and bombs, the Japs were being wiped out. "You sit," said N'Goni. "You watch. Me, too."

He hunkered down, grinning.

"Grand stand seat," said Foster.

COURTESY

This story was first sent to Horace Gold of Galaxy Science Fiction *in mid-September 1950, but after Gold rejected it, Cliff sent it to Fred Pohl, then apparently acting as Cliff's agent. John W. Campbell Jr., purchased it via Pohl the following March, paying $225, and it was published in the August 1951 issue of Campbell's magazine, Astounding Science Fiction.*

"Courtesy" is a morality tale, one that I believe represents yet another aspect of Cliff Simak's reactions to World War II, so recently ended: the need to avoid thinking, and acting, as if you're a member of a superior race. Yet "Courtesy" represents a puzzle for Simak fans, for while it's one of the few stories in which Cliff apparently used characters who would reappear in a later story—"Junkyard," published in 1953—you will see that if the stories are related, they were, strangely, not written and published in the correct order. (It's true that Cliff sometimes reused character names, but this is not one of those cases; it is clear that they were the same characters; I lean toward the idea that Cliff actually began "Junkyard" first, but there is absolutely no evidence to support that speculation.)

—dww

The serum was no good. The labels told the story.

Dr. James H. Morgan took his glasses off and wiped them carefully, cold terror clutching at his innards. He put the spectacles back on, probing at them with a thick, blunt finger to settle them into correct position. Then he took another look. He had been right the first time. The date on the serum consignment was a good ten years too old.

He wheeled slowly, lumbered a few ponderous steps to the tent flap and stood there, squat body framed in the triangular entrance, pudgy hands gripping the canvas on either side.

Outside, the fantastic lichen moors stretched to gray and bleak horizons. The setting sun was a dull red glow in the west—and to the east, the doctor knew, night already was beginning to close in, with that veil of purplish light that seemed to fall like a curtain upon the land and billow rapidly across it.

A chill wind blew out of the east, already touched with the frigidity of night, and twitched the canvas beneath the doctor's fingers.

"Ah, yes," said Dr. Morgan, "the merry moors of Landro."

A lonely place, he told himself. Not lonely only in its barrenness nor in its alien wildness, but with an ingrained loneliness that could drive a man mad if he were left alone with it.

Like a great cemetery, he thought, an empty place of dead. And yet without the cemetery's close association, without the tenderness and the inevitability of a cemetery. For a cemetery held in scared trust the husks of those who once had lived and this place was an emptiness that held no memory at all.

But not for long, said Dr. Morgan. Not for long now.

He stood looking at the barren slope that rose above the camp and he decided that it would make an eminently satisfactory cemetery.

All places looked alike. That was the trouble. You couldn't tell one place from another. There were no trees and there were no bushes, just a fuzzy-looking scrub that grew here and there, clothing the naked land in splotches, like the ragged coat that a beggar wears.

Benny Falkner stopped on the path as it topped the rise and stood rigid with the fear that was mounting in him. Fear of the coming night and of its bitter cold, fear of the silent hills and the shadowed swales, and the more distant and yet more terrible fear of the little natives that might this very moment be skulking on the hillside.

He put up his arm and wiped the sweat off his brow with his tattered sleeve. He shouldn't have been sweating, he told himself, for it was chilly now and getting colder by the minute. In another hour or two it would be cold enough to freeze a man unprotected in the open.

He fought down the terror that choked his throat and set his teeth a-chatter and for an instant stood stock-still to convince himself he was not panic-stricken.

He had been going east and that meant he must go west to reach the camp again. Although the catch was that he couldn't be absolutely sure he had been going east all the time—he might have trended north a little or even wandered south. But the deviation couldn't have been enough, he was sure, to throw him so far off that he could not spot the camp by returning straight into the west.

Sometime soon he should sight the smoke of the Earthmen's camp. Any ridge, the next ridge, each succeeding hummock in the winding trail, he had assured himself, would bring him upon the camp itself. He would reach higher ground and there the camp would be, spread out in front of him, with the semicircle of white canvas gleaming in the fading light and the thin trail of smoke rising from the larger cook tent where Bat Ears Brady would be bellowing one of his obscene songs.

But that had been an hour ago when the sun still stood a good two hands high. He remembered now, standing on the ridge-top, that he had been a little nervous, but not really apprehensive. It had been unthinkable, then, that a man could get himself lost in an hour's walk out of camp.

Now the sun was gone and the cold was creeping in and the wind had a lonely sound he had not noticed when the light was good.

One more rise, he decided. One more ridge, and if that is not the one, I'll give up until morning. Find a sheltered place somewhere, a rock face of some sort that will give me some protection and reflect a campfire's heat—if I can find anything with which to make a campfire.

He stood and listened to the wind moaning across the land behind him and it seemed to him there was a whimper in the sound, as if the wind were anxious, that it might be following on his track, sniffing out his scent.

Then he heard the other sound, the soft, padding sound that came up the hill toward him.

Ira Warren sat at his desk and stared accusingly at the paperwork stacked in front of him. Reluctantly he took some of the papers off the stack and laid them on the desk.

That fool Falkner, he thought. I've told them and I've told them that they have to stick together, that no one must go wandering off alone.

A bunch of babies, he told himself savagely. Just a bunch of drooling kids, fresh out of college, barely dry behind the ears and all hopped up with erudition, but without any common sense. And not a one of them would listen. That was the worst of it, not a one of them would listen.

Someone scratched on the canvas of the tent.

"Come in," called Warren.

Dr. Morgan entered.

"Good evening, commander," he said.

"Well," said Warren irritably, "what now?"

"Why, now," said Dr. Morgan, sweating just a little. "It's the matter of the serum."

"The serum?"

"The serum," said Dr. Morgan. "It isn't any good."

"What do you mean?" asked Warren. "I have troubles, doctor. I can't play patty-cake with you about your serum."

"It's too old," said Morgan. "A good ten years too old. You can't use old serum. You see, it might . . ."

"Stop chattering," commanded Warren, sharply. "The serum is too old, you say. When did you find this out?"

"Just now."

"You mean this very moment?"

Morgan nodded miserably.

Warren pushed the papers to one side very carefully and deliberately. He placed his hands on the desk in front of him and made a tent out of his fingers.

"Tell me this, doctor," said Warren, speaking cautiously, as if he were hunting in his mind for the exact words which he must use, "how long has this expedition been on Landro?"

"Why," said Morgan, "quite some time, I'd say." He counted mental fingers. "Six weeks, to be exact."

"And the serum has been here all that time?"

"Why, of course," said Morgan. "It was unloaded from the ship at the same time as all the other stuff."

"It wasn't left around somewhere, so that you just found it? It was taken to your tent at once?"

"Of course it was," said Morgan. "The very first thing. I always insist upon that procedure."

"At any time in the last six weeks, at any given moment in any day of that whole six weeks, you could have inspected the serum and found it was no good? Isn't that correct, doctor?"

"I suppose I could have," Morgan admitted. "It was just that . . ."

"You didn't have the time," suggested Warren, sweetly.

"Well, not that," said Morgan.

"You were, perhaps, too pressed with other interests?"

"Well, not exactly."

"You were aware that up to a week ago we could have contacted the ship by radio and it could have turned back and took us off. They would have done that if we had let them know about the serum."

"I know that."

"And you know now that they're outside our radio range. We can't let them know. We can't call them back. We won't have any contact with the human race for the next two years."

"I," said Morgan, weakly, "I . . ."

"It's been lovely knowing you," Warren told him. "Just how long do you figure it will be before we are dead?"

"It will be another week or so before we'll become susceptible to the virus," Morgan said. "It will take, in certain stubborn cases, six weeks or so for it to kill a man."

"Two months," said Warren. "Three, at the outside. Would you say that was right, Dr. Morgan?"

"Yes," said Morgan.

"There is something that I want you to tell me," Warren said.

"What is it?" Morgan asked.

"Sometime when you have a moment, when you have the time and it is no inconvenience to you, I should like to know just how it feels to kill twenty-five of your fellow men."

"I," said Morgan, "I . . ."

"And yourself, of course," said Warren. "That makes twenty-six."

Bat Ears Brady was a character. For more than thirty years now he had been going out on planetary expeditions with Commander Ira Warren, although Warren had not been a commander when it started, but a second looey. Today they were still together, a team of toughened planet-checkers. Although no one on the outside would have known that they were a team, for Warren headed the expedition and Bat Ears cooked for them.

Now Warren set out a bottle on his desk and sent for Bat Ears Brady.

Warren heard him coming for some time before he finally arrived. He'd had a drink or two too many and he was singing most obscenely.

He came through the tent entrance walking stiff and straight, as if there were a chalked line laid out for him to follow. He saw the bottle on the desk and picked it up, disregarding the glasses set beside it. He lowered the bottle by a good three inches and set it back again. Then he took the camp chair that had been placed there for him.

"What's the matter now?" he demanded. "You never send for me unless there's something wrong."

"What," asked Warren, "have you been drinking?"

Bat Ears hiccupped politely. "Little something I cooked up."

He regarded Warren balefully. "Use to be we could bring in a little something, but now they say we can't. What little there is you keep under lock and key. When a man gets thirsty, it sure tests his ingen . . . ingen . . . ingen . . ."

"Ingenuity," said Warren.

"That's the word," said Bat Ears. "That's the word, exactly."

"We're in a jam, Bat Ears," said Warren.

"We're always in a jam," said Bat Ears. "Ain't like the old days, Ira. Had some he-men then. But now . . ."

"I know what you mean," said Warren.

"Kids," said Bat Ears, spitting on the floor in a gesture of contempt. "Scarcely out of didies. Got to wipe their noses and . . ."

"It isn't that kind of a jam," said Warren. "This is the real McCoy. If we can't figure this one out, we'll all be dead before two months are gone."

"Natives?" asked Bat Ears.

"Not the natives," Warren told him. "Although more than likely they'd be glad to do us in if there was a chance."

"Cheeky customers," said Bat Ears. "One of them sneaked into the cook tent and I kicked him off the reservation real unceremonious. He did considerable squalling at me. He didn't like it none."

"You shouldn't kick them, Bat Ears."

"Well, Ira, I didn't really kick him. That was just a figure of speech, kind of. No sir, I didn't kick him. I took a shovel to him. Always could handle a shovel some better than my feet. Reach farther and . . ."

He reached out and took the bottle, lowered it another inch or two.

"This crisis, Ira?"

"It's the serum," Warren told him. "Morgan waited until the ship had got too far for us to contact them before he thought to check the serum. And it isn't any good—it's about ten years too old."

Bat Ears sat half stunned.

"So we don't get our booster shots," said Warren, "and that means that we will die. There's this deadly virus here, the . . . the—oh, well, I can't remember the name of it. But you know about it."

"Sure," said Bat Ears. "Sure I know about it."

"Funny thing," said Warren. "You'd expect to find something like that on one of the jungle planets. But, no, you find it here. Something about the natives. They're humanoid. Got the same kind of guts we got. So the virus developed an ability to attack a humanoid system. We are good, new material for it."

"It don't seem to bother the natives none now," said Bat Ears.

"No," said Warren. "They seem to be immune. One of two things: They've found a cure or they've developed natural immunity."

"If they've found a cure," said Bat Ears, "we can shake it out of them."

"And if they haven't," said Warren, "if adaptation is the answer—then we're dead ducks for sure."

"We'll start working on them," said Bat Ears. "They hate us and they'd love to see us croak, but we'll find some way to get it out of them."

"Everything always hates us," Warren said. "Why is that, Bat Ears? We do our best and they always hate us. On every planet that Man has set a foot on. We try to make them like us, we do all we can for them. But they resent our help. Or reject our friendliness. Or take us for a bunch of suckers—so that finally we lose our patience and we take a shovel to them."

"And then," said Bat Ears, sanctimoniously, "the fat is in the fire."

"What I'm worried about is the men," said Warren. "When they hear about this serum business . . ."

"We can't tell them," said Bat Ears. "We can't let them know. They'll find out, after a while, of course, but not right away."

"Morgan is the only one who knows," said Warren, "and he blabs. We can't keep him quiet. It'll be all over camp by morning."

Bat Ears rose ponderously. He towered over Warren as he reached out a hand for the bottle on the desk.

"I'll drop in on Morgan on my way back," he said. "I'll fix it so he won't talk."

He took a long pull at the bottle and set it back.

"I'll draw a picture of what'll happen to him if he does," said Bat Ears.

Warren sat easily in his chair, watching the retreating back of Bat Ears Brady. Always there in a pinch, he thought. Always a man that you can depend on.

Bat Ears was back in three minutes flat. He stood in the entrance of the tent, no sign of drunkenness upon him, his face solemn, eyes large with the thing he'd seen.

"He croaked himself," he said.

That was the solemn truth.

Dr. James H. Morgan lay dead inside his tent, his throat sliced open with a professional nicety that no one but a surgeon could have managed.

About midnight the searching party brought in Falkner.

Warren stared wearily at him. The kid was scared. He was all scratched up from floundering around in the darkness and he was pale around the gills.

"He saw our light, sir," said Peabody, "and let out a yell. That's the way we found him."

"Thank you, Peabody," said Warren. "I'll see you in the morning. I want to talk to Falkner."

"Yes, sir," said Peabody. "I am glad we found him, sir."

Wish I had more like him, thought Warren. Bat Ears, the ancient planet-checker; Peabody, an old army man, and Gilmer, the grizzled supply officer. Those are the ones to count on. The rest of them are punks.

Falkner tried to stand stiff and straight.

"You see, sir," he told Warren, "it was like this: I thought I saw an outcropping . . ."

Warren interrupted him. "You know, of course, Mr. Falkner, that it is an expedition rule you are never to go out by yourself; that under no circumstances is one to go off by himself."

"Yes, sir," said Falkner, "I know that . . ."

"You are aware," said Warren, "that you are alive only by some incredible quirk of fate. You would have frozen before morning if the natives hadn't got you first."

"I saw a native, sir. He didn't bother me."

"You are more than lucky, then," said Warren. "It isn't often that a native hasn't got the time to spare to slit a human's throat. In the five expeditions that have been here before us, they have killed a full eighteen. Those stone knives they have, I can assure you, make very ragged slitting."

Warren drew a record book in front of him, opened it and made a very careful notation.

"Mr. Falkner," he said, "you will be confined to camp for a two-week period for infraction of the rules. Also, during that time, you shall be attached to Mr. Brady."

"Mr. Brady, sir? The cook?"

"Precisely," said Warren. "He probably shall want you to hustle fuel and help with the meals and dispose of garbage and other such light tasks."

"But I was sent on this expedition to make geologic observations, not to help the cook."

"All very true," admitted Warren. "But, likewise, you were sent out under certain regulations. You have seen fit to disregard those regulations and I see fit, as a result, to discipline you. That is all, Mr. Falkner."

Falkner turned stiffly and moved toward the tent flap.

"By the way," said Warren, "I forgot to tell you. I'm glad that you got back."

Falkner did not answer.

Warren stiffened for a moment, then relaxed. After all, he thought, what did it matter? Within another few weeks nothing would matter for him and Falkner, nor for any of the rest.

The chaplain showed up the first thing in the morning. Warren was sitting on the edge of his cot, pulling on his trousers, when the man came in. It was cold and Warren was shivering despite the sputtering of the little stove that stood beside the desk.

The chaplain was very precise and businesslike about his visit.

"I thought I should talk with you," he said, "about arranging services for our dear departed friend."

"What dear departed friend?" asked Warren, shivering and pulling on a shoe.

"Why, Dr. Morgan, of course."

"I see," said Warren. "Yes, I suppose we shall have to bury him."

The chaplain stiffened just a little.

"I was wondering if the doctor had any religious convictions, any sort of preference."

"I doubt it very much," said Warren. "If I were you, I'd hold it down to minimum simplicity."

"That's what I thought," said the chaplain. "A few words, perhaps, and a simple prayer."

"Yes," said Warren. "A prayer by all means. We'll need a lot of prayer."

"Pardon me, sir?"

"Oh," Warren told him, "don't mind me. Just wool-gathering, that's all."

"I see," said the chaplain. "I was wondering, sir, if you have any idea what might have made him do it."

"Who do what?"

"What made the doctor commit suicide."

"Oh, that," said Warren. "Just an unstable character, I guess."

He laced his shoes and stood up.

"Mr. Barnes," he said, "you are a man of God, and a very good one from what I've seen of you. You may have the answer to a question that is bothering me."

"Why," said Mr. Barnes, "why I . . ."

"What would you do," asked Warren, "if you suddenly were to find out you had no more than two months to live?"

"Why," said Mr. Barnes, "I suppose that I would go on living pretty much the way I always have. With a little closer attention to the condition of my soul, perhaps."

"That," said Warren, "is a practical answer. And, I suppose, the most reasonable that anyone can give."

The chaplain looked at him curiously. "You don't mean, sir . . ."

"Sit down, Barnes," said Warren. "I'll turn up the stove. I need you now. To tell you the solemn truth, I've never held too much with this business of having you fellows with the expedition. But I guess there always will be times when one needs a man like you."

The chaplain sat down.

"Mr. Barnes," said Warren, "that was no hypothetical question I asked. Unless God performs some miracle we'll all be dead in another two months' time."

"You are joking, sir."

"Not at all," said Warren. "The serum is no good. Morgan waited to check it until it was too late to get word to the ship. That's why he killed himself."

He watched the chaplain closely and the chaplain did not flinch.

"I was of a mind," said Warren, "not to tell you. I'm not telling any of the others—not for a while, at least."

"It takes a little while," said Mr. Barnes, "to let a thing like that soak in. I find it so, myself. Maybe you should tell the others, let them have a chance . . ."

"No," said Warren.

The chaplain stared at him. "What are you hoping for, Warren? What do you expect to happen?"

"A miracle," said Warren.

"A miracle?"

"Certainly," said Warren. "You believe in miracles. You must."

"I don't know," said Mr. Barnes. "There are certain miracles, of course—one might call them allegorical miracles, and sometimes men read into them more than was ever meant."

"I am more practical than that," said Warren, harshly. "There is the miracle of the fact that the natives of this place are humanoid like ourselves and they don't need any booster shots. There is a potential miracle in the fact that only the first humans who landed on the planet ever tried to live on Landro without the aid of booster shots."

"Since you mention it," said the chaplain, "there is the miracle of the fact that we are here at all."

Warren blinked at him. "That's right," he said. "Tell me, why do you think we're here? Divine destiny, perhaps. Or the immutable performance of the mysterious forces that move Man along his way."

"We are here," said Barnes, "to carry on the survey work that has been continued thus far by parties here before us."

"And that will be continued," said Warren, "by the parties that come after us."

"You forget," the chaplain said, "that all of us will die. They will be very wary of sending another expedition to replace one that has been wiped out."

"And you," said Warren, "forget the miracle."

* * *

The report had been written by the psychologist who had accompanied the third expedition to Landro. Warren had managed, after considerable digging in the file of quadruplicates, to find a copy of it.

"Hog wash," he said and struck the papers with his fist.

"I could of told you that," said Bat Ears, "before you ever read it. Ain't nothing one of them prissy punks can tell an old-timer like me about these abor . . . abor . . . abor . . ."

"Aborigines," said Warren.

"That's the word," said Bat Ears. "That's the word I wanted."

"It says here," declared Warren, "that the natives of Landro have a keen sense of dignity, very delicately tuned—that's the very words it uses—and an exact code of honor when dealing among themselves."

Bat Ears snorted and reached for the bottle. He took a drink and sloshed what was left in the bottom discontentedly.

"You sure," he asked, "that this is all you got?"

"You should know," snapped Warren.

Bat Ears wagged his head. "Comforting thing," he said. "Mighty comforting."

"It says," went on Warren, "that they also have a system of what amounts to protocol, on a rather primitive basis."

"I don't know about this proto-whatever-you-may-call-it," said Bat Ears, "but that part about the code of honor gets me. Why, them dirty vultures would steal the pennies off a dead man's eyes. I always keep a shovel handy and when one of them shows up . . ."

"The report," said Warren, "goes into that most exhaustively. Explains it."

"Ain't no need of explanation," insisted Bat Ears. "They just want what you got, so they sneak in and take it."

"Says it's like stealing from a rich man," Warren told him. "Like a kid that sees a field with a million melons in it. Kid can't see anything wrong with taking one melon out of all that million."

"We ain't got no million melons," said Bat Ears.

"It's just an analogy," said Warren. "The stuff we have here must look like a million melons to our little friends."

"Just the same," protested Bat Ears, "they better keep out of my cook tent . . ."

"Shut up," said Warren savagely. "I get you here to talk with you and all you do is drink up my liquor and caterwaul about your cook tent."

"All right," said Bat Ears. "All right. What do you want to know?"

"What are we doing about contacting the natives?"

"Can't contact them," said Bat Ears, "if we can't find them. They were around here, thicker than fleas, before we needed them. Now that we need them, can't find hide nor hair of one."

"As if they might know that we needed them," said Warren.

"How would they know?" asked Bat Ears.

"I can't tell you," Warren said. "It was just a thought."

"If you do find them," asked Bat Ears, "how you going to make them talk?"

"Bribe them," said Warren. "Buy them. Offer them anything we have."

Bat Ears shook his head. "It won't work. Because they know all they got to do is wait. If they just wait long enough, it's theirs without the asking. I got a better way."

"Your way won't work, either."

"You're wasting your time, anyhow," Bat Ears told him. "They ain't got no cure. It's just adap . . . adap . . ."

"Adaptation."

"Sure," said Bat Ears. "That's the word I meant."

He took up the bottle, shook it, measured it with his thumb and then, in a sudden gesture, killed it.

He rose quickly to his feet. "I got to sling some grub together," he said. "You stay here and get her figured out."

Warren sat quietly in the tent, listening to his footsteps going across the compound of the camp.

There was no hope, of course. He must have known that all along, he told himself, and yet he had postponed the realization of it. Postponed it with talk of miracles and hope that the natives might have the answer—and the native answer, the native cure, he admitted now, was even more fantastic than the hope of a miracle. For how could one expect the little owl-eyed people would know of medicine when they did not know of clothing, when they still carried rudely-chipped stone knives, when their campfire was a thing very laboriously arrived at by the use of stricken flint?

They would die, all twenty-five of them, and in the days to come the little owl-eyed natives would come boldly marching in, no longer skulking, and pick the camp to its last bare bone.

Collins was the first to go. He died hard, as all men die hard when infected by the peculiar virus of Landro. Before he was dead, Peabody had taken to his bed with the dull headache that heralded the onset of the malady. After that the men went down like tenpins. They screamed and moaned in delirium, they lay as dead for days before they finally died, while the fever ate at them like some ravenous animal that had crept in from the moors.

There was little that anyone could do. Make them comfortable, keep them bathed and the bedding washed and changed, feed them broth that Bat Ears made in big kettles on the stove, be sure there was fresh, cold water always available for the fever-anguished throats.

At first the graves were deep and wooden crosses were set up, with the name and other information painted on the cross bar. Then the graves were only shallow holes because there were less hands to dig them and less strength within the hands.

To Warren it was a nightmare of eternity—a ceaseless round of caring for his stricken men, of helping with the graves, of writing in the record book the names of those who died. Sleep came in snatches when he could catch it or when he became so exhausted that he tottered in his tracks and could not keep his eyelids open. Food was something that Bat Ears brought and set in front of him and he gulped without knowing what it was, without tasting what it was.

Time was a forgotten thing and he lost track of days. He asked what day it was and no one knew nor seemed to care. The sun came up and the sun went down and the moors stretched to their gray horizons, with the lonely wind blowing out of them.

Vaguely he became aware of fewer and fewer men who worked beside him, of fewer stricken men upon the cots. And one day he sat down in his tent and looked across at another haggard face and knew it was nearly over.

"It's a cruel thing, sir," said the haggard face.

"Yes, Mr. Barnes," said Warren. "How many are there left?"

"Three," said the chaplain, "and two of them are nearly gone. Young Falkner seems to be better, though."

"Any on their feet?"

"Bat Ears, sir. Just you and I and Bat Ears."

"Why don't we catch it, Barnes? Why are we still here?"

"No one knows," the chaplain told him. "I have a feeling that we'll not escape it."

"I know," said Warren. "I have that feeling, too."

Bat Ears lumbered into the tent and set a pail upon the table. He reached into it and scooped out a tin cup, dripping, and handed it to Warren.

"What is it, Bat Ears?" Warren asked.

"Something I cooked up," said Bat Ears. "Something that you need."

Warren lifted the cup and gulped it down. It burned its way clear into his stomach, set his throat afire and exploded in his head.

"Potatoes," said Bat Ears. "Spuds make powerful stuff. The Irish found that out, years and years ago."

He took the cup from Warren, dipped it again and handed it to Barnes.

The chaplain hesitated.

Bat Ears shouted at him. "Drink it, man. It'll put some heart in you."

The minister drank, choked, set the cup back on the table empty.

"They're back again," said Bat Ears.

"Who's back?" asked Warren.

"The natives," said Bat Ears. "All around us, waiting for the end of us."

He disdained the cup, lifted the pail in both his hands and put it to his lips. Some of the liquor splashed out of the corners of his mouth and ran darkly down his shirt.

He put the pail back on the table, wiped his mouth with a hairy fist.

"They might at least be decent about it," he declared. "They might at least keep out of sight until it is all over. Caught one sneaking out of Falkner's tent. Old gray buck. Tried to catch him, but he outlegged me."

"Falkner's tent?"

"Sure. Snooping around before a man is dead. Not even waiting till he's gone. Didn't take nothing, though, I guess. Falkner was asleep. Didn't even wake him."

"Asleep? You sure?"

"Sure," said Bat Ears. "Breathing natural. I'm going to unsling my gun and pick off a few of them, just for luck. I'll teach them . . ."

"Mr. Brady," asked Barnes, "you are certain Falkner was sleeping naturally? Not in a coma? Not dead?"

"I know when a man is dead," yelled Bat Ears.

Jones and Webster died during the night. Warren found Bat Ears in the morning, collapsed beside his stone-cold stove, the empty liquor pail beside him. At first he thought the cook was only drunk and then he saw the signs upon him. He hauled him across the floor and boosted him onto his cot, then went out to find the chaplain.

He found him in the cemetery, wielding a shovel, his hands red with broken blisters.

"It won't be deep," said Mr. Barnes, "but it will cover them. It's the best that I can do."

"Bat Ears has it," Warren told him.

The chaplain leaned on his shovel, breathing a little hard from digging.

"Queer," he said. "Queer, to think of him. Of big, brawling Bat Ears. He was a tower of strength."

Warren reached for the shovel.

"I'll finish this," he said, "if you'll go down and get them ready. I can't . . . I haven't the heart to handle them."

The chaplain handed over the shovel. "It's funny," he said, "about young Falkner."

"You said yesterday he was a little better. You imagined it?"

Barnes shook his head. "I was in to see him. He's awake and lucid and his temperature is down."

They stared at one another for a long time, each trying to hide the hope that might be upon his face.

"Do you think . . ."

"No, I don't," said Barnes.

But Falkner continued to improve. Three days later he was sitting up. Six days later he stood with the other two beside the grave when they buried Bat Ears.

And there were three of them. Three out of twenty-six.

The chaplain closed his book and put it in his pocket. Warren took up the shovel and shoveled in the dirt. The other two watched him silently as he filled the grave, slowly, deliberately, taking his time, for there was no other task to hurry him—filled it and mounded it and shaped it neat and smooth with gentle shovel pats.

Then the three of them went down the slope together, not arm in arm, but close enough to have been arm in arm—back to the white tents of the camp.

Still they did not talk.

It was as if they understood for the moment the dedicatory value of the silence that lay upon the land and upon the camp and the three that were left out of twenty-six.

Falkner said: "There is nothing strange about me. Nothing different than any other man."

"There must be," insisted Warren. "You survived the virus. It hit you and you came out alive. There must be a reason for it."

"You two," said Falkner, "never even got it. There must be some reason for that, too."

"We can't be sure," said Chaplain Barnes, speaking softly.

Warren rustled his notes angrily.

"We've covered it," he said. "Covered everything that you can remember—unless you are holding back something that we should know."

"Why should I hold back anything?" demanded Falkner.

"Childhood history," said Warren. "The usual things. Measles, a slight attack of whooping cough, colds—afraid of the dark. Ordinary eating habits, normal acceptance of schools and social obligations. Everything as if it might be someone else. But there has to be an answer. Something that you did . . ."

"Or," said Barnes, "even something that he thought."

"Huh?" asked Warren.

"The ones who could tell us are out there on the slope," said Barnes. "You and I, Warren, are stumbling along a path we are not equipped to travel. A medical man, a psychologist, even an alien psychologist, a statistician—any one of them would have had something to contribute. But they are dead. You and I are trying to do something we have no training for.

We might have the answer right beneath our noses and we would not recognize it."

"I know," said Warren. "I know. We only do the best we can."

"I have told you everything I can," said Falkner, tensely. "Everything I know. I've told you things I would not tell under any other circumstances."

"We know, lad," said Barnes gently. "We know you have."

"Somewhere," persisted Warren, "somewhere in the life of Benjamin Falkner there is an answer—an answer to the thing that Man must know. Something that he has forgotten. Something that he has not told us, unintentionally. Or, more than likely, something that he has told us and we do not recognize."

"Or," said Barnes, "something that no one but a specialist could know. Some strange quirk in his body or his mind. Some tiny mutation that no one would suspect. Or even . . . Warren, you remember, you talked to me about a miracle."

"I'm tired of it," Falkner told them. "For three days now you have gone over me, pawed me, questioned me, dissected every thought . . ."

"Let's go over that last part again," said Warren wearily. "When you were lost."

"We've gone over it," said Falkner, "a hundred times already."

"Once again," said Warren. "Just once again. You were standing there, on the path, you say, when you heard the footsteps coming up the path."

"Not footsteps," said Falkner. "At first I didn't know they were footsteps. It was just a sound."

"And it terrified you?"

"It terrified me."

"Why?"

"Well, the dark and being lost and . . ."

"You'd been thinking about the natives?"

"Well, yes, off and on."

"More than off and on?"

"More than off and on," Falkner admitted. "All the time, maybe. Ever since I realized I was lost, perhaps. In the back of my mind."

"Finally you realized they were footsteps?"

"No. I didn't know what they were until I saw the native."

"Just one native?"

"Just one. An old one. His coat was all gray and he had a scar across his face. You could see the jagged white line."

"You're sure about that scar?"

"Yes."

"Sure about his being old?"

"He looked old. He was all gray. He walked slowly and he had a limp."

"And you weren't afraid?"

"Yes, afraid, of course. But not as afraid as I would have expected."

"You would have killed him if you could?"

"No, I wouldn't have killed him."

"Not even to save your life?"

"Oh, sure. But I didn't think of that. I just . . . well, I just didn't want to tangle with him, that is all."

"You got a good look at him?"

"Yes, a good look. He passed me no farther away than you are now."

"You would recognize him again if you saw him?"

"I did recognize . . ."

Falkner stopped, befuddled.

"Just a minute," he said. "Just a minute now."

He put up his hand and rubbed hard against his forehead. His eyes suddenly had a stricken look.

"I did see him again," he said. "I recognized him. I know it was the same one."

Warren burst out angrily: "Why didn't you tell . . ."

But Barnes rushed in and headed him off:

"You saw him again. When?"

"In my tent. When I was sick. I opened my eyes and he was there in front of me."

"Just standing there?"

"Standing there and looking at me. Like he was going to swallow me with those big yellow eyes of his. Then he . . . then he . . ."

They waited for him to remember.

"I was sick," said Falkner. "Out of my head, maybe. Not all there. I can't be sure. But it seemed that he stretched out his hands, his paws rather—that he stretched them out and touched me, one paw on each side of my head."

"Touched you? Actually, physically touched you?"

"Gently," said Falkner. "Ever so gently. Just for an instant. Then I went to sleep."

"We're ahead of our story," Warren said impatiently. "Let's go back to the trail. You saw the native—"

"We've been over that before," said Falkner bitterly.

"We'll try it once again," Warren told him. "You say the native passed quite close to you when he went by. You mean that he stepped out of the path and circled past you . . ."

"No," said Falkner, "I don't mean that at all. I was the one who stepped out of the path."

You must maintain human dignity, the manual said. Above all else, human dignity and human prestige must be upheld. Kindness, yes. And helpfulness. And even brotherhood. But dignity was ahead of all.

And too often human dignity was human arrogance.

Human dignity did not allow you to step out of the path. It made the other thing step out and go around you. By inference, human dignity automatically assigned all other life to an inferior position.

"Mr. Barnes," said Warren, "it was the laying on of hands."

The man on the cot rolled his head on the pillow and looked at Warren, almost as if he were surprised to find him there. The thin lips worked in the pallid face and the words were weak and very slow in coming.

"Yes, Warren, it was the laying on of hands. A power these creatures have. Some Christ-like power that no human has."

"But that was a divine power."

"No, Warren," said the chaplain, "not necessarily. It wouldn't have to be. It might be a very real, a very human power, that goes with mental or spiritual perfection."

Warren hunched forward on his stool. "I can't believe it," he said. "I simply can't. Not those owl-eyed things."

He looked up and glanced at the chaplain. Barnes' face had flushed with sudden fever and his breath was fluttery and shallow. His eyes were closed and he looked like a man already dead.

There had been that report by the third expedition's psychologist. It had said dignity and an exact code of honor and a rather primitive protocol. And that, of course, would fit.

But Man, intent upon his own dignity and his own prestige, had never accorded anyone else any dignity. He had been willing to be kind if his kindness were appropriately appreciated. He stood ready to help if his help were allowed to stand as a testament to his superiority. And here on Landro he had scarcely bothered to be either kind or helpful, never dreaming for a moment that the little owl-eyed native was anything other than a stone age creature that was a pest and nuisance and not to be taken too seriously even when he turned out, at times, to be something of a menace.

Until one day a frightened kid had stepped out of a path and let a native by.

"Courtesy," said Warren. "That's the answer: courtesy and the laying on of hands."

He got up from the stool and walked out of the tent and met Falkner coming in.

"How is he?" Falkner asked.

Warren shook his head. "Just like the others. It was late in coming, but it's just as bad."

"Two of us," said Falkner. "Two of us left out of twenty-six."

"Not two," Warren told him. "Just one. Just you."

"But, sir, you're all . . ."

Warren shook his head.

"I have a headache," he said. "I'm beginning to sweat a little. My legs are wobbly."

"Maybe . . ."

"I've seen it too many times," said Warren, "to kid myself about it."

He reached out a hand, grasped the canvas and steadied himself.

"I didn't have a chance," he said. "I stepped out of no paths."

THE VOICE IN THE VOID

One of the earliest of Clifford Simak's stories, "The Voice in the Void" is a melodramatic account of obsession, set largely on a fictional version of the planet Mars that probably indicates Cliff Simak had read the John Carter novels of Edgar Rice Burroughs. One of Cliff's journals shows that a story named "The Bones of Kell-Rabin" was sent to Hugo Gernsback's Wonder Stories on January 12—but no year is indicated in that entry. However, since the story then appeared in the Spring 1932 issue of Wonder Stories Quarterly, one can only conclude that either the story was rushed into print—or that it was purchased the preceding year (which would indicate that it had been written in 1930, which in turn might make it Cliff's oldest known story—perhaps information will turn up one day to clarify that matter).

A different journal entry indicates that Cliff was paid $37 "on account" in June 1932, which would have, by itself, been a terribly small price for a story of this length: Does this mean he received a larger total price for the story, and was paid in installments? Again, it cannot be told from the available record. Or was Gernsback having difficulty in making payments?

The format of the magazine at that time was to include a line drawing of each author at the beginning of his story. The drawing of Cliff shows a very young face; and I believe it was drawn by legendary science fiction artist Frank R. Paul, who was the magazine's art director, and who apparently also created the cover and all interior illustrations. That same issue included stories by Manley Wade Wellman and Jack Williamson.

—dww

"I would give my left eye to have a chance at studying the bones of Kell-Rabin," I said.

Kenneth Smith grunted.

"You would give more than your left eye," he grumbled. "Yes, you would give a damn sight more than your left eye, whether you want to or not."

Ice tinkled in his glass as he drank and then twirled the goblet in his hand.

We were sitting on the terrace of the Terrestrial Club and far in the distance, on the Mount of Athelum, we could see the lights of the Temple of Saldebar, where reposed the famous bones that were worshipped by the entire Martian nation. In the shallow valley at our feet flowed the multi-colored lights of Dantan, the great Martian city, second to the largest on the planet and first in importance in interplanetary trade.

Several miles to the north the huge, revolving beacons of the space port, one of the largest in the universe, flashed, cutting great swaths in the murky night, great pencils of light that could be seen hundreds of miles above the face of the planet, a lamp set in the window to guide home the navigators of icy space.

It was a beautiful and breathtaking scene, but I was not properly impressed. There were others on the terrace, talking and smoking, drinking and enjoying the pure beauty of the scene stretched out before them. Try as hard as I might, however, to keep from doing so, my eyes would stray from the lighted city and the lights of the port to the faint glimmer that came like a feeble candle beam from the Temple of Saldebar, set on the top of the highest, and one of the few remaining mountains of the Red Planet.

I was thinking dangerous thoughts. I knew they were dangerous. It is always dangerous for an outlander to become too interested in the sacred things of an alien race.

"Yes," continued my friend slowly, "you would give more than a left eye. If you went monkeying around up there you would probably lose both of your eyes, one at a time in the most painful manner possible. Probably they'd put salt in where your eyes had been. Probably you'd lose your tongue too and they'd probably carve you up considerable and try a little fire and some acid. By the time they got ready to kill you, which they would do artistically, you'd be glad for death."

"I gather," I retorted, "that it would be dangerous to try for a look at Kell-Rabin's skeleton, then."

"Dangerous! Say, it would be plain suicide. You don't know these Martians as I do. You have studied them and pried into their history, but I have been high-balling around from space port to space port for a dozen years or more and I have come to know them differently. A fine people to trade with and as courteous and polite as you would want, but they have tabus and Kell-Rabin is their biggest. You know that as well as I. They're a funny people to look at. It takes some time to get acquainted with them, but they aren't a bad lot. Get their dander up, though, and look out! Why, it isn't safe to speak the name of Kell-Rabin. I, for one, wouldn't think of uttering it where a Martian could hear me."

"We'll grant all that," I replied, "but will you stop to consider for an instant what it would mean to me, who have spent my life studying the Martian race, to know what sort of a man or thing this Kell-Rabin may have been. One glimpse of those bones might serve to settle once for all the origin of the present Martian race; it might serve to determine whether or not the race descended along practically the same lines as we of the Earth; it might even open new angles of thought to the entire situation."

"And," grumbled Ken, "have you ever stopped to consider that the bones of Kell-Rabin are to the Martians what a bit of wood from the true cross would be to a Christian or a hair from the beard of the Prophet would mean to a Moslem? Did you ever consider that every man with a drop of Martian blood in his veins would fight to the death to protect the relic against foreign hands?"

"You're too serious about it," I told him, "I know how much chance I'll ever have of seeing them."

"Well," replied my friend, "someday I may knock off for a while and try my hand at rifling the tomb."

"If you do," I said, "let me know. I'll be anxious to have a look."

He laughed and rose to his feet. I heard his footsteps go ringing across the floor of the terrace.

I sat in my chair and gazed out at the feeble gleam of the Martian temple, set there on its mountain, towering above the weird landscape of the fourth planet. I thought upon the temple and the bones of Kell-Rabin.

In the mighty temple of Saldebar, the revered skeleton has lain for ages, from time that had long since been forgotten. Through all of recorded Martian history, a history many thousands of years older than that of the Earth, the bones had lain there, guarded by the priests and worshipped by an entire planet. In the mass of legend and religion that had become attached to the Most Holy Relic, the true identity of Kell-Rabin had been lost. The only persons who might have any idea of what that mythical thing had been were the priests and perhaps even they did not know.

"Quit thinking about it," I told myself fiercely, but I could not.

Exactly three weeks later I was served with deportation papers because I had attempted, in a perfectly legitimate manner through the civil and ecclesiastical authorities, to obtain permission to study the Temple of Saldebar under the supervision of the Priestly Council.

I had shown, the deportation papers stated, "an unusual and disconcerting curiosity in the Martian religion." The papers also specifically stated that I was not to return to Mars under the pain of death.

It was a terrible blow to me. For years I had worked on Mars. I was recognized as one of the greatest living authorities on modern Martian civilization and in the course of my work, I had gathered a great deal of information concerning the ancient history of the planet.

I had Martian friends in high offices, but I found they were no longer my friends when I attempted to approach them, hoping they might intercede with a word in my favor. All but one absolutely refused to see me and that one openly insulted me, with a dirty smirk on his face as he did it, almost as if he was glad misfortune had fallen my way.

The Earth ambassador shook his head when I talked with him.

"There's nothing I can do for you, Mr. Ashby," he said. "I regret deeply my inability. You know the Martians, however. No one should know them better than you. You have committed a mistake. To them it was the greatest breach of faith possible. There is nothing I can do."

As I stood upon the deck of the liner, whirling rapidly away from the planet I had devoted my life to, I silently, and unconsciously, shook a fist at its receding bulk.

"Someday—sometime—," I muttered, but that was merely to soothe my tortured pride. I never really meant to do anything.

I saw the familiar, sun-tanned face of Kenneth Smith in the visor of the visaphone.

"Well," he said, "I have them!"

"Have what, Ken?" I asked.

"I have," he said slowly, "the bones of Kell-Rabin!"

My heart seemed to rise up in my throat and choke me. My face must have gone the shade of cold ashes and my mouth was suddenly so dust-dry that I could not speak.

A great fear, mingled with an equally great elation, rose in me and seemed to overwhelm me. I stared, open mouthed, gasping, into the visor. My hand trembled and I think that my entire body shook like a leaf in a gale.

"You look as if you had seen a ghost," jeered Ken on the other end of the connection.

I gulped and attempted to speak. At last I succeeded. My voice was hardly more than a whisper.

"I have," I said, "I have seen the ghosts of legions of Martians rising from their graves in protest."

"Let them rise," snarled the man in the visor, "we have the damned bones, haven't we. We'll make them squeal plenty to get them back."

There was a hardness, a grimness, a death-head quality in his voice that had never been there before.

"Why, what is the matter, Ken?" I asked, "Where have you been?"

"I have been in the Grondas Desert in Mars," he said. "Prospecting. Found a deposit of pitchblende that was simply lousy with radium. It would have made me one of the richest men in the universe."

"Why, that's good news . . ."

"It isn't good news," replied Ken and the hardness was in his voice again. "The Martian government took it from me and I only got out by the skin of my teeth. Some damn clause or other in an old treaty about foreigners not being allowed any radium rights on the planet."

"That's too bad," I comforted.

"Too bad," he grinned like a foul monster of the pit. "It is not too bad. The Martians will pay ten times what that pitchblende deposit was worth to get these blessed bones back. The laugh is on the other horse now. In the meantime come over and have a look. I am staying at the Washington. The box is still shut. I thought you would enjoy opening it."

I snapped off the connection and clutched at the edge of the desk. I was alternately hot and cold. This meant . . . what did it mean? Kenneth Smith had robbed the Martian nation of the thing that was most highly prized on the entire planet. Not only Kenneth Smith but myself. Not for a moment did I doubt but our short talk on the terrace of the Terrestrial Club three years before had prompted my friend's mad theft. My words had suggested to him the supreme revenge which he had taken on the crooked little men of Mars, our neighbors in space and our friends by treaty.

I felt little remorse. Given the chance I would probably have done the same thing, not merely because of my desire to inspect those famous bones, but for much the same reason as had prompted Ken. My summary dismissal from Mars and the closing of its hospitality to me forever had been a great blow to my pride and the hurt still rankled deeply. The Martians had played rotten tricks on both myself and my friend. I did not think of any possible wrong that we may have done the Martians. In fact, from that angle of it, I felt a satisfaction that became keener every moment. This, in a way, was my revenge as much as Ken's.

I felt, however, an inexplicable terror, a dreadful foreboding. The fountain-head of the Martian religion had been profaned and I could imagine what would be the fate of those who had stolen the Holy Remains, if captured by the Martians. That they immediately had discovered the theft and were even now on the trail, I did not doubt. I shivered in sheer physical horror at thinking of the sinister little crooked folks seeking me out.

They would demand that the Terrestrial authorities deliver us to their courts as a last resort, but only as a last resort. The Martians are a proud people and would not readily disclose a tale that would make them the laughing stock of the universe. It was with the priests of Mars themselves that my friend and I would be concerned.

I laughed and jerked open a drawer in the desk. My hand reached in and closed about something that was metallic and cold.

I drew it out and slipped it into one of my pockets. There might be need of a weapon and the little electro-gun that hurled living thunderbolts was the most effective weapon the worlds had developed. Not even the Martians, for all their centuries of a wonderful mechanical civilization, had anything that would compare with it. The gun was an Earth secret and only Earthmen carried it.

I rose to my feet and laughed again, the bitter laugh of a conqueror who knows that his victory is empty, that he may, before the next dawn, face a firing squad. It was a great victory, a supreme insult to the Martians. Neither my friend nor I had any cause to love the people of the ruddy planet and both of us had ample for which to hate them. It had been foolish of Ken to steal the bones of Kell-Rabin, but it had been a master stroke . . . if one did not count the consequences.

I let myself out and rode to the ground floor. From there I took an aero-taxi straight to the Washington.

Ken let me in and bolted the door behind me. Then we grasped hands and stood for a long time looking into one another's eyes.

"You shouldn't have done it, Ken," I said.

"Don't worry so much about it," he replied, "I would have done it anyhow. I just remembered what you had said, how anxious you were to see those bones. I would have thought of it, anyhow, for after that radium affair, I sat down and tried hard to think of how I could best humiliate the whole nation that had palmed that sort of deal off on me. Only, if it hadn't been for you, I would have dropped the cursed box out in space somewhere. If they could find it out there, say, half way between Earth and Mars, I wouldn't have begrudged it to them. As it is, I have brought it here. You can study those damned bones to your heart's content."

He turned to lead the way to an inner room of the suite.

"It was the rottenest thing imaginable," he was telling me. "They let me find that deposit and then took it away from me.

Confiscated it . . . threatened me with death if I made a fuss about it. Said they were letting me off easy, because there is a ten-year imprisonment clause in that old treaty to deal with any foreigner who does not immediately report such a discovery to the proper officials. They knew I was working on it all the time and never a word did they say."

He halted and wheeled to face me.

"For two years I worked there in that blazing hell of a desert. I went hungry and thirsty part of the time and went through the sieges of desert fever. I fought heat and red dust, poisonous reptiles and insects, loneliness and near-insanity. I lost three fingers on my left hand when I poisoned them on some sort of a damn desert weed. I found it, tons upon tons of it. I have no idea how many and fairly rotten with radium. One cargo alone would have put me at the top of the world.

"All I would have had to do was snap my fingers and the solar system would bow its knee. I worked, went through two years of Martian desert; I lost my youth, three fingers, and two years of living . . . for what? For what, I ask you? So that some bloated Martian official might glut his hideous belly, so that he might weigh down some simpering female with precious stones, and give great gifts to the priests who guarded the skeleton of a thing that should have been dust long ago!"

His face was livid with rage. The man was insane! This was not the Ken Smith I had last seen only a few years before. It was another man, a man crazed by the horrible heat and the ghastly loneliness of the red reaches of Mars, a man embittered beyond human endurance by the scurvy injustice of an alien people who never had and never could understand the people of the Earth.

He jerked his arm above his head and pointed at the ceiling, and through the ceiling, out into the blind darkness of space where among the swarms of celestial lights a red star glowed.

"When they find out," he shouted, "they'll fear! Damn them, their stinking little souls will shrivel up inside of them. They will know the blasted hope and the terror that I have known. They are a religious people and I have taken their religion! I, the man they ruined, have taken the thing that is most precious to them. Someday, if they don't find out, I'll let them know, let them know that I rattled the musty bones of Kell-Rabin in their holy box and laughed at the sound they made!"

There was no doubt of it. The man was mad, a raving lunatic.

"And if they want them badly, as badly as I think they do," he said in a whisper, "perhaps I'll return them . . . at ten times the worth of my radium mine. I'll bankrupt them. I'll make them grub in their dirty soil for the next hundred years to pay the price I'll ask. And always they will know that a man of the Earth has rattled the bones of Kell-Rabin! That will hurt!"

"Man," I shouted at him, "are you entirely insane? They know now, they must know. Why, the box is gone. Even now they must be searching throughout the whole solar system for it."

"They do not know," replied my friend, "I took steps. I knew I would have no chance, even in my own ship, to make a getaway if they found out at once. There is another box, exactly like the one that holds the bones of Kell-Rabin, in the Temple of Saldebar, but it is an empty box . . . a box that I made and put there. I secreted myself in the temple and took photographs with an electrocamera and with those photos as my guide, I worked for weeks to make another box just like it, except for one thing. On one corner of that other box there is carved a message, a message to the priests of Mars, and when one of them finds that message, they will know that the bones of Kell-Rabin are gone."

A sonorous voice filled the room.

"We have found the message, Kenneth Smith," it said, "and we are here to take the Holy Relic and you."

We whirled about and there, standing just within the room, was a priest of Mars, dressed in all his picturesque habiliments. In his hand he held a vicious little heat weapon.

Looking beyond him I saw that the lock of the door had been melted away. Funny how a man will notice a little thing like that even in the most exciting moments.

The priest was slow with his gun. I believe that, even with my gun in my pocket, I could have beaten him to it. Priests are not supposed to be compelled to use a gun.

I knew, as I faced him, that quick death from his weapon was preferable to capture, and my hand went to my pocket. It was not more than half way out when a thunderous crash split the air.

Kenneth Smith held his gun in his hand. It was as if it had been there all the time. He was fast with his weapon, too fast for the Martian priest.

The priest was crumpled on the floor, a charred mass of flesh. The odor of burned hair and skin mingled with the sharp tang of ionized air.

There was a scurry in the other room and through the doorway we saw another priest bounding toward the hall. We fired simultaneously and the figure collapsed in mid-air to lie smoking on the floor.

"That's frying them!" I gasped, the words jerked out of my mouth by the suddenness of the events.

"We have to get out of here," snapped Ken. "Quick, up to the roof. It's only two stories up. I have a small flier there."

Chapter II
Fugitives

Dropping his gun in his pocket, he raced into the adjoining room. While I stood, stunned and hardly knowing where to go, he re-appeared and under his arm was tucked a box about three feet in length.

He grasped me by the arm and we hurdled the two smoking bodies to gain the corridor. Doors were opening and heads were popping out of the rooms. Below us we heard the hurried tramp of feet and one of the elevator dials showed that a cage was rapidly ascending.

We bounded for the stairs and clattered upward. As we gained the roof an excited horde of people burst from the elevator on the floor below us. One man got in our way as we raced across the roof to the little red plane that belonged to Ken. I bowled him over with a straight left and we hurried on.

We scrambled into the plane and Ken stepped on the starter. The motors whined and the machine stirred. Toward us raced a number of people. Two of them, a few feet in advance of the others, reached the plane and threw themselves upon it in a vain attempt to retard its progress. As we gathered speed they rolled off and the machine zoomed up.

We broke every traffic rule that was ever written as we spun crazily off the landing field at the top of the hotel and hurtled into the upper levels. Irate taxi-pilots shouted at us and more than one man at the controls of passenger planes and freighters must have held their breath as we zigzagged past them at a speed that was prohibited in these crowded levels above the city. Twice traffic planes speeded after us and each time we eluded them. No pilot other than Kenneth Smith, space rover extraordinary, could have sent that little red ship on its mad flight and come out with a whole skin.

In half an hour we had cleared the city and were flying over the country. We knew that the murder of the Martian priests had been discovered and that the description of our plane, and possibly a description of our persons, was being broadcast the length and breadth of the land. Every police ship would on an outlook for us.

Night, however, was coming on and it was on this fact that we relied for a clean getaway. A half hour before darkness fell, when twilight was creeping over the lower valleys of the earth, we sighted a golden circle on the wing of a ship far behind us, upon which we had turned our 'scope and knew that the police were on our trail. Before the other ship could gain on us appreciably, darkness cloaked us and, flying without lights, we tore madly on.

An hour later the moon slipped above the horizon and by its light we saw that we had reached the Rocky Mountains and were flying over their jagged ranges.

We held a council of war. A wide search was being conducted for us. The killing of the two priests, on the face of it, must have appeared to be one of the most heinous crimes imaginable, one that was of interplanetary importance, and no stone would be left unturned to apprehend us. The red plane was easily recognizable. There was only one thing to do; abandon the ship before we were sighted.

A moment later two figures, one clutching a wood and metal box, plunged down out of the speeding ship, dropped sickeningly for a moment and then gently floated as the valves of the parachutes were turned on. A red plane, throttle wide open, stick lashed back, and with no occupants plunged on its mad course. Two months later I learned that the wreck had been found the next morning some hundred miles from where we had leaped into space.

It was a wild and desolate place where we had chosen to drop out of the plane. Easily we guided ourselves to earth and closed the parachute valves as our feet touched ground. There was the strong, aromatic scent of pine in the air and a strong breeze sighed dismally through the tree-tops. Rocks rolled under my feet as I moved.

We found a dense thicket of a low growing evergreen shrub and hiding ourselves in it, fell into a troubled sleep, waking when the slanting rays of the sun reached between the needles and touched our faces.

Several times that morning, as we tried to decide what to do, I was tempted to pry loose the cover and view the contents of the box which was reputed to contain the bones of the famous Kell-Rabin. I was afraid to do so, however. I feared that, upon being exposed to the air, the precious bones would disintegrate into dust. The box, when it was opened, must be in a laboratory, where proper preservatives and apparatus would be directly at hand. Opening the box there, in that wild mountainous region, was too much of a gamble. I decided to wait.

Hunger at last drove us forth and we were fortunate enough to bring down a small buck with a reduced charged from Ken's electro-gun. We had no salt, but ate the meat, charred over the fire, like ravenous wolves. We found berries and ate them.

For weeks we staggered through the mountains, lugging our precious box. Neither of us would have thought of discarding it, for to Ken it meant revenge and a fabulous fortune in ransom and to me it meant a chance to probe deeper into the mysteries of the Martian race and a revenge, which I desired only a little less than my half-mad friend. So, although it galled our shoulders and was a dead weight that made our hard way even harder, we clung tenaciously to it.

We grew beards and I developed a tan that was only a shade lighter than Ken had acquired on the parched deserts of Mars. Pounds of superfluous flesh fell from us and our faces became thinner. I doubt if anyone other than close acquaintances would have known us.

So at last we came to a lonely little town set in the hills and while Ken mounted guard over the box at its outskirts, I entered the town. There I purchased a shabby old-fashioned trunk from the hardware and furniture dealer and appropriate clothes from the one clothing store the place boasted.

That evening, when the east bound plane soared down out of the sky it found two mountaineers, bewhiskered and ragged, who were silent, as all strong men of the open spaces are supposed to be, but who made it known they had struck it "rich" and were going to the cities for a spree. Their only baggage consisted of one trunk of ancient vintage.

In Chicago we purchased a strong box and in it placed the box containing the Martian bones. Half an hour later the strong box was placed in a safety deposit vault in the First Lunar bank and duplicate keys were delivered to Ken and myself. We did not deem it wise to have the box in our possession until the police had dropped their search for us. Reasoning that we would hardly be expected to return so shortly to the city from which we had escaped, we decided to remain there.

The day we placed the box in the vault, we checked out of the hotel. We next visited a certain man who lived in one of the least fashionable parts of the city. We left behind us a sum of money, but walked away entirely different men. We were no longer Kenneth Smith and Robert Ashby whom the world had known nor were we the bearded mountaineers who had boarded the east bound flier with a single trunk as baggage. Our features were a work of art. There were little plates, which could be removed instantly, but which caused no discomfort, in our nostrils and in our cheeks. Our hair was cut differently and trained to lie just so, under the persuasion of an intricate machine. It was a simple disguise and an effective one. During the next few weeks I met friends of mine face to face on the street and there was not even the faintest gleam of recognition in their eyes.

We established residence in a modest little residential district and bided our time. When the murder of the two Martian priests had blown over, we would act.

And then one day Ken did not return to our lodgings. I waited for him for hours, then started a systematic and careful search. A week brought no results. He had not been arrested, his body had not been found, he was in no hospital, he had not taken any plane.

I was forced to face the apparent facts. The Martians had captured my friend!

A death sentence awaited me the moment I set foot on Martian soil. I had been absolutely forbidden to visit the planet again.

But I did return. I held my breath as I was passed through the customs office. Would my disguise, which had been so effective on Earth, continue to serve me on Mars? The examination, however, was perfunctory, and I was passed. I had declared myself a business man on a pleasure trip, one of the innumerable swarm of tourists who each year shake off the shackles of a prosaic Earth to enjoy the weird offerings of the alien planet.

I stood once more on the soil of the Red Planet. Once more I was face to face with the nation before which Ken Smith and myself had thrown the gauge of battle. My business was a grim one, a mission of rescue, perhaps of revenge. My destination was the Temple of Saldebar.

My friend had told me much of the temple. Hour after hour we had talked of it. Printed indelibly upon my mind was the route which my friend had twice followed when he had filched the bones of Kell-Rabin. Carefully I laid my plans which were, necessarily, a duplication of the same plans which Ken had made and carried out successfully. For the second time in the history of the planet an alien was planning to enter the Holy of Holies by the same route that the first had followed.

The Mount of Athelum was shrouded in darkness. Two hours before the sun had slipped over the rim of the planet and it would be another hour before Deimos, the larger moon of Mars, would rise.

I shivered in the cold wind that roared up from the desert below and wrapped my black cloak tighter about me. In their holsters at my belt were two electro-guns and in my hand, attached to my wrist by a leather thong was a stick with a weighted end, an ugly and a silent weapon. In my jacket pocket rested a small flash and a package of concentrated food wafers. I did not know for how long I would have to lurk in the great dark temple which reared its massive walls before me, before I found he whom I sought or was at last convinced he was not there.

It was past the usual hour for worship and still I waited. I had no desire to enter the place when it swarmed with pilgrims and worshippers. I preferred to wait until there was no longer any doubt that the temple was occupied only by the priests. It was also necessary that I strike at the hour when guards were changed, for once a clubbed guard was discovered a general search would be started and I would have to go into hiding and hope for the best. That I could get in the building without clubbing one or more of the guards, I knew, was an impossibility.

Like a great glittering jewel set in the black pool of the night, I could see the lights of Dantan in the distance and I chucked with a fiendish glee when I tried to imagine what an uproar the city would be in if the populace of Mars and of the Earth knew of the theft of the holy bones and the sacrilege of the temple. The matter of the theft had been kept a secret. The Martian government and the priestly clan did not relish publicity on a thing of that sort.

Someday, perhaps, as the one final act of revenge, I would broadcast the news to the ends of the solar system. I would set every land, from the little mining settlements on Mercury to the last trading outposts in the frozen fastnesses of Pluto on ear with the news. The Martian and his religion would become the laughing stock of the universe. Perhaps, then, too late, the high officials and the priests would wish that they had dealt more leniently with myself and my friend. It was something good to think about as I squatted in the darkness outside the temple, waiting my time to strike. Perhaps I was a bit insane. Probably I still am.

A ringing voice cried out in the darkness and a light flashed briefly in a niche in the temple wall. Another voice answered. There was a ceremonial clash of swords, which the priests carried while on guard as emblems of their post.

Guards were being changed. From far down the temple wall came another challenge and another reply, followed by the clash of steel. It was all ceremony and custom. The setting of the guard, like the carrying of the sword, was a survival from dim, forgotten days.

On this night, however, I thought grimly, there would be need of guards.

Softly I moved forward to gain the denser shadow of the wall and with my left hand touching the rough stones, crept slowly along it edge. Several times I stopped to stare and listen, straining my eyeballs and ears. My presence, I was convinced, was unsuspected, but I was taking no chances. A Martian temple of any sort, and especially the Temple of Saldebar, is a dangerous place for an Earthman.

My clutching fingers, feeling along the wall slightly above and before my head, found a break in the stone and I knew that I had reached the postern gate which I had selected for my entrance to the temple.

Holding my breath for fear that the guard on duty there might hear it, I peered cautiously around the edge of the niche in which the gate was set. Like a graven image, upright, holding the ritualistic position of a Martian temple guard, the fellow stood there directly in front of the gate. The point of the massive sword rested on the stone flagging at his feet and both hands gripped the hilt.

I gathered myself together, gripped the edge of the wall tightly with my fingers to aid in directing my leap, took a firmer grip on the end of the lead-weighted club, and sprang.

The guard never lifted the point of the sword from the ground. I doubt if he recognized me as an Earthman at all. As I loomed in front of him, my club, which had whirled through an arc as I leaped, descended viciously on his skull. I caught his falling body with my left arm and my right hand closed in an iron grip over his mouth to strangle any sound that he might make. Easily I laid him on the flagging and moved to the door. With my hand on the heavy latch I stopped a moment to consider donning the clothes of the dead guard, but decided not to do so. His robes would hinder my movements and my greater size would betray me as quickly as my earthly dress.

The hinges of the door creaked slightly as I let myself in, but the slight sound must have gone unheeded, for nothing happened, although I waited for long minutes, poised to flee upon the slightest indication of any disturbance.

The corridor into which the door led was pitch black and when I closed the door behind me I was seized for a moment with that indescribable terror that descends upon one when facing danger in darkness. For a split second I wanted to use my flash, but I knew, even as I wanted to do it, that even the faintest glimmer of light might betray me and foil my plans.

From my talks with Ken, who had twice passed this way to rob the temple of its precious relic, I was fairly well acquainted with the route which I was to take to gain the great hall in the center of the temple. I knew that the corridor in which I stood ran straight ahead for a matter of two hundred paces and then veered sharply, almost at a right angle, to the left.

I was to follow the corridor until I gained another, which was more extensively used and which was lighted. There was little danger, I knew, to be expected in the dark corridor. It was after I had gained the second corridor that I would have to exercise the utmost caution. With my hand trailing along the wall of the corridor, I moved forward, tiptoeing so that the sound of my footsteps would be deadened.

I came to the turn in the corridor and saw a faint light in the distance where it entered the second corridor. Cautiously I moved forward, keeping sharp watch on all sides.

Chapter III
The Man Without a Body

Near to the floor on the left wall my eyes made out a small patch of light and I stopped stock still to study it and try to determine its origin. I was unable to do so until I slithered across from the right wall, which I was hugging, to the left side and then I saw that the patch of light came from a small oblong chink in the right wall. Apparently the wall separated the corridor from another room and a chunk of stone had fallen from it.

Straining my ears, I heard a mumble of voices. Martian voices, apparently coming from the room from which the light streamed through the hole in the wall.

Determined to find what was transpiring in the room, I slid forward along the wall.

Only a matter of half a dozen feet from the hole, I was suddenly arrested in my tracks. My foot was lifted to take another step forward and I did not lower it. I was like a pointer who has suddenly run afoul of a bird. I believe that my ears actually moved forward a little, as I tried to catch again the words which I had heard.

Then, distinctly and as if the speaker were almost at my elbow, came other words, spoken in English and in a voice that I knew . . . the voice of the man I sought, Ken Smith!

"No, damn you. You'll rot in Hell before I tell you. I rattled them in their filthy box. Rattled them and laughed when I heard them rattle. I rattled them, do you understand, blast your filthy souls. They're only bones, musty, rotten bones, like the bones of my body over there will be in a few weeks and like your bones will be when you die . . ."

The voice had risen, shriller and shriller, to suddenly break in a terrible scream of pain that brought cold perspiration out of every pore in my body.

The screaming ended and I heard the rumble of a Martian voice.

"Kenneth Smith, you will tell us where the holy skeleton of Kell-Rabin is. Not until then will we give you a merciful release. Remember, we could leave you here, with the current turned on, high . . . higher than it was just now, and forget about you for years. Perhaps then you would tell us. You are immortal, you will never die. Could you endure an eternity of torture?"

Again I heard the voice of my friend, high and shrill.

"I will tell you where the bones are . . . I will tell you."

I could almost see the breathless suspense of those who were on the other side of the wall.

". . . I will tell you where the bones of Kell-Rabin are—when your stinking planet has dissolved into bloody dust and floats among the stars."

The rumble of Martian voices boomed out like the angry beat of a drum. The screaming began again, rising until it seemed that it would burst the ear-drums.

With a leap I was at the hole in the wall and my fingers hooked themselves on the edge of a great block. With all my strength I tore at it and felt it give beneath my hands. Frantically I tugged and it came free. Madly I battered at other blocks, pulling them out, fighting madly to clear a space large enough to admit my body.

All the time the horrible agonized screaming beat upon my brain and urged me to greater effort. The screaming, too, drowned out the sound of crunching masonry and falling blocks of stone.

A last block came free and I leaped through the gap. Even as I leaped, my hands sought the holsters and before my feet hit the floor I had both electro-guns out.

It was a strange tableau that confronted me. On a table to one side of the room lay a naked human body, with the skull split open, the face gone, and the neck horribly mangled. On another table, about which were grouped five Martian priests, stood a small machine, attached by two wires to a transparent cylinder about three feet in height.

It was the cylinder, however, that held my eye and struck terror deep into my soul. It was filled with some sort of milky liquid and in the liquid floated a naked, pulsating human brain. Just below the brain hung a face, the face of Ken Smith! His features were distorted in pain, from the cylinder rose the shrill screams of torture. Below the face trailed a portion of the spinal cord and what were apparently the voice organs.

I was mad with terror and anguish at the scene before me. In two leaps I was at the table where the cylinder sat, had swept away the astonished priest who stood in my way, and flipped up the switch of the tiny mechanism beside the cylinder. Abruptly the transparency of the cylinder faded and the screaming was cut short. As I swung away from the table to face the priests, who were swiftly recovering from their astonishment at my appearance, I saw, out of the corner of my eye, that the cylinder had assumed a solid shape, a dull-grey, metallic shade.

The priests surged forward, but as I jabbed the two guns forward, they fell back, murmuring.

"One word out of you," I hissed scarcely above a whisper, "and I'll fry you where you stand."

They understood. They had no arms and they knew the reputation of the electro-guns. They knew, too, that a Terrestrial, discovered in a Martian temple, would be desperate and that he would not hesitate to kill and kill ruthlessly.

I racked my brain. I was in a quandary. If I killed the priests and made a break, I might be able to win my way out of the temple. I had found my friend, however, and I could not leave him behind. When I went, the cylinder and the little machine that operated it, must go also. I could not leave Ken Smith, or what was left of Ken Smith, to suffer indescribable torture at the hands of these fiends. If the worst came to pass, I would train one of the guns on the cylinder and deliberately blast what I had seen in its milky contents out of existence. It would be better that way than leaving it there in the hands of the Martians.

My glance fell on the mutilated body that lay on the second table. It was, I knew, the body of Ken Smith. He had said something about "my body over there." The beastly men of Mars had stolen his brain and placed it in a cylinder! They had said something about him being immortal.

The crooked little men before me had assumed the stoical expression that characterized the Martian race. All of them were draped in the robes of high office. I smiled grimly and they flinched at my smile. I had thought of what a rare bag of birds I had flushed. Their lives lay in a balance, lay at the end of my two gun-finger tips and they knew it.

"Show me how this mechanism works," I ordered the foremost one in a guarded whisper.

The priest hesitated, but I made a peremptory motion with one of the guns and he stepped quickly forward.

"One wrong move," I warned him grimly, "and every one of you sizzle. I am here and I am leaving soon, with this cylinder. Maybe I'll let you live, maybe I won't."

The expressions on their faces never changed. They had courage, you have to say that much for them.

"What do you wish to know of the machine?" asked the Martian who had stepped forward.

"I want to talk to the man in the cylinder," I said. "I don't want to torture him, you understand. I want to talk to him."

The priest reached out a hand toward the machine, but I waved him back.

"No," I said. "You tell me what to do. If you direct me falsely . . ."

I did not finish my threat. He beat me to it. He licked his thin lips and nodded his head.

I laid one of my guns on the table, where I could snatch it up at a second's notice, and reached out my hand to the machine.

"You must turn that red indicator back of the green reading," said the Martian. "Back of that the brain in the cylinder has full exercise of its faculties and experiences no ill effects. Above that mark torture begins. The machine is very simple . . ."

"Yes," I said, "it must be. But I am not interested in the machine. I want to talk to my friend. Now what do I do."

"All that is necessary is to close the switch you opened."

My fingers closed over the switch and pushed it home. My back was to the cylinder and I could not see what transpired, but no scream came and I knew that the priest must have informed me correctly.

"You there, Ken?" I asked.

"Right here, Bob," came the well-remembered voice.

"Listen closely, Ken," I said. "We haven't got much time. Something may happen any moment. Have you any suggestions for getting out of here."

"The way out through the corridor is clear?" asked the voice of my friend.

"So far as I know. The guard is dead."

"Then roast the priests and on your way out give me a shot. Promise, though, to finish the priests first. After what they did to me . . . You understand. Eye for eye. Blast their brains, rob them of this eternal life they've given me. And be sure I'm done before you leave."

"No, Ken," I said, "I'm taking you."

"You're crazy, Bob."

"I may be crazy," I retorted, half angrily, "but either both of us go out of here or neither of us go."

"But, Bob . . ."

"We haven't time to argue. You know the ropes better than I do. Any suggestions?"

"Alright, then. Shut me off. Disconnect the cylinder from the machine and stick the machine in your pocket. You will need it . . . or rather, I will. It is run on a connection with any electric current. Disconnect it from the temple wiring. Wipe out the priests and stick me under your arm. That's all. If we get out, we get out. If we don't, crack me up before you wash out."

"That's talking," I cheered him. "What these animals have done to you doesn't make any difference. We're still pals."

"Sure, we're pals. Only you'll have to do all the fighting from now on."

My fingers were on the switch.

"Just a second, Bob. I've thought of something. Think you can carry two of these tanks?"

"How heavy are they?"

"I don't know. Not so heavy, though."

The priests were moving uneasily and I shouted a sharp command at them.

"If you can do it," droned the voice of my friend, "run into that room just across from you. You can see the door. There's racks of tanks in there. Brains of dead priests, you know. Take one of them. He may be a great help."

"Okeh," my hand started to lift the switch.

"Don't forget the priests. Damn them, give them . . ."

The voice snapped short as I pulled the switch free.

A latch clicked behind me and I swung about. In the doorway which opened from the second corridor stood another priest. Amazement was written all over his features. He was opening his mouth to scream a warning when I got him.

The blast had scarcely left the muzzle of the gun, when I twisted back on my heel and not a moment too soon. All five of the priests were rushing me. The muzzle of the gun was not more than a few inches from the breast of the foremost one when I depressed the trigger. The priest was bathed for a second in a lurid blue flame that lapped over him from head to foot; for an instant he wavered in front of me, shriveled and blackened and then fell, his charred body breaking into pieces as it fell. The gun crackled and roared and I imagine that the noise could be heard even in the farthest corners of the temple. The electro-gun is not a silent weapon.

Two of the priests died only a few feet from me and the third almost touched my throat with his skinny, twisted hands before I could stick the gun into his stomach and give him everything it had. He simply evaporated in a flash of electrical energy that almost knocked me off my feet.

Staggering from the shock, I caught sight of the last of the priestly quintet rushing for the open door. My finger caught on the regulator and pushed it far over as I fired. It was unintentional, but it was lucky for me that it happened. Set at full charge, the gun hurled a living thunderbolt across the room that snuffed the fleeing priest out of existence and blasted the entire opposite wall of the room into the outer corridor. Other masonry, falling with resounding crashes, completely blocked the passage.

The room reeked with the charnel odor of burned flesh and the sickening stench of burning ozone. My ears were dulled by the thunder of the electro-gun in that vaulted room and my senses were reeling from the effects of the electrical charges set off at close quarters. With deafening crashes the masonry was still falling in the outer passage. I heard faint cries from some other quarter of the building and knew that the priests of Mars were aroused and racing toward this section of the temple.

Stumbling to the table I wrenched loose the connections from the machine and thrust it in my pocket. I lifted the cylinder and was surprised to find it so light.

Then I remembered. I was to take another cylinder. Had I the time? My friend had a good reason for wanting me to get one of the other cylinders. I was confident of being able to fight my way through.

I resolved to try it. Setting the cylinder back on the table, I ran toward the door which Ken had indicated. Halfway to it I jerked out one of the guns. There was no need of fumbling with a lock now. Every second counted. Training the gun on the lock as I ran, I pressed the trigger. The heavy charge blasted away a section of the door and, running at full tilt, I struck it, driving it open. I sprawled into a room that was so large it at first bewildered me. In huge racks that left only alleyways between them, were piled cylinder on cylinder, identically like the one in which the brain of Ken Smith reposed.

I clutched at the one nearest at hand, hauled it from its resting place and fled back into the other room.

I could hear the enraged babble of the priests as they worked frantically to clear the corridor which my shot had blocked. There was no one in sight.

With a cry of triumph, I swept up the cylinder which contained all that was left of my friend, and raced for the breach I had made between the room and the dark corridor.

Once in it, I ran swiftly until I believed myself to be near the sharp turn. Throwing caution to the winds, I brought out my flash and cut the darkness with a swath of light. Behind me I heard a shrill yell and a flame pistol spat, but the distance was too great and the livid tongue of fire that it flung out fell far short.

With fear riding my shoulders, I tore on. The pistol continued to spit. At the sharp turn in the corridor, I halted and pocketed my flash, hauling forth one of my guns. Quickly I stepped out from behind the projecting wall and as quickly stepped back. In that swift second of action I had swept the corridor behind me clean with an electric charge that incinerated all in its path.

Like a drunken man, I staggered out of the door into the cold night. I almost stumbled over the body of the dead guard, but righted myself and fled on. Behind me rose a babble of fear and anger as the enraged and terrified priests sought, too late, to cut off my escape.

The darkness soon swallowed me and a half hour later I was in a swift plane, which I had securely hidden the day before, headed for the wildernesses deep in the Arantian Desert. In the seat beside me were lashed two cylinders, identical in shape and size, but one held the brain of an Earthman and the other the brain of a Martian.

Chapter IV
In the Desert

"It's no use, Ken," I said. "We've tried every way. It was just our luck that I had to pick a Martian who died years before the Terrestrials came to Mars. Even at that, he may know as much about it as any of the present day priests. He has coughed up splendidly, especially when I threatened to smash his cylinder with a hammer. These Martians seem to love their eternal life in the cylinders. That made him turn himself inside out. But all that he knows is how a brain is put into the cylinder. He claims that it is impossible to take one out and put it back into a body again."

I sat beside the cylinder in which floated the brain and face of Kenneth Smith.

"Yes, Bob," came the voice of my friend out of the cylinder, the lips in the face moving ever so slightly, "it looks as if I am here for the rest of my life, which our Martian friend assures us is for eternity, once you get inside one of these things. Funny how they can do a thing like that. Some sort of a chemical that keeps the brain alive. I suppose Tarsus-Egbo has told you what it is."

"Yes, he has. Was a bit reluctant about it, but I shoved the indicator up and let him howl for exactly fifteen minutes by the chronometer. When I shut it off, he was ready to tell me everything he knew about the composition of the stuff."

"What do you plan to do now, Bob?"

"That's a hard question, Ken. I'd like to try to take you back to Earth with me again, but that is almost an impossibility, at least for a few years. The Martians are going through every outgoing ship with a fine toothed comb. Probably I could slip out myself—but a man caught with one of these tanks! Boy, it would be just too bad! If we could get back to Earth we could go right on living as usual. Both of us are hunted men on Mars, for the desecration of the temple and on Earth for killing the two Martian priests, but we could manage somehow. I'm sticking by you, though, no matter what happens."

"Stout chap," said Ken. "If I ever get to be too much of a burden, just hit the tank a crack and go about your way."

"You know I'll never do that, Ken. We're pals, aren't we. If the Martians had stuck me instead of you into a tank, you would have acted just as I am acting now. I'd be a poor friend if I quit you now."

Silence reigned as we sat there, looking out over the red wilderness of sand and thorns that stretched for mile on interminable mile all about us.

"If something happens," I assured him, "well, something, you know. If a Martian ship would show up or if . . . well, you understand . . . I promise to hit you a clip. I will make sure you won't fall into their hands again."

"That's it," said Ken, "Just say 'So long, fellow, I hate to do this, but it's the best way' and swing the hammer. Be sure to swing it hard enough. This stuff may be tough, hard to break, you know."

The sun was sinking low in the sky and a chill was creeping over the crimson desert. I stirred and slowly rose.

"I guess I'd better get a bite to eat. I'll be back right away."

"Take your time," said Ken, "I enjoy this scene. Leave me turned on. You might shift me a little bit toward the west. I like to watch the sun go down."

"All right, old fellow."

I patted the cylinder and shifted it slightly so that my friend could watch the setting of the sun.

We had been in hiding for weeks. No place on Mars could have been more suitable as a hide-out than this mighty desert, a desert of red sand, peopled only by wicked thorn shrubs and poisonous insects and reptiles.

We had been hopeful at first of obtaining useful information from the brain of the Martian I had stolen from the temple. Particularly I had wanted to find if there was a way of removing Ken's brain from the cylinder and replacing it again in a human body. If there had been, the matter of finding a man willing to give his body and a surgeon to perform the operation would not have been too hard a task. Apparently, however, there was no way of doing it. Once the brain was in a cylinder it was there to stay . . . forever. Solemnly the Martian had assured me that the milky chemical in which the brain floated contained enough concentrated foodstuffs to nourish the brain and its few attached parts almost indefinitely. When the cylinder was not attached to the machine the brain was in a state of suspended animation and took none of the nourishment.

I had suggested that I could go back to the temple again and attempt to select a cylinder which contained the brain of a priest who had died only a few years before, hoping that, since Tarsus-Egbo had died, there may have been some advancement in the science of the cult and that a way now might be known of performing the operation.

Ken had absolutely forbidden this. He had pointed out the danger. The temple was sure to be under unusually heavy guard as a result of our former adventures under its roof and I would have only one chance in a hundred of getting out if, in fact, I could even get in. He had also pointed out that there was no reason to believe the priests would know any way of replacing a brain in a body. To be placed in the cylinder seemed the highest ambition of the Martian priests. It meant eternal life, the thing most highly prized by them. Why, then, Ken asked, should they attempt to find a way of replacing a brain in a body when life in the cylinder seemed to be the greatly preferred type of existence? Sadly, I felt that I had to agree with him.

I think, too, that Ken did not wish to be parted from me. He felt keenly his helplessness. He depended entirely upon me. He feared that, left alone, he might be recaptured by the Martians. I shuddered to think of what might happen to him if such a thing occurred.

It was uncanny at first, talking to my friend's brain inside the cylinder, but, realizing that we must accept the situation, we had maintained our friendship on its old standards. Ken joked about his helplessness, while I chose to ignore that he was anything other than the old Kenneth Smith whom I had once known in a human body.

I had eaten and was just lighting up for an after-meal smoke, when my friend hailed me. I hurried to the side of the cylinder.

"What is it, Ken?"

"Take a look over there, Bob. Straight ahead of me, the only way I can look. I've been trying to figure out if I see something or not. I would swear that I could, a white speck of some sort. Just between those two hills where the sun is setting."

I strained my eyes, but could see nothing. I told him so.

"Something funny about that," commented Ken, "I am certain that I see something. Looks like a building of some sort. It may be that my senses have been sharpened by being put into this tank. They're all I've got left to use and they may be developing. I've been watching that thing for a long time and I am convinced it's not my imagination."

"But what would a building be doing out here in the middle of the desert, a good 500 miles from any habitation?"

"I don't know," said Ken. "This is an old planet. There's lots of strange things on it. Get out Tarsus-Egbo and hook him up. He may have developed even better eyesight than I have. If my theory is right, it should be a great deal better. He's been tanked up longer than I have."

I walked to the ship and brought forth the second cylinder.

"I won't have you disconnected for long," I told Ken, "Just long enough to look up the Martian and see if he can tell me anything."

"Hook us up together, just wire him up to the same terminals I'm hooked up to. I have been thinking about it. I am certain, from what I know of the machine, that two or even more cylinders could be hooked up at the one time."

"You really think so? I don't want something to go wrong."

"I am certain of it. About all I can do, in the shape I'm in, is to think and I believe I have it all figured out. I'd like to talk to Tarsus-Egbo. It would be a marvelous sensation talking to another pickled brain."

"Well . . . if you are sure . . ."

"Go ahead, Bob. Nothing will happen."

Securing two short wires, I quickly connected the Martian's cylinder, holding my breath. At the least sign of anything wrong I was prepared to rip the wires away, but nothing did happen. The second cylinder glowed softly and took on its milky transparency.

The Martian blinked his eyes, as if awakening from a deep slumber.

"Kor," I greeted him solemnly in Martian.

He replied as solemnly.

I shifted the cylinder so that the Martian faced my friend.

Rapidly Ken spoke to him and the Martian replied gravely.

"Shift my cylinder so that I may see. My eyes are good. Strange man, your theory is correct. Being placed in the cylinder does sharpen one's senses. I am certain I can see it, if there is anything there."

I shifted the cylinder and Ken, speaking softly, directed Tarsus-Egbo's gaze.

"I also see it," said the Martian, "It is a pyramid, one of the many which existed here on these deserts in my day, but which, before my death had been largely destroyed by my people."

"Why destroyed by your people?" asked Ken.

"For two reasons," replied the Martian. "They are structures that were built by an ancient people who subscribed to a blasphemous religion and who used the pyramids as temples. It was only just that they should be destroyed. Those who destroyed them also found a great reward, for the pyramids invariably conceal great riches. Piety and hope of gain spurred my people on to their destruction. The sight of this one maddens me. I had thought that, by now, all would have been destroyed. It is an insult to Kell-Rabin, an insult to all of Mars that it should stand there. It is the filthy manifestation of a loathsome cult that once held sway over our beautiful land."

I thought that I heard a faint chuckle come from Ken's cylinder, but I was not sure, for he spoke immediately.

"What would you say, Tarsus-Egbo, if my friend destroyed that pyramid over there? Would he be able to do it? Do you think he would find great riches there?"

"It would be a great service to Mars if he did so," said the Martian. "I would thank him and the high priest would thank him. Perhaps we would even accord him the honor of being placed in one of the cylinders when he dies, even as you have been accorded that honor. I would forgive him the wrong that he had done me in his insane quest for knowledge and would thank him if he destroyed the pyramid."

"But," replied Ken, "my friend does not care for your thanks nor for the thanks of the high priest. In fact," I was sure of the chuckle this time, "he would not even care to meet the high priest. I even doubt if he would care to be placed in a cylinder. He is interested only in the great riches which he might find in the pyramid."

"If that is all he wishes," rumbled Tarsus-Egbo, "he will find them there. Riches that will make his brain swim. Jewels that are like fire and jewels that are like ice and others that are blue as the outer reaches of the sky. There too, he will find . . ."

"Wait," droned Ken, "Do you realize that you are in the power of my friend. Do you know that he might be very angry if he did not find riches such as you have described in the pyramid? Do you know that he might be so enraged that he would break your cylinder and destroy your immortality? My friend is quick to anger and it is best not to play upon his temper."

"He will find riches, great riches, in the pyramid," insisted the Martian, terror-stricken.

"But how do you know that some of your own people have not taken them? Just because the pyramid is there, does not necessarily mean that the riches must also be there."

"They are there," insisted the Martian, "If my people had found the place, it would not be standing now."

"I guess that's about all he can tell us, Bob," said Ken and I unhooked the Martian's cylinder.

"This is a new one to me," I told my friend, "I studied the Martians a great deal before they kicked me out, but this is the first time I ever heard about these incredibly ancient people."

"It was natural that you wouldn't hear about it," Ken pointed out. "It was something closely connected with their religion and you will have to admit that you can't find out much about this religion of Mars. What we have found out has been against their will and we have paid heavily for it."

"This puts a different face on the whole matter," I said.

Ken did not reply for a moment, then he spoke.

"I get you. With riches such as Tarsus-Egbo described, one can get anything one may happen to want. Those riches, Bob, if we can get them, will mean a lot to us. It will mean that we can continue to play our old hand against Mars. It will mean that, after all, we may not have to relinquish our revenge. It may mean that you can, at last, with safety, study the bones of Kell-Rabin. It is worth a try."

"Yes, worth a try," I said, "and we are going to make that try tonight. We can fly over there in a few minutes."

"That's talking now. Wish that I had a couple of hands to help you. Too bad. Two can do more than one. About all I can do is sit to one side and keep up the conversation."

"That's all right, old man," I consoled him, "Now I will have to unhook you. I'll connect the machine to the generator inside the plane and hook you up again so that you won't miss the trip over there."

"Don't go to so much trouble," protested Ken, "I am trouble enough as it . . ."

"Shut up, you," I rejoined, and pulled the switch, effectively silencing him.

I had worked for an hour with what few tools I had at hand to open the sealed door of the great pyramid, which towered blackly up into the cold night of the Martian desert. Above me rolled the two moons of the planet and thousands of stars pricked out on the blue-black sky. The night desert wind sang weirdly around the corners of the pyramid. The atomic engine of the plane whined softly, operating the light generator to which I had hooked the machine which motivated the cylinder that contained the brain of Ken Smith.

"I think I am moving a big one now," I told the cylinder, and the voice of my friend came distinctly to me, cheering me on.

The huge stone moved ever so slightly and I threw all my weight against the steel bar which I was using. It moved just a bit more and again I heaved. Bit by bit I worked it out, until I was certain that a few more heaves would pry it away.

"I have it almost out now," I told Ken, "and I am going to move you out of the way a bit. I don't want anything to happen to you."

"It would be hard luck to get cracked up now, just when we are on the verge of a great discovery," he chuckled.

"The Martian may have been lying," I told him.

"He wasn't," protested Ken. "He was telling the truth. That crack about you busting him up if he lied would have made him change his story in a hurry. Funny how those fellows set so much store on long life. If something doesn't happen to me before, I am going to hire somebody to tap me over the head when I get to be about two hundred years old."

Laughingly, I picked up the cylinder and moved it several feet away, then went back to my task. Several more heaves brought the block of stone away and it fell, burying itself deep into the sand. The second stone was less trouble to pry away and after that the third and fourth one came still more easily. At last I had a hole large enough to pass through into the interior of the structure.

With my flashlight trained before me, I clambered through and dropped softly to the floor, which was paved with huge slabs of stone similar to those of which the pyramid was built.

The circle of light which I flashed before me revealed a huge block of stone, apparently an altar, set in the middle of the room. It was not the altar, however, that drew my attention. Piled in a heap before the altar were five great chests. The treasure chests!

My heart leaped up into my throat and I ran forward. Seizing one of the chests, I attempted to lift the lid, but found that I was unable to do so. Grasping it under my arm, I staggered to the door, for the chest was heavy, and heaving the chest outside, leaped after it.

With my bar, I attacked the lid and with a rending of metal and the splintering of breaking wood, it came away. Living fire seemed to leap from it to strike me in the face and I threw up my arms across my eyes and stepped back.

CHAPTER V

The Last Defiance

There before me lay the treasure of the ancient people of Mars! Treasure that had lain for centuries under the sacred walls of the ghostly pyramid!

Tarsus-Egbo had spoken true! Here was a planet's ransom! Here was wealth undreamed of! Here lay jewels that flashed in the soft light of the two moons and seemed to glow and move and writhe like animate things.

Ken was shrieking at me.

"It's the treasure, Bob! It's the treasure! We are rich men, rich men! Trillionaires! Now we can carry on. Now we can thrust the bones of Kell-Rabin down the throat of the Martian nation! Now we can make them pay, pay, pay . . . pay, damn then, for my radium, and for my body, and for all the hell that they have made us pass through! We have them, we have them . . . right by the bloody throat!"

The sight of the gleaming jewels had awakened the old hatred, the old desire for revenge. They represented power, power to strike back at Mars. Almost had we forgotten our plans of revenge . . . but always, now I realized, they had lurked in the back of our brains, awaiting release, the release which the jewels had given them. I seemed to see the jewels through a red haze of weird emotion. Ken was right! With them we had Mars by the throat, we could stuff the musty bones of Kell-Rabin down the throats of the high officials and the priests!

Insane? Of course, we were insane. I think we had always been; I, since my deportation from Mars and Ken since the confiscation of his radium deposits.

"Yes, it's the treasure, Ken," I choked. "It is the treasure and there are four other chests just like this one inside the pyramid!"

I ran forward and thrust my hands deep into the box. I brought them away with a handful of stones that glimmered and glinted and flashed blue and red and green and white fire. Some rolled away and lay sparkling and shining in the sands.

"Look, Ken," I screamed. "Look at them. Why, damn it, man, with these we can buy out the entire planet. We can buy Mars and blow it to hell if we want to."

I threw a handful on the sand in front of him and raced back to the pyramid. One after the other I threw out the boxes and with the bar ripped away their lids. They were filled to overflowing with jewels some not much larger than peas, others the size of my fist. Offerings, perhaps, made to some ancient god; offerings made by a people who were wind blown dust millennia ago.

"Are you sure that is all?" asked Ken.

"Isn't that enough?" I asked.

"More than enough," agreed my friend, "but if there are more, we want them."

Once again I crawled back into the pyramid room. Slowly I explored it, from one end to the other and came at last to the rear of the great stone altar. Hardly thinking of what I was doing, I lifted a booted foot and kicked at the altar. I half remembered wondering if it was a solid block or if it was hollow.

As my foot struck the altar, it moved. What appeared to be pivoted stone set in the back of the block, swung aside and out of the aperture toppled a long, narrow box. I leaped aside out of its way and it struck the stone floor with a crash, splitting wide open.

I screamed and fell back, still holding my light directed on the broken box. Out of it rolled something that was round and white and as it rolled I saw that it was a human skull.

Shaking like a leaf, I moved nearer to the broken box and with my foot swept away the splintered wood. My light revealed a human skeleton, the skeleton of a Terrestrial! Still horrified, I stooped down and examined the bones. They were in a poor state of preservation, but easily identified as the bones of an Earthman, not of a Martian. Rising, I walked to where the skull lay, picked it up and examined the teeth. There were thirty-two. Thirty-two teeth, and the most any Martian could boast were twenty-four. The skull was crumbling away even as I held it. It must have been inconceivably old.

I ran from the pyramid. The skeleton of a Terrestrial in an ancient Martian pyramid, which had been closed, which had not been viewed by mortal eyes, for thousands upon thousands of years! What did it mean? What awful secret lay back of it? Terrestrials had landed on Mars in the first space car only a few hundred years before. Yet, I had found an ancient skeleton . . . My mind whirled and my senses reeled at the astounding possibilities which the thing suggested.

Terrestrials, then, had visited Mars before! Other civilizations than our own had risen to great heights, only to fall into nothingness. Could it have been men of Atlantis, or men of Mu, or men of a nation that was forgotten before those other two arose?

Other Earthly races had visited Mars . . . but why had I found the skeleton of one in a pyramid associated with an ancient religion, ancient even to the aged planet of Mars? Could it have been possible . . . could Terrestrials have been regarded as gods? Could the proud races of Mars . . . could the proud religion . . . ?

I stumbled out of the pyramid and tilting my head back, roared in laughter at the two moons which swung above the dead reaches of the desert.

Many things have happened in the past five years, and as I think of it, I remember that it was just five years ago today that Ken Smith and myself, with the jewels and the cylinder which contained Tarsus-Egbo, the Martian, secretly left Mars on the ship of a space captain who was willing to take a few risks for a double handful of jewels. We reached Earth safely, the captain landing us in a remote section of the Rocky Mountain district.

For a year we remained in hiding and discussed our plans. At last, satisfied that both the Earth and Mars had lost all trace of us, I securely hid the jewels, except for a pocketful, with the two cylinders in a cave and journeyed to the outside.

This time there was no need for a disguise. As I look in the glass now I can scarcely believe that I am only slightly over forty. My hair is snow white and my face is the face of an old man, lined with deep wrinkles and scarred with care.

In Chicago I experienced some trouble in retrieving the box which contained the bones of Kell-Rabin from its place in the safety deposit vault, but the papers I presented were all in good order and there was no reason for raising too great an objection, so it was finally handed over to me.

There was much to do and I set about doing it. I realized that my time might be short, so I wasted none of it. There were draftsmen, electricians, radio experts, laborers, orders for steel and other materials, all to be attended to, and I attended to them. It cost money, but the jewels that we possessed represented a colossal fortune and cost meant nothing if it purchased haste and efficient workmanship.

A month ago, I dismissed the last workman whom I had employed to build the huge broadcasting station ten miles from where I sit and write this. It is the most powerful station in the universe, greater even than those mighty stations on Jupiter. It is the pride of the Earth. I am hailed far and wide all over the planet as one of Earth's greatest benefactors. With that station a message may be flung to the farthest limits of the universe, out to where icy Pluto swings in the outer void and where the sun is no more than a star among many stars.

If only the Earth suspected what would be the first message that is to be hurled out from that station, it would be destroyed immediately by governmental orders. If only Mars suspected, a fleet of warships would leave the surface of that planet within the next few hours, bound for Earth.

The Earth will call me a traitor to the solar system, Mars will list my name on the blackest sheet of the most infamous book, my own people will believe me crazy. I am crazy, crazy with suffering, crazy with a mad desire to humble a cruel and haughty nation. There is a method in my insanity, a terrible, cold, calculating method. And the world does not suspect. The Martians, who have praised my philanthropic work, do not suspect.

Crazy, you say, insane, a raving maniac. How, I ask you, have I come to be insane? Would not any man lose his mind if he sat day after day, face to face with the brain of a friend encased in a metal cylinder? Remembering other days, when this thing in the cylinder walked on two legs, laughed and joked, enjoyed a good smoke . . .

I must hasten, however. There is little time left.

For the past four years I have lived in dread, dread that someone would recognize me, that I would be unveiled as the murderer of the Martian priests in the Chicago hotel or as the man who had blasphemed the Martian religion and profaned the Temple of Saldebar.

I have kept to myself. I have gained the reputation of being shy, modest, retiring. I have not allowed myself to be photographed, I have granted no interviews. I have remained the Great Enigma and become the better known and gained more publicity because of it.

It was not that I cared for myself, for life is no longer valuable to me. It was fear that I would be discovered before the hour had struck, before I had completed all my plans. Now the hour is near and if I live a few more hours the world will never find me.

Only a few hours now. My plans are well laid, all arrangements are made. The broadcasting station is completed. Here in the cragged hills of North American's greatest mountains, there is a great vault, carved from the everlasting rock. Tonight Dr. John E. Barston, the world's greatest surgeon, will perform an important operation in that vault. When he leaves, he will take with him a chest half filled with jewels, all that is left of the great Martian treasure. He will take them with him as the price of silence. The men who built the vault are silenced, too, on the criminal colonies on Mercury. It took several handfuls of the jewels to do that.

At last revenge is in my grasp. In a few hours Mars will be the butt of the entire universe. In a few hours the Martian religion will be a joke.

The Martians, who excluded me from their planet, who stole my friend's radium deposits and then stole his body, the Martians, who made Kenneth Smith and me outcasts of the solar system, shall feel the point of our wrath. I am striking at them where it will hurt most. I am taking from them their proud religion, I am tumbling their card house down about the ears of their beastly priests. I am stealing their faith as they stole the body of Kenneth Smith.

Good old Ken! We were pals ten years ago and we are still pals. He has played a wonderful game. He has pretended that it didn't matter. It has been hard for him, as it has been hard for me. He has depended on me so much. It is I who have turned him on and off, who have shifted his cylinder so that he may rest his eyes on a different scene. With the passing of the years his senses and his brain have grown stronger. His reasoning power has increased until he thinks in almost pure logic. His one passion is revenge, revenge on the Martian race, and I am giving that to him.

I have here an electrical transcription of my own voice. In a short time, I shall turn on the power to its fullest in the great station and shall set before the microphone a machine to transcribe the metal cylinder that lies before me, to repeat the transcription over and over again so that all may hear, may hear my voice in a declaration that will seal the doom of the Martian religion. I shall lock the doors of the station and before they batter them down every living soul in the universe will know my story. Every person will know how the bones of Kell-Rabin were filched from the Temple of Saldebar, how the Martian race has worshipped almost six years before an empty box. They will know of the skeleton that I found in the pyramid in the Arantian desert and of the religious frenzy that has driven the Martians to destroy every one of these pyramids they can find.

They will know, too, the truth about Kell-Rabin, whose bones were worshipped for uncounted centuries as the Holy Relics and the Revered Remains. They will know that the bones of Kell-Rabin *are the bones of a Terrestrial, of a human being who must have lived on Earth millions of years before Mu rose out of the sea. They will know that a Terrestrial was worshipped as a god by the Martian race and that his bones were religiously placed in a box to be worshipped long after he had died . . . and from the fact that the bones in the old pyramid and the bones of Kell-Rabin were both Terrestrial skeletons they may draw their own conclusions.*

The Martians, what of them? When my words flash out to the mining stations of Mercury and the trading outposts of Pluto, where, then, will be the proud religion of Mars? Crumpled, dissolved, gone! Gone, as are Ken Smith's radium deposits and his body. My words will rob them of the thing they have held dear, all their teachings will be for nothing, all their creeds will be empty words whistling in the wind.

A Martian has worshipped a Terrestrial! The Martian race, believing they have worshipped a god too great to give attention to the lesser races, will know that they have worshipped, not a god at all, but a man from Earth, one of the despised, money-grabbing, business-like men of the third planet.

When that is done I shall hurry to keep my last earthly appointment. The appointment will be with Dr. Barston in the vault that is chiseled from the living stone. Weeks ago I placed in his hands complete directions, given me by Tarsus-Egbo, for the process of transferring a human brain to one of the cylinders. One of the cylinders, especially constructed under directions and specifications also given me by the Martian, now rests in the vault.

There, in the vault, I shall lie down on an operating table and Dr. Barston will take my brain from its cavity and place it in the cylinder and when he leaves, with a jewel chest under his arm, there will be three cylinders, all standing in a row . . . waiting for what?

He will close the door of stone behind him and the automatic bolts will shoot home. The three of us, Kenneth Smith, Tarsus-Egbo, and myself, will remain behind, awaiting our fate.

Perhaps, in millions of years, men wonderfully advanced in science, will find us and mayhaps they will know how to release us from the cylinders and give us bodies again. Perhaps men will never come and we will remain forever in the deep sleep of seeming death. Perhaps we will never be aroused from that sleep, perhaps no one will ever attach the machine to our cylinders. If anyone of intelligence gains entrance to our vault, he will find there, imprinted on metal pages, definite information which should be easy for him to follow.

Life holds no more for me. I might as well be dead. It is Ken's idea, however, and I am going through with it. It was my suggestion that I destroy his cylinder and kill myself when vengeance was accomplished, but he suggested this other way, and it may be the better way.

Only a few minutes remain. I must soon start for the broadcasting station. Then I must hurry to keep my appointment with Dr. Barston.

My last thought shall be, I know, whether or not I will ever live again, or if, when I go under the anaesthetic, my days are ended. It matters little either way. My vengeance will then have been complete.

When the knife cuts into my skull, all the universe will be listening to my final words, and the name of Kell-Rabin will be bandied about in laughter from world to world.

SENSATIONAL DISAPPEARANCE
FIRE IN NEW INTERPLANETARIAN RADIO STUDIO
VEILS DEEP MYSTERY

By *Amalgamated Press*

Ventnor, Calif., October 5th—As the new gigantic interplanetarian station IXXB went on the air tonight for the first time, the whole universe held its breath for what its new and generous owner, Mr. Robert Humphrey would have to say. Much mystery had surrounded the building of this station and untold wealth had been poured into it, yet no one seems to have the confidence of the silent Humphrey who intimated that the mystery would be speedily ended with the first broadcast.

Mr. Humphrey had spent much time in arranging his inauguration address, and instead of facing the microphone himself, he had preferred to make a record of his voice and it is understood that a number of these had been made as he was not satisfied with the first one. He intended to have the first broadcast letter-perfect, and it was personally "edited" by him a number of time to make it 100% perfect.

The station, as is well known, was to go on the air last night at 8 o'clock sharp, and the populace of not only our own earth but all the other planets were at a fever pitch to hear this first broadcast. The reason of course, was that Mr. Humphrey had spent millions in the week before the broadcast was to come off in newspapers, radio broadcasting on other stations, and, as a matter of fact, he used every means of publicity he could to draw attention to the first broadcast of his station. Sensational copy was used in all his advertising to make sure that everybody would listen. Such sentences as "The Greatest Dramatic Story Ever Told in the Universe," "Revelations That Will Set the Universe Agog," had caused heated speculation as to what the first broadcast would be.

A few minutes before 8 o'clock, when the memorable event was to come off, a heavy thunderstorm was at its height near this city, and at exactly five seconds before 8, a lightning bolt struck the studio of the immense station. The listeners heard the announcer introduce Mr. Humphrey whose voice from the record had just gone on the air, with the words, "Ladies and Gentlemen, I am about to make the most dramatic revelation of the ages . . ." This terminated the broadcast because when the lightning struck it set fire to the studio, and inasmuch as the announcer and the two control men at the studio had been stunned, the fire immediately gained some headway and the record was destroyed in the ensuing blaze.

There was no duplicate record, but strangest of all, Bob Humphrey was not in the building, and he is strangely missing. The mystery has now deepened, as for sixteen hours no word has been had from Humphrey. It is certain that if he had been near the scene, he would have been able, in person, to make his announced broadcast or supply another record. The fire was not so extensive, and the main radio generating plant was not damaged excepting the studio, and the station could have gone on the air within three hours after the fire. Yet, there is no word from Humphrey. His station staff hint that he bid them good-bye in the afternoon telling them that "they might have to get new positions after tomorrow." Foul play is feared.

RETROGRADE EVOLUTION

This story was named "The Googles Are a Funny Race" when Clifford D. Simak sent it to Sam Moskowitz in November 1952. The following April, Cliff was paid $270 for it, at about the same time that the story, having been renamed, was published in the second issue of Hugo Gernsback's doomed magazine, Science Fiction Plus.

Gernsback, perhaps abusing his status as one of the founding fathers of magazine science fiction, included in that same issue a long editorial in which he excoriated "pseudo science-fiction," by which he meant stories, represented as science fiction, that were based on "science" that was not possible—an attitude that would, a few months later, lead him to take unusual liberties with a different Simak story, "Target Generation" (you can find that story in volume seven of this series, which is entitled A Death in the House and Other Stories).

But for the purpose of publishing "Retrograde Evolution," Gernsback made a number of changes to Cliff's story—including one that likely amuses the modern reader: he changed the name of the alien race featured in the story, "Googles," to "Kzyzz"—a name, he explained in a dreadful footnote purportedly written by the author of the story, which was given them because of the "strange sibilant sound" they made while eating. I do not believe for an instant that the change was Cliff's idea, and I will always wonder what his reaction was to Gernsback's alterations—the situation, after all, was complicated, since it was Gernsback who had published the very first piece of Cliff's fiction to appear before the public, more than two decades earlier . . . In any case, along with deleting the footnote, I've reversed that change, and several others, for this publication.

—dww

The trader had saved some space in the cargo hold for the *babu* root which, ounce for ounce, represented a better profit than all the other stuff he carried from the dozen planets the ship had visited.

But something had happened to the *Google* villages on the planet Zan. There was no *babu* root waiting for the ship and the trader had raged up and down, calling forth upon all *Googles* dire malefactions combed from a score of languages and cultures.

High in his cubbyhole, one level down from the control room and the captain's quarters, Steve Sheldon, the space ship's assigned co-ordinator, went through reel after reel of records pertaining to the planet and studied once again the bible of his trade, Dennison's *Key to Sentient Races.* He searched for a hidden clue, clawing through his close-packed memory for some forgotten fact which might apply.

But the records were not much help.

Zan, one of the planets by-passed on the first wave of exploration, had been discovered five centuries before. Since that time traders had made regular visits there to pick up *babu* root. In due time the traders had reported it to Culture. But Culture, being busy with more important things than a backwoods planet, had done no more than file the report for future action, and then, of course, had forgotten all about it.

No survey, therefore, had ever been made of Zan, and the record reels held little more than copies of trading contracts, trading licenses, applications for monopolies and hundreds of sales invoices covering the five hundred years of trade. Interspersed here and there were letters and reports on the culture of the

Googles and descriptions of the planet, but since the reports were by obscure planet-hoppers and not by trained observers they were of little value.

Sheldon found one fairly learned dissertation upon the *babu* root. From that paper he learned that the plant grew nowhere else but on Zan and was valuable as the only known cure for a certain disease peculiar to a certain sector of the galaxy. At first the plant had grown wild and had been gathered by the *Googles* as an article of commerce, but in more recent years, the article said, some attempts had been made to cultivate it since the wild supply was waning.

Sheldon could pronounce neither the root's drug derivative nor the disease it cured, but he shrugged that off as of no consequence.

Dennison devoted less than a dozen lines to Zan and from them Sheldon learned no more than he already knew: *Googles* were humanoid, after a fashion, and with Type 10 culture, varying from Type 10-A to Type 10-H; they were a peaceful race and led a pastoral existence; there were thirty-seven known tribal villages, one of which exercised benevolent dictatorship over the other thirty-six. The top-dog village, however, changed from time to time, apparently according to some peaceful rotational system based upon a weird brand of politics. *Googles* were gentle people and did not resort to war.

And that was all the information there was. It wasn't much to go on.

But, for that matter, Sheldon comforted himself, no co-ordinator ever had much to go on when his ship ran into a snag. A co-ordinator did not actually begin to function constructively until everyone, including himself, was firmly behind the eight-ball.

Figuring the way out from behind the eight-ball was a co-ordinator's job. Until he faced dilemma, a yard wide and of purest fleece, he was hardly needed. There was, of course, the matter of riding herd on traders to see that they didn't cheat, beyond a reasonable limit, the aliens with whom they traded, of seeing that they violated no alien tabus and outranged no alien ethics, that they abided by certain restraints and observed minimum protocol, but that was routine policing—just ordinary chores.

Now, after an uneventful cruise, something had finally happened—there was no *babu* root and Master Dan Hart of the starship *Emma* was storming around and raising hell and getting nowhere fast.

Sheldon heard him now, charging up the stairs to the co-ordinator's cubbyhole. Judging the man's temper by the tumult of his progress, Sheldon swept the reels to one side of the desk and sat back in his chair, settling his mind into that unruffled calm which went with his calling.

"Good day to you, Master Hart," said Sheldon when the irate skipper finally entered.

"Good day to you, Co-ordinator," said Hart, although obviously, it pained him to be civil.

"I've been looking through the records," Sheldon told him. "There's not much to go on."

"You mean," said Hart, with rage seething near the surface, "that you've no idea of what is going on."

"Not the slightest," said Sheldon cheerfully.

"It's got to be better than that," Hart told him. "It's got to be a good deal better than that, Mister Co-ordinator. This is one time you're going to earn your pay. I carry you for years at a good stiff salary, not because I want to, but because Culture says I have to, and during all that time there's nothing, or almost nothing, for you to do. But now there is something for you to do. Finally there is something to make you earn your pay. I've put up with you, had you in my hair, stumbled over you, and I've held my tongue and temper, but now that there's a job to do, I'm going to see you do it."

He thrust out his head like an angry turtle. "You understand that, don't you, Mister Co-ordinator?"

"I understand," said Sheldon.

"You're going to get to work on it," said Hart. "You'll get on it right away."

"I'm working on it now."

"Indeed," said Master Hart.

"I've satisfied myself," said Sheldon, "that there's nothing in the records."

"And what do you do now?"

"Observe and think," said Sheldon.

"Observe and think!" yelped Hart, stricken to the core.

"Maybe try a hunch or two," said Sheldon. "Eventually we'll find out what's the trouble."

"How long?" asked Hart. "How long will all this mummery take?"

"That's something I can't tell you."

"So you can't tell me that. I must remind you, Mister Coordinator, that time spells money in the trading business."

"You're ahead of schedule," Sheldon told him calmly. "You've shaved everything on the entire cruise. You were brusque in your trading almost to the point of rudeness despite the standards of protocol that Culture has set up. I was forced time after time to impress upon you the importance of that protocol. There were other times when I let you get away with murder. You've driven the crew in violation of Labor's program of fair employment. You've acted as if the devil were only a lap behind you. Your crew will get a needed rest while we untangle this affair. The loss of time won't harm you."

Hart took it because he didn't know quite how far he could push the quiet man who sat behind the desk. He shifted his tactics.

"I have a contract for the *babu*," he said, "and the license for this trade route. I don't mind telling you I'd counted on the *babu*. If you don't shake loose that *babu*, I'll sue . . ."

"Don't be silly," Sheldon said.

"They were all right five years ago," said Hart, "the last trip we were here. A culture just can't go to pot in that length of time."

"What we have here," said Sheldon, "is something more complicated than mere going to pot. Here we have some scheme, some plan, something deliberate.

"The Type 10 culture village stands there to the west of us, just a mile or two away, deserted, with its houses carefully locked and boarded up. Everything all tidy, as if its inhabitants had moved away for a short time and meant to come back in the not too distant future. And a mile or two outside that Type 10 village we have instead another village and a people that average Type 14."

"It's crazy," Hart declared. "How could a people lose four full culture points? And even if they did, why would they move from a Type 10 village to a collection of reed huts? Even barbarian conquerors who capture a great city squat down and camp in the palaces and temples—no more reed huts for them."

"I don't know," said Sheldon. "It's my job to find out."

"And how to correct it?"

"I don't know that, either. It may take centuries to correct."

"What gets me," said Hart, "is that god-house. And the greenhouse behind it. There's *babu* growing in that greenhouse."

"How do you know it's *babu*?" Sheldon demanded. "All you've ever seen of *babu* was the root."

"Years ago," said Hart, "one of the natives took me out and showed me. I'll never forget it. There was a patch of it that seemed to cover acres. There was a fortune there. But I couldn't pull up a single plant. They were saving it, they said, until the root grew bigger."

"I've told the men," said Sheldon, "to keep clear of that god-house and now, Hart, I'm telling you. And that means the greenhouse, too. If I catch anyone trying to get at *babu* root or anything else growing in that greenhouse, there'll be hell to pay."

A short time after Hart left, the chief of the Google village climbed the stairs to call on the co-ordinator.

He was a filthy character, generously inhabited by vermin. He didn't know what chairs were for, and squatted on the floor. So Sheldon left his chair and squatted down to face him, but immediately shuffled back a step or two, for the chief was rather high.

Sheldon spoke in Google lingo haltingly, for it was the first time he had used it since co-ordinator college days. There is, he supposed, not a man on the ship that could not speak it better than I, for each of the crew was on Zan before and this is my first trip.

"The chief is welcome," Sheldon said.

"Favor?" asked the chief.

"Sure, a favor," Sheldon said.

"Dirty stories," said the chief. "You know some dirty stories?"

"One or two," said Sheldon. "But I'm afraid they're not too good."

"Tell 'em," said the chief, busily scratching himself with one hand. With the other he just as busily picked mud from between his toes.

So Sheldon told him the one about the woman and the twelve men marooned on an asteroid.

"Huh?" said the chief.

So Sheldon told him another one, much simpler and more directly obscene.

"That one all right," said the chief, not laughing. "You know another one?"

"That's all I know," said Sheldon, seeing no point in going on. "Now you tell me one," he added, for he figured that one should do whatever possible to get along with aliens, especially when it was his job to find what made them tick.

"I not know any," said the chief. "Maybe someone else?"

"Greasy Ferris," Sheldon told him. "He's the cook, and he's got some that will curl your hair."

"So good," said the chief, getting up to go.

At the door he turned. "You remember another one," he said, "you be sure to tell me."

Sheldon could see, without half trying, that the chief was serious about his stories.

Sheldon went back to his desk, listening to the soft padding of the chief's feet doing down the catwalk. The communicator chirped. It was Hart.

"The first of the scout boats are in," he said. "They reported on five other villages and they are just the same as this. The *Googles* have deserted their old villages and are living in filthy huts just a mile or two away. And every one of those reed-hut villages has a god-house and a greenhouse."

"Let me know as soon as the other boats come in," said Sheldon, "although I don't suppose we can hope for much. Their reports probably will be the same."

"Another thing," said Hart. "The chief asked us to come down to the village for a pow-wow tonight. I told him that we'd come."

"That's some improvement," Sheldon said. "For the first few days they didn't notice us. Either didn't notice us or ran away."

"Any ideas yet, Mister Co-ordinator?"

"One or two."

"Doing anything about them?"

"Not yet," said Sheldon. "We have lots of time."

He clicked off the squawk box and sat back. Ideas? Well, one maybe. And not a very good one.

A purification rite? An alien equivalent of a return to nature? It didn't click too well. For, with a Type 10 culture, the *Googles* never strayed far enough from nature to want to return to it.

Take a Type 10 culture. Very simple, of course, but fairly comfortable. Not quite on the verge of the machine age, but almost—yes, just short of the machine age. A sort of golden age of barbarism. Good substantial villages with a simple commerce and sound basic economics. Peaceful dictatorship and pastoral existence. Not too many laws to stumble over. A watered-down religion without an excess of tabus. One big happy family with no sharp class distinction.

And they had deserted that idyllic life.

Crazy? Of course it was crazy.

As it stands now the Googles seem barely to get along. Their vocabulary is limited; why, I speak the language even better than the chief, Sheldon told himself.

Their livelihood was barely above the survival level. They hunted and fished, picked some fruit and dug some roots, and went a little hungry—and all the time the garden patches outside the deserted villages lay fallow, waiting for the plow and hoe, waiting for the seed, but with evidence of having been worked only a year or so before. And in those patches undoubtedly they had grown the *babu* plants as well as vegetables. But the *Googles* now apparently knew nothing of plow or hoe or seed. Their huts were ill-made and dirty. There was family life, but on a moral level that almost turned one's stomach. Their weapons were of stone and they had no agricultural implements.

Retrogression? No, not just simple retrogression. For even in the retrogression, there was paradox.

In the center of the Type 14 village to which the *Googles* had retreated stood the god-house, and back of the god-house stood the greenhouse with *babu* growing in it. The greenhouse was built of glass and nowhere else in the Type 14 village was there any sign of glass. No Type 14 alien could have built that greenhouse, nor the god-house, either. No mere hut, that god-house, but a building made of quarried stone and squared timbers, with its door locked tight by some ingenious means that no one yet had figured out. Although, to tell the truth, no one had spent much time on it. On an alien planet, visitors don't monkey with a god-house.

"I swear," said Sheldon, talking aloud to himself, "that the god-house was never built by that gang out there. It was built, if I don't miss my guess, before the retrogression. And the greenhouse, too."

On Earth when we go away for a vacation and have potted flowers or plants that we wish to keep alive, we take them to a neighbor or a friend to care for them, or make arrangements for someone to come in and water them.

And when we go on vacation from a Type 10 culture back to Type 14, and we have some *babu* plants that are valuable seed stock, what do we do with them? We can't take them to a neighbor, for our neighbor, too, is going on vacation. So we do the best we can. We build a greenhouse and rig it up with a lot of automatic gadgets that will take care of the plants until we come back to care for them ourselves.

And that meant, that almost proved, that the retrogression was no accident.

The crew slicked themselves up for the pow-wow, putting on clean clothes, taking baths and shaving. Greasy hauled out his squeeze box and tried a tune or two by way of warming up. A gang of would-be singers in the engine room practiced slow harmony, filling the ship with their caterwauling. Master Hart caught one of the tube-men with a bottle that had been smuggled aboard. He broke the man's jaw with one well-directed lick, a display of enthusiastic discipline which Sheldon told Hart was just a bit extreme.

Sheldon put on a semi-dress outfit, feeling slightly silly at dressing up for a tribe of savages, but he salved his conscience with the feeling that, after all, he was not going all the way with a full-dress uniform.

He was putting on his coat when he heard Hart come down from his quarters and turn toward his cubbyhole.

"The rest of the scouts came in," said Hart from the door.

"Well?"

"They are all the same. Every single tribe has moved out of its old village and set up a bunch of hovels built around a higher culture god-house and a greenhouse. They're dirty and half starving, just like this bunch out here."

"I suspected it," said Sheldon.

Hart squinted at him, as if he might be calculating where he best could hang one.

"It's logical," said Sheldon. "Certainly you see it. If one village went native for a certain reason, so would all the rest."

"The reason, Mister Co-ordinator, is what I want to know."

Sheldon said calmly, "I intend to discover it."

And he thought: It was for a reason, then. If all of them went native, it was for some purpose, according to some plan! And to work out and co-ordinate such a plan among thirty-seven villages would call for smooth-working communication, far better than one would look for in a Type 10 culture.

Feet pounded on the catwalk, thundering up. Hart swung around to face the door, and Greasy, charging into it, almost collided with him.

The cook's eyes were round with excitement and he was puffing with his run.

"They're opening the god-house," he gasped. "They just got the—"

"I'll have their hides for this," Hart bellowed. "I issued orders not to fool around with it."

"It isn't the men, sir," said Greasy. "It's the *Googles*. They've opened up their god-house."

Hart swung around to Sheldon.

"We can't go," he said.

"We have to go," Sheldon said. "They've invited us. At this particular moment, we can't offend them."

"Side-arms, then," said Hart.

"With orders not to use them except as a last resort."

Hart nodded. "And some men stationed up here with rifles to cover us if we have to run for it."

"That sounds sensible," said Sheldon.

Hart left at the double.

Greasy turned to go.

"Just a minute, Greasy. You saw the god-house standing open?"

"That I did, sir."

"And what were you doing down there?"

"Why, sir . . ." From his face, Sheldon could see that Greasy was fixing up a lie.

"I'm not the skipper," Sheldon said. "You can talk to me."

The cook grinned. "Well, you see, it was like this. Some of them *Googles* were cooking up some brew and I gave them some pointers, just to help along a bit. They were doing it all wrong, sir, and it seemed a pity to have their drinking spoiled by ignorance. So . . ."

"So, tonight you went down to get your cut."

"That, sir, was about the way it was."

"I see," said Sheldon. "Tell me, Greasy, have you been giving them some pointers on other things as well?"

"Well, I told the chief some stories."

"Did he like them?"

"I don't know," said Greasy. "He didn't laugh, but he seemed to like them all right."

"I told him one," said Sheldon. "He didn't seem to get it."

"That might be the case," said Greasy. "If you'll pardon me, sir, a lot of your stories are a bit too subtle."

"That's what I thought," said Sheldon. "Anything else?"

"Anything—oh, I see. Well, there was one fixing up a reed to make a flute and he was doing it all wrong . . ."

"So you showed him how to make a better flute?"

"That I did," said Greasy.

"I am sure," said Sheldon, "that you feel you've put in some powerful licks for progress, helping along a very backward race."

"Huh," said Greasy.

"That's all right," said Sheldon. "If I were you, I'd go easy on that brew."

"That's all you want of me?" asked Greasy, already halfway out the door.

"That's all I want," said Sheldon. "Thanks, Greasy."

A better brew, thought Sheldon. A better brew and a better flute and a string of dirty stories.

He shook his head. None of it, as yet, added up to anything.

Sheldon squatted on one side of the chief and Hart squatted on the other. Something about the chief had changed. For one thing, he was clean. He no longer scratched and he was no longer high. There was no mud between his toes. He had trimmed both his beard and hair, scraggly as they were, and had combed them out—a vast improvement over the burrs and twigs and maybe even birds' nests once lodged in them.

But there was something more than cleanliness. Sheldon puzzled over it even as he tried to force himself to attack the dish of food that had been placed in front of him. It was a terrible-looking mess and the whiff he had of it wasn't too encouraging, and to make matters worse, there were no forks.

Beside him, the chief slurped and gurgled, shoveling food into his mouth with a swift, two-handed technique. Listening to his slurping, Sheldon realized what else was different about him. The chief spoke better now. Just that afternoon he had talked a pidgin version of his own tongue, and now he talked with a command of the language that amounted almost to fluency!

Sheldon shot a glance around the circle of men squatted on the ground. Each Earthman was seated with a *Google* to each side of him, and between the slurping and the slopping, the natives made a point of talking to the Earthmen. *Just like the Chamber of Commerce boys do when they have guests*, thought Sheldon—*doing their best to make their guest content and happy and very must at home.* And that was a considerable contrast with the situation when the ship first had landed, when the natives had peeked out of doorways or had merely grunted, when they'd not actually run away.

The chief polished his bowl with circling fingers, then sucked his fingers clean with little moans of delight. Then he turned to

Hart and said, "I observe that in the ship you eat off an elevated structure. I have puzzled over that."

"A table," mumbled Hart, having hard going with his fingers.

"I do not understand," said the chief, and Hart went on to tell him what a table was, and its advantage over squatting on the ground.

Sheldon, seeing that everyone else was eating, although with something less than relish, dipped his fingers in the bowl. *Mustn't gag, he* told himself. *No matter how bad it is, I mustn't gag.*

But it was even worse than he had imagined and he did gag. But no one seemed to notice.

After what seemed interminable hours of gastronomical torture, the meal was done, and during that time Sheldon told the chief about knives and forks and spoons, about cups, about chairs, pockets in trousers and coats, clocks and watches, the theory of medicine, the basics of astronomy, and the quaint Earthian custom of hanging paintings on a wall. Hart told him about the principles of the wheel and the lever, the rotation of crops, sawmills, the postal system, bottles for the containment of liquid and the dressing of building stone.

Just encyclopedias, thought Sheldon. *My God, the questions that he asks. Just encyclopedias for a squatting, slurping savage of a Type 14 culture. Although, wait a minute now—was it still 14? Might it not, within the last half day, have risen to a Type 13? Washed, combed, trimmed, with better social graces and a better language—it's crazy, he told himself. Utterly and absolutely insane to think that such a change could take place in the span of half a day.*

From where he sat he could look across the circle directly at the god-house with its open door. And staring at the black maw of the doorway, in which there was no hint of life or light, he wondered what was there and what might come out of it—or go into it. For he was certain that within the doorway lay the key to the enigma of the *Googles* and their retrogression, since it seemed that the god-house itself must have been erected in preparation for the retrogression. *No Type 14 culture*, he decided, *could have erected it.*

After the meal was over, the chief rose and made a short speech, telling them that he was glad the visitors could eat with the tribe that night, and that now they would have some entertainment. Then Hart stood up and made a speech, saying they were glad to be on Zan and that his men had come prepared to offer a small matter of entertainment in return, if the chief would care to see it. The chief said he and his people would. Then he clapped his hands as a signal and about a dozen *Google* girls came out and marched around in the center of the circle, going through a ritual figure, weaving and dancing without benefit of music. Sheldon saw that the *Googles* watched intently, but none of it made much sense to him, well-grounded as he was on alien ritual habits.

Finally it was over. One or two misguided Earthmen clapped, but quickly subsided into embarrassed silence when everyone else sat in deathly quiet.

Then a *Google* with a reed pipe—*perhaps the very one,* Sheldon thought, *upon which Greasy had done his consultative engineering*—squatted in the center of the circle and piped away with a weird inconsistency that would have put to shame even the squeakiest of Earthly bagpipers. It lasted for a long time and seemed to get nowhere but this time the ship's crew, perhaps in relief at the ending, finally, of the number, whooped and clapped and yelled and whistled as if for an encore, although Sheldon was fairly sure they meant quite the opposite.

The chief turned to Sheldon and asked what the men were doing. Sheldon had a reasonably hard time explaining to him the custom of applause.

The two numbers, it turned out, were the sum total of the entertainment program whomped up by the *Googles*, and Sheldon would have liked to ask the chief if that was all the village could muster, a fact which he suspected, but he refrained from inquiring.

The ship's crew took over, then.

The engine-room gang gathered together, with their arms around each other's shoulders in the best barbershop tradition and sang half a dozen songs, with Greasy laboring away on the squeeze box to accompany them. They sang old songs of Earth, the songs all spacemen sing, with unshed tears brightening their eyes.

It wasn't long before others of the crew joined in, and in less than an hour the ship's entire complement was howling out the songs, beating the ground with the flats of their hands to keep time and flinging back their heads to yelp the Earth words into the alien sky.

Then someone suggested they should dance. One of the tubemen called the sets while Greasy humped lower over his squeeze box, pumping out "Old Dan Tucker" and "Little Brown Jug" and "The Old Gray Mare" and others of their kind.

Just how it happened Sheldon didn't see, but all at once there were more sets. The *Googles* were dancing, too, making a few mistakes, but their Earthmen teachers guided them through their paces until they got the hang of it.

More and more of them joined in, and finally the entire village was dancing, even the chief, while Greasy pumped away, with the sweat streaming down his face. The Google with the reed pipe came over after a while and sat down beside Greasy. He seemed to have got the technique of how to make the music too, for his piping notes came out loud and clear, and he and Greasy hunkered there, playing away like mad while all the others danced. The dancers yelled and hollered and stamped the ground and turned cartwheels which were totally uncalled for and strictly out of place. But no one seemed to care.

Sheldon found himself beside the god-house. He and Hart were alone, pushed outward by the expanding dance space.

Said Hart: "Mister Co-ordinator, isn't that the damnedest thing that you have ever seen."

Sheldon agreed. "One thing you have to say about it: The party is a wingding."

Greasy brought the news in the morning when Sheldon was having breakfast in his cubbyhole.

"They've dragged something out of that there god-house," Greasy said.

"What is it, Greasy?"

"I wouldn't know," said Greasy. "And I didn't want to ask."

"No," said Sheldon, gravely. "No, I can appreciate you wouldn't."

"It's a cube," said Greasy. "A sort of latticework affair and it's got shelves, like, in it, and it don't make no sense at all. It looks something like them pictures you showed me in the book one time."

"Diagrams of atomic structure?"

"That's exactly it," said Greasy. "Except more complicated."

"What are they doing with it?"

"Just putting it together. And puttering around with it. I couldn't tell exactly *what* they were doing with it."

Sheldon mopped up his plate and shoved it to one side. He got up and shrugged into his coat. "Let's go down and see," he said.

There was quite a crowd of natives around the contraption when they arrived, and Sheldon and Greasy stood on the outskirts of the crowd, keeping quiet and saying nothing, being careful not to get in the way.

The cube was made of rods of some sort and was about twelve feet on each side, and the rods were joined together with a peculiar disc arrangement. The whole contraption looked like something a kid with a full-blown imagination might dream up with a super-tinker-toy set.

Within the cube itself were planes of glasslike material, and these, Sheldon noticed, were set with almost mathematical precision, great attention having been paid to the exact relationship between the planes.

As they watched, a heavy box was brought out of the god-house by a gang of *Googles*, who puffed and panted as they lugged it to the cube. They opened the box and took out several objects, carved of different materials, some wood, some stone, others of unfamiliar stuff. These they set in what appeared to be prescribed positions upon the various planes.

"Chess," said Greasy.

"What?"

"Chess," said Greasy. "It looks like they're setting up a game of chess."

"Could be," said Sheldon, thinking, *if it is a chess game, it is the wildest, most fantastic, toughest game I have ever seen.*

"They got some screwy chess games, now," said Greasy. "Fairy chess, they call it, with more squares to the board and more pieces, different than the ones you use just regular. Me, I never could rightly get the hang of even normal chess."

The chief saw them and came over.

"We are very confident," he said. "With the help you gave us, we can't help but win."

"That is gratifying," Sheldon said.

"These other villages," said the chief, "haven't got a ghost. We have them pegged dead center. This will be three times, hand-running."

"You are to be congratulated," said Sheldon, wondering what it was all about.

"It's been a long time," said the chief.

"So it has," said Sheldon, still very much at sea.

"I must go now," said the chief. "We start now."

"Wait a second," Sheldon asked him. "You are playing a game?"

"You might call it that," the chief admitted.

"With these other villages—all the other villages?"

"That's right," said the chief.

"How long does it take? With all those villages, you and the other thirty-six . . ."

"This one won't take long," the chief declared, with a knowing leer.

"Good luck, chief," said Sheldon and watched him walk away.

"What's going on?" asked Greasy.

"Let's get out of here," said Sheldon. "I have work to do."

Hart hit the ceiling when he learned the kind of work that Sheldon had to do.

"You can't third-degree my men!" he shouted. "I won't have it. They haven't done a thing."

"Master Hart," said Sheldon, "you will have the men line up. I'll see them in my quarters, one at a time, and I won't third-degree them. I just want to talk to them."

"Mister Co-ordinator," said Hart, "I'll do the talking for them."

"You and I, Master Hart," said Sheldon, "did our talking last night. Much too much of it."

For hours on end, Sheldon sat in his cubbyhole while the men filed in one at a time and answered the questions that he shot at them:

"What questions did the *Googles* ask you?"

"How did you answer them?"

"Did they seem to understand?"

Man by man the notes piled up, and at last the job was done.

Sheldon locked the door, took a bottle from his desk and had a liberal snort; then he put the bottle back again and settled down to work, going through the notes.

The communicator beeped at him.

"The scouts are in," said Hart's voice, "and every single village has one of those cubes set up in front of their god-house. They're sitting around it in a circle and they seem to be playing some sort of game. Every once in a while someone gets up from the circle and makes a move on one of the planes in the cube and then goes back and sits down again."

"Anything else?"

"Nothing else," said Hart. "That was what you wanted, wasn't it?"

"Yes," said Sheldon, "I guess that was what I wanted."

"Tell me one thing," asked Hart. "Who are they playing?"

"They're playing one another."

"One another what?"

"The villages," said Sheldon. "The villages are playing against one another."

"You mean thirty-seven villages?"

"That's what I mean."

"Would you tell me just how in hell thirty-seven villages can play one single game?"

"No, I can't," said Sheldon. But he had the terrible feeling that he could. That he could make a guess at least.

When it had become apparent that the retrogression was a planned affair, he remembered, he had wondered about the problem of communications which would have been necessary to have thirty-seven villages simultaneously retrogress. It would have taken, he had told himself, a higher order of communications than one would expect to find in a Type 10 culture.

And here it was again—an even tougher communications job, an odd, round-robin game in which these same thirty-seven villages played a game upon a complicated board.

There is one answer for it, he told himself. *It simply couldn't be, but there is no other answer for it—telepathy—and that is almost unthinkable in a Type 10 culture, let alone a Type 14.*

He clicked off the squawk box and went back to work. He took a large sheet of paper to serve as a master chart and thumbtacked it to the desk, then started on the notes, beginning with the top one and going through to the very last. And when he had finished the chart, he sat back and looked at it, then put in a call for Hart.

Five minutes later Hart climbed the stairs and knocked at the door. Sheldon unlocked it and let him in. "Sit down, Hart," he said.

"You have something?"

"I think I have," said Sheldon. He gestured at the sheet thumbtacked on the desk. "It's all there."

Hart stared at the chart. "I don't see a thing."

"Last night," said Sheldon, "we went to the *Google* pow-wow, and in the short time we spent there, we gave that particular village the most complete and comprehensive outline of a Type 10 culture that you have ever seen. But what really scares me is that we went somewhere *beyond* Type 10. I haven't worked it out completely, but it looks nearer Type 9M than Type 10."

"We what?"

"They pumped it out of us," said Sheldon. "Each of our men was questioned about certain cultural matters, and in not a single instance was there duplication. Each of the set of questions asked was a different set of questions. Just as if those *Googles* were assigned certain questions."

"What does it mean?" asked Hart.

"It means," said Sheldon, "that we have interfered in one of the slickest social setups in the entire galaxy. I hope to God . . ."

"Slick social setup! You mean the *Googles*?"

"I mean the *Googles*," Sheldon said.

"But they never amounted to anything," Hart said. "They never will amount to anything. They . . ."

"Think hard," said Sheldon, "and try to tell me what is the most outstanding thing about the Google culture. We have a history of five hundred years of trade with them. During those five hundred years there is one fact about them that sticks up like a bandaged thumb."

"They're dumb," said Hart.

"Not from here, they aren't."

"They never got anywhere," said Hart. "Weren't even going anywhere, far as I could see."

"That's part of it," said Sheldon. "Static culture."

"I'll be damned," said Hart, "if I'll play guessing games with you. If you have something on your mind . . ."

"I have *peace* on the mind," said Sheldon. "In all the five hundred years we've known the *Googles*, there has been no dissension among them. They've never fought a war. That is something that cannot be said for any other planet."

"They are just too dumb to fight," said Hart.

"Too *smart* to fight," said Sheldon. "The *Googles*, Master Hart, have done something no other people, no other culture, has ever been able to do in all galactic history. They've found a way in which to outlaw war!"

For thousands upon thousands of years, empire after empire had been built among the stars and upon the many planets that circled round the stars.

And one by one, lonely and beaten, each empire had fallen, and one by one other empires had risen to take their place and in their turn had fallen. And those that existed in this day would fall in time.

This is the old, old cycle, Sheldon told himself, *the ancient disease of force and arrogance and desperation—the ageless pattern of cultural development.*

Never had a day existed since the first beginning that there had not been war at one place or another within the galaxy.

War came about because of economic pressure, mostly, although there were other causes—the ambitions of a certain being or of a certain race, the strange death-wish psychology which bloomed in certain cultures, an overweening racism, or a religion that spoke in terms of blood and death, rather than in terms of love and life.

Break down the causes of war, Sheldon thought, and we would find a pattern—certain factors which made for war and certain other factors which made for victory, once war had been invoked.

Now, suppose we made a study of war, its causes and the winning of it. Suppose we worked out the relevant relationships which each factor held to all the other factors, and not only that, but the relevant power of certain groups of factors against other groups of factors—factors of racial ingenuity and technology, of the human spirit, of logistics, of cultural development and the urge to protect and retain that culture, and hatred or the capacity to hate, all the many factors, tangible and intangible, which went into the making and the winning of a war.

And broken down into concrete terms, what would some of those factors be? What factors pushed a culture to the point of war? What factors made a victor? Certainly not just steel and firepower, certainly not courage alone, or generalship alone, or logistics or any other thing that could stand alone.

There would be other things as well, little, inconsequential, homely items, like sitting in a chair instead of squatting on the floor to eat, or using a knife and fork and not fingers. And other things, like dirty stories and better-drinking likker and a better pipe fashioned from a reed. For into all of these would go certain principles—the principle involved in the making of a better beer might light the way to manufacture a chemical that could be used in war; the perverted wit that shaped a dirty story might be turned to more destructive use in the propaganda section; the knowledge that made a better musical instrument might be extended to fashion an instrument that was not musical, but deadly.

It would be abilities such as these which would supply the economic pressure that might start a war, or contribute to that sense of superiority and intolerance and invincibility which might incline a tribe to war.

And if we watched the factors which represented these and other abilities, we would know when a war was about to pop.

And it was these same basic abilities and attitudes, plus a million other factors, which would determine who would win if a war should start.

Knowing this, we could assign certain actual values to all these cultural factors, although the value, as in a hand of cards, would be increased or decreased as they occurred in combination.

Sheldon got up and paced the tiny room, three steps up and three steps back.

Suppose then, he thought, *we made a game of it—a game of war, with all the factors represented by game pieces assigned sliding values. Suppose we played a game instead of fighting a war. Suppose we let the game decide which side would have won if there had been a war.*

Suppose, furthermore, that we watched cultures and detected the rise of those factors which finally lead to war. Suppose we could say that if the rise of certain factors should continue, war would then be inevitable in five years or ten.

Suppose we could do this—then we could catch a war before it started. We could see the danger signals and we would know the crisis point. And when we reached the crisis point, we played a game—we did not fight a war.

Except, Sheldon told himself, *it wouldn't work.*

We could play a game and decide a war, and once it had been decided, the factors that made for war would still be there; the crisis point would stand. We would be right back where we started; we would not have gained a thing. For the game, while it might decide who would have won the war, would not upset or correct the economic pressure, would not erase the crisis point.

No doubt the game could show which side would have won. It could predict, with a small percentage error, the outcome of a war. But it could not wipe out excess populations, it could not wrest trade advantages from the opposing side—it wouldn't do the job.

It wouldn't work, he told himself. *It was a beautiful theory, a great idea, but it just wouldn't work.*

We'd have to do more than play a game. We'd have to do a great deal more than play a game.

Besides determining who would have won the war if there had been a war, we would have to remove voluntarily the factors which had brought about the war—the solid, substantial facts of economic pressure, of intolerance, of all the other factors which would be involved.

It wasn't only the matter of playing a game, but of paying a price as well. There would be a price for peace and we'd have to pay the price.

For there would be more than one set of factors.

There would be the set that showed a war was coming. And there would be another set which would show that beyond a certain point the hard-won formula for peace simply wouldn't work.

It would work, perhaps, for a Type 10 culture, but beyond that, the factors involved might get so complicated that the formula would collapse under its own weight. A Type 10 culture might be able to deal with a factor which represented the cornering of the market on a certain food, but they could not deal with a factor which represented the complexity of galactic banking.

The formula might work for a Type 10 culture, but it might not work for Type 9; it might be utterly worthless for Type 8.

So the *Googles* not only played the game, but they paid the price of peace. And the price of peace was to run the other way. They retreated from advancement. They went clear back to 14 and they stayed there for a while, then went forward rather swiftly, but not as far as they were before they retrogressed. They went back voluntarily, and they stayed back, so they wouldn't fight a war.

They went back not because war was less likely in a Type 14 culture than in a Type 10 culture, but they went back so that the formula, once it had been used, would be effective; they stayed back so that they had some room to advance before they again reached the point beyond which the formula would break down.

But how would they go back? How would they retreat from a 10 to a 14 culture? Retrogress—sure they would retrogress. They would leave their comfortable village and go back and live in squalor and all the time the gameboard and the pieces and the position values they had earned in their Type 10 existence would be safely locked away inside the god-house. There would come the day when they had advanced far enough so they could play the game, and they played it then, according to the rules and with what they had—unless they hit the jackpot, and a spaceship from a higher culture landed in their midst and handed them on a silver platter, as it were, a load of atom bombs to be used in a bow-and-arrow war.

Sheldon sat down at his desk, and held his head in his hands.

How much, he asked himself, *how much more did we give them than they had before? Have we wrecked the formula? Have we given them so much that this village just outside the ship can bust the formula wide open? How much tolerance would there be? How far could they advance before a Type 10 culture and still be within the safety limit?*

He got up and paced the floor again.

It's probably all right, he told himself. *They've played the game for five hundred years we know of—for how many thousands of years more than that we simply cannot know. They would not willingly break down the formula; they would know the limit. For there must be a deeply ingrained fear of war within their very culture, or otherwise they would not continue to subscribe to the formula. And it's a simple formula, really. Simple. Like falling off a log! Except—how did a people deliberately retrogress?*

Hypnotism? Hypnotism wouldn't work, for what would happen to the hypnotist? He'd remain as a random and dangerous factor.

A clever machine, perhaps, except the *Googles* had no machines at all. So it couldn't be machines.

Drugs, maybe.

There was a root, and out of the root a drug was made to fight a disease peculiar to a certain sector of the galaxy—the *babu* root. Zan was the only place where the *babu* plant was grown.

"Good Lord" said Sheldon, "I didn't think of that. I read about it. What was that disease?"

He dug out his reels and put them in the viewer and found the dissertation on the use of the *babu* root, and he found the name of the disease, which was unpronounceable. He looked through the index of his reels and found a reel with the medical information, and there were few lines on that strange disease:

. . . nervous disorder, with high emotional tensions involved, in many cases stressing a sense of guilt, arising from the inability to forget past experiences. The drug induces a complete state of forgetfulness, from which the patient gradually recovers, retaining basic precepts, rather than the welter of detailed experiences, the impingement of which contributes to his condition.

That's it, of course! That's the perfect answer!

The *Googles* ate of the *babu* root, perhaps ceremonially, and they forgot, and in the forgetting they sloughed their culture from them, retrogressing four entire culture points. Then, after a time, the effect of the *babu* root would gradually wear away and they would remember, and remembering, advance up the cultural scale. They would remember, not the details of their former culture, but only its basic precepts, and in that way they'd not climb as high as they had been before. In that way they'd leave a margin through which they would advance toward the next crisis. Then once again, they'd eat of the *babu* root and once again war would be averted.

For, while the game would determine who would have won the war if one had been fought, the forgetting and the slow recovery from the *babu* would wipe out the cause of war, would remove the crisis point.

The formula worked because, even before they played the game, the factors of war would have been upset and the crisis point have already disappeared.

"God forgive us," Sheldon said, "our little grasping souls."

He went back to the desk and sat down. With a hand that suddenly was heavy, he reached out and thumbed up the communicator for a call to Hart.

"What is it now?" rasped Hart.

"Get out of here," Sheldon ordered. "Get off this planet as quickly as you can."

"But the root . . ."

"There isn't any root," said Sheldon. "Not any more, there isn't any root."

"I have a contract."

"Not now," said Sheldon. "It is null and void, contrary to galactic interests."

"Contrary!" He could hear Hart choking on his rage. "Look here, Co-ordinator, they need that root out in sector 12. They need . . ."

"They'll synthesize it," Sheldon said. "If they want it they'll have to synthesize it. There is something more important . . ."

"You can't do this," said Hart.

"I can," said Sheldon. "If you think I can't, try me out and see."

He snapped the toggle down and waited, sweating out the issue.

Then minutes passed before he heard the men running in the ship below, preparing for blast-off.

He watched the planet fade behind them as the ship fled into space.

Courage, he said to himself, thinking of the *Googles*, the bare, cold courage of it. *I hope it's not too late. I hope we didn't tempt them too far. I hope they can offset the damage that we did.*

There must have been a day when the *Googles* were a great race, building a great civilization—greater, perhaps, than any culture now in the galaxy. For it would have taken a fantastically advanced people to have done what they have done. It was no job for a Type 10 culture, nor for a Type 6 culture, which is the best that Earth itself can boast.

It had taken intelligence and great compassion, sharp analytical ability, and sober objectivity to figure out the factors and how they could be used.

And it had taken courage beyond imagination to activate the course those ancient *Googles* had worked out—to trade a culture that might have reached Type 2 or 3, for a Type 10 culture, because their plan for peace would not work beyond a Type 10 culture.

Once having worked, it must now continue working. All the courage of the race must not now be lost. It is a formula that must not be allowed to fail. It must not be allowed to fail because of the profit that traders made out of the *babu* root. It must not be allowed to fail through contact with other uncouth creatures who might be higher on the cultural yardstick, but who are without the common sense and the courage of the *Googles*.

And another thing—we must not run the chance that the *babu* root became a mere article of commerce. We could not blind the *Googles* to the greater value of the root, the value in which lay the greatest hope the galaxy had known.

Sheldon went back to the chart he'd made and checked through the information which the *Googles* had pumped out of the crew, and it added up to just slightly more than a Type 10 culture—a Type 9R, perhaps. And that was dangerous, but probably not too much so, for the Type 10A, if the *Googles* ever got that far, probably still represented a certain margin of safety. And there was the matter of the lag in the culture, due to the *babu*-eating, which would probably add an additional safety margin.

But it had been close. Too close for comfort. It demonstrated another factor, the factor of temptation—and that was something that could not be allowed to continue.

He went back to the record reels and spent hours studying the invoices, and once again he saw the cold, stark courage and the insistent dedication of the *Googles*.

There was not a single item on any of the invoices which went beyond a Type 10 culture.

Imagine, he told himself, *settling for a better hoe when they could have had atomic engines!*

Imagine, for five hundred years, refusing merchandise and comfort that would have made the Googles a greater people and a happier and more leisured people.

Greater and happier—and, more than likely, dead.

Once long ago, in mighty cities now hidden in the dust of the planet's surface, the *Googles* must have learned the terrible bitterness of a most artful and accomplished war and must have recoiled from the death and agony and the blind futility, and the knowledge of that day still dwelt within the minds of the *Googles* of today.

And that knowledge the galaxy could not afford to lose.

Sheldon picked up the chart and rolled it into a cylinder and slipped a couple of rubber bands around it. He put the reels away.

For five hundred years the *Googles* had held out against the lure of traders who would have given them anything they asked for the *babu* root. Traders who, even if they had known the truth, still would have willingly and thoughtlessly wrecked the protective Type 10 culture for the sake of profit.

They had held out for five hundred years. How much longer could they hold out? Not forever, certainly. Perhaps not for a great deal longer.

The chief and his tribe had weakened momentarily in acquiring information beyond the Type 10 culture limit. Might that not mean that already the moral fiber was weakening, that the years of trading had already sown their poison?

And if the *Googles* had not held out—if they did not hold out—the galaxy then would be the poorer and the bloodier.

For the day would come, many years from now perhaps, when it might be safe to make a survey, to conduct a study of this great thing the *Googles* had accomplished.

And out of that study certainly would come the first great step toward peace throughout the galaxy, a hint as to how the principle might apply without the stultifying need of a static culture.

But the study itself could not be made for many years. Not until the random factors of the last five hundred years of trade had been swept away.

He sat down at the desk, pulled out the voice-writer, and inserted a sheet of paper.

He spoke a heading which the machine printed quickly:

RECOMMENDATION FOR THE INDEFINITE CLOSING OF THE PLANET ZAN TO ALL VISITORS AND TRADERS.

WAY FOR THE HANGTOWN REBEL!

"Way for the Hangtown Rebel!" was originally published in the May 1945 issue of Ace-High Western Stories. *Cliff Simak's journals do not mention that he ever wrote a story with that title, and it seems likely that the title was a concoction of the editorial staff of the magazine—but one journal does show that Cliff was paid $150 in 1945 for a story called "Gunsmoke Letter," and the action in this story is indeed precipitated by a letter (of course, that could be said about "Gunsmoke Interlude," too . . .).*

Another point of interest is the fact that the saloon owner in this story was named Joe Carson—Carson was the first name of Cliff's younger brother, and his name turns up in a number of Cliff's stories, particularly in the early years of Cliff's career . . .

—dww

CHAPTER ONE

Hemp Greeting for a Stranger

The gallows were grim and shining new with the yellowness of lumber that had never braved the elements. Like a deliberate signboard of warning, they stood in the vacant lot, gleaming in the sun.

Steve Burns' hands tightened on the reins and even though the day was bright and warm, he felt the coldness of the challenging gallows.

"Getting fancy," he told himself, staring at the gallows. Most places were satisfied with a good stout cottonwood. But not Skull Crossing—they had this man-made apparatus that was evidently ready for business.

Slowly Burns swung the horse around and headed down the street.

Burns pulled up in front of the livery barn and spoke to an oldster tipped back on a chair.

"Got some extra hay and oats?" he asked.

"Yup," the man told him and then added, "the saloon's just down that dirt street."

Burns grinned and slid from the gray, handing over the reins.

"Was looking at that contraption up the street," he said. "Must be expecting some heavy business."

The livery man spat through a broken front tooth. "Already got the business. Fixing to string up some ornery hombres the sheriff caught out in the hills. Mex gang that's been raising hell for a year or two. Dang near cleaned out the valley."

"Noticed some abandoned ranches coming in," said Burns. "Wondered what it was all about."

"Yup," declared the man. "Getting so it wasn't safe to go out nights. Hay stacks burned. People killed. Cattle all run off."

"So the ranchers up and left," said Burns.

"That's it, stranger. Spent a lot of time trying to hunt down the lobos, but they never found their hideout. Bad country, them hills out back where they holed up."

"But the sheriff found the gang."

The livery man spat through the broken tooth again. "Tell you how it is, stranger. Sheriff sort of works up a little extra steam every time election date gets close."

"Think I'll head for a drink," said Burns and walked down the empty street.

After the blaze of sun outside, the interior of the Longhorn bar was a place of shadows. Burns stopped just inside the swinging doors, stood blinking until forms began to take dim shape. The bartender leaned on the bar, staring out the window. In one corner some men were playing cards and others stood around and watched.

Burns strode toward the bar. "Set it out," he told the barkeep. "I aim to cut some dust out of my throat."

The bartender moved deliberately, reaching for a bottle.

"Burns!" The word snapped like a whip across the room.

Steve spun from the bar, hands streaking for his guns.

In the dim light he saw one of the men who had been watching the game coming toward him.

The man's face was a blur and his body blended with the shadows that still hung in the corner. But there was no mistaking the poise of the body, no question about those moving hands, already hitting leather.

Burns' mind clicked blank with sudden concentration, everything else wiped out except that figure in the center of the room. Time stretched taut in the brittle silence and Burns, watching the smudge of the other's face, knew that his own hands were moving swiftly, that his guns were coming out . . . as if by rote.

Burns dodged swiftly and behind him he heard the crash of shattered glass as a bullet swept past his cheek and hit the backbar.

Then Steve's own guns were now talking, bucking against his wrists, coughing with a twin precision that set the glasses to jiggling on the bar.

Before him the smudge of face bent forward, hung for a single instant as the shadowy body jerked to the impact of the bullets, then slid to the floor.

Steve let his hands fall to his side, smelled the acrid smoke that trickled from his gun barrels, stared at the black, hunched thing in the center of the room.

Men were stirring out of the corner, plainer now that his eyes had become accustomed to the gloom, moving slowly and cautiously, with their hands hanging at their sides.

Feet pounded on the porch outside and the batwing doors smashed open. A huge man entered and walked toward Steve Burns. Wary, with thumbs hooked in his gunbelt, and the sunlight from the open doors striking fire against the nickel-plated star pinned upon his vest.

He stopped six feet away and stared, eyes squinted until they were little more than slits. He nodded at the guns.

"You're handy with them things."

"Only when I have to be," Burns answered.

"How come that Kagel knew you?"

"I wouldn't know," Steve replied.

"He called you by name," the sheriff growled. "You must have met him somewhere."

Burns shook his head. "He had my name, all right. But I don't recognize his handle. Maybe it's a new one."

"Maybe if we rolled him over," suggested a voice and Burns' eyes flicked toward the man who'd spoken. Squat, square of shoulders, smooth. Pearl stickpin gleaming in the black cravat that bunched above the ornate vest.

Slowly Steve holstered his guns. "Let's take a look," he said. "I'll tell you if I know him."

It was the last thing that he wanted to do, he admitted to himself. But it was a thing he had to do. One suspicious move and the burly sheriff would be making trouble.

They moved across the floor to stand above the dead man. Callously, the sheriff turned the body over with his toe and it flopped grotesquely on its back, arms flung out, limp head lolling.

Burns' face felt stiff, as if a mask had enclosed his flesh. He couldn't show the slightest flicker of expression, he knew, for the sheriff would be watching with those squinted eyes.

Slowly he shook his head. "Never saw him before," he said. "Can't imagine who he is."

And that, he told himself, was the damnest lie he had ever told. For there was no doubt about the dead man on the floor. His name wasn't Kagel, of course, and he looked some older than the day that he had left Devil's Gulch, swearing vengeance on the man who drove him out.

"I think I'll get that drink," said Burns.

"Just a minute," the sheriff called.

Burns stood silent, while the star-man squinted at him.

"Figuring on staying for a while?" the sheriff asked.

"Hadn't thought about it, sheriff."

"Take my advice," the lawman told him. "Have a drink and get some grub. Have a sleep if you really need it. But then you better slope."

Burns reached into a vest pocket, hauled out a sack of tobacco. His fingers shook a little as he thumbed the book of leaves.

"Ordering me out?" he said.

"I'm giving you some time."

"I think I'll stay a while," Burns told him calmly.

The sheriff's face flushed and his fingers twitched impatiently toward his guns, but his thumbs stayed anchored on the belt.

Burns spilled tobacco into the paper. "You see," he said, "this is the first place I was ever ordered out of. If I let it happen to me, folks might get the idea I was just a saddle tramp."

"I told you to vamoose," the sheriff rumbled. "We got our bellies plumb full of slickers that come in with their guns tied down."

Burns lifted the cigarette to his mouth, licked the flap, twirled it shut. His lips scarcely moved as he spoke. "Sheriff, the only way I ever argue is with my guns. Maybe you would like to . . ."

"Hold it," warned the man with the fancy vest. He addressed the sheriff. "Look, Egan, he didn't pick the fight, Kagel called him. Must have been out of his head or something. Burns here says he never saw the man before."

"That's what he says," declared the sheriff, "but it sounds damn funny to me."

"He had to defend himself," argued the other. "Kagel had the first shot. He already had his guns half out when he yelled at Burns. Under those circumstances, I don't see why Burns can't stick around long as he's a mind to."

The sheriff started to speak, stammered. "All right," he finally said. "All right, I guess that he can stay."

He swung on Burns like a raging grizzly. "Only don't go flourishing them guns. This here county is cleaning up and we don't stand for off-hand shooting."

Burns grinned sourly. "Just tell the boys not to prod me none."

Brusquely the sheriff turned on his heel and headed for the door. Steve stood, looking after him. Funny, he told himself. Damn funny. That big bear of a sheriff folding up to fancy vest.

Fingers tapped him on the elbow and he turned around.

"Name is Carson," said the man with the fancy vest, holding out his hand. "Joe Carson. Own this place."

Burns put out his hand and shook. Carson's hand was flabby and his handclasp matched it.

"Don't mind the sheriff," said Carson. "It's near election time and he is on the prod. Always is, come election time. Looking for things that will help the votes."

"Like rounding up the cow thieves?"

"Something like that," Carson agreed. "Probably had those rustlers staked out for months ahead and hauled them in when it would do some good."

Burns moved to the bar, Carson at his elbow.

"Good shooting," the bartender told him. "Seen lots of it in my day. But nothing quite like that."

"Thanks," said Burns. "Slow, though. He got in the first one."

"And smashed up the backbar," declared the bartender, bitterly. "Damn it all, I do hate messy shooting. Neat and clean, I says. That's the way to do it."

"Go ahead, drink up," invited Carson. "The bottle's on the house."

Burns poured a drink and downed it.

"Maybe you're looking for a job," asked Carson. "If you are, I'd like to talk to you."

Burns hesitated. "Well, not a job exactly. I'm looking for a man."

"Not Kagel?" asked Carson.

Burns shook his head. "A friend. Name of Custer—Bob Custer. Used to live around here."

"You won't find him, mister," the bartender told Burns. "He up and pulled his freight a month or two ago."

"One of the ranchers that were driven out?"

The bartender nodded.

Burns downed a second drink of whiskey. "Doesn't sound like Bob," he protested. "All hell couldn't scare him out."

"None of them had a thing to stay for," Carson said. "Their cattle were gone and some of their places burned. They tried banding together, but it didn't do no good. Didn't have the men to protect themselves. When they were one place, the gang would strike at another. Only outfit that survived was Newman's Lazy K. Newman had men enough to fight off the wild bunch."

Burns shook his head, bewildered. "Funny that a bunch of cow thieves would go in for burning and killings. Mostly they're just interested in cows."

"Ranchers picked off a few of them," said Carson. "Got their dander up. For a while . . ."

The batwings flapped and a voice drawled. "Just take it easy, gents. Keep on doing what you're doing."

Burns stiffened and the whiskey in the glass he held slopped onto the bar. In the mirror, he saw Carson's face go white. The bartender stood frozen with a rag in one hand and a wet glass in the other.

"We're holding up the bank," the man in the doorway said, "and we don't want any trouble."

From down the street came the sound of a single shot.

"Somebody," said the man in the doorway, "thought that we were fooling."

"Apparently you aren't," Burns told him.

"If you think we are," replied the voice, "just turn around and try me."

Burns spun on his heels, knees folding beneath him so that he slid toward the floor, hands going for his guns. A bullet chunked in the wood above his head and the sound of the bandit's coughing gun crashed through the stillness of the bar.

"Take it easy, bub," said the bandit slowly. "Take it easy, bub. Stay right where you are."

Burns' guns, almost clear of leather, slid back as his fingers loosened.

"Take it easy, bub . . . take it easy, bub . . ."

The voice didn't sound exactly right, muffled by the blue bandanna mask, but the words were right. How long had it been since he'd heard those words? Five years or more . . . seven . . . maybe more than that.

"O.K.," said Burns. "I was a fool to try it."

He hunkered on his heels, hands on the floor, studying the man. Tall, straight, with a jaunty angle to his hat and wisps of tawny hair sticking out beneath it. The gun hand was steady and the figure tensed, but the voice had been cool, full of self assurance.

A ripple of shots came from down the street. A horse's hoofs started up and drummed into the distance.

"Steady," said the man in the doorway. "Don't get fidgety. One move and I'll fill you with lead!"

Queer to be sitting here, thought Burns, while a bank robbery's going on just a door or two away. Like spectators watching a horse race—or like a dream where a man sees something happening and can't raise a hand to stop it.

Someone was shouting now, yelling out orders. A sixgun banged and a rifle barked. Hoofs drummed again, hoofs that became a thunder in the street.

The man in the door moved swiftly. A quick heel sounded on the steps and just outside a man yelled to a horse. The rolling rush of hoofs went past the saloon and thundered down the street. Gunfire broke loose, went along the street in a ragged wave.

Burns leaped to his feet, bounded for the still-swinging doors.

Two dozen horsemen were racing out of town, horses hunched down and humping like scared rabbits, kicking up a cloud of dust, while guns from doors and windows sent a hail of lead after them. There were no answering shots. There was no need of any. The retreating bandits were already out of range.

Burns heard Carson come out of the door behind him. Together they stood side by side, watching the swirl of dust move out of sight.

Burns shook his head. "Big bunch," he said. "Bank robbers as a rule don't ride that many together."

"Smart way of doing it," said Carson, almost admiringly. "Ride in and take over the town. Have it over and done with before a man can make a move."

Down the street Sheriff Egan was bellowing, rounding up a posse. Up the street a few enthusiastic souls still banged away.

"Looks like the sheriff will have a chance to win another vote or two," Burns said in a low tone.

CHAPTER TWO

Gun the Man Down!

The bartender had said that Bob Custer had pulled freight. But the barkeep had been wrong. For the man who had stood with leveled gun in the doorway of the Longhorn bar had been Bob Custer.

Even with the mask covering his face, you couldn't mistake a jasper like Bob Custer, Steve told himself. Not with the jaunty angle to his hat, the tawny hair that refused to stay in place, the words he used . . .

"Take it easy, bub," he'd said and those had been words that he had used before. Words that he had used when the two of them had ridden together before Burns took the job in Devil's Gulch.

He had recognized Steve and had deliberately used that expression to keep his old partner from using his guns.

Sitting on the edge of the bed in his hotel room, Steve smoothed the faded letter on his knee, read the words again as the lamp on the little table guttered in the wind:

> *Dear Steve: If you ever figure on leaving Devil's Gulch why not ramble this way. I got a spread in a nice, quiet valley and sure could use a partner again . . .*

A nice, quiet valley! Well, maybe it had been, when Bob had written that letter, almost two years before.

Carefully Steve folded the letter, replaced it in his wallet and walked to the window. Dusk was falling over Skull Crossing and the orange and yellow glow of lighted windows ran along the street. The thump of boots upon the sidewalk came to Burns' ears as he stood staring out of the window. A horseman galloped past and it seemed to Burns that he could smell the acrid dust the pony's hoofs had raised in its haste.

If you ever figure on leaving Devil's Gulch . . . Somehow, Bob Custer, even then, two years ago, must have known that the day would come when a man couldn't go on living in a town where the ghosts of dead men walked in broad daylight. He knew even then that Steve would want to hang up his guns and get away from the constant whispering of, "That's Steve Burns, he shot about fifty men—cleaned up Devils' Gulch—he's poison with a gun."

"Good evening," said a voice from the doorway and Burns swung from the window, saw the man leaning against the jamb.

"You the gent," asked the man, "who perforated Kagel?"

Burns nodded, watching the man warily. A youngish fellow with slicked back hair and a bulldog pipe hanging from his mouth.

"I'm Humphrey," said the man. "Jay Humphrey. Editor of the *Tribune.* Got the room just across the hall from you. Saw your door was open."

"Glad to know you, Humphrey," said Burns, but he didn't try to make his voice sound as if he were.

"Understand your name is Burns," said Humphrey. "Wouldn't be Steve Burns, would you, from Devil's Gulch?"

"That's right," Burns told him, tight-lipped. "You aren't gunning for me, too?"

"Hell, no," protested Humphrey. "I just record the news. I never try to make it."

Burns hauled out his tobacco sack, started to build a smoke.

"Catch the bank robbers?" he asked.

Humphrey shook his head. "Egan came back with the posse just a while ago. The bandits got away into the hills. Osborne's sorer than a boil."

"Osborne the banker?" asked Burns.

"That's correct," said Humphrey. "Egan's sending out to the Lazy K for help. Figures on taking everyone he can lay his hands on out into the hills tomorrow."

Burns snapped a matchhead on his thumb nail, lit the smoke. "I can imagine that Osborne is sore," he said. "The sheriff will never catch that gang, waiting until morning."

He grinned at Humphrey. "You don't sound too sore yourself. Must not have lost much money in the holdup."

"Not a dime," said Humphrey. "The only ones that had money in the bank were the Lazy K, Carson and old man Osborne himself. Rest of us just use the bank for borrowing."

"High interest, I suppose," said Burns.

"It isn't interest," Humphrey told him. "It's highway robbery."

He straightened from the door jamb. "Got to be going," he said. "Got some work to do. Don't suppose you'll be riding with the posse in the morning?"

Burns hoisted his eyebrows. "Why should I? It's no skin off my nose what happens to the town. I ride in peaceable and what happens to me? Someone tries to plug me."

"Don't blame you," said Humphrey. "Drop into the office sometime. I got a bottle hid away for my friend."

Burns stood in the center of the room, listening to the sound of the man's feet going down the hall.

Humphrey had come for something. That, he knew, was certain. Some information. Something that he wanted to know. He hadn't asked any questions, except about that Devil's Gulch business and about riding with the posse. But that last had been a funny one. Men just passing through seldom rode with posses.

Humphrey couldn't suspect that he knew Bob Custer . . . probably no one in town even suspected Custer had been involved in the holdup. And that only made the visit more senseless than ever.

Burns let smoke trickle from his nostrils, knitted his brow.

Funny, that Custer could be tangled with a bank gang. Never had a wild streak in him. Always wanting to stop somewhere and settle down.

Bob Custer and some other ranchers were driven out of the valley by a bunch of cow thieves that didn't act the way cow thieves should act. Cow thieves as a rule don't burn and kill. They gather them some critters and get the hell out as fast as they can go.

Custer took part in the holdup of a bank, but it was a funny sort of holdup. Not the way bank men ordinarily work. The bunch was too big for one thing and . . .

Burns jumped as the door creaked, hand reaching for his gun. But even as his fingers touched the grip, he stopped, frozen in astonishment.

A girl stood in the room, back against the door, hands behind her, looking at him with blue eyes that seemed to sparkle in the smoky lamplight.

"You Steve Burns?" she asked.

Burns nodded, staring at her. The faded levis she wore were splotched with dust and the sleeves of the blue work shirt were so long she'd turned up the cuffs. Brown hair spilled around her shoulders and her hat hung at her back by a thong around her throat.

"Bob Custer sent me," she said quietly.

Burns rose slowly, fumbled his hat off his head and stood with it in his hand.

"I was figuring maybe that he would get in touch with me," he said, "but I never thought he would send a girl."

"I was the only one that could come. It would be too dangerous for any of the others. But no one would pay any attention to me. Probably wouldn't even know me."

Her eyes laughed at him. "Besides, I sneaked around in back after it was getting dark."

"Look, miss," pleaded Burns. "Maybe you would just slow up a bit and let me get it straight. About it being dangerous. About the bank robbery this . . ."

"That's what Bob wants to talk to you about," declared the girl. "He's afraid you'll think that he really is a bandit—that all of us are out robbing banks and shooting folks and . . ."

"You were doing a right good job of it today," said Burns.

Her hand reached out and gripped his arm. "But don't you see that's what Bob wants to talk to you about. Wants to explain how we are hiding in the hills, fighting back against the men who drove us off our land."

"Wait a second," gasped Burns. "You mean that Carson, Osborne and the Lazy K were the ones who drove the ranchers out?"

"Only Carson, really," the girl told him. "He's the town boss here. Osborne plays in with him and Newman out at the Lazy K is just the foreman. Carson owns the ranch and uses it as a hideout for his gunslicks."

"I should have guessed it," Burns said, almost as if talking to himself. "I should have spotted it right off. The phoney story about the rustlers and the burning . . ."

Steps came rapidly along the hall and Burns, reaching out, pulled the girl away from the door, stepped toward it, hand reaching for a gun.

Breathlessly they waited, but the steps went past, turned in at another door farther down the hall.

"You got to get out of here," Burns whispered. "There's too much chance of someone spotting you."

"Bob asked me to bring you out to the hills," the girl whispered back. "You'll come, won't you?"

"Sure, I'll come. What the hell. Bob Custer's the best friend I ever had. If he's in trouble, it's time I was sitting in and calling for a hand."

"I'll meet you on the road just west of town." She started for the door, but Burns halted her with a gesture. Swiftly, he stepped to the table, blew out the lamp.

"I'll be there just as soon as I can get my horse," he said.

He heard the doorknob turned.

"Just a minute," he said.

"Yes?"

"Since you know my name, miss, maybe . . ."

"Ann," she said.

The door opened and closed softly and her footsteps were faint tappings.

Burns stood for a moment, listening, then socked his hat on his head, walked out of the room and down the stairs. There was no sign of Ann. Probably, he told himself, she sneaked out the back way. Probably had her horse out there, back of the hotel.

There was no one in the lobby and he strode across it, came out on the porch.

The town was quiet. Somewhere a drunken puncher gurgled on a song and two horses stood slack-hipped at a hitch rack across the street.

Steve shucked up his gunbelt, stepped swiftly from the porch and headed for the livery barn.

A whining thing brushed past him and thudded into the hotel's side. A heavy rifle coughed hollowing in the night.

Burns flung himself toward the dark alley between the hotel and barber shop, hands clawing for his guns even as his legs drove him toward the place of safety.

The rifle coughed again and another bullet chewed into the siding, throwing bright splinters that flashed like tiny spears of light in the glow that came from the window just above them.

Burns hit the alley running and kept on, stumbling in the darkness.

And as he ran, thoughts hammered in his skull.

Someone knew who he was. Probably Carson had planted that rifleman in the building across the street.

The livery stable, he remembered, was to the west. He had to reach there quickly, get his horse and ride—west out of town to meet the girl.

A sudden thought stopped him in his stride. That girl! Was she really who she said she was? How was he to be sure that Custer had sent her? Maybe she was nothing more than bait to Carson's trap. A ruse to get him out of the hotel. If he rode to meet her, that might be another trap.

He shook his head, befuddled. He'd been a blundering fool, should have demanded some proof of the girl's identity. But it was too late now.

Carson was out to get him—for no one else would have planted that rifleman. Probably out to get anyone who rode into town and looked as if he might be troublesome.

Carson had said a word for him, he remembered, but that probably meant nothing now. Maybe Carson had figured on hiring him for one of his gunslicks until he'd shown too much interest in the empty valley and had asked about Bob Custer.

There was no one in sight at the alley's end and Burns swung to the west, slipped along the buildings, gun out, eyes and ears alert for danger.

From the street behind him came the uproar of shouting voices. Probably, he thought, grimly, those rifle shots had emptied every business place.

"Got to be fast about it," he told himself. "Another minute and the whole town will be on top of me."

Out of the silence ahead a pebble clicked and Burns froze against the building. Behind him the boards gave way and pushed inward as his shoulder pressed against them. In the darkness there was another sound, the slither of a foot, of a man moving up ahead coming toward him.

Steve froze tighter against the building, felt the boards against his back swing farther inward. Putting his hand behind him, he pushed and a hinge squealed faintly, like the sound of a cricket in the grass.

It was a door, he knew. A door leading into the rear of one of the buildings, although he could not know which one.

Backing silently into the darkness, he felt the floor beneath his boots, ducked swiftly into the cavernous blackness.

From outside came the scuff of boots, the scuff of several boots. More than one man out there, he told himself.

Reaching out with his toe, he found the door's edge, exerted gentle pressure. The door swung easily. The hinges squeaked just once then the latch clicked softly.

Relaxing from the strung-up tension of a moment before, he caught the sweetish smell of whiskey in the darkness, heard the subdued mumble of voices that came from just behind him.

His eyes made out the shapes of things piled against the wall. Kegs and cases and a pile of empty bottles, thrown helter-skelter in the corner.

A voice came higher than the others, cutting through the mumble.

"But, damn it, Egan, Gardner never misses. He's pure death with that gun of his. That's why I picked him for the job."

The sheriff's throaty rumble answered. "But he did miss, Carson. Shot twice and missed slick and clean each time. The boys are out hunting down the hombre."

Straightening up, Burns tiptoed back into the darkness, nearer to the sound of the voices.

The sheriff said: "Just wait. You'll hear a gunshot pretty quick. That'll be the end of him."

"The end of someone else more than likely," growled Carson. "You don't seem to get it into your thick skull who this man is. Steve Burns, the toughest marshal that ever packed a star. Cleaned up Devil's Gulch single-handed and you know what kind of a place that was. A jasper like that would have to ride in just when we'd gotten things to rolling. Wonder if Custer sent for him . . ."

The back door, the one Burns had latched a moment or so before, burst open with a crash.

Burns wheeled, stepped swiftly backward, felt his body wedge between two piles of cases.

"Hey!" yelled a voice. "Hey, in there!"

There were three figures in the doorway and one of them was

struggling, fighting furiously and silently to break from the clutch of the other two.

The sheriff's voice boomed. "That's Gardner. They got him!"

A door opened and a flood of light splashed into the room, lighting up the three who struggled in the doorway.

From his position between the cases, Steve Burns gasped and his guns jerked up.

The one who stood between the other two, the one who had been fighting to get free, was the girl with the blue eyes, the girl Bob Custer had sent to guide him to the hills!

CHAPTER THREE
Satan's Law and Order

Across the room, Burns saw Ann's mouth shape a warning cry, saw the blank astonishment that slipped like a mask across the face of one of the men who stood beside her. He sensed rather than saw the lightning move that brought a gun flashing from the holster of the other man.

In that timeless space while the flashing gun was moving, Burns twisted his wrist and thumbed the hammer. The gun bucked in his hand and across the room the other gun was spinning in the lamplight that flooded from the inner door.

Spinning like a wheel of light while in the doorway the man who had drawn it was wilting like a sack from which the grain was pouring.

Shuffling feet scraped swiftly across the floor and Burns spun clear of the packing cases, pivoting on his toes. The burly sheriff was almost on top of him, his drawn six-gun dwarfed almost to toy size by the ham-like fist that clutched it.

The sheriff's gun crashed in the closeness of the room and Burns felt a slash of fire rip across his ribs. Savagely he lashed out at the charging figure and his sixgun barrel slapped across the sheriff's face.

The lawman staggered in midstride and stumbled. His gun dropped from his hands and his face suddenly was red with blood that spouted from his nose. Burns danced out of his way, brought up with a jolt against a pile of cases stacked against the wall.

Egan skidded to his knees, sprawled upon the floor.

The room crashed again with spitting thunder and a bullet crunched into a case scant inches from Burns' head. Quickly Burns ducked, knees bending beneath him, dropping his body to a crouching position.

Through the gunsmoke that filled the place, Burns saw Carson standing to one side of the doorway. A crooked smile was on his lips and his gun was leveling for another shot.

Swiftly Burns angled his own sixgun around, thumbed the hammer. The shot was wild, but it spoiled the saloon man's aim. Carson's bullet plowed a furrow along the floor, hurling shining splinters in the murky light.

Another gun crashed and the half open door beside which Carson was standing jumped on its hinges at the impact of the bullet.

Carson jerked back, moving swiftly, dived for the safety of an empty case standing on the floor.

Steve spun on his heels, leaping for the back door. He saw Ann standing in the doorway, gun in hand, smoke still drooling from its muzzle. The man who had stood beside her, the one with the look of blank astonishment on his face, was huddled on the floor.

"Quick!" Burns yelled at her. "Outside!"

She hesitated for a second, staring at him.

With a single bound, he was at the door and reaching out for her. Lifting her, he swung her into the darkness, set her roughly on her feet. From behind them a sixgun snarled.

"Run!" gasped Burns. "The livery stable. Two horses. I'll hold them off."

She clung to him. "I hit him," she said. "He was just standing there and I grabbed the gun out of his holster and hit him on the head."

Burns shoved her away. "The barn," he shouted at her. "Get us horses!"

The girl was running and Steve loped after her, watchful, guns ready to be used.

Another gun barked from a building's corner and Burns heard the bullet whine through the grass at ankle height. He held his fire.

"They can't be sure where we are," he told himself. "No use showing them."

Ahead of him he saw Ann's shadowy figure duck into an open door, knew it must be the rear entrance to the livery barn. Reaching it, he stood in the darkness by the door, waiting, watching. But there was no sign of pursuit. Perhaps no one knew exactly where they'd gone. Perhaps most of them didn't even know what was happening. Of the gang back in the saloon's back room, Carson would be the only one in any shape to tell them. One man was dead, another had been knocked out by the girl, and the sheriff would need a little while to get his wits together.

Swiftly, Steve ducked into the door, ran down the aisle that smelled of hay, of oiled leather, of sweaty saddle blankets.

One horse was sidling along the aisle and Burns spoke to it soothingly. The animal snorted and backed away. Leaping, Burns caught the reins.

"Where are you?" he shouted at the girl and her voice came back.

"Here. I got another horse."

She was backing it out of the stall.

Burns flicked his eyes up and down the row of stalls, wishing for his own gray, although his mind told him there was no time to wait, no time to choose. No time even to get on saddles.

They'd have to ride without them. Bridles was the best that they could do.

If he only knew where his own horse had been put. If only . . .

"Hey, what's going on?" a voice called sharply.

Burns swung around. It was the livery man, striding toward him.

Burns jerked up his gun.

"See this?" he asked.

The livery man stopped abruptly.

"Just turn around and walk ahead of us," Burns told him. "Real slow. And shed your artillery as you go."

Slowly the man swung around, hands fumbling at his gun belt.

"One wrong move," warned Burns, "and I'll blow you plumb to hell."

The gun belt dropped from off the man's waist and the man himself plodded on ahead, hands half raised.

Behind him, Burns heard the soft, muffled thud of his own horse and the girl's.

"When we get to the door," Burns told Ann, "we'll climb these ponies and hit the street full gallop. Swing to the west and keep on going. If there's any shooting, don't try to shoot back. I'll take care of that."

To the livery man, he said: "That's far enough for you. Just stand where you are and don't let out a yelp."

Burns swung abruptly, leaped for the back of his horse. The animal, accustomed to a saddle, crouched in fright, then sprang for the doorway, burst into the street.

Deftly, Burns swung the horse around, brought his sixgun up to a firing position. Someone stormed out of a restaurant doorway, yelling at him and from far up the street a rifle started up with hollow coughing.

The sound of hoofs swept out of the barn and went past him. Out of the corner of his eye, Steve caught a quick glimpse of the girl, bent low on the saddleless horse, thundering down the street.

A bullet hummed over his head and another skipped along the sidewalk, like a stone on water, gouging out clouds of splinters as it went.

In front of the Longhorn bar men were running for their horses. Others were leaping for their saddles.

With a yell, Steve reined his horse around, taking the direction the girl had gone. Lighted windows spun past as the horse stretched out and ran as if his life depended on it.

Then the town of Skull Crossing was behind him and he was following the drumfire of hoofbeats that he knew was the other horse ahead.

The moon rode just above the eastern horizon and flooded the valley with a crystal light.

Burns frowned. If only the night could have been dark, Ann and he might have had a better chance. But with the moon almost full, pursuit would be easy. Soon the horses and their riders would be streaming out upon their trail.

The horse thundered down an incline, splashed across a shallow stream, plunged up the other bank and breasted the rise.

Ann and her mount were no longer to be seen, but the trail was plain and the horse followed it unerringly. If there's a place to turn off, Burns told himself, she'll stop there and wait for me.

The horse suddenly shied as a running figure came out of the shadows. Burns' hand, snaking for his gun-butt, stopped short. The running figure, he saw, was Ann. She was stumbling down the trail in the moonlight, waving as if to stop him.

She had lost her hat and the shirt was ripped open at the shoulder. Dirt smudges marched across her face.

"The horse," she gasped. "Threw me off. Scared of a snake . . ."

He reached down a hand and she grasped it.

"Up you come," he said, and heaved.

The horse shied and reared, and Burns talked to it soothingly.

"Hang on," he said to Ann.

Her arms tightened around his waist. "I'm all right," she told him. "If I'd had a saddle he never would have thrown me. But he jumped so quick that I just flew off."

"You hurt?"

"Skinned up some. That's all. Landed on my shoulder and skidded."

"We got to keep moving," Burns told her. "There's a big gang in town. Running for their horses when I left."

"The Lazy K mob," said Ann. "Egan must have sent for them."

The horse was stretching out again, running with an easy lope that ate up ground.

"You'll have to tell me when to leave the trail," said Burns.

"I will," she said.

They crossed another stream that tumbled from the hills down into the valley and the horse lunged up the bank.

"We sure got you in a mess," said Ann. "I know Bob didn't figure it this way. He just wanted to talk to you. Wanted to get you straightened out. Didn't want you to ride away thinking he had taken to robbing banks."

"I would have dealt me a hand anyhow," Burns told her, "just as soon as I got the lay. Didn't like Carson from the very first. A greasy sort of hombre."

They rode in silence for a moment.

"I came to see Bob anyway," said Burns. "Got a letter from him a couple of years ago. Said he needed a partner. Figured maybe that he still did. Figured maybe I could find a place where I could hang up the guns."

He laughed shortly. "Guess I'll need them for a while."

For a long while nothing further was spoken, then Ann said: "I hear something."

Straining his ears, Steve heard it, too. Heard it above the whistle of wind in his ears, the steady beat of the pony's feet—a distant drum of hoofs.

"That's the posse," said Burns. "I was hoping they'd hold off for a while."

At the end of ten minutes they turned off the trail, plunged into the tangle of hills that crowded against the valley.

The horse stumbled beneath them, regained his stride. But it was not as smooth and firm as it had been before—nor quite as fast.

Behind them the drum of hoofs was closer, louder. Once a man yelled and the yell cut above the rolling sound of pursuit.

The horse stumbled again, then went on, but this time the stride was broken, limping.

Burns pulled to a halt and slid off.

"Go on," he yelled at the girl. "Tell Bob I'll try to hold them off."

"But, Steve . . ."

"Go on!" he yelled. "Ride!"

He hit the horse with his hat and the animal leaped away. The girl, he saw, had grabbed the reins, was bending low. Then the hoofs clattered up a rocky gorge and pounded into the distance.

For a moment Burns stood at the mouth of the gorge, eyes taking in the scene. Not too bad a place to make a stand, he told himself, and yet it could be better.

But there was one thing clear. He had to stop them, hold them up a while for Ann to make her getaway. Had to try to hold out until Bob Custer could send his men sweeping down upon the posse.

Swiftly he ran up the gorge, dodging around the boulders, heading for a tangle of rock and juniper to one side of the gorge. As he ran he heard the nearing thunder of the posse.

Jerking loose his guns, he leaped behind the rocks and junipers, crouched waiting, breath whistling in his throat.

Suddenly the horses and their riders burst over the brow of the hill, stormed down toward the gorge. Twenty five or thirty of them, Burns made out, counting swiftly. Too many—more than he'd thought there'd be.

Moistening his lips, he lifted the guns. The palms of his hands were wet and he wrapped his fingers with a tighter grip.

They charged up the gorge in a massed bunch and Burns tensed in his hiding place. Slowly, deliberately, his trigger fingers tightened.

The first rider reached the boulder that he had marked and Burns' guns were hammering in his grip, spitting fire, blasting the night wide open with their talk.

Screams and yells burst out and the posse swirled madly for a moment with horses rearing and fighting the bits, men fighting to break free from the riders who were packed around them.

One man threw up his arms, his scream was drowned by the gurgle of blood welling in his throat. A horse jack-rabbited up the hillside, kicking at the bouncing thing that dragged beside it, foot caught in the stirrup.

Then, suddenly, the gorge was clear—clear except for three sprawled figures. One was bigger than the other two and that one, Burns knew, was a horse that one of his bullets had caught.

Horses were galloping wildly, reins dragging, while men raced like scurrying shadows for a patch of undergrowth, for a boulder, for anything that might serve as shelter from the storm of lead.

Flat on his belly, Burns fed cartridges into his guns. A gun coughed angrily and a bullet howled off a boulder, turning end over end into the moonlight night.

Another gun spat like a startled cat and the bullet crunched with a chewing sound through the screen of juniper, smacked into the earth. A third gun talked and then a fourth. Lead snarled and whined.

Huddled against the biggest boulder, Burns held his fire. Let them shoot. Let them burn a little powder. After a while they'll wonder what they're shooting at—now they're just shooting blind, working off some steam.

A branch, clipped by one of the buzzing bullets, fell on top of his hat and he shook it off with a jerk of his head. Another plowed ground three inches from his boot.

It was more than he had bargained for, he admitted grimly. Twenty men or more against his guns. Right in the middle of the jackpot and plumb out of blue chips.

The guns quieted and there were rustling noises—the sound of men moving forward, working closer to his position, crawling up the hill so they could get above him.

Squinting through the tangle of junipers, he waited. Out in the moonlight a stealthy figure moved, inching along like a drifting shadow. Burns brought one gun up, waited tensely. The shadow moved again and the gun in his hand barked into the night. The shadow screamed and jerked half upright, then fell back, a huddled shape sprawling on the hillside.

Guns shrieked and hammered and the junipers danced wildly with the bullets. Hugging the ground, Burns felt the breath of death wing past, whispering in his ear. Sand geysered and sprayed into his face. A burning thing raked across his elbow. Screaming lead slid wildly from the boulders and went yowling away. They were doing their best to get him.

Another shadow moved and Burns jerked up his gun, triggered swiftly. The shadow yelled, leaped from the ground, became a running man. Burns' trigger finger worked again and the man bent in the middle, hit the ground with his shoulders and pinwheeled into the gully.

Guns yammered and the hillside and gully were full of winking muzzles that spat out leaden death.

The boulders and thicket of juniper lay no more than ten feet from the lip of the dry stream bed that sluiced down the gully.

The guns were quiet again. They were waiting for a moving target.

Burns crouched, gathering his feet beneath him. Then he moved, straight toward the dry wash, hurling himself across the moonlit space.

One gun cracked and then he was over the edge, tumbling down into the darkness, steeling himself against the boulders and gravel that would bite into his body.

His shoulder crashed into something soft and yielding, something that grunted and swore, something that lumbered out of his way.

Scrambling to his feet, Burns swung around, face to face with Sheriff Egan.

The impact had knocked the gun from the sheriff's hand and the sheriff was ambling toward him with a huge fist cocked.

Burns swung up his gun, but even as he did the fist exploded in his face and he felt himself lifted from his feet and sailing backward. He crashed into the gravelly bank behind him and for a moment his head seemed to burst and spin with screaming colors. Then he was crawling on his hands and knees, gasping for breath, while his stomach churned with an icy coldness and his knees and arms were so weak they ached.

A savage voice cut across his brain: "You damn fool, why didn't you shoot him?"

The sheriff growled and Carson's voice said: "Well, then, by Lord, I will."

A third voice came. "If you shoot him, Carson, it'll be the last thing you ever do. I'll drill you where you stand."

Cold seconds dripped by, breathless and taut.

The voice that had threatened Carson came again and this time Burns' befuddled brain remembered it—the voice of the man who had stood propped against the door jamb with the pipe hanging from his mouth.

"Law and order, Carson. That's what you're pulling for and it's what I'm pulling for and we're going to have it if I have to shoot you to get it."

Leather rasped as Carson holstered his gun.

"O.K., Humphrey," he said. "You win. Law and order, it is. He'll get a trial."

"Hell of a lot of good it'll do him," the sheriff growled.

A boot prodded him viciously.

"Come on, get up," someone rasped. "You're lucky. We're heaving you in jail."

CHAPTER FOUR
The Scapegoats Vamoose

Steve hunkered in a corner of the single room that served as the Skull Crossing jail. He glared sourly at the two barred windows which let in some moonlight.

From the opposite corner came the sound of breathing, deep and regular—not of one alone, but of several people. Burns listened carefully, but the breathing rose and fell with monotonous regularity of sleep.

Funny, how sound those hombres can sleep, Burns told himself. Never figured anyone could sleep that good when he was going to be hung. His elbow was sore where the bullet had nicked it back there in the gully and his stomach still was squeamish—but he'd done the thing he'd set out to do. They'd never find Ann now.

Funny how that newspaper hombre had up and saved the beans. If it hadn't been for that, Burns knew, Carson would have shot him in cold blood out there in the gully.

Burns shook his head. Queer setup. Carson and the sheriff were in cahoots, that much as least was certain. But they had the town buffaloed into thinking they were bringing law and order to Skull Crossing.

Rounding up those cow thieves over there in the corner had been a master stroke that convinced the town on this law and order business and assured the sheriff's re-election. Fixing up that gallows was another thing. Lots more impressive than a cottonwood. Sort of civilized and fancy. Make the people think justice had finally come to stay.

One of the men stirred in the corner and Burns suddenly realized that the regular breathing had stopped.

"Hey, amigo," a voice whispered. "What they throw you in for?"

"I shot somebody," Burns told him.

"Ah, that's bad," the voice said. "We only steal the cows and look at us. They hang us for only steal some cows."

He shuffled out of the darkness and came into the moonlight. Other men followed him, three of them, and squatted down behind him when he stopped in front of Burns.

"Who you shoot?" he asked.

Burns shook his head. "I wouldn't know. I'm not acquainted here."

"I hope it was the sheriff."

"Not the sheriff," said Burns. "I only hit the sheriff. In the face with a gun."

"Hear that?" said the man to the other three. "He hit the sheriff, right in his big, fat face."

"You tell him, Raymond," said one of the others.

"Shut up!" snapped Raymond.

Raymond hunkered down to face Burns. The moonlight fell across his face and Burns saw that it was dirty and wolfish, a man who would cut your throat when you weren't looking.

"You want to stay in here?" he asked.

Burns shook his head. "I don't intend to stay."

Raymond traced a pattern on the dirt floor with a grimy finger.

"You figure out a way to leave?" he asked.

"Not yet," said Burns. "I will."

"How much you give to go?"

Steve's mouth snapped tight. "I haven't any money."

Raymond's finger retraced the pattern carefully.

"You see some people in town?" he asked.

Burns nodded.

"Man with scar across his face," said Raymond. "Call himself Gunderson, maybe. Maybe something else."

"What about him?" asked Burns.

"He get us into this," snarled Raymond. "He come to us, he say easy pickings here. So we come and we have easy pickings and then one day he leave us and the sheriff come."

Raymond made a motion with his forefinger across his throat, made a noise like a spurting jugular.

"We think he sell us out," he said.

"You think he'd still stick around here if he'd sold you out?"

Raymond's face wrinkled like a worried hound dog's. "Something funny," he said. "Something smell. Judge, he won't let us tell about this man in court. Judge, he won't let us say a thing. Like maybe judge he know about this man and don't want us to spill the beans."

"Red headed man?" asked Burns. "Scar across his face. Finger missing on his left hand."

"That's him. That's him. You know him."

"He jumped me this afternoon," said Burns.

"And you? Of course, you kill him?"

"Of course," said Burns.

Raymond let the breath out of his lungs slowly.

"You hear that?" he asked the other three.

He swung back on Burns.

"Name of Gunderson? You sure?"

"Name of Kagel," said Burns. "But that doesn't make any difference. I knew him once before and his name was Taylor."

"Man of many names," said Raymond quickly.

"He sure took you for a ride," Burns told them. "Helped Carson hang it on you. Carson had to find some scapegoat to explain the range terror that he used to drive the ranchers out and so he got Kagel or Gunderson or whatever you want to call him to fix you fellows up as the fall guys."

Raymond's eyes narrowed. "Tricked?"

"That's it," said Burns. "Carson's outfit stole and burned and killed and you were blamed for it—they're hanging you for it."

Raymond rocked quietly on his toes and laughed softly to himself.

"No, we not hang. We got it all fixed up."

He rose to his feet. "Come," he said.

He shuffled toward the other end of the room and Burns followed, trailed by the other three. A packing box stood near one corner and Raymond indicated it.

"Table," he said. "Play the monte on him."

He laid hands on the box, grunted, shoved it to one side.

"Look," he said, pointing.

Burns knelt on the dirt floor, staring. A dark hole gaped up at him. Behind him he heard Raymond chuckling.

"We dig," said Raymond. "We dig like hell. Use old pie plate. Hide dirt under blankets. Tonight we finish him. Now we go."

He clapped a friendly hand on Burns' shoulder.

"You kill the gringo dog. You go, too."

"A while ago," said Burns, "you talked of money."

Raymond spread his hands, embarrassed. "But that was before we know about this gringo. You save us the trouble of finding him and doing what was needed. You leave with us. You ride with us."

"I leave with you," said Burns, "but I won't ride with you. I got other things to do."

"As you wish," said Raymond. "I go first. You follow me."

The tunnel was small—just big enough for a man to squeeze his way, dark and earthy. Slowly Burns worked his way along with clawing hands and kicking boots, thrusting himself along the downward dip, along the level run that passed beneath the walls of the jail, then up, with the stars shining through the opening above him.

Raymond reached down a hand and Burns caught it and was hauled up. The hole emerged a matter of six feet or so beyond the rear of the building, just within the limit of the shadow cast by the moon that now was sliding down the western sky.

Burns squatted on his heels, ears alert, eyes busy with the shadows, while Raymond hovered over the hole, lending help to his three companions.

Getting to their feet the five of them moved into the deeper darkness next to the building.

"We go now," Raymond said softly. "We get some horses. You sure," urged Raymond, "that you stay here?"

"I have to stay," Burns told him. "I got some folks to see."

Raymond held out his hand. "Adios," he said.

"Adios," said Burns, "and look. Lay off the gray horse. He's mine."

"You betcha," said Raymond. "We pass up the gray one."

"And take it easy," warned Burns. "Don't bring the whole town down on top of us. Better ride east. That west country, toward the hills, may be full of Carson's gunslicks."

"Sure Mike," said Raymond.

He moved away and his three companions followed. Burns stood watching them. A few yards away they stopped again, lifted hands in salute. Burns waved back at them, then turned and cat-walked swiftly through the darkness behind the buildings.

A smoky lantern set on the dump burned dimly in the back room of the *Tribune.* Humphrey, perched on a high-legged stool, was busy setting type, the bulldog pipe clenched between his jaws.

Standing just outside the window, Burns stared in at the editor, then moved softly to the back door.

From down the street came a startled yelp, a shot, then the wild clatter of hoofs building up some distance. Another shot boomed hollowly and silence came again, a thick and breathless silence that hung above the town.

The back door shrilled open on screeching hinges and Humphrey appeared within the frame staring at the darkness.

"I'm coming in," Burns told him softly, "and don't make a squawk."

Humphrey started, then saw Burns.

"Oh, it's you again."

Burns strode across the doorway, shut the door behind him.

"I thought I heard some shooting out in back," said Humphrey.

"It was up in front," Burns told him. "The cow thieves just escaped."

He clacked his tongue. "And that pretty gallows, standing out there waiting."

Humphrey relit his pipe, eyes fixed on Burns, face lighted up by the flaring match.

"You haven't got a gun back here?" asked Burns.

"Nope," said Humphrey. "Got one up in front."

"Just was going to warn you not to try to use it if you had," Burns told him. "I came to do some talking."

Humphrey motioned at the pot-bellied stove in the center of the room and the battered coffee pot that perched on top of it.

"How about a cup?" he asked.

Burns nodded.

Humphrey paced to the stove, lifted the pot.

"Don't ever be a newspaperman," he said. "Hell of a job. You work all hours of the day and night."

"I just sort of wanted to ask you," declared Burns, "why you stepped in and saved my hide tonight."

Humphrey wrinkled his brow. "Revulsion, I guess. Get tired every now and then of Carson's high handed ways. Runs the town, you know. Have to play ball with him, but shooting a man in cold blood is just a bit too much."

"Aren't you just a bit afraid he'll think it over some and get hostile about you pulling a gun on him?"

"Maybe," admitted Humphrey. "But, hell, that's the only kind of language a hombre like Carson understands. And if he wants to argue about it, he knows where to find me."

Humphrey sucked noisily on his pipe, squinted quizzically at Burns. "Aren't you taking a chance, my friend? Sitting around like this with me."

"You mean you figure I'd ought to be building up some miles—why I'm still hanging around these parts?"

Humphrey nodded. "That is precisely the thought that went across my mind."

"Can't do it," Burns told him. "Got a date with Carson."

"What you so steamed up over Carson for?" demanded Humphrey. "Here you ride cold into town and before a day is over you've worked up a feud with our leading citizen."

"I'm against anyone who drives his neighbors out," said Burns. "Don't take very kindly to shooting up a peaceful valley and running off cattle and burning houses. Don't seem very honest to me."

"Well, I be damned," declared Humphrey. "Why didn't I think of it before. Seems natural now, of course. Figured everything wasn't on the square, but I never figured Carson would have the gall to do a thing like that."

"He covered up his tracks right good," said Burns. "Seems to have most of the people fooled. Reckon you all thought it was a gang of night riders."

Humphrey hesitated. "Yes, I guess so. Although it seemed sort of funny to me that four puny Mexicans could raise quite so much unadulterated hell."

"They didn't," Burns told him. "Carson's gunslicks out on the Lazy K were the ones that did it. Them Mexicans were just the scapegoats. Served two purposes really. Covered up Carson's tracks and served as bait to keep Carson's sheriff snug in his office. Carson could have fixed up a crooked election and elected him anyway, but it was simpler this way. Easier to fool the people into voting for him."

Humphrey squinted at Burns in the dim lantern light. "How come you dealt yourself a hand?" he asked. "Custer or some of the others send for you?"

"Nope," Burns told him, "I'm looking for a place to hang up my guns."

"Far as I can see you ain't fixing on hanging them up right away."

Fists hammered on the front door and Humphrey spun about.

"Quick," he hissed at Burns. "Out you go."

Burns did not move, stood watching Humphrey walk swiftly for the door. Then he stepped out of sight of the door, into the shadow of the shop.

The front door grated open and a voice boomed at Humphrey.

"Thought I'd find you here."

"Come in, Osborne," said Humphrey.

Osborne—that would be the banker, Burns knew. Soft footed, he ducked around the press and type cabinets, moved closer to the door between the front and back rooms.

A chair creaked under Osborne's weight and the man spoke again.

"I suppose you know that Burns escaped."

"Hadn't heard of it," said Humphrey. "Been back in the shop, catching up on some work I had to do."

"Well, he did," growled Osborne. "Took the Mexicans with him."

"Imagine Egan is fit to be tied," said Humphrey.

"Carson is the one that's really sore," said Osborne. "If you hadn't interfered out there tonight Burns would have been out of the way for good and all."

The banker cleared his throat. "I been sitting up going over the bank records," he said. "I find you owe us quite a bit of money."

"A thousand dollars," said Humphrey.

"Plus interest," Osborne pointed out.

"You told me to forget the whole thing until I was in shape to pay it."

"Right," said Osborne. "We liked you. But in view of the present situation, something will have to be done about it. The note already is ninety days overdue."

"There isn't a thing I can do about it," said Humphrey.

"Then I'll have to start some action," said the banker. "I been letting it ride along because you seemed a smart young fellow . . ."

"Because," asked Humphrey, "I kept my mouth shut?"

Silence swept the office, a tense and terrible silence.

"Kept my mouth shut," said Humphrey, finally, "about you and Carson and Egan taking over the valley."

Osborne sighed and his chair creaked.

"I'm sorry," he said. "It would have been nice to have let you keep on living. Just running you out of town would have been enough. But after this . . ."

Burns' hand snatched out for a short steel bar that lay on the make-up stone, was at the door in two quick strides—all poised.

Osborne still sat in the chair across the desk from Humphrey, but he held a sixgun in his hand. Humphrey, half risen from his chair, was frozen, half standing, hands clenching the desk edge, white face staring at the weapon's muzzle.

Burns hurled the bar with terrific force. It whistled in the air, whirling end for end, smashed with a crunching sound into the banker's gun arm.

The arm flopped down and dangled, the gun spilling from the trailing fingers to clatter on the floor beside the fallen bar. Osborne sat motionless, as if stunned, still staring straight ahead.

Slowly Humphrey straightened up, then stooped and opened a desk drawer. When his hand came out it held a gun.

"If you so much as open your mouth," he told Osborne, "I'll fill you full of this!"

Burns slouched in the doorway. "What're we going to do with the ornery cuss," he asked, "now that we got him?"

"Personally," said Humphrey, "I favor hanging, but we can't do that without due process of law. And Carson's crooked judge would turn him loose."

Osborne's lips moved in his frightened face, but Humphrey twitched the gun and he did not speak.

"Better tie him up," said Burns, "and cache him some place. Probably be a good witness against Carson and his gang. His kind always turn state evidence."

"There's an old shed out back," said Humphrey. "Keep my paper stock in there."

"Good place," decided Burns. "We got to be careful tying him up. That one arm of his is broke surer than hell."

CHAPTER FIVE
Hang Your Guns!

The jail office was dark and Burns ducked quickly inside, slid to one side of the door, flat against the wall, and listened. There was no sound of breathing, nothing to indicate there was a second person in the room.

Probably all of them out chasing the Mexicans, Burns told himself. Probably think they are chasing me, too.

Unmoving, he stood flattened against the wall and gradually his eyes adjusted themselves to the darkness until he could make out the dimness of furniture—the battered desk, the swivel chair in front of it, the dull gleam of a spittoon at one corner of it.

Something else gleamed on the desk and Burns sucked in his breath. There they were—just where Egan had tossed them.

Swiftly, he strode across to the desk, picked up the gunbelt and the guns. He strapped the belt around him, took the guns out one by one and checked them. Still loaded, except for two empties in one that he had used back there in the hills before he made the dash for the dry wash. After he had reloaded he put them back in the holsters.

The sound of racing hoofs tensed him where he stood. Instinctively, he started for the door and then turned back. There was no time for that, he knew.

Like a trapped animal, he stood in the center of the room and probed the darkness for some way of escape. A spidery ladder in the hallway between the office and the cell-room caught his eye. A ladder! Probably leading up to an attic above the office, maybe a place for the jailer to sleep and cook his meals.

The hoof-beats were nearer now and there was more than one horse.

Burns leaped for the hallway, scrambled frantically up the ladder. A dark hole loomed above him, just wide enough for his shoulders to squeeze through. His hands clawed at the smooth boards of the floor and he hoisted himself into the attic even as the hoof beats came to an explosive halt just outside the jail.

He lay flat on the floor and listened to the tramp of heavy feet as they came into the office, heard the mumble of many voices.

A closer sound, a stealthy padding, edged into his brain and he moved swiftly, alarm growing in his mind, but even as he moved, hands came out of the darkness and closed around his throat.

Maddened by unreasoning fear, Burns fought to break away, arching his back, twisting, bucking like a locoed horse, tearing at the hands that throttled him. But the fingers held and tightened while the breath whistled in his throat and darkness churned within his brain.

From somewhere far away he heard the rasp of a striking match, a tiny, terrible sound that penetrated through the buzzing in his skull—the rattle of a lamp chimney being lifted. Then light flared in his face and even as he fought he knew that someone in the sheriff's office had lit a lamp and the light was sifting through the attic hole.

The fingers were steel bands now that shut off even the whistle in his throat and inside his head the black ball grew and even while he still clawed feebly at the constricting fingers, the blackness exploded with a shrieking roar and was a pinwheel of light that hissed within his brain.

He felt himself pitching forward, head slamming on the floor—then, suddenly, the fingers had left his throat and there was an arm around his shoulders, lifting him into a sitting position. He gulped great breaths of air and inside his brain the pinwheel slowed down and there was a soft voice in his ear, a frightened voice.

"Take it easy, bub," the voice said. "Just take it easy, now. I didn't know it was you. So help me, I didn't know."

Words rose to Burns' tongue, but his tongue refused to say them. He choked and gasped, gulped for air.

Bob Custer! Custer choking him, not knowing who it was. he sat up straighter and stared at the man who squatted face to face with him.

In the office below boots crunched across the floor.

A voice said sharply: "Be still, can't you. I tell you I heard something up there in the attic."

The sheriff's voice rumbled back: "Ah, hell, Carson, you're spooky, that's all. This Burns has got you on the prod."

"Spooky, eh," said Carson, viciously. "Where are Burns' guns?"

"On the desk," the sheriff said. "Right where I left them, on the . . ."

His rumble trailed off and ran down. "Maybe," the sheriff agreed, reluctantly, "you did hear something after all."

Crouched beside the ladder hole, Burns and Custer heard the sheriff stalk into the corridor, could sense the man standing down below, staring at the hole.

His bellow came up to them. "Burns, you better come down. If you don't we'll plumb come up and root you out."

Custer's voice was sharp and crisp. "You got two of us to root out, sheriff. You better bring plenty of men along when you come to do it. Men that are ready to die!"

Boots scuffed hurriedly back along the corridor and Carson shrieked angrily: "Go on up and get them! What are you standing there for?"

"First man that does, gets it in the guts," said Custer and although he did not speak above an ordinary tone, there was no doubt that those in the office heard him.

A gun coughed sullenly from downstairs and a bullet splintered the floor a good ten feet from the attic hole, plunked against the roof.

Burns rubbed his aching throat.

"What was you doing, messing around a jail?"

"Figured you might be in it," Custer told him. "Ann told me you stood off the posse and when I got there I couldn't find hide nor hair of you. Figured, then, they hadn't killed you outright."

"Why didn't you bring your men?"

"Couldn't. Got worried about things, you see, and started back alone. Met Ann on the trail."

In the office another gun crashed and another bullet chewed its way through the attic floor.

"We sure are in one hell of a fix," Burns said, dolefully. "Cooped up in this place. Sooner or later they'll figure out a way to smoke us out."

Other guns were bellowing now, bullets chunking faster and faster through the flooring.

The sheriff was bellowing. "Stop that shooting! You ain't doing any good. You ain't coming within a mile of them."

Carson's voice dripped acid at him. "Just how do you plan to get them, sheriff?"

"Starve them out," the sheriff told him. "They can't get out, nohow. All we got to do is just sit . . ."

"I have a better way," snapped Carson. His feet moved purposefully across the floor.

"Hey," the sheriff yelled, "you can't do that. You'll burn down the place."

"Sure," said Carson. "That's exactly what I mean to do."

The light that sifted up through the attic hole danced weirdly as Carson lifted the lamp, poised it for the throw.

"No!" screamed the sheriff.

Glass crashed in the corridor below the hole and a sheet of flame puffed out, flame that flared, then licked swiftly up the walls.

Burns leaped to his feet, stood stricken as the ladder hole became a fiery mouth . . . a mouth that gushed flame and smoke, lighting up the attic.

Custer grabbed at his arm.

"Quick," he gasped. "Through the roof."

Burns jerked his arm free. "They'd pot us like squirrels," he said.

Swiftly he ran his eye around the room, saw the hatchet lying on the rickety table. With a leap, he was at the table, snatching up the hatchet.

"The floor," he yelled.

Smoke billowed down upon them and the flame, funneled through the ladder hole, reached and curled against the roof.

Kneeling, Burns inserted the hatchet blade in a crack between two flooring boards, pried with all his might. Nails creaked protestingly.

"Grab hold," he yelled at Custer. "Pull!"

* * *

He coughed as smoke swept down to the end of the room.

A glowing spark fell on the back of his neck, burned agonizingly.

Cooler air puffed up from the cell room as Custer ripped away a board, flung it to one side. Nails screeched again as Burns pried at another board. Squealing thinly, it came loose.

"Drop down," Burns yelled at Custer.

"But . . ."

"Get down there!" shrieked Burns. "It's the only way."

He reached out, tugged at Custer, and the man let himself down, dropped to the earth floor.

Hurling the hatchet away, Burns followed him, thudded on the floor. Staggering, he righted himself, stood for a moment to get his bearing in the flame lighted room.

The box that had served as a table stood in its corner and beside it gaped the tunnel.

"Follow me," said Burns.

On his hands and knees he crawled into the hole, wriggled his way along, saw the circle of light appear ahead of him.

Cautiously, he poked his head out.

Flames leaping from the roof of the jail lighted up the night and in the flickering light, Burns saw two men standing off to one side, guns in hand, watching the roof intently.

Waiting for us to chop our way out, he told himself. Swell chance we'd had if we'd tried to do it.

Gathering his body together, bracing his hands, he flung himself out of the tunnel, stumbled as he hit the ground, fought desperately to keep his balance. Hands clawing at his guns, he spun on his toes.

Yelling, the two men were swinging around to face him and his guns came up.

Flame speared out at him and lead chugged past his cheek. Then his guns were hammering, left and right, left and right—with that old rhythmic cadence that spelled sudden death.

Out in the flame lighted night the two men were staggering, one of them slumping like a sack, the other fighting to keep on his feet, fighting to bring up his gun again. Still fighting, he tilted forward, slammed downward on his face.

A mighty fist slapped Burns in his shoulder and he stumbled, spinning sidewise with the impact of the blow. Behind him a sixgun bellowed angrily and a whining thing threw a shower of dust and pebbles as it struck the ground before him.

Another gun was growling, coughing with jerky gasps and Burns, still dizzy from the blow, righted himself and faced around, lifted his guns. But only one hand, the right one, came up. The other dangled and the gun had fallen from his fingers. His shoulder was numb and his forearm tingled and a tiny rivulet of blood was trickling through his shirt.

Sheriff Egan was lumbering toward him, guns in both fists, and as he walked he staggered, uncertainly, like a blind man who has lost his cane.

Beside the tunnel's mouth Custer crouched, gun leaping in his hand, the muzzle flare splashing angrily against the flame-etched night.

The sheriff stumbled again and then sat down, like a huge tired bear. The guns dropped out of his hands and his arms hung limp and he sat there watching them. As the flames flared up from the burning jail, Burns saw that a look of stupid wonder had spread across his face.

Custer was up now and racing toward the darkness, away from the fiery pillar, yelling as he ran.

"Come on, Steve! They'll be after us like a swarm of . . ."

A gun belched out of the darkness and Custer went limp even as he ran, struck the ground like a sodden sack, somersaulted and lay still.

Steve started forward.

"Bob!" he shrieked. "Bob!"

The hidden gun snarled again and a mighty hand swept the

hat from Burns' head, swept it off and sent it wheeling on its rim toward the burning jail.

Steve spun on his toe in midstride, jerking his body to one side. The gun out in the darkness was a drooling mouth of red and Burns heard the bullet whisper past. His gun hand jerked up and his finger tightened. The sixgun bellowed—yammering at the point where the red mouth had opened in the night.

Even before the hammer clicked on an empty cartridge, Burns was running, head down, legs driving like pistons beneath him, his numbed left shoulder and arm a dead weight that seemed to unbalance him as he ran.

A patch of weeds loomed ahead and he hurled himself for them, smashed into them, wriggled frantically forward and then lay still.

Gasping, he hugged the earth, awkwardly reloaded the sixgun with his one good hand.

Above him the weeds whispered in a rising dawn wind and the licking flames from the jail sent flickering shadows across his hiding place.

He grasped the sixgun with a fierce grip, felt a dull rage burning through his body.

Bob Custer was dead, shot down by someone who had raced out into the darkness to trap them between his guns and the flaming building. Someone who had waited until they stood there outlined against the fire.

The grass rustled in the tiny puffs of breeze and Burns lifted himself cautiously, staring through the weeds. Directly in front of him, not more than a dozen feet away, was a wooden post. Slowly, realization dawning in his brain, his eyes followed it up to the grim crossbar of new, unweathered lumber.

It was the gallows—the gallows that he had seen riding in the afternoon before. The gallows that had been waiting to hang four men who now were free, but who had been ticketed to die for a thing they'd never done.

Just four more men who had been slated to die so that Carson might hold the valley he'd swept with steel and fire—

A voice, thinned by distance, came to his ear:

"He's in there somewhere. Over by the gallows. I want you men to cover that ground. Run him out . . ."

A whiplash report broke off the words and a bullet screeched off the gallows post. Another gun roared and the weeds bent before the storm of hissing lead.

Steve dropped back to the ground, hugged it tight.

That had been Carson's voice—Carson rounding up his men like pack of hounds to hunt him down. Men who would cover every inch of the weed patch with bullets to flush him out.

It had been Carson who had been out there in the darkness, Carson whose bullet had cut down Bob Custer—Carson who had planted the rifleman in the window across from the hotel—Carson who had wanted to shoot him in cold blood out there in the hills. He had quite a few debts to settle with him.

Bullets rattled in the weed stalks, plunked into the ground, hissed through the grass.

Burns' fist tightened on his gun and there was a tightness in his throat and his tongue was saying something that was almost a prayer:

"Just let me get one good shot at him—just one good shot—that's all I ask—just one good shot . . ."

He crawled in unison to the words that rattled in his brain, as if they were a march to go on his hands and knees.

Crawled, not away from the flaming, jabbering guns, but toward them, crawling with grim determination, spurred on by hate and the hope of vengeance.

I'm the only one left, he thought. The only one left to stand up for Bob Custer and the things he stood for. For homes and grazing cattle, for Saturday nights in town, for a place to hang one's guns.

Long ago, he thought, I was looking for a place to hang my guns. Because I was sick of gunsmoke, sick of bloodshed, sick of fighting. But there'll never be a place now to hang those guns—they'll keep on talking till my hands can't hold them.

He gathered his feet under him, tensing for the effort that would heave his body upward. A bullet kicked dust in his face. Another clipped weeds above his head.

From far away came a drumming sound, a rhythmic sound that beat faintly through the night—a sound that grew and hammered as an undertone to the snarling of the guns that swept the weed patch.

Steve heaved himself clear of the weeds, snapped up his gun.

Before him, advancing like a line of skirmishers, were dark figures, etched against the glowing pile of coals where the jail had stood.

His gun bounced in his fist and one of the dark figures threw up its hands and yelled, pitched forward.

A bullet twitched at Burns' shirt and the sixgun barked again. Another of the men in front of him jerked backwards, folding up and falling. Like a shadow show, thought Burns.

Fingernails of fire raked across his legs and droning lead stirred the air whining past his cheek. In front of him specks of flame were dancing, like fireflies in the night.

A man was lunging at him—a man with a white shirt and a black tie whipping in the wind. Flame lanced from the hand of the lunging figure and pain lashed across Burns' ribs.

Carson—Carson coming at him! Carson with his white shirt and fancy vest and the bunched cravat that had come loose and was flapping in the wind.

Steve felt the gun buck against his wrist, heard Carson's sudden cry, saw the man stumbling on unsteady feet.

There were other cries—cries and the drum of hoofs. Hoofs that came thundering down the street and stormed across the vacant ground back of the smouldering jail. The high clear sound of hoofs and the yells of men and the shapes of running horses that charged the line of skirmishers. Charged them with whoops of vengeance and the spat of gunfire and the slow drift of powder-smoke blue against the glow.

Burns felt his knees buckling beneath him, felt the gun slip reluctantly from fingers that slowly went lax—held himself erect with sheer determination, watching Carson staggering toward him.

Carson's right hand, Burns saw, was a bloody smear where the bullet had smashed bone and flesh. But his left hand was in his coat pocket, fumbling . . .

Bells of alarm rang through Burns' brain and he drove his beaten body forward in a spring even as Carson's hand came out of the pocket and steel glimmered as he lifted it to strike.

Burns felt his body smashing into Carson's, saw the gleaming knife start its downward thrust, threw up his arm to ward off the blow. The knife point caught his wrist and slashed downward to the elbow, but Carson was stumbling backward, giving ground, knocked off his balance by the body block.

With a yell of rage Steve twisted his wrist, caught Carson's hand in a steel trap grip, wrenched with a savage jerk. The knife flew from suddenly deadened fingers and Carson was going down, Burns on top of him.

The red haze in front of Burns' eyes spun in a tightening circle and the black crept in, constricting the red until it was no more than a spinning ball.

Hands were on his shoulder, lifting him, tearing loose his fingers, dragging him back to a sense of consciousness.

"Take it easy, bub," a voice said. "We want to have a few to bring into court."

Burns struggled with the hands, fighting to get free.

"Bob," he mumbled. "It can't be you. You're dead."

"Not so you'd notice," Custer told him. "The bullet nicked me on the head. Knocked me out. Woke up good as new."

Burns shook off the hands, struggled to his feet, stood there swaying, suddenly aware of the crowd that hemmed him in, aware of the throb that beat across his shoulder.

Straight before him he saw a face, a face half covered by bushy whiskers.

"Stranger," said the whiskers, "you sure will do to ride the river with."

Burns tried to make his tongue work, but somehow it failed.

"I'm Randall," said the man. "Jim Randall. Ann's father. Guess I can tell you this crowd will do almost anything you want."

Burns croaked at him. "Shucks, I don't want nothing, Randall. Maybe just a peg somewhere to hang my guns."

"We cleaned them out," said Randall. "Those that ain't dead are high-tailing it out of here so fast they're burning up the grass. Now we can come back and settle down."

A small figure in a torn shirt and dusty levis pushed past Randall, ran toward Burns.

"You shouldn't have done it," cried Ann. "You shouldn't have stayed back there on the trail . . ."

Burns put out his one good arm and drew her close. "That was just the start of it," he said. "This is the end."

He looked at Randall. "Maybe there's a place," he asked, "Where a man could stake a homestead?"

Randall regarded the two of them smilingly.

"I wouldn't wonder a bit," he said, "but what there is."

FINAL GENTLEMAN

What rough beast . . . ?

In May 1958, Clifford D. Simak began writing a story he initially called "Ghost Writer," and I believe that story would be published in the January 1960 issue of the Magazine of Fantasy & Science Fiction under the title "Final Gentleman." The writing was a struggle, particularly because Cliff was involved, during much of that time, with a number of crises, including several other writing projects and a move to a new home—"Did more writing on Ghost Writer tonight," he recorded in his journal on July 15, when he was involved in revising it at Horace Gold's request. "Rough going, but then, it always is."

Gold would ultimately reject the story, as would John W. Campbell Jr., of Astounding; and although Bob Mills of the Magazine of Fantasy & Science Fiction would take the story, he would want even more revisions, and would not accept the story until April 1959.

The story is, I think, as autobiographical as any piece of fiction that Cliff ever wrote: It is about a writer of fiction who, going into retirement, comes to realize that his entire career has been manipulated by an alien force—a force that once, in the dim past, made the much younger writer an offer perhaps reminiscent of the Temptation of Christ.

But, no, that's not the "autobiographical" aspect I see in "Final Gentleman." Rather, I was referring to the story's portrayal of the loneliness that pervades every aspect of Hollis Harrington's life.

And it was Harrington's emotional connection to the idea of Neanderthal Man—a connection also to be found in Cliff Simak's life and writings—that saved him.

—dww

After thirty years and several million words there finally came a day when he couldn't write a line.

There was nothing more to say. He had said it all.

The book, the last of many of them, had been finished weeks ago and would be published soon and there was an emptiness inside of him, a sense of having been completely drained away.

He sat now at the study window, waiting for the man from the news magazine to come, looking out across the wilderness of lawn, with its evergreens and birches and the gayness of the tulips. And he wondered why he cared that he would write no more, for certainly he had said a great deal more than most men in his trade and most of it more to the point than was usual, and cloaked though it was in fictional garb, he'd said it with sincerity and, he hoped, convincingly.

His place in literature was secure and solid. And, perhaps, he thought, this was the way it should be—to stop now at the floodtide of his art rather than to go into his declining years with the sharp tooth of senility nibbling away the bright valor of his work.

And yet there remained the urge to write, an inborn feeling that to fail to write was treachery, although to whom it might be traitorous he had no idea. And there was more to it than that: An injured pride, perhaps, and a sense of panic such as the newly blind must feel.

Although that was foolishness, he told himself. In his thirty years of writing, he had done a lifetime's work. And he'd made a *good* life of it. Not frivolous or exciting, but surely satisfying.

He glanced around the study and thought how a room must bear the imprint of the man who lives within it—the rows of calf-bound books, the decorous neatness of the massive oaken desk, the mellow carpet on the floor, the old chairs full of comfort, the sense of everything firmly and properly in place.

A knock came. "Come in,"' said Harrington.

The door opened and old Adams stood there, bent shoulders, snow white hair—the perfect picture of the old retainer.

"It's the gentleman from *Situation*, sir."

"Fine," said Harrington. "Will you show him in?"

It wasn't fine—he didn't want to see this man from the magazine. But the arrangements had been made many weeks before and there was nothing now but to go through with it.

The man from the magazine looked more like a businessman than a writer, and Harrington caught himself wondering how such a man could write the curt, penetrating journalistic prose which had made *Situation* famous.

"John Leonard, sir," said the man, shaking hands with Harrington.

"I'm glad to have you here," said Harrington, falling into his pat pattern of hospitality. "Won't you take this chair? I feel I know you people down there. I've read your magazine for years. I always read the Harvey column immediately it arrives."

Leonard laughed a little. "Harvey," he said, "seems to be our best known columnist and greatest attraction. All the visitors want to have a look at him."

He sat down in the chair Harrington had pointed out.

"Mr. White," he said, "sends you his best wishes."

"That is considerate of him," said Harrington. "You must thank him for me. It's been years since I have seen him."

And thinking back upon it, he recalled that he'd met Preston White only once, all of twenty years ago. The man, he remembered, had made a great impression upon him at the time—a forceful, driving, opinionated man, an exact reflection of the magazine he published.

"A few weeks ago," said Leonard. "I talked with another friend of yours. Senator Johnson Enright."

Harrington nodded. "I've known the senator for years and have admired him greatly. I suppose you could call it a dissimilar association. The senator and I are not too much alike."

"He has a deep respect and affection for you."

"And I for him,"' said Harrington. "But this secretary of state business. I am concerned . . ."

"Yes?"

"Oh, he's the man for it, all right," said Harrington. "Or I would suppose he is. He is intellectually honest and he has a strange, hard streak of stubbornness and a rugged constitution, which is what we need. But there are considerations . . ."

Leonard showed surprise. "Surely you do not . . ."

Harrington waved a weary hand. "No, Mr. Leonard, I am looking at it solely from the viewpoint of a man who has given most of his life to the public service. I know that Johnson must look upon this possibility with something close to dread. There have been times in the recent past when he's been ready to retire, when only his sense of duty has kept him at his post."

"A man," said Leonard positively, "does not turn down a chance to head the state department. Besides, Harvey said last week he would accept the post."

"Yes, I know," said Harrington. "I read it in his column."

Leonard got down to business. "I won't impose too much upon your time," he said. "I've already done the basic research on you."

"It's quite all right," said Harrington. "Take all the time you want. I haven't a single thing to do until this evening, when I have dinner with my mother."

Leonard's eyebrows raised a bit. "Your mother is still living?"

"Very spry," said Harrington, "for all she's eighty-three. A sort of Whistler's mother. Serene and beautiful."

"You're lucky. My mother died when I was still quite young."

"I'm sorry to hear of it," said Harrington. "My mother is a gentlewoman to her fingertips. You don't find many like her now.

I am positive I owe a great deal of what I am to her. Perhaps the thing I'm proudest of is what your book editor, Cedric Madison, wrote about me quite some years ago. I sent a note to thank him at the time and I fully meant to look him up someday, although I never did. I'd like to meet the man."

"What was it that he said?"

"He said, if I recall correctly, that I was the last surviving gentleman."

"That's a good line." Leonard said. "I'll have to look it up. I think you might like Cedric. He may seem slightly strange at times, but he's a devoted man, like you. He lives in his office, almost day and night."

Leonard reached into his briefcase and brought out a sheaf of notes, rustling through them until he found the page he wanted.

"We'll do a full-length profile on you," he told Harrington. "A cover and an inside spread with pictures. I know a great deal about you, but there still are some questions, a few inconsistencies."

"I'm not sure I follow you."

"You know how we operate," said Leonard. "We do exhaustive checking to be sure we have the background facts, then we go out and get the human facts. We talk with our subject's boyhood chums, his teachers, all the people who might have something to contribute to a better understanding of the man himself. We visit the places he has lived, pick up the human story, the little anecdotes. It's a demanding job, but we pride ourselves on the way we do it."

"And rightly so, young man."

"I went to Wyalusing in Wisconsin," said the man from the magazine. "That's where the data said that you were born."

"A charming place as I remember it," said Harrington. "A little town, sandwiched between the river and the hills."

"Mr. Harrington."

"Yes?"

"You weren't born there."

"I beg your pardon?"

"There's no birth record at the county seat. No one remembers you."

"Some mistake," said Harrington. "Or perhaps you're joking."

"You went to Harvard, Mr. Harrington. Class of 27."

"That is right. I did."

"You never married, sir."

"There was a girl. She died."

"Her name," said Leonard, "was Cornelia Storm."

"That was her name. The fact's not widely known."

"We are thorough, Mr. Harrington, in our background work."

"I don't mind," said Harrington. "It's not a thing to hide. It's just not a fact to flaunt."

"Mr. Harrington."

"Yes."

"It's not Wyalusing only. It's all the rest of it. There is no record that you went to Harvard. There never was a girl named Cornelia Storm."

Harrington came straight out of his chair.

"That is ridiculous!" he shouted. "What can you mean by it?"

"I'm sorry," Leonard said. "Perhaps I could have found a better way of telling you than blurting it all out. Is there anything—"

"Yes, there is," said Harrington. "I think you'd better leave."

"Is there nothing I can do? Anything at all?"

"You've done quite enough," said Harrington. "Quite enough, indeed."

He sat down in the chair again, gripping its arms with his shaking hands, listening to the man go out.

When he heard the front door close, he called to Adams to come in.

"Is there something I can do for you?" asked Adams.

"Yes. You can tell me who I am."

"Why, sir," said Adams, plainly puzzled, "you're Mr. Hollis Harrington."

"Thank you, Adams," said Harrington. "That's who I thought I was!"

Dusk had fallen when he wheeled the car along the familiar street and drew up to the curb in front of the old, white-pillared house set well back from the front of wide, tree-shaded grounds.

He cut the engine and got out, standing for a moment to let the sense of the street soak into him—the correct and orderly, the aristocratic street, a refuge in this age of materialism. Even the cars that moved along it, he told himself, seemed to be aware of the quality of the street, for they went more slowly and more silently than they did on other streets and there was about them a sense of decorum one did not often find in a mechanical contraption.

He turned from the street and went up the walk, smelling in the dusk the awakening life of gardens in the springtime, and he wished that it were light, for Henry, his mother's gardener, was quite famous for his tulips.

As he walked along the path, with the garden scent, he felt the strange sense of urgency and of panic drop away from him, for the street and house were in themselves assurances that everything was exactly as it should be.

He mounted the brick steps and went across the porch and reached out his hand for the knocker on the door.

There was a light in the sitting room and he knew his mother would be there, waiting for him to arrive, but that it would be Tilda, hurrying from the kitchen, who would answer to his knock, for his mother did not move about as briskly as she had.

He knocked and waited and as he waited he remembered the happy days he'd spent in this house before he'd gone to Harvard, when his father still was living. Some of the old families still lived here, but he'd not seen them for years, for on his visits lately he'd scarcely stirred outdoors, but sat for hours talking with his mother.

The door opened, and it was not Tilda in her rustling skirts and her white starched collar, but an utter stranger.

"Good evening," he said. "You must be a neighbor."

"I live here," said the woman.

"I can't be mistaken," said Harrington. "This is the residence of Mrs. Jennings Harrington."

"I'm sorry," said the woman. "I do not know the name. What was the address you were looking for?"

"2034 Summit Drive."

"That's the number," said the woman, "but Harrington—I know of no Harringtons. We've lived here fifteen years and there's never been a Harrington in the neighborhood."

"Madam," Harrington said, sharply, "this is most serious—"

The woman closed the door.

He stood on the porch for long moments after she had closed the door, once reaching out his hand to clang the knocker again, then withdrawing it. Finally he went back to the street.

He stood beside the car, looking at the house, trying to catch in it some unfamiliarity—but it was familiar. It was the house to which he'd come for years to see his mother; it was the house in which he'd spent his youth.

He opened the car door and slid beneath the wheel. He had trouble getting the key out of his pocket and his hand was shaking so that it took a long time for him to insert it in the ignition lock.

He twisted the key and the engine started. He did not, however, drive off immediately, but sat gripping the wheel. He kept staring at the house and his mind hurled back the fact again and yet again that strangers had lived behind its walls for more than fifteen years.

Where, then, were his mother and her faithful Tilda? Where, then, was Henry, who was a hand at tulips? Where the many evenings he had spent in that very house? Where the conversations in the sitting room, with the birch and maple burning in the fireplace and the cat asleep upon the hearth?

There was a pattern, he was reminded—a deadly pattern—in all that had ever happened to him; in the way that he had lived, in the books that he had written, in the attachments he had had and, perhaps, more important, the ones he had not had. There was a haunting quality that had lurked behind the scenes, just out of sight, for years, and there had been many times he'd been aware of it and wondered at it and tried to lay his fingers on it—but never a time when he'd ever been quite so acutely aware of it as this very moment.

It was, he knew, this haunted factor in his life which kept him steady now, which kept him from storming up the walk again to hammer at the door and demand to see his mother.

He saw that he had stopped shaking, and he closed the window and put the car in gear.

He turned left at the next corner and began to climb, street after street.

He reached the cemetery in ten minutes' time and parked the car. He found the topcoat in the rear seat and put it on. For a moment, he stood beside the car and looked down across the town, to where the river flowed between the hills.

This, he told himself, at least is real, the river and the town. This no one could take away from him, or the books upon the shelf.

He let himself into the cemetery by the postern gate and followed the path unerringly in the uncertain light of a sickle moon.

The stone was there and the shape of it unchanged; it was a shape, he told himself, that was burned into his heart. He knelt before it and put out his hands and laid them on it and felt the moss and lichens that had grown there and they were familiar, too.

"Cornelia," he said. "You are still here, Cornelia."

He fumbled in his pocket for a pack of matches and lit three of them before the fourth blazed up in a steady flame. He cupped the blaze between his hands and held it close against the stone.

A name was graven there.

It was not Cornelia Storm.

Senator Johnson Enright reached out and lifted the decanter.

"No, thanks," said Harrington. "This one is all I wish. I just dropped by to say hello. I'll be going in a minute."

He looked around the room in which they sat and now he was sure of it—sure of the thing that he had come to find. The study was not the same as he had remembered it. Some of the bright was gone, some of the glory vanished. It was faded at the edges and it seemed slightly out of focus and the moose head above the mantle was somehow just a little shabby, instead of grand and notable.

"You come too seldom," said the senator, "even when you know that you are always welcome. Especially tonight. The family are all out and I'm a troubled man."

"This business of the state department?"

Enright nodded. "That is it exactly. I told the President, yes, I would take it if he could find no one else. I almost pleaded with him to find another man."

"You could not tell him no?"

"I tried to," said the senator. "I did my best to tell him. I, who never in my life have been at a loss for words. And I couldn't do it. Because I was too proud. Because through the years I have built up in me a certain pride of service that I cannot turn my back upon."

The senator sat sprawling in his chair and Harrington saw that there was no change in him, as there had been in the room within which they sat. He was the same as ever—the iron-gray unruly mop of hair, the woodchopper face, the snaggly teeth, the hunched shoulders of a grizzly.

"You realize, of course," said Enright, "that I have been one of your most faithful readers."

"I know," said Harrington. "I am proud of it."

"You have a fiendish ability," said the senator, "to string words together with fishhooks hidden in them. They fasten into you and they won't let loose and you go around remembering them for days."

He lifted up his glass and drank.

"I've never told you this before," he said. "I don't know if I should, but I suppose I'd better. In one of your books you said that the hallmark of destiny might rest upon one man. If that man failed, you said, the world might well be lost."

"I think I did say that. I have a feeling . . ."

"You're sure," asked the senator, reaching for the brandy, "that you won't have more of this?"

"No, thanks," said Harrington.

And suddenly he was thinking of another time and place where he'd once gone drinking and there had been a shadow in the corner that had talked with him—and it was the first time he'd ever thought of that. It was something, it seemed, that had never happened, that could not remotely have happened to Hollis Harrington. It was a happening that he would not—could not—accept, and yet there it lay, cold and naked in his brain.

"I was going to tell you," said the senator, "about that line on destiny. A most peculiar circumstance, I think you will agree. You know, of course, that one time I had decided to retire."

"I remember it," said Harrington. "I recall I told you that you should."

"It was at that time," said the senator, "that I read that paragraph of yours. I had written out a statement announcing my retirement at the completion of my term and intended in the morning to give it to the press. Then I read that line and asked myself what if I were that very man you were writing of. Not, of course, that I actually thought I was."

Harrington stirred uneasily. "I don't know what to say. You place too great a responsibility upon me."

"I did not retire," said the senator. "I tore up the statement."

They sat quietly for a moment, staring at the fire flaming on the hearth.

"And now," said Enright, "there is this other thing."

"I wish that I could help," said Harrington, almost desperately. "I wish that I could find the proper words to say. But I can't, because I'm at the end myself. I am written out. There's nothing left inside me."

And that was not, he knew, what he had wished to say. *I came here to tell you that someone else has been living in my mother's house for more than fifteen years, that the name on Cornelia's headstone is not Cornelia's name. I came here to see if this room had changed and it has changed. It has lost some of its old baronial magic . . .*

But he could not say it. There was no way to say it. Even to so close a friend as the senator it was impossible.

"Hollis, I am sorry," said the senator.

It was all insane, thought Harrington. He was Hollis Harrington. He had been born in Wisconsin. He was a graduate of Harvard and—what was it Cedric Madison had called him—the last surviving gentleman.

His life had been correct to the last detail, his house correct, his writing most artistically correct—the result of good breeding to the fingertips.

Perhaps just slightly too correct. Too correct for this world of 1962, which had sloughed off the final vestige of the old punctilio.

He was Hollis Harrington, last surviving gentleman, famous writer, romantic figure in the literary world—and written out, wrung dry of all emotion, empty of anything to say since he had finally said all that he was capable of saying.

He rose slowly from his chair.

"I must be going, Johnson. I've stayed longer than I should."

"There is something else," said the senator. "Something I've always meant to ask you. Nothing to do with this matter of myself. I've meant to ask you many times, but felt perhaps I shouldn't, that it might somehow . . ."

"It's quite all right," said Harrington. "I'll answer if I can."

"One of your early books," said the senator. "*A Bone to Gnaw,* I think."

"That," said Harrington, "was many years ago."

"This central character," said the senator. "This Neanderthaler that you wrote about. You made him seem so human."

Harrington nodded. "That is right. That is what he was. He was a human being. Just because he lived a hundred thousand years ago—"

"Of course," said the senator. "You are entirely right. But you had him down so well. All your other characters have been sophisticates, people of the world. I have often wondered how you could write so convincingly of that kind of man—an almost mindless savage."

"Not mindless," said Harrington. "Not really savage. A product of his times. I lived with him for a long time, Johnson, before I wrote about him. I tried to put myself into his situation, think as he did, guess his viewpoint. I knew his fears and triumphs. There were times, I sometimes think, that I was close to being him."

Enright nodded solemnly. "I can well believe that. You really must be going? You're sure about that drink?"

"I'm sorry, Johnson. I have a long way to drive."

The senator heaved himself out of the chair and walked with him to the door.

"We'll talk again," he said, "and soon. About this writing business. I can't believe you're at the end of it."

"Maybe not," said Harrington. "It may all come back."

But he only said this to satisfy the senator. He knew there was no chance that it would come back.

They said good-night and Harrington went trudging down the walk. And that was wrong—in all his life, he'd never trudged before.

His car was parked just opposite the gate and he stopped beside it, staring in astonishment, for it was not his car.

His had been an expensive, dignified model, and this one was not only one of the less expensive kinds, but noticeably decrepit.

And yet it was familiar in a vague and tantalizing way.

And here it was again, but with a difference this time, for in this instance he was on the verge of accepting unreality.

He opened the door and climbed into the seat. He reached into his pocket and found the key and fumbled for the ignition lock. He found it in the dark and the key clicked into it. He twisted, and the engine started.

Something came struggling up from the mist inside his brain. He could feel it struggle and he knew what it was. It was Hollis Harrington, final gentleman.

He sat there for a moment and in that moment he was neither final gentleman nor the man who sat in the ancient car, but a younger man and a far-off man who was drunk and miserable.

He sat in a booth in the farthest, darkest corner of some unknown establishment that was filled with noise and smell and in a corner of the booth that was even darker than the corner where he sat was another one, who talked.

He tried to see the stranger's face, but it either was too dark or there was no face to see. And all the time the faceless stranger talked.

There were papers on the table, a fragmented manuscript, and he knew it was no good and he tried to tell the stranger how it was no good and how he wished it might be good, but his tongue was thick and his throat was choked.

He couldn't frame the words to say it, but he felt it inside himself—the terrible, screaming need of putting down on paper the conviction and belief that shouted for expression.

And he heard clearly only one thing that the stranger said.

"I am willing," said the stranger, "to make a deal with you."

And that was all there was. There was no more to remember.

And there it stood—that ancient, fearsome thing—an isolated remembrance from some former life, an incident without a past or future and no connection with him.

The night suddenly was chilly and he shivered in the chill. He put the car in gear and pulled out from the curb and drove slowly down the street.

He drove for half an hour or more and he was still shivering from the chilly night. A cup of coffee, he thought, might warm him and he pulled the car up to the curb in front of an all-night quick-and-greasy. And realized with some astonishment that he could not be more than a mile or two from home.

There was no one in the place except a shabby blonde who lounged behind the corner, listening to a radio.

He climbed up on a stool.

"Coffee, please," he said and while he waited for her to fill the cup he glanced about the place. It was clean and cozy with the cigarette machines and the rack of magazines lined against the wall.

The blonde set the cup down in front of him.

"Anything else?" she asked, but he didn't answer, for his eye had caught a line of printing across the front of one of the more lurid magazines.

"Is that all?" asked the blonde again.

"I guess so," said Harrington. "I guess that's all I want."

He didn't look at her; he was still staring at the magazine.

Across the front of it ran the glaring lines:

THE ENCHANTED WORLD OF
HOLLIS HARRINGTON!

Cautiously he slid off the stool and stalked the magazine. He reached out quickly and snatched it from the rack before it could elude him. For he had the feeling, until he had it safely in his hand, that the magazine would be like all the rest of it, crazy and unreal . . . He took it back to the counter and laid it down and stared at the cover and the line stayed there. It did not change; it did not go away. He extended his thumb and rubbed the printed words and they were real enough.

He thumbed swiftly through the magazine and found the article and staring out at him was a face he knew to be his own, although it was not the kind of face he had imagined he would have—it was a somewhat younger, darker face that tended to untidiness, and beneath that face was another face that was without a doubt a face of great distinction. And the caption that ran between them asked a question: *Which one of these men is really Hollis Harrington?*

There was as well a picture of a house that he recognized in all its ramshackleness and below it another picture of the same house, but highly idealized, gleaming with white paint and surrounded by neatly tended grounds—a house with character.

He did not bother with the reading of the caption that ran between the houses. He knew what it would say.

And the text of the article itself:

Is Hollis Harrington really more than one man? Is he in actuality the man he thinks he is, a man he has created out of his own mind, a man who moves in an incredibly enchanted world of good living and good manners? Or is this attitude no more than a carefully cultivated pose, an exceptional piece of perfect showmanship? Or could it be that to write in the manner that he does, to turn out the sleekly tailored, thoughtful, often significant prose that he has been writing for more than thirty years, it is necessary that he create for himself another life than the one he really lives, that he has forced himself to accept this strange internal world of his and believe in it as a condition to his continued writing . . . .

A hand came out and spread itself across the page so he could not read and he looked up quickly. It was the hand of the waitress and he saw there was a shining in her eyes that was very close to tears.

"Mr. Harrington,"' she said. "Please, Mr. Harrington. Please don't read it, sir."

"But, miss . . ."

"I told Harry that he shouldn't let them put in that magazine. I told him he should hide it. But he said you never came in here except on Saturdays."

"You mean," asked Harrington, "that I've been here before?"

"Almost every Saturday," she told him, surprised. "Every Saturday for years. You like our cherry pie. You always have a piece of our cherry pie."

"Yes, of course," he said.

But, actually, he had no inkling of this place, unless, good God, he thought, unless he had been pretending all the time that it was some other place, some gold-plated eatery of very great distinction.

But it was impossible, he told himself, to pretend as big as that. For a little while, perhaps, but not for thirty years. No man alone could do it unless he had some help.

"I had forgotten," he told the waitress. "I'm somewhat upset tonight. I wonder if you have a piece of that cherry pie."

"Of course," the waitress said.

She took the pie off the shelf and cut a wedge and slid it on the plate. She put the plate down in front of him and laid a fork beside it.

"I'm sorry, Mr. Harrington," she said. "I'm sorry I didn't hide the magazine. You must pay no attention to it—or to anything. Not to any of the things that people say or what other people write. All of us around here are so proud of you."

She leaned across the counter toward him.

"You mustn't mind," she said. "You are too big to mind."

"I don't believe I do," said Hollis Harrington.

And that was the solemn truth, for he was too numb to care. There was in him nothing but a vast wonderment that filled his being so there was room for nothing else.

"I am willing," the stranger in the corner of the booth had told him many years ago. "I am willing to make a deal with you."

But of the deal he had no recollection, no hint of terms or of the purpose of it, although possibly he could guess.

He had written for all of thirty years and he had been well paid for it—not in cash and honor and acclaim alone—but in something else as well. In a great white house standing on a hill with a wilderness of grounds, with an old retainer out of a picture book, with a Whistler's mother, with a romantic bittersweetness tied to a gravestone symbol.

But now the job was done and the pay had stopped and the make-believe had ended.

The pay had stopped and the delusions that were a part of it were gone. The glory and the tinsel had been stripped out of his mind. No longer could he see an old and battered car as a sleek, glossy machine. Now, once again, he could read aright the graving on a stone. And the dream of a Whistler's mother had vanished from his brain—but had been once so firmly planted that on this very evening he actually had driven to a house and an address that was a duplicate of the one imprinted on his imagination.

He had seen everything, he realized, overlain by a grandeur and a lustre out of story books.

But was it possible, he wondered. Could it be made to work? Could a man in all sanity play a game of make-believe for thirty years on end? Or might he be insane?

He considered it calmly and it seemed unlikely, for no insanity could have written as he had written; that he had written what he thought he had was proved by the senator's remarks tonight.

So the rest had been make-believe; it could be nothing else. Make-believe with help from that faceless being, whoever he might be, who had made a deal with him that night so long ago.

Although, he thought, it might not take much help. The propensity to kid one's self was strong in the human race. Children were good at it; they became in all reality all the things they pretended that they were. And there were many adults who made themselves believe the things they thought they should believe or the things they merely wanted to believe for their peace of mind.

Surely, he told himself, it would be no great step from this kind of pretending to a sum total of pretending.

"Mr. Harrington," asked the waitress, "don't you like your pie?"

"Certainly," said Harrington, picking up the fork and cutting off a bite.

So pretending was the pay, the ability to pretend without conscious effort a private world in which he moved alone. And perhaps it was even more than that—perhaps it was a prior condition to his writing as he did, the exact kind of world and life in which it had been calculated, by whatever means, he would do his best.

And the purpose of it?

He had no idea what the purpose was.

Unless, of course, the body of his work was a purpose in itself.

The music in the radio cut off and a solemn voice said: "We interrupt our program to bring you a bulletin. The Associated Press has just reported that the White House has named Senator Johnson Enright as secretary of state. And now, we continue with our music . . . ."

Harrington paused with a bite of pie poised on the fork, halfway to his mouth.

"The hallmark of destiny," he quoted, "may rest upon one man!"

"What was that you said, Mr. Harrington?"

"Nothing. Nothing, miss. Just something I remembered. It's really not important."

Although, of course, it was.

How many other people in the world, he wondered, might have read a certain line out of one of his books? How many other lives might have been influenced in some manner from the reading of a phrase that he had written?

And had he had help in the writing of those lines? Did he have actual talent or had he merely written the thoughts that lay in other minds? Had he had help in writing as well as in pretending? Might that be the reason now he felt so written out?

But however that might be, it was all over now. He had done the job and he had been fired. And the firing of him had been as efficient and as thorough as one might well expect—all the mumbo-jumbo had been run in competent reverse, beginning with the man from the magazine this morning. Now here he sat, a humdrum human being perched upon a stool, eating cherry pie.

How many other humdrum humans might have sat, as he sat now, in how many ages past, released from their dream-life as he had been released, trying with no better luck than he was having to figure out what had hit them? How many others, even now, might still be living out a life of make-believe as he had lived for thirty years until this very day?

For it was ridiculous, he realized, to suppose he was the only one. There would be no point in simply running a one-man make-believe.

How many eccentric geniuses had been, perhaps, neither geniuses nor eccentric until they, too, had sat in some darkened corner with a faceless being and listened to his offer?

Suppose—just suppose—that the only purpose in his thirty years had been that Senator Johnson Enright should not retire from public life and thus remain available to head the state department now? Why, and to whom, could it be so important that one particular man got one certain post? And was it important enough to justify the use of one man's life to achieve another's end?

Somewhere, Harrington told himself, there had to be a clue. Somewhere back along the tangled skein of those thirty years there must be certain signposts which would point the way to the man or thing or organization, whatever it might be.

He felt dull anger stirring in him, a formless, senseless, almost hopeless anger that had no direction and no focal point.

A man came in the door and took a stool one removed from Harrington.

"Hi, Gladys," he bellowed.

Then he noticed Harrington and smote him on the back. "Hi, there, pal," he trumpeted. "Your name's in the paper."

"Quiet down, Joe," said Gladys. "What is it that you want?"

"Gimme a hunk of apple pie and a cuppa coffee."

The man, Harrington saw, was big and hairy. He wore a Teamsters badge.

"You said something about my name being in the paper."

Joe slapped down a folded paper.

"Right there on the front page. The story there with your picture in it."

He pointed a grease-stained finger.

"Hot off the press," he yelped and burst into gales of laughter.

"Thanks," said Harrington.

"Well, go ahead and read it," Joe urged boisterously. "Or ain't you interested."

"Definitely," said Harrington.

The headline said:

NOTED AUTHOR WILL RETIRE

"So you're quitting," blared the driver. "Can't say I blame you, pal. How many books you written?"

"Fourteen," said Harrington.

"Gladys, can you imagine that! Fourteen books! I ain't even read that many books in my entire life . . ."

"Shut up, Joe," said Gladys, banging down the pie and coffee.

The story said:

Hollis Harrington, author of See My Empty House, which

won him the Nobel prize, will retire from the writing field with the publication of his latest work, Come Back, My Soul.

The announcement will be made in this week's issue of Situation magazine, under the byline of Cedric Madison, book editor.

Harrington feels, Madison writes, that he has finally, in his forthcoming book, rounded out the thesis which he commenced some thirty years and thirteen books ago . . .

Harrington's hand closed convulsively upon the paper, crumpling it.

"Wassa matter, pal?"

"Not a thing," said Harrington.

"This Madison is a jerk," said Joe. "You can't believe a thing he says. He is full of . . ."

"He's right," said Harrington. "I'm afraid he's right."

But how could he have known? He asked himself. How could Cedric Madison, that queer, devoted man who practically lived in his tangled office, writing there his endless stream of competent literary criticism, have known a thing like this? Especially, Harrington told himself, since he, himself, had not been sure of it until this very morning.

"Don't you like your pie?" asked Joe. "And your coffee's getting cold."

"Leave him alone," said Gladys, fiercely. "I'll warm up his coffee."

Harrington said to Joe: "Would you mind if I took this paper?"

"Sure not, pal. I'm through with it. Sports is all I read."

"Thanks," said Harrington. "I have a man to see."

The lobby of the *Situation* building was empty and sparkling—the bright, efficient sparkle that was the trademark of the magazine and the men who made it.

The 12-foot globe, encased in its circular glass shield, spun slowly and majestically, with the time-zone clocks ranged around its base and with the keyed-in world situation markers flashing on its surface.

Harrington stopped just inside the door and glanced around, bewildered and disturbed by the brightness and the glitter. Slowly he oriented himself. Over there the elevators and beside them the floor directory board. There the information counter, now unoccupied, and just beyond it the door that was marked:

HARVEY
Visiting Hours
9 to 5 on Week Days

Harrington crossed to the directory and stood there, craning his neck, searching for the name. And found it.

CEDRIC MADISON . . . 317

He turned from the board and pressed the button for the elevator.

On the third floor the elevator stopped and he got out of it and to his right was the newsroom and to his left a line of offices flanking a long hall.

He turned to the left and 317 was the third one down. The door was open and he stepped inside. A man sat behind a desk stacked high with books, while other books were piled helter-skelter on the floor, and still others bulged the shelves upon the walls.

"Mr. Madison?" asked Harrington and the man looked up from the book that he was reading.

And suddenly Harrington was back again in that smoky, shadowed booth where long ago he'd bargained with the faceless being—but no longer faceless. He knew by the aura of the man and the sense of him, the impelling force of personality, the disquieting, obscene feeling that was a kind of psychic spoor.

"Why, Harrington!" cried the faceless man, who now had

taken on a face. "How nice that you dropped in! It's incredible that the two of us . . ."

"Yes, isn't it," said Harrington.

He scarcely knew he said it. It was, he realized, an automatic thing to say, a putting up of hands to guard against a blow, a pure and simple defense mechanism.

Madison was on his feet now and coming around the desk to greet him, and if he could have turned and run, Harrington would have fled. But he couldn't run; he was struck and frozen; he could make no move at all beyond the automatic ones of austere politeness that had been drilled into him through thirty years of simulated aristocratic living.

He could feel his face, all stiff and dry with the urbane deadpan that he had affected—and he was grateful for it, for he knew that it would never do to show in any way that he had recognized the man.

"It's incredible that the two of us have never met," said Madison, "I've read so much of what you've written and liked so much everything I've read."

"It's good of you to say so," said the urbane, unruffled part of Harrington, putting out his hand. "The fault we have never met is entirely mine. I do not get around as much as I really should."

He felt Madison's hand inside his own and closed his fingers on it in a sense of half-revulsion, for the hand was dry and cold and very like a claw. The man was vulture-like—the tight, dessicated skin drawn tight across the death-head face, the piercing, restless eyes, the utter lack of hair, the knife-like slash of mouth.

"You must sit down," said Madison, "and spend some time with me. There are so many things we have to talk about."

There was just one empty chair; all the others overflowed with books. Harrington sat down in it stiffly, his mouth still dry with fear.

Madison scurried back behind the desk and hunched forward in his chair.

"You look just like your pictures," he declared.

Harrington shrugged. "I have a good photographer—my publisher insists."

He could feel himself slowly coming back to life, recovering from the numbness, the two of him flowing back together into the single man.

"It seems to me," he said, "that you have the advantage of me there. I cannot recall I've ever seen your picture."

Madison waved a waggish finger at him. "I am anonymous," he said. "Surely you must know all editors are faceless. They must not intrude themselves upon the public consciousness."

"That's a fallacy, no doubt," Harrington declared, "but since you seem to value it so much, I will not challenge you."

And he felt a twinge of panic—the remark about editorial facelessness seemed too pat to be coincidental.

"And now that you've finally come to see me," Madison was saying, "I fear it may be in regard to an item in the morning papers."

"As a matter of fact," Harrington said smoothly, "that is why I'm here."

"I hope you're not too angry."

Harrington shook his head. "Not at all. In fact, I came to thank you for your help in making up my mind. I had considered it, you see. It was something I told myself I should do, but . . ."

"But you were worried about an implied responsibility. To your public, perhaps; perhaps even to yourself."

"Writers seldom quit," said Harrington. "At least not voluntarily. It didn't seem quite cricket."

"But it was obvious," protested Madison. "It seemed so appropriate a thing for you to do, so proper and so called-for, that I could not resist. I confess I may have wished somewhat to influence you. You've tied up so beautifully what you set out to say so many years ago in this last book of yours that it would be a shame to spoil it by attempting to say more. It would be different, of course, if you had need of money from continued writing, but your royalties—"

"Mr. Madison, what would you have done if I had protested?"

"Why, then," said Madison, "I would have made the most abject apology in the public prints. I would have set it all aright in the best manner possible."

He got up from the desk and scrabbled at a pile of books stacked atop a chair.

"I have a review copy of your latest book right here," he said. "There are a few things in it I'd like to chat about with you."

He's a clue, thought Harrington, watching him scrabble through the books—but that was all he was. There was more, Harrington was sure, to this business, whatever it might be, than Cedric Madison.

He must get out of here, he knew, as quickly as he could, and yet it must be done in such a manner as not to arouse suspicion. And while he remained, he sternly warned himself, he must play his part as the accomplished man of letters, the final gentleman.

"Ah, here it is!" cried Madison in triumph.

He scurried to the desk, with the book clutched in his hand.

He leafed through it rapidly.

"Now, here, in chapter six, you said . . ."

The moon was setting when Harrington drove through the massive gates and up the curving driveway to the white and stately house perched upon its hill.

He got out of the car and mounted the broad stone steps that ran up to the house. When he reached the top, he halted to gaze down the moon-shadowed slope of grass and tulips, whitened birch and darkened evergreen, and he thought it was the sort of thing a man should see more often—a breathless moment of haunting beauty snatched from the cycle that curved from birth to death.

He stood there, proudly, gazing down the slope, letting the moonlit beauty, the etching of the night soak into his soul.

This, he told himself, was one of those incalculable moments of experience which one could not anticipate, or afterwards be able to evaluate or analyze.

He heard the front door open and slowly turned around.

Old Adams stood in the doorway, his figure outlined by the night lamp on the table in the hall. His snow-white hair was ruffled, standing like a halo round his head, and one frail hand was clutched against his chest, holding together the ragged dressing gown he wore.

"You are late, sir," said Adams. "We were growing a bit disturbed."

"I am sorry," said Harrington. "I was considerably delayed."

He mounted the stoop and Adams stood aside as he went through the door.

"You're sure that everything's all right, sir?"

"Oh, quite all right," said Harrington. "I called on Cedric Madison down at *Situation.* He proved a charming chap."

"If it's all right with you, sir, I'll go back to bed. Knowing you are safely in, I can get some sleep."

"It's quite all right," said Harrington. "Thanks for waiting up."

He stood at the study door and watched Adams trudge slowly up the stairs, then went into the study, turning on the lights.

The place closed in around him with the old familiarity, with the smell of comfort and the sense of being home, and he stood gazing at the rows of calf-bound books, and the ordered desk, the old and home-like chairs, the worn, mellow carpet.

He shrugged out of his topcoat and tossed it on a chair and became aware of the folded paper bulging in his jacket pocket.

Puzzled, he pulled it out and held it in front of him and the headline hit him in the face. The room changed, a swift and subtle changing. No longer the ordered sanctuary, but a simple workroom for a writing man. No longer the calf-bound volumes in all their elegance upon the shelves, but untidy rows of tattered, dog-eared books. And the carpet was neither worn nor mellow; it was utilitarian and almost brand new.

"My God!" gasped Harrington, almost prayerfully.

He could feel the perspiration breaking out along his forehead and his hands suddenly were shaking and his knees like water.

For he had changed as well as the room had changed; the room had changed because of the change in him.

He was no longer the final gentleman, but that other, more real person he had been this evening. He was himself again; had been jerked back to himself again, he knew, by the headlines in the paper.

He glanced around the room and knew that it finally was right, that all its starkness was real, that this had been the way the room had always been, even when he had made it into something more romantic.

He had found himself this very evening after thirty years and then—he sweat as he thought about it—and then he had lost himself again, easily and without knowing it, without a twitch of strangeness.

He had gone to see Cedric Madison, with this very paper clutched within his hands, had gone without clear purpose—almost, he told himself, as if he were being harried there.

And he had been harried for too long. He had been harried into seeing a room different than it was; he had been made to read a myth-haunted name upon a strange gravestone; he had been deluded into thinking that he had supper often with his mother who had long been dead; he had been forced to imagine that a common quick-and-greasy was a famous eatery—and, of course, much more than that.

It was humiliating to think upon, but there was more than mere humiliation—there was a method and a purpose and now it was important, most immediately important, to learn that method and that purpose.

He dropped the paper on the floor and went to the liquor cabinet and got a bottle and a glass. He sloshed liquor in the glass and gulped it.

You had to find a place to start, he told himself, and you worked along from there—and Cedric Madison was a starting point, although he was not the whole of it. No more, perhaps, than a single clue, but at least a starting point.

He had gone to see Cedric Madison and the two of them had sat and talked much longer than he planned, and somewhere in that talk he'd slid smoothly back into the final gentleman.

He tried to drive his mind and memory along the pathway of those hours, seeking for some break, hunting for the moment he had changed, but there was nothing. It ironed out flat and smooth.

But somewhere he had changed, or more likely had been changed, back into the masquerade that had been forced upon him long years in the past.

And what would be the motive of that masquerade? What would be the reason in changing a man's life, or, more probably, the lives of many men?

A sort of welfare endeavor, perhaps. A matter of rampant dogoodism, an expression of the itch to interfere in other people's lives.

Or was there here a conscious, well-planned effort to change the course of world events, to so alter the destiny of mankind as to bring about some specific end-result? That would mean that whoever, or whatever, was responsible possessed a sure method of predicting the future, and the ability to pick out the key factors in the present which must be changed in order effectively to change that future in the desired direction.

From where it stood upon the desk the phone snarled viciously.

He swung around in terror, frightened at the sound.

The phone snarled a second time.

He strode to the desk and answered. It was the senator.

"Good," said the senator. "I did not get you up."

"No. I was just getting ready to turn in."

"You heard the news, of course."

"On the radio," said Harrington.

"The White House called . . ."

"And you had to take it."

"Yes, of course, but then . . ."

There was a gulping, breathing sound at the other end as if the senator were on the verge of strangling.

"What's the matter, Johnson? What is going—"

"Then," said the senator, "I had a visitor."

Harrington waited.

"Preston White," said the senator. "You know him, of course."

"Yes. The publisher of *Situation*."

"He was conspiratorial," said the senator. "And a shade dramatic. He talked in whispers and very confidentially. As if the two of us were in some sort of deal."

"But what—"

"He offered me," said the senator, almost strangling with rage, "the exclusive use of Harvey—"

Harrington interrupted, without knowing why—almost as if he feared to let the senator go on.

"You know," he said, "I can remember, many years ago—I was just a lad—when Harvey was installed down in the *Situation* office."

And he was surprised at how well he could remember it—the great hurrah of fanfare. Although at that time, he recalled, no one had put too much credence in the matter, for *Situation* was then notorious for its circulation stunts. But it was different now. Almost everyone read the Harvey column and even in the most learned of circles it was quoted as authority.

"Harvey!" spat the senator. "A geared-up calculator! A mechanical predicter!"

And that was it, Harrington thought wildly. That was the very thing for which he had been groping!

For Harvey was a predicter. He predicted every week and the magazine ran a column of the predictions he spewed out.

"White was most persuasive," said the senator. "He was very buddy-buddy. He placed Harvey at my complete disposal. He said that he would let me see all the predictions that he made immediately he made them and that he'd withhold from publication any that I wished."

"It might be a help, at that," said Harrington.

For Harvey was good. Of that there was no question. Week after week he called the shots exactly, right straight down the line.

"I'll have none of it!" yelled the senator. "I'll have no part of Harvey. He is the worst thing that could have happened so far as public opinion is concerned. The human race is entirely capable, in its own good judgment, of accepting or rejecting the predictions of any human pundit. But our technological society has developed a conditioning factor that accepts the infallibility of machines. It would seem to me that *Situation*, in using an analytical computer, humanized by the name of Harvey, to predict the trend of world events, is deliberately preying upon public gullibility. And I'll have no part of it. I will not be tarred with—"

"I knew White was for you," said Harrington. "I knew he favored your appointment, but—"

"Preston White," said the senator, "is a dangerous man. Any powerful man is a dangerous man, and in our time the man who is in a position to mould public opinion is the most powerful of them all. I can't afford to be associated with him in any way at all. Here I stand, a man of some forty years of service, without, thank God, a single smudge upon me. What would happen to me if someone came along and pegged this man White—but good? How would I stand then?"

"They almost had him pegged," said Harrington, "that time years ago when the congressional committee investigated him. As

I remember, much of the testimony at that time had to do with Harvey."

"Hollis," said the senator, "I don't know why I trouble you. I don't know why I phoned you. Just to blow off steam, I guess."

"I am glad you did," said Harrington. "What do you intend to do?"

"I don't know," said the senator. "I threw White out, of course, so my hands theoretically are clean, but it's all gone sour on me. I have a vile taste in my mouth."

"Sleep on it," said Harrington. "You'll know better in the morning."

"Thanks, Hollis, I think I will," said the senator. "Good night."

Harrington put up the phone and stood stiff beside the desk.

For now it all was crystal clear. Now he knew without a doubt exactly who it was that had wanted Enright in the state department.

It was precisely the kind of thing, he thought, one could expect of White.

He could not imagine how it had been done—but if there had been a way to do it, White would have been the one to ferret out that way.

He'd engineered it so that Enright, by reading a line out of a book, had stayed in public life until the proper time had come for him to head the state department.

And how many other men, how many other situations, stood as they did tonight because of the vast schemings of one Preston White?

He saw the paper on the floor and picked it up and looked at the headline, then threw it down again.

They had tried to get rid of him, he thought, and it would have been all right if he'd just wandered off like an old horse turned out to pasture, abandoned and forgotten. Perhaps all the others had done exactly that. But in getting rid of him, in getting rid of anyone, they must have been aware of a certain danger. The only safe and foolproof way would have been to keep him on, to let him go on living as the final gentleman until his dying day.

Why had they not done that? Was it possible, for example, that there were limitations on the project, that the operation, whatever its purpose, had a load capacity that was now crammed to its very limit? So that, before they could take on someone else, they must get rid of him?

If that were true, it very well could be there was a spot here where they were vulnerable.

And yet another thing, a vague remembrance from that congressional hearing of some years ago—a sentence and a picture carried in the papers at the time. The picture of a very puzzled man, one of the top technicians who had assembled Harvey, sitting in the witness chair and saying: "But, senator, I tell you no analytical computer can be anywhere near as good as they claim Harvey is."

And it might mean something and it might not, Harrington told himself, but it was something to remember, it was a hope to which to cling.

Most astonishing, he thought placidly, how a mere machine could take the place of thinking man. He had commented on that before, with some asperity, in one of his books—he could not recall which one. As Cedric Madison had said this very evening . . .

He caught himself in time.

In some dim corner of his brain an alarm was ringing, and he dived for the folded paper he had tossed onto the floor.

He found it, and the headline screamed at him and the books lost their calf-bound elegance and the carpeting regained its harsh newness, and he was himself once more.

He knelt, sobbing, on the floor, the paper clutched in a shaky hand.

No change, he thought, no warning!

And a crumpled paper the only shield he had.

But a powerful shield, he thought.

Try it again! he screamed at Harvey. *Go ahead and try!*

Harvey didn't try.

It had *been* Harvey. And, he told himself, of course he didn't know.

Defenseless, he thought, except for a folded paper with a headline set in 18 point caps.

Defenseless, with a story that no one would believe even if he told it to them.

Defenseless, with thirty years of eccentricity to make his every act suspect.

He searched his mind for help and there was no help. The police would not believe him and he had few friends to help, for in thirty years he had made few friends.

There was the senator—but the senator had troubles of his own.

And there was something else—there was a certain weapon that could be used against him. Harvey only had to wait until he went to sleep. For if he went to sleep, there was no doubt he'd wake the final gentleman and more than likely then remain the final gentleman, even more firmly the final gentleman than he'd ever been before. For if they got him now, they'd never let him go.

He wondered, somewhat vaguely, why he should fight against it so. The last thirty years had not been so bad; the way they had been passed would not be a bad way, he admitted, being honest with himself, to live out the years that he had left in him.

But the thought revolted him as an insult to his very humanness. He had a right to be himself, perhaps even an obligation to remain himself, and he felt a deep-banked anger at the arrogance that would make him someone else.

The issue was straightly drawn, he knew. Two facts were crystal clear: Whatever he did, he must do himself; he must expect no help. And he must do it now before he needed sleep.

He clambered to his feet, with the paper in his hand, squared his shoulders and turned toward the door. But at the door he halted, for a sudden, terrible truth had occurred to him.

Once he left the house and went out into the darkness, he would be without his shield. In the darkness the paper would be worthless since he would not be able to read the headline.

He glanced at his watch and it was just after three. There were still three hours of darkness and he couldn't wait three hours.

He needed time, he thought. He must somehow buy some time. Within the next few hours he must in some way manage to smash or disable Harvey. And while that, he admitted to himself, might not be the whole answer, it would give him time.

He stood beside the door and the thought came to him that he might be wrong—that it might not be Harvey or Madison or White. He had put it all together in his mind and now he'd managed to convince himself. He might, he realized, have hypnotized himself almost as effectively as Harvey or someone else had hypnotized him thirty years ago.

Although probably it had not been hypnotism.

But whatever it might be, he realized, it was a bootless thing to try to thresh out now. There were more immediate problems that badly needed solving.

First of all he must devise some other sort of shield. Defenseless, he'd never reach the door of the *Situation* lobby.

Association, he thought—some sort of association—some way of reminding himself of who and what he was. Like a string around his finger, like a jingle in his brain.

The study door came open and old Adams stood there, clutching his ragged robe together.

"I heard someone talking, sir."

"It was I," said Harrington. "On the telephone."

"I thought, perhaps," said Adams, "someone had dropped in. Although it's an unearthly time of night for anyone to call."

Harrington stood silent, looking at old Adams, and he felt some of his grimness leave him—for Adams was the same. Adams had not changed. He was the only thing of truth in the entire pattern.

"If you will pardon me," said Adams, "your shirt tail's hanging out."

"Thanks," said Harrington. "I hadn't noticed. Thanks for telling me."

"Perhaps you had better get on to bed, sir. It is rather late."

"I will," said Harrington, "in just another minute."

He listened to the shuffling of old Adams' slippers going down the hall and began tucking in his shirt tail.

And suddenly it struck him: Shirt tails—they'd be better than a string!

For anyone would wonder, even the final gentleman would wonder, why his shirt tails had a knot in them.

He stuffed the paper in his jacket pocket and tugged the shirt tails entirely free. He had to loosen several buttons before there was cloth enough to make a satisfactory knot.

He made it good and hard, a square knot so it wouldn't slip, and tight enough so that it would have to be untied before he took off the shirt.

And he composed a silly line that went with the knotted shirt tails:

I tie this knot because I'm not the final gentleman.

He went out of the house and down the steps and around the house to the shack where the garden tools were kept.

He lighted matches until he found the maul that he was looking for. With it in his hand, he went back to the car.

And all the time he kept repeating to himself the line:

I tie this knot, because I'm not the final gentleman.

The *Situation* lobby was as brilliant as he remembered it and as silent and deserted and he headed for the door that said HARVEY on it.

He had expected that it would be locked, but it wasn't, and he went through it and closed it carefully behind him.

He was on a narrow catwalk that ran in a circle, with the wall behind him and the railing out in front. And down in the pit circled by the catwalk was something that could be only Harvey.

. . . *Hello, son,* it said, or seemed to say, inside his brain.

Hello, son. I'm glad that you've come home again.

He stepped forward to the railing eagerly and leaned the maul against it and gripped the railing with both hands to stare down into the pit, enveloped in the feel of father-love that welled up from the thing that squatted in the pit—the old pipe-tweed coat-grizzled whisker love he'd forgotten long ago.

A lump came in his throat and tears smarted in his eyes and he forgot the barren street outside and all the lonely years.

The love kept welling up—the love and understanding and the faint amusement that he should have expected anything but love from an entity to which he had been tied so intimately for all of thirty years.

You did a good job, son. I am proud of you. I'm glad that you've come home to me again.

He leaned across the railing, yearning toward the father squatting in the pit, and one of the rails caught against the knotted shirt tail and shoved it hard against his belly.

Reflexes clicked within his brain and he said, almost automatically: *I tie this knot because I'm not . . .*

And then he was saying it consciously and with fervor, like a single chant.

I tie this knot because I'm not the final gentleman.

I tie this knot because I'm not . . .

He was shouting now and the sweat streamed down his face and he fought like a drunken man to push back from the railing, and still he was conscious of the father, not insistent, not demanding, but somewhat hurt and puzzled by this ingratitude.

Harrington's hand slipped from the top rail and the fingers

touched the handle of the maul and seized and closed upon it and lifted it from the floor to throw.

But even as he lifted it, the door catch snicked behind him and he swung around.

Cedric Madison stood just inside the door and his death-head face wore a look of utter calm.

"Get him off my back!" yelled Harrington. "Make him let loose of me or I will let you have it."

And was surprised to find that he meant every word of it, that a man as mild as he could find it in his heart to kill another man without a second thought.

"All right," said Madison, and the father-love was gone and the world stood cold and hard and empty, with just the two of them standing face to face.

"I'm sorry that this happened, Harrington. You are the first . . ."

"You took a chance," said Harrington. "You tried to turn me loose. What did you expect I would do—moon around and wonder what had happened to me?"

"We'll take you back again. It was a pleasant life. You can live it out."

"I have no doubt you would. You and White and all the rest of—"

Madison sighed, a very patient sigh. "Leave White out of this," he said. "The poor fool thinks that Harvey . . ."

He stopped what he meant to say and chuckled.

"Believe me, Harrington, it's a slick and foolproof setup. It is even better than the oracle at Delphi."

He was sure of himself, so sure that it sent a thrill of apprehension deep through Harrington, a sense of being trapped, of being backed into a corner from which he never could escape.

They had him cold, he thought, between the two of them—Madison in front and Harvey at his rear. Any second now Harvey would throw another punch at him and despite all that he had said, despite the maul he gripped, despite the knotted shirt tails and the silly rhyme, he had grave doubts that he could fight it off.

"I am astonished that you are surprised," Madison was saying smoothly. "For Harvey has been in fact a father to you for all these many years, or the next thing to a father, maybe better than a father. You've been closer to him, day and night, than you've ever been to any other creature. He has watched over you and watched out for you and guided you at times and the relationship between the two of you has been more real than you can ever guess."

"But why?" asked Harrington and he was seeking furiously for some way out of this, for some defense that might be more substantial than a knotted shirt.

"I do not know how to say this so you will believe it," Madison told him earnestly, "but the father-feeling was no trick at all. You are closer at this moment to Harvey and perhaps even to myself than you can ever be to any other being. No one could work with you as long as Harvey worked with you without forming deep attachments. He, and I, have no thought but good for you. Won't you let us prove it?"

Harrington remained silent, but he was wavering—even when he knew that he should not waver. For what Madison had said seemed to make some sense.

"The world," said Madison, "is cold and merciless. It has no pity for you. You've not built a warm and pleasant world and now that you see it as it is no doubt you are repelled by it. There is no reason you should remain in it. We can give you back the world you've known. We can give you security and comfort. Surely you would be happy then. You can gain nothing by remaining as you are. There is no disloyalty to the human race in going back to this world you love. Now you can neither hurt nor harm the race. Your work is done . . ."

"No!" cried Harrington.

Madison shook his head. "Your race is a queer one, Harrington."

"My race!" yelled Harrington. "You talk as if—"

"There is greatness in you," said Madison, "but you must be pushed to bring it out. You must be cheered and coddled, you must be placed in danger, you must be given problems. You are like so many children. It is my duty, Harrington, my sworn, solemn duty to bring out the greatness in you. And I will not allow you nor anyone to stand against the duty."

And the truth was there, screaming through the dark, dread corridors of belated recognition. It had been there all the time, Harrington told himself, and he should have seen it.

He swung up the maul in a simple reflex action, as a gesture of horror and revulsion, and he heard his screaming voice as if it were some other voice and not his own at all: "Why, damn you, you aren't even human!"

And as he brought the maul up in its arc and forward, Madison was weaving to one side so that the maul would miss, and his face and hands were changing and his body, too—although changing was perhaps not the word for it. It was a relaxing, rather, as if the body and the face and hands that had been Madison were flowing back again into their normal mould after being held and prisoned into human shape. The human clothes he wore ripped apart with the pressure of the change and hung on him in tatters.

He was bigger, or he seemed to be, as if he had been forced to compress his bigness to conform to human standards, but he was humanoid and there was no essential change in his skull-like face beyond its taking on a faintly greenish cast.

The maul clanged to the floor and skidded on the steel face of the catwalk and the thing that had been Madison was slouching forward with the alien sureness in it. And from Harvey poured a storm of anger and frustration—a father's storming anger at a naughty child which must now stand in punishment. And the punishment was death, for no naughty child must bar the great and solemn duty of a sworn and dedicated task. In that storming fury, even as it rocked his mind, Harrington sensed an essential oneness between machine and alien, as if the two moved and thought in unison.

And there was a snarling and a coughing sound of anger and Harrington found himself moving toward the alien thing with his fingers spread and his muscles tensed for the seizing and the rending of this enemy from the darkness that extended out beyond the cave. He was shambling forward on bowed and sturdy legs and there was fear deep-rooted in his mind, a terrible, shriveling fear that drove him to his work. But above and beyond that fear there was as well the knowledge of the strength within his own brute body.

For a moment he was aghast at the realization that the snarling and the coughing was coming from himself and that the foam of fighting anger was dripping from his jaws. Then he was aghast no longer, for he knew with surety who he was and all that he might have been or might ever have thought was submerged and swept away in sheer bestiality and the driving urge to kill.

His hands reached out and caught the alien flesh and tore at it and broke it and ripped it from the bones, and in the wild, black job of killing scarcely felt or noticed the raking of the other's talons or the stabbing of the beak.

There was a screaming somewhere, a piercing sound of pain and agony from some other place, and the job was done.

Harrington crouched above the body that lay upon the floor and wondered at the growling sounds which still rumbled in his throat.

He stood erect and held out his hands and in the dim light saw that they were stained with sticky red, while from the pit he heard Harvey's screams dwindle into moaning.

He staggered forward to the railing and looked down into the pit and streams of some dark and stringy substance were pouring out of every crack and joint of Harvey—as if the life and intelligence were draining out of him.

And somewhere a voice (a voice?) was saying: *You fool! Now look at what you've done! What will happen to you now?*

"We'll get along," said Harrington—ordinary Harrington, not the final gentleman, nor yet Neanderthaler.

There was a gash along one arm and the blood was oozing out and soaking the fabric of his torn coat and one side of his face was wet and sticky, but he was all right,

We kept you on the road, said the dying voice, now faint and far away. *We kept you on it for so many ages . . .*

Yes, thought Harrington. Yes, my friend, you're right. Once the Delphian oracle and how many cons before that? And clever—once an oracle and in this day an analytical computer. And where in the years between—in monastery? in palace? in some counting house?

Although, perhaps, the operation need not have been continuous. Perhaps it was only necessary at certain crisis points.

And what the actual purpose? To guide the toddling footsteps of humanity, make man think as they wanted him to think? Or to shape humanity to the purpose of an alien race? And what the shape of human culture if there had been no interference?

And he, himself, he wondered—was he the summer-up, the man who had been used to write the final verdict of the centuries of patterning? Not in his words, of course, but in the words of these other two—the one down in the pit, the other on this catwalk. Or were there two of them? Might there have been only one? Was it possible, he wondered, that they were the same—the one of them no more than an extension of the other? For when Madison had died, so had Harvey.

"The trouble with you, friend," he said to the thing lying on the floor, "was that you were too close to human in many ways yourself. You got too confident and you made mistakes."

And the worst mistake of all had been when they'd allowed him to write a Neanderthaler into that early story.

He walked slowly toward the door and stopped at it for a moment to look back at the twisted form that lay huddled on the floor. They'd find it in an hour or two and think at first, perhaps, that it was Madison. Then they'd note the changes and know that it could not be Madison.

And they'd be puzzled people, especially since Madison himself would have disappeared. They'd wonder, too, what had happened to Harvey, who'd never work again. And they'd find the maul!

The maul! Good God, he thought. I almost left the maul!

He turned back and picked it up and his mind was churning with the fear of what might have happened had he left it there. For his fingerprints would be all over it and the police would have come around to find out what he knew.

And his fingerprints would be on the railing, too, he thought. He'd have to wipe them off.

He took out his handkerchief and began to wipe the railing, wondering as he did it why he went to all the trouble, for there would be no guilt associated with this thing he'd done.

No *guilt?* he asked himself.

How could he be sure?

Had Madison been a villain or a benefactor?

There was no way, he knew, that anyone could be sure.

Not yet, at least. Not so shortly after. And now perhaps there'd never be any way to know. For the human race had been set so firmly in the track that had been engineered for it, it might never deviate. For the rest of his days he'd wonder about the rightness and the wrongness of this deed he'd done.

He'd watch for signs and portents. He'd wonder if every piece of disturbing news he read might have been averted by this alien that now lay upon the floor. He'd come fighting out of sleep at night, chased by nightmares of an idiot doom that his hand had brought about.

He finished polishing the railing and walked to the door. He polished the knob most carefully and shut the door behind him. And, as a final gesture, he untied the shirt tails.

There was no one in the lobby and no one in the street, and he stood looking up and down the street in the pale cold light of morning.

He cringed against it—against the morning light and against this street that was a symbol of the world. For there seemed to him to be a crying in the street, a crying of his guilt.

There was a way, he knew, that he could forget all this—could wipe it from his mind and leave it all behind him. There was a path that even at this hour led to comfort and security and even, yes, to smugness, and he was tempted by it. For there was no reason that he shouldn't. There was no point in not doing it. No one except himself stood either to gain or to lose.

But he shook his head stubbornly, as if to scare the thought away.

He shifted the maul from one hand to the other and stepped out to cross the street. He reached the car and opened the back door and threw the maul in on the floor.

And he stood there, empty-handed now, and felt the silence beating in long rolls, like relentless surf pounding through his head.

He put up his hands to keep his head from bursting and he felt a terrible weakness in him. He knew it was reaction—nerves suddenly letting go after being taut too long.

Then the stifling silence was no more than an overriding quietness. He dropped his hands.

A car was coming down the street, and he watched it as it parked across from him a short distance up the street.

From it came the shrilling voice of a radio tuned high:

". . . In his note to the President, refusing the appointment, Enright said that after some soul-searching he was convinced it would be better for the country and the world if he did not accept the post. In Washington, foreign policy observers and the diplomatic corps are reported in a dither. What, after all, they ask, could soul-searching have to do with the state department?

"And here is another piece of news this morning that is likewise difficult to assess. Peking announces a reshuffling of its government, with known moderates taking over. While it is too early yet to say, the shift could result in a complete reversal of Red China's policies—"

The radio shut off abruptly and the man got out from the car. He slammed the door behind him and went striding down the street.

Harrington opened the front door and climbed behind the wheel. He had the strangest sense that he had forgotten something. He tried to remember what it was, but it was gone entirely.

He sat with his hands clutched upon the wheel and he felt a little shiver running through his body. Like a shiver of relief, although he could not imagine why he should feel relief.

Perhaps over that news about Enright. he told himself. For it was very good news. Not that Enright was the wrong man for the post, for he surely was the right one. But there came a time when a man had the right and duty to be himself entirely.

And the human race, he told himself, had that same right.

And the shift of government in China was a most amazing thing. As if, he thought, evil geniuses throughout the world might be disappearing with the coming of the dawn.

And there was something about geniuses, he told himself, that he should remember. Something about how a genius came about.

But he could not recall it.

He rolled down the window of the car and sniffed the brisk, fresh breeze of morning. Sniffing it, he consciously straightened his body and lifted up his chin. A man should do a thing like this more often, he told himself contentedly. There was something in the beginning of a day that sharpened up one's soul.

He put the car in gear and wheeled it out into the street.

Too bad about Madison, he thought. He was really, after all, a very decent fellow.

Hollis Harrington, final gentleman, drove down the morning street.

PROJECT MASTODON

Originally published in the March 1955 issue of Galaxy Science Fiction, *this story comes from the time of the Cold War, when the looming threat of nuclear war was oppressing many, including newspapermen—and so represents another variation on Cliff Simak's occasional theme of the use of time travel to find sanctuary. But those purported historians of science fiction who state that this story was later expanded to create the novel Mastodonia clearly have never read both.*

—dww

The chief of protocol said, "Mr. Hudson of—ah—Mastodonia."

The secretary of state held out his hand. "I'm glad to see you, Mr. Hudson. I understand you've been here several times."

"That's right," said Hudson. "I had a hard time making your people believe I was in earnest."

"And are you, Mr. Hudson?"

"Believe me, sir, I would not try to fool you."

"And this Mastodonia," said the secretary, reaching down to tap the document upon the desk. "You will pardon me, but I've never heard of it."

"It's a new nation," Hudson explained, "but quite legitimate. We have a constitution, a democratic form of government, duly elected officials and a code of laws. We are a free, peace-loving people and we are possessed of a vast amount of natural resources and—"

"Please tell me, sir," interrupted the secretary, "just where are you located?"

"Technically, you are our nearest neighbors."

"But that is ridiculous!" exploded Protocol.

"Not at all," insisted Hudson. "If you will give me a moment, Mr. Secretary, I have considerable evidence."

He brushed the fingers of Protocol off his sleeve and stepped forward to the desk, laying down the portfolio he carried.

"Go ahead, Mr. Hudson," said the secretary. "Why don't we all sit down and be comfortable while we talk this over?"

"You have my credentials, I see. Now here is a propos—"

"I have a document signed by a certain Wesley Adams."

"He's our first president," said Hudson. "Our George Washington, you might say."

"What is the purpose of this visit, Mr. Hudson?"

"We'd like to establish diplomatic relations. We think it would be to our mutual benefit. After all, we are a sister republic in perfect sympathy with your policies and aims. We'd like to negotiate trade agreements and we'd be grateful for some Point Four aid."

The secretary smiled. "Naturally. Who doesn't?"

"We're prepared to offer something in return," Hudson told him stiffly. "For one thing, we could offer sanctuary."

"Sanctuary!"

"I understand," said Hudson, "that in the present state of international tensions, a foolproof sanctuary is not something to be sneezed at."

The secretary turned stone cold. "I'm an extremely busy man."

Protocol took Hudson firmly by the arm. "Out you go."

General Leslie Bowers put in a call to State and got the secretary.

"I don't like to bother you, Herb," he said, "but there's something I want to check. Maybe you can help me."

"Glad to help you if I can."

"There's a fellow hanging around out here at the Pentagon, trying to get in to see me. Said I was the only one he'd talk to, but you know how it is."

"I certainly do."

"Name of Huston or Hudson or something like that."

"He was here just an hour or so ago," said the secretary. "Crackpot sort of fellow."

"He's gone now?"

"Yes. I don't think he'll be back."

"Did he say where you could reach him?"

"No, I don't believe he did."

"How did he strike you? I mean what kind of impression did you get of him?"

"I told you. A crackpot."

"I suppose he is. He said something to one of the colonels that got me worrying. Can't pass up anything, you know—not in the Dirty Tricks Department. Even if it's crackpot, these days you got to have a look at it."

"He offered sanctuary," said the secretary indignantly. "Can you imagine that!"

"He's been making the rounds, I guess," the general said. "He was over at AEC. Told them some sort of tale about knowing where there were vast uranium deposits. It was the AEC that told me he was heading your way."

"We get them all the time. Usually we can ease them out. This Hudson was just a little better than the most of them. He got in to see me."

"He told the colonel something about having a plan that would enable us to establish secret bases anywhere we wished, even in the territory of potential enemies. I know it sounds crazy . . . ."

"Forget it, Les."

"You're probably right," said the general, "but this idea sends me. Can you imagine the look on their Iron Curtain faces?"

The scared little government clerk, darting conspiratorial glances all about him, brought the portfolio to the FBI.

"I found it in a bar down the street," he told the man who took him in tow. "Been going there for years. And I found this portfolio laying in the booth. I saw the man who must have left it there and I tried to find him later, but I couldn't."

"How do you know he left it there?"

"I just figured he did. He left the booth just as I came in and it was sort of dark in there and it took a minute to see this thing laying there. You see, I always take the same booth every day and Joe sees me come in and he brings me the usual and—"

"You saw this man leave the booth you usually sit in?"

"That's right."

"Then you saw the portfolio."

"Yes, sir."

"You tried to find the man, thinking it must have been his."

"That's exactly what I did."

"But by the time you went to look for him, he had disappeared."

"That's the way it was."

"Now tell me—why did you bring it here? Why didn't you turn it in to the management so the man could come back and claim it?"

"Well, sir, it was like this. I had a drink or two and I was wondering all the time what was in that portfolio. So finally I took a peek and—"

"And what you saw decided you to bring it here to us."

"That's right. I saw—"

"Don't tell me what you saw. Give me your name and address and don't say anything about this. You understand that we're grateful to you for thinking of us, but we'd rather you said nothing."

"Mum's the word," the little clerk assured him, full of vast importance.

The FBI phoned Dr. Ambrose Amberly, Smithsonian expert on paleontology.

"We've got something, Doctor, that we'd like you to have a look at. A lot of movie film."

"I'll be most happy to. I'll come down as soon as I get clear. End of the week, perhaps?"

"This is very urgent, Doctor. Damnest thing you ever saw. Big, shaggy elephants and tigers with teeth down to their necks. There's a beaver the size of a bear."

"Fakes," said Amberly, disgusted. "Clever gadgets. Camera angles."

"That's what we thought first, but there are no gadgets, no camera angles. This is the real McCoy."

"I'm on my way," the paleontologist said, hanging up.

Snide item in smug, smart-aleck gossip column: Saucers are passé at the Pentagon. There's another mystery that's got the high brass very high.

II

President Wesley Adams and Secretary of State John Cooper sat glumly under a tree in the capital of Mastodonia and waited for the ambassador extraordinary to return.

"I tell you, Wes," said Cooper, who, under various pseudonyms, was also the secretaries of commerce, treasury and war, "this is a crazy thing we did. What if Chuck can't get back? They might throw him in jail or something might happen to the time unit or the helicopter. We should have gone along."

"We had to stay," Adams said. "You know what would happen to this camp and our supplies if we weren't around here to guard them."

"The only thing that's given us any trouble is that old mastodon. If he comes around again, I'm going to take a skillet and bang him in the brisket."

"That isn't the only reason, either," said President Adams, "and you know it. We can't go deserting this nation now that we've created it. We have to keep possession. Just planting a flag and saying it's ours wouldn't be enough. We might be called upon for proof that we've established residence. Something like the old homestead laws, you know."

"We'll establish residence sure enough," growled Secretary Cooper, "if something happens to that time unit or the helicopter."

"You think they'll do it, Johnny?"

"Who do what?"

"The United States. Do you think they'll recognize us?"

"Not if they know who we are."

"That's what I'm afraid of."

"Chuck will talk them into it. He can talk the skin right off a cat."

"Sometimes I think we're going at this wrong. Sure, Chuck's got the long-range view and I suppose it's best. But maybe what we ought to do is grab a good, fast profit and get out of here. We could take in hunting parties at ten thousand a head or maybe we could lease it to a movie company."

"We can do all that and do it legally and with full protection," Cooper told him, "if we can get ourselves recognized as a sovereign nation. If we negotiate a mutual defense pact, no one would dare get hostile because we could squawk to Uncle Sam."

"All you say is true," Adams agreed, "but there are going to be questions. It isn't just a matter of walking into Washington and getting recognition. They'll want to know about us, such as our population. What if Chuck has to tell them it's a total of three persons?"

Cooper shook his head. "He wouldn't answer that way, Wes. He'd duck the question or give them some diplomatic double-talk. After all, how can we be sure there are only three of us? We took over the whole continent, remember."

"You know well enough, Johnny, there are no other humans back here in North America. The farthest back any scientist will place the migrations from Asia is 30,000 years. They haven't got here yet."

"Maybe we should have done it differently," mused Cooper. "Maybe we should have included the whole world in our proclamation, not just the continent. That way, we could claim quite a population."

"It wouldn't have held water. Even as it is, we went a little further than precedent allows. The old explorers usually laid claim to certain watersheds. They'd find a river and lay claim to all the territory drained by the river. They didn't go grabbing off whole continents."

"That's because they were never sure of exactly what they had," said Cooper. "We are. We have what you might call the advantage of hindsight."

He leaned back against the tree and stared across the land. It was a pretty place, he thought—the rolling ridges covered by vast grazing areas and small groves, the forest-covered, ten-mile river valley. And everywhere one looked, the grazing herds of mastodon, giant bison and wild horses, with the less gregarious fauna scattered hit and miss.

Old Buster, the troublesome mastodon, a lone bull which had been probably run out of a herd by a younger rival, stood at the edge of a grove a quarter-mile away. He had his head down and was curling and uncurling his trunk in an aimless sort of way while he teetered slowly in a lazy-crazy fashion by lifting first one foot and then another.

The old cuss was lonely, Cooper told himself. That was why he hung around like a homeless dog—except that he was too big and awkward to have much pet-appeal and, more than likely, his temper was unstable.

The afternoon sun was pleasantly warm and the air, it seemed to Cooper, was the freshest he had ever smelled. It was, altogether, a very pleasant place, an Indian-summer sort of land, ideal for a Sunday picnic or a camping trip.

* * *

The breeze was just enough to float out from its flagstaff before the tent the national banner of Mastodonia—a red rampant mastodon upon a field of green ferns.

"You know, Johnny," said Adams, "there's one thing that worries me a lot. If we're going to base our claim on precedent, we may be way off base. The old explorers always claimed their discoveries for their nations or their king, never for themselves."

"The principle was entirely different," Cooper told him. "Nobody ever did anything for himself in those days. Everyone was always under someone else's protection. The explorers either were financed by their governments or were sponsored by them or operated under a royal charter or a patent. With us, it's different. Ours is a private enterprise. You dreamed up the time unit and built it. The three of us chipped in to buy the helicopter. We've paid all of our expenses out of our own pockets. We never got a dime from anyone. We never represented anyone. What we found is ours."

"I hope you're right," said Adams uneasily.

Old Buster had moved out from the grove and was shuffling warily toward the camp. Adams picked up the rifle that lay across his knees.

"Wait," said Cooper sharply. "Maybe he's just bluffing. It would be a shame to plaster him; he's such a nice old guy."

Adams half raised the rifle.

"I'll give him three steps more," he announced. "I've had enough of him."

Suddenly a roar burst out of the air just above their heads. The two leaped to their feet.

"It's Chuck!" Cooper yelled. "He's back!"

The helicopter made a half-turn of the camp and came rapidly to Earth.

Trumpeting with terror, Old Buster was a dwindling dot far down the grassy ridge.

III

They built the nightly fires circling the camp to keep out the animals.

"It'll be the death of me yet," said Adams wearily, "cutting all this wood."

"We have to get to work on that stockade," Cooper said. "We've fooled around too long. Some night, fire or no fire, a herd of mastodon will come busting in here and if they ever hit the helicopter, we'll be dead ducks. It wouldn't take more than just five seconds to turn us into Robinson Crusoes of the Pleistocene."

"Well, now that this recognition thing has petered out on us," said Adams, "maybe we can get down to business."

"Trouble is," Cooper answered, "we spent about the last of our money on the chain saw to cut this wood and on Chuck's trip to Washington. To build a stockade, we need a tractor. We'd kill ourselves if we tried to rassle that many logs bare-handed."

"Maybe we could catch some of those horses running around out there."

"Have you ever broken a horse?"

"No, that's one thing I never tried."

"Me, either. How about you, Chuck?"

"Not me," said the ex-ambassador extraordinary bluntly.

Cooper squatted down beside the coals of the cooking fire and twirled the spit. Upon the spit were three grouse and half a dozen quail. The huge coffee pot was sending out a nose-tingling aroma. Biscuits were baking in the reflector.

"We've been here six weeks," he said, "and we're still living in a tent and cooking on an open fire. We better get busy and get something done."

"The stockade first," said Adams, "and that means a tractor."

"We could use the helicopter."

"Do you want to take the chance? That's our getaway. Once something happens to it . . ."

"I guess not," Cooper admitted, gulping.

"We could use some of that Point Four aid right now," commented Adams.

"They threw me out," said Hudson. "Everywhere I went, sooner or later they got around to throwing me out. They were real organized about it."

"Well, we tried," Adams said.

"And to top it off," added Hudson, "I had to go and lose all that film and now we'll have to waste our time taking more of it. Personally, I don't ever want to let another saber-tooth get that close to me while I hold the camera."

"You didn't have a thing to worry about," Adams objected. "Johnny was right there behind you with the gun."

"Yeah, with the muzzle about a foot from my head when he let go."

"I stopped him, didn't I?" demanded Cooper.

"With his head right in my lap."

"Maybe we won't have to take any more pictures," Adams suggested.

"We'll have to," Cooper said. "There are sportsmen up ahead who'd fork over ten thousand bucks easy for two weeks of hunting here. But before we could sell them on it, we'd have to show them movies. That scene with the saber-tooth would cinch it."

"If it didn't scare them off," Hudson pointed out. "The last few feet showed nothing but the inside of his throat."

Ex-ambassador Hudson looked unhappy. "I don't like the whole setup. As soon as we bring someone in, the news is sure to leak. And once the word gets out, there'll be guys lying in ambush for us—maybe even nations—scheming to steal the know-how, legally or violently. That's what scares me the most about those films I lost. Someone will find them and they may guess what it's all about, but I'm hoping they either won't believe it or can't manage to trace us."

"We could swear the hunting parties to secrecy," said Cooper.

"How could a sportsman keep still about the mounted head of a saber-tooth or a record piece of ivory? And the same thing would apply to anyone we approached. Some university could raise dough to send a team of scientists back here and a movie company would cough up plenty to use this place as a location for a caveman epic. But it wouldn't be worth a thing to either of them if they couldn't tell about it.

"Now if we could have gotten recognition as a nation, we'd have been all set. We could make our own laws and regulations and be able to enforce them. We could bring in settlers and establish trade. We could exploit our natural resources. It would all be legal and aboveboard. We could tell who we were and where we were and what we had to offer."

"We aren't licked yet," said Adams. "There's a lot that we can do. Those river hills are covered with ginseng. We can each dig a dozen pounds a day. There's good money in the root."

"Ginseng root," Cooper said, "is peanuts. We need *big* money."

"Or we could trap," offered Adams. "The place is alive with beaver."

"Have you taken a good look at those beaver? They're about the size of a St. Bernard."

"All the better. Think how much just one pelt would bring."

"No dealer would believe that it was beaver. He'd think you were trying to pull a fast one on him. And there are only a few states that allow beaver to be trapped. To sell the pelts—even if you could—you'd have to take out licenses in each of those states."

"Those mastodon carry a lot of ivory," said Cooper. "And if we wanted to go north, we'd find mammoths that would carry even more . . ."

"And get socked into the jug for ivory smuggling?"

They sat, all three of them, staring at the fire, not finding anything to say.

The moaning complaint of a giant hunting cat came from somewhere up the river.

IV

Hudson lay in his sleeping bag, staring at the sky. It bothered him a lot. There was not one familiar constellation, not one star that he could name with any certainty. This juggling of the stars, he thought, emphasized more than anything else in this ancient land the vast gulf of years which lay between him and the Earth where he had been—or would be—born.

A hundred and fifty thousand years, Adams had said, give or take ten thousand. There just was no way to know. Later on, there might be. A measurement of the stars and a comparison with their positions in the twentieth century might be one way of doing it. But at the moment, any figure could be no more than a guess.

The time machine was not something that could be tested for calibration or performance. As a matter of fact, there was no way to test it. They had not been certain, he remembered, the first time they had used it, that it would really work. There had been no way to find out. When it worked, you knew it worked. And if it hadn't worked, there would have been no way of knowing beforehand that it wouldn't.

Adams had been sure, of course, but that had been because he had absolute reliance in the half-mathematical, half-philosophic concepts he had worked out—concepts that neither Hudson nor Cooper could come close to understanding.

That had always been the way it had been, even when they were kids, with Wes dreaming up the deals that he and Johnny carried out. Back in those days, too, they had used time travel in their play. Out in Johnny's back yard, they had rigged up a time machine out of a wonderful collection of salvaged junk—a wooden crate, an empty five-gallon paint pail, a battered coffee maker, a bunch of discarded copper tubing, a busted steering wheel and other odds and ends. In it, they had "traveled" back to Indian-before-the-white-man land and mammoth-land and dinosaur-land and the slaughter, he remembered, had been wonderfully appalling.

But, in reality, it had been much different. There was much more to it than gunning down the weird fauna that one found.

And they should have known there would be, for they had talked about it often.

He thought of the bull session back in university and the little, usually silent kid who sat quietly in the corner, a law-school student whose last name had been Pritchard.

And after sitting silently for some time, this Pritchard kid had spoken up: "If you guys ever do travel in time, you'll run up against more than you bargain for. I don't mean the climate or the terrain or the fauna, but the economics and the politics."

They all peered at him, Hudson remembered, and then had gone on with their talk. And after a short while, the talk had turned to women, as it always did.

He wondered where that quiet man might be. Some day, Hudson told himself, I'll have to look him up and tell him he was right.

We did it wrong, he thought. There were so many other ways we might have done it, but we'd been so sure and greedy—greedy for the triumph and the glory—and now there was no easy way to collect.

On the verge of success, they could have sought out help, gone to some large industrial concern or an educational foundation or even to the government. Like historic explorers, they could have obtained subsidization and sponsorship. Then they would have had protection, funds to do a proper job and they need not have operated on their present shoestring—one beaten-up helicopter and one time unit. They could have had several and at least one standing by in the twentieth century as a rescue unit, should that be necessary.

But that would have meant a bargain, perhaps a very hard one, and sharing with someone who had contributed nothing but the money. And there was more than money in a thing like this—there were twenty years of dreams and a great idea and the dedication to that great idea—years of work and years of disappointment and an almost fanatical refusal to give up.

Even so, thought Hudson, they had figured well enough. There had been many chances to make blunders and they'd made relatively few. All they lacked, in the last analysis, was backing.

Take the helicopter, for example. It was the one satisfactory vehicle for time traveling. You had to get up in the air to clear whatever upheavals and subsidences there had been through geologic ages. The helicopter took you up and kept you clear and gave you a chance to pick a proper landing place. Travel without it and, granting you were lucky with land surfaces, you still might materialize in the heart of some great tree or end up in a swamp or the middle of a herd of startled, savage beasts. A plane would have done as well, but back in this world, you couldn't land a plane—or you couldn't be certain that you could. A helicopter, though, could land almost anywhere.

In the time-distance they had traveled, they almost certainly had been lucky, although one could not be entirely sure just how great a part of it was luck. Wes had felt that he had not been working as blindly as it sometimes might appear. He had calibrated the unit for jumps of 50,000 years. Finer calibration, he had said realistically, would have to wait for more developmental work.

Using the 50,000-year calibrations, they had figured it out. One jump (conceding that the calibration was correct) would have landed them at the end of the Wisconsin glacial period; two jumps, at its beginning. The third would set them down toward the end of the Sangamon Interglacial and apparently it had—give or take ten thousand years or so.

They had arrived at a time when the climate did not seem to vary greatly, either hot or cold. The flora was modern enough to give them a homelike feeling. The fauna, modern and Pleistocenic, overlapped. And the surface features were little altered from the twentieth century. The rivers ran along familiar paths, the hills and bluffs looked much the same. In this corner of the Earth, at least, 150,000 years had not changed things greatly.

Boyhood dreams, Hudson thought, were wondrous. It was not often that three men who had daydreamed in their youth could follow it out to its end. But they had and here they were.

Johnny was on watch, and it was Hudson's turn next, and he'd better get to sleep. He closed his eyes, then opened them again for another look at the unfamiliar stars. The east, he saw, was flushed with silver light. Soon the Moon would rise, which was good. A man could keep a better watch when the Moon was up.

He woke suddenly, snatched upright and into full awareness by the marrow-chilling clamor that slashed across the night. The very air seemed curdled by the savage racket and, for a moment, he sat numbed by it. Then, slowly, it seemed—his brain took the noise and separated it into two distinct but intermingled categories, the deadly screaming of a cat and the maddened trumpeting of a mastodon.

The Moon was up and the countryside was flooded by its light. Cooper, he saw, was out beyond the watchfires, standing there and watching, with his rifle ready. Adams was scrambling out of his sleeping bag, swearing softly to himself. The cooking fire had burned down to a bed of mottled coals, but the watchfires still were burning and the helicopter, parked within their circle, picked up the glint of flames.

"It's Buster," Adams told him angrily. "I'd know that bellowing of his anywhere. He's done nothing but parade up and down and bellow ever since we got here. And now he seems to have gone out and found himself a saber-tooth."

Hudson zipped down his sleeping bag, grabbed up his rifle and jumped to his feet, following Adams in a silent rush to where Cooper stood.

Cooper motioned at them. "Don't break it up. You'll never see the like of it again."

Adams brought his rifle up.

Cooper knocked the barrel down.

"You fool!" he shouted. "You want them turning on us?"

Two hundred yards away stood the mastodon and, on his back, the screeching saber-tooth. The great beast reared into the air and came down with a jolt, bucking to unseat the cat, flailing the air with his massive trunk. And as he bucked, the cat struck and struck again with his gleaming teeth, aiming for the spine.

Then the mastodon crashed head downward, as if to turn a somersault, rolled and was on his feet again, closer to them now than he had been before. The huge cat had sprung off.

For a moment, the two stood facing one another. Then the tiger charged, a flowing streak of motion in the moonlight. Buster wheeled away and the cat, leaping, hit his shoulder, clawed wildly and slid off. The mastodon whipped to the attack, tusks slashing, huge feet stamping. The cat, caught a glancing blow by one of the tusks, screamed and leaped up, to land in spread-eagle fashion upon Buster's head.

Maddened with pain and fright, blinded by the tiger's raking claws, the old mastodon ran—straight toward the camp. And as he ran, he grasped the cat in his trunk and tore him from his hold, lifted him high and threw him.

"Look out!" yelled Cooper and brought his rifle up and fired.

For an instant, Hudson saw it all as if it were a single scene, motionless, one frame snatched from a fantastic movie epic—the charging mastodon, with the tiger lifted and the sound track one great blast of bloodthirsty bedlam.

Then the scene dissolved in a blur of motion. He felt his rifle thud against his shoulder, knowing he had fired, but not hearing the explosion. And the mastodon was almost on top of him, bearing down like some mighty and remorseless engine of blind destruction.

He flung himself to one side and the giant brushed past him. Out of the tail of his eye, he saw the thrown saber-tooth crash to Earth within the circle of the watchfires.

He brought his rifle up again and caught the area behind Buster's ear within his sights. He pressed the trigger. The mastodon staggered, then regained his stride and went rushing on. He hit one of the watchfires dead center and went through it, scattering coals and burning brands.

Then there was a thud and the screeching clang of metal.

"Oh, no!" shouted Hudson.

Rushing forward, they stopped inside the circle of the fires.

The helicopter lay tilted at a crazy angle. One of its rotor blades was crumpled. Half across it, as if he might have fallen as he tried to bull his mad way over it, lay the mastodon.

Something crawled across the ground toward them, its spitting, snarling mouth gaping in the firelight, its back broken, hind legs trailing.

Calmly, without a word, Adams put a bullet into the head of the saber-tooth.

V

General Leslie Bowers rose from his chair and paced up and down the room. He stopped to bang the conference table with a knotted fist.

"You can't do it," he bawled at them. "You can't kill the project. I *know* there's something to it. We can't give it up!"

"But it's been ten years, General," said the secretary of the army. "If they were coming back, they'd be here by now."

The general stopped his pacing, stiffened. Who did that little civilian squirt think he was, talking to the military in that tone of voice!

"We know how you feel about it, General," said the chairman of the joint chiefs of staff. "I think we all recognize how deeply you're involved. You've blamed yourself all these years and there is no need of it. After all, there may be nothing to it."

"Sir," said the general, "I *know* there's something to it. I thought so at the time, even when no one else did. And what we've turned up since serves to bear me out. Let's take a look at these three men of ours. We knew almost nothing of them at the time, but we know them now. I've traced out their lives from the time that they were born until they disappeared—and I might add that, on the chance it might be all a hoax, we've searched for them for years and we've found no trace at all.

"I've talked with those who knew them and I've studied their scholastic and military records. I've arrived at the conclusion that if any three men could do it, they were the ones who could. Adams was the brains and the other two were the ones who carried out the things that he dreamed up. Cooper was a bulldog sort of man who could keep them going and it would be Hudson who would figure out the angles.

"And they knew the angles, gentlemen. They had it all doped out.

"What Hudson tried here in Washington is substantial proof of that. But even back in school, they were thinking of those angles. I talked some years ago to a lawyer in New York, name of Pritchard. He told me that even back in university, they talked of the economic and political problems that they might face if they ever cracked what they were working at.

"Wesley Adams was one of our brightest young scientific men. His record at the university and his war work bears that out. After the war, there were at least a dozen jobs he could have had. But he wasn't interested. And I'll tell you why he wasn't. He had something bigger—something he wanted to work on. So he and these two others went off by themselves—"

"You think he was working on a temporal—" the army secretary cut in.

"He was working on a time machine," roared the general. "I don't know about this 'temporal' business. Just plain 'time machine' is good enough for me."

"Let's calm down, General," said the JCS chairman. "After all, there's no need to shout."

The general nodded. "I'm sorry, sir. I get all worked up about this. I've spent the last ten years with it. As you say, I'm trying to make up for what I failed to do ten years ago. I should have talked to Hudson. I was busy, sure, but not that busy. It's an official state of mind that we're too busy to see anyone and I plead guilty on that score. And now that you're talking about closing the project—"

"It's costing us money," said the army secretary.

"And we have no direct evidence," pointed out the JCS chairman.

"I don't know what you want," snapped the general. "If there was any man alive who could crack time, that man was Wesley Adams. We found where he worked. We found the workshop and we talked to neighbors who said there was something funny going on and—"

"But ten years, General!" the army secretary protested.

"Hudson came here, bringing us the greatest discovery in all history, and we kicked him out. After that, do you expect them to come crawling back to us?"

"You think they went to someone else?"

"They wouldn't do that. They know what the thing they have found would mean. They wouldn't sell us out."

"Hudson came with a preposterous proposition," said the man from the state department.

"They had to protect themselves!" yelled the general. "If you had discovered a virgin planet with its natural resources intact, what would you do about it? Come trotting down here and hand it over to a government that's too 'busy' to recognize—"

"General!"

"Yes, sir," apologized the general tiredly. "I wish you gentlemen could see my view of it, how it all fits together. First there were the films and we have the word of a dozen competent paleontologists that it's impossible to fake anything as perfect as those films. But even granting that they could be, there are certain differences that no one would ever think of faking, because no one ever knew. Who, as an example, would put lynx tassels on the ears of a saber-tooth? Who would know that young mastodon were black?

"And the location. I wonder if you've forgotten that we tracked down the location of Adams' workshop from those films alone. They gave us clues so positive that we didn't even hesitate—we drove straight to the old deserted farm where Adams and his friends had worked. Don't you see how it all fits together?"

"I presume," the man from the state department said nastily, "that you even have an explanation as to why they chose that particular location."

"You thought you had me there," said the general, "but I have an answer. A good one. The southwestern corner of Wisconsin is a geologic curiosity. It was missed by all the glaciations. Why, we do not know. Whatever the reason, the glaciers came down on both sides of it and far to the south of it and left it standing there, a little island in a sea of ice.

"And another thing: Except for a time in the Triassic, that same area of Wisconsin has always been dry land. That and a few other spots are the only areas in North America which have not, time and time again, been covered by water. I don't think it necessary to point out the comfort it would be to an experimental traveler in time to be certain that, in almost any era he might hit, he'd have dry land beneath him."

The economics expert spoke up: "We've given this matter a lot of study and, while we do not feel ourselves competent to rule upon the possibility or impossibility of time travel, there are some observations I should like, at some time, to make."

"Go ahead right now," said the JCS chairman.

"We see one objection to the entire matter. One of the reasons, naturally, that we had some interest in it is that, if true, it would give us an entire new planet to exploit, perhaps more wisely than we've done in the past. But the thought occurs that any planet has only a certain grand total of natural resources. If we go into the past and exploit them, what effect will that have upon what is left of those resources for use in the present? Wouldn't we, in doing this, be robbing ourselves of our own heritage?"

"That contention," said the AEC chairman, "wouldn't hold true in every case. Quite the reverse, in fact. We know that there was, in some geologic ages in the past, a great deal more uranium than we have today. Go back far enough and you'd catch that uranium before it turned into lead. In southwestern Wisconsin, there is a lot of lead. Hudson told us he knew the location of vast uranium deposits and we thought he was a crackpot talking through his hat. If we'd known—let's be fair about this—if we had known and believed him about going back in time, we'd have snapped him up at once and all this would not have happened."

"It wouldn't hold true with forests, either," said the chairman of the JCS. "Or with pastures or with crops."

The economics expert was slightly flushed. "There is another thing," he said. "If we go back in time and colonize the land we find there, what would happen when that—well, let's call it retroactive—when that retroactive civilization reaches the beginning of our historic period? What will result from that cultural collision? Will our history change? Is what has happened false? Is all—"

"That's all poppycock!" the general shouted. "That and this other talk about using up resources. Whatever we did in the past—or are about to do—has been done already. I've lain awake nights, mister, thinking about all these things and there is no answer, believe me, except the one I give you. The question which faces us here is an immediate one. Do we give all this up or do we keep on watching that Wisconsin farm, waiting for them to come back? Do we keep on trying to find, independently, the process or formula or method that Adams found for traveling in time?"

"We've had no luck in our research so far, General," said the quiet physicist who sat at the table's end. "If you were not so sure and if the evidence were not so convincing that it had been done by Adams, I'd say flatly that it is impossible. We have no approach which holds any hope at all. What we've done so far, you might best describe as flounder. But if Adams turned the trick, it must be possible. There may be, as a matter of fact, more ways than one. We'd like to keep on trying."

"Not one word of blame has been put on you for your failure," the chairman told the physicist. "That you could do it seems to be more than can be humanly expected. If Adams did it—*if* he did, I say—it must have been simply that he blundered on an avenue of research no other man has thought of."

"You will recall," said the general, "that the research program, even from the first, was thought of strictly as a gamble. Our one hope was, and must remain, that they will return."

"It would have been so much simpler all around," the state department man said, "if Adams had patented his method."

The general raged at him. "And had it published, all neat and orderly, in the patent office records so that anyone who wanted it could look it up and have it?"

"We can be most sincerely thankful," said the chairman, "that he did not patent it."

VI

The helicopter would never fly again, but the time unit was intact.

Which didn't mean that it would work.

They held a powwow at their camp site. It had been, they decided, simpler to move the camp than to remove the body of Old Buster. So they had shifted at dawn, leaving the old mastodon still sprawled across the helicopter.

In a day or two, they knew, the great bones would be cleanly picked by the carrion birds, the lesser cats, the wolves and foxes and the little skulkers.

Getting the time unit out of the helicopter had been quite a chore, but they finally had managed and now Adams sat with it cradled in his lap.

"The worst of it," he told them, "is that I can't test it. There's no way to. You turn it on and it works or it doesn't work. You can't know till you try."

"That's something we can't help," Cooper replied. "The problem, seems to me, is how we're going to use it without the whirlybird."

"We have to figure out some way to get up in the air," said Adams. "We don't want to take the chance of going up into the twentieth century and arriving there about six feet underground."

"Common sense says that we should be higher here than up ahead," Hudson pointed out. "These hills have stood here since Jurassic times. They probably were a good deal higher then and have weathered down. That weathering still should be going on. So we should be higher here than in the twentieth century—not much, perhaps, but higher."

"Did anyone ever notice what the altimeter read?" asked Cooper.

"I don't believe I did," Adams admitted.

"It wouldn't tell you, anyhow," Hudson declared. "It would just give our height then and now—and we were moving, remember—and what about air pockets and relative atmosphere density and all the rest?"

Cooper looked as discouraged as Hudson felt.

"How does this sound?" asked Adams. "We'll build a platform twelve feet high. That certainly should be enough to clear us and yet small enough to stay within the range of the unit's force-field."

"And what if we're two feet higher here?" Hudson pointed out.

"A fall of fourteen feet wouldn't kill a man unless he's plain unlucky."

"It might break some bones."

"So it might break some bones. You want to stay here or take a chance on a broken leg?"

"All right, if you put it that way. A platform, you say. A platform out of what?"

"Timber. There's a lot of it. We just go out and cut some logs."

"A twelve-foot log is heavy. And how are we going to get that big a log uphill?"

"We drag it."

"We try to, you mean."

"Maybe we could fix up a cart," said Adams, after thinking a moment.

"Out of what?" Cooper asked.

"Rollers, maybe. We could cut some and roll the logs up here."

"That would work on level ground," Hudson said. "It wouldn't work to roll a log uphill. It would get away from us. Someone might get killed."

"The logs would have to be longer than twelve feet, anyhow," Cooper put in. "You'd have to set them in a hole and that takes away some footage."

"Why not the tripod principle?" Hudson offered. "Fasten three logs at the top and raise them."

"That's a gin-pole, a primitive derrick. It'd still have to be longer than twelve feet. Fifteen, sixteen, maybe. And how are we going to hoist three sixteen-foot logs? We'd need a block and tackle."

"There's another thing," said Cooper. "Part of those logs might just be beyond the effective range of the force-field. Part of them would have to—have to, mind you—move in time and part couldn't. That would set up a stress . . ."

"Another thing about it," added Hudson, "is that we'd travel with the logs. I don't want to come out in another time with a bunch of logs flying all around me."

"Cheer up," Adams told them. "Maybe the unit won't work, anyhow."

VII

The general sat alone in his office and held his head between his hands. The fools, he thought, the goddam knuckle-headed fools! Why couldn't they see it as clearly as he did?

For fifteen years now, as head of Project Mastodon, he had lived with it night and day and he could see all the possibilities as clearly as if they had been actual fact. Not military possibilities alone, although as a military man, he naturally would think of those first.

The hidden bases, for example, located within the very strongholds of potential enemies—within, yet centuries removed in time. Many centuries removed and only seconds distant.

He could see it all: The materialization of the fleets; the swift, devastating blow, then the instantaneous retreat into the fastnesses of the past. Terrific destruction, but not a ship lost nor a man.

Except that if you had the bases, you need never strike the blow. If you had the bases and let the enemy know you had them, there would never be the provocation.

And on the home front, you'd have air-raid shelters that would be effective. You'd evacuate your population not in space, but time. You'd have the sure and absolute defense against any kind of bombing—fission, fusion, bacteriological or whatever else the labs had in stock.

And if the worst should come—which it never would with a setup like that—you'd have a place to which the entire nation could retreat, leaving to the enemy the empty, blasted cities and the lethally dusted countryside.

Sanctuary—that had been what Hudson had offered the then-secretary of state fifteen years ago—and the idiot had frozen up with the insult of it and had Hudson thrown out.

And if war did not come, think of the living space and the vast new opportunities—not the least of which would be the opportunity to achieve peaceful living in a virgin world, where the old hatreds would slough off and new concepts have a chance to grow.

He wondered where they were, those three who had gone back into time. Dead, perhaps. Run down by a mastodon. Or stalked by tigers. Or maybe done in by warlike tribesmen. No, he kept forgetting there weren't any in that era. Or trapped in time, unable to get back, condemned to exile in an alien time. Or maybe, he thought, just plain disgusted. And he couldn't blame them if they were.

Or maybe—let's be fantastic about this—sneaking in colonists from some place other than the watched Wisconsin farm, building up in actuality the nation they had claimed to be.

They had to get back to the present soon or Project Mastodon would be killed entirely. Already the research program had been halted and if something didn't happen quickly, the watch that was kept on the Wisconsin farm would be called off.

"And if they do that," said the general, "I know just what I'll do."

He got up and strode around the room.

"By God," he said, "I'll show 'em!"

VIII

It had taken ten full days of back-breaking work to build the pyramid. They'd hauled the rocks from the creek bed half a mile away and had piled them, stone by rolling stone, to the height of a full twelve feet. It took a lot of rocks and a lot of patience, for as the pyramid went up, the base naturally kept broadening out.

But now all was finally ready.

Hudson sat before the burned-out campfire and held his blistered hands before him.

It should work, he thought, better than the logs—and less dangerous.

Grab a handful of sand. Some trickled back between your fingers, but most stayed in your grasp. That was the principle of the pyramid of stones. When—and if—the time machine should work, most of the rocks would go along.

Those that didn't go would simply trickle out and do no harm. There'd be no stress or strain to upset the working of the force-field.

And if the time unit didn't work?

Or if it did?

This was the end of the dream, thought Hudson, no matter how you looked at it.

For even if they did get back to the twentieth century, there would be no money and with the film lost and no other taken to replace it, they'd have no proof they had traveled back beyond the dawn of history—back almost to the dawn of Man.

Although how far you traveled would have no significance. An hour or a million years would be all the same; if you could span the hour, you could span the million years. And if you could go back the million years, it was within your power to go back to the first tick of eternity, the first stir of time across the face of emptiness and nothingness—back to that initial instant when nothing as yet had happened or been planned or thought, when all the vastness of the Universe was a new slate waiting the first chalk stroke of destiny.

Another helicopter would cost thirty thousand dollars—and they didn't even have the money to buy the tractor that they needed to build the stockade.

There was no way to borrow. You couldn't walk into a bank and say you wanted thirty thousand to take a trip back to the Old Stone Age.

You still could go to some industry or some university or the government and if you could persuade them you had something on the ball—why, then, they might put up the cash after cutting themselves in on just about all of the profits. And, naturally, they'd run the show because it was their money and all you had done was the sweating and the bleeding.

"There's one thing that still bothers me," said Cooper, breaking the silence. "We spent a lot of time picking our spot so we'd miss the barn and house and all the other buildings . . . ."

"Don't tell me the windmill!" Hudson cried.

"No. I'm pretty sure we're clear of that. But the way I figure, we're right astraddle that barbed-wire fence at the south end of the orchard."

"If you want, we could move the pyramid over twenty feet or so."

Cooper groaned. "I'll take my chances with the fence." Adams got to his feet, the time unit tucked underneath his arm. "Come on, you guys. It's time to go."

They climbed the pyramid gingerly and stood unsteadily at its top.

Adams shifted the unit around, clasped it to his chest.

"Stand around close," he said, "and bend your knees a little. It may be quite a drop."

"Go ahead," said Cooper. "Press the button."

Adams pressed the button.

Nothing happened.

The unit didn't work.

IX

The chief of Central Intelligence was white-lipped when he finished talking.

"You're sure of your information?" asked the President.

"Mr. President," said the CIA chief, "I've never been more sure of anything in my entire life."

The President looked at the other two who were in the room, a question in his eyes.

The JCS chairman said, "It checks, sir, with everything we know."

"But it's incredible!" the President said.

"They're afraid," said the CIA chief. "They lie awake nights. They've become convinced that we're on the verge of traveling in time. They've tried and failed, but they think we're near success. To their way of thinking, they've got to hit us now or never, because once we actually get time travel, they know their number's up."

"But we dropped Project Mastodon entirely almost three years ago. It's been all of ten years since we stopped the research. It was twenty-five years ago that Hudson—"

"That makes no difference, sir. They're convinced we dropped the project publicly, but went underground with it. That would be the kind of strategy they could understand."

The President picked up a pencil and doodled on a pad.

"Who was that old general," he asked, "the one who raised so much fuss when we dropped the project? I remember I was in the Senate then. He came around to see me."

"Bowers, sir," said the JCS chairman.

"That's right. What became of him?"

"Retired."

"Well, I guess it doesn't make any difference now." He doodled some more and finally said, "Gentlemen, it looks like this is it. How much time did you say we had?"

"Not more than ninety days, sir. Maybe as little as thirty."

The President looked up at the JCS chairman.

"We're as ready," said the chairman, "as we will ever be. We can handle them—I think. There will, of course, be some—"

"I know," said the President.

"Could we bluff?" asked the secretary of state, speaking quietly. "I know it wouldn't stick, but at least we might buy some time."

"You mean hint that we have time travel?"

The secretary nodded.

"It wouldn't work," said the CIA chief tiredly. "If we really had it, there'd be no question then. They'd become exceedingly well-mannered, even neighborly, if they were sure we had it."

"But we haven't got it," said the President gloomily.

X

The two hunters trudged homeward late in the afternoon, with a deer slung from a pole they carried on their shoulders. Their breath hung visibly in the air as they walked along, for the frost had come and any day now, they knew, there would be snow.

"I'm worried about Wes," said Cooper, breathing heavily. "He's taking this too hard. We got to keep an eye on him."

"Let's take a rest," panted Hudson.

They halted and lowered the deer to the ground.

"He blames himself too much," said Cooper. He wiped his sweaty forehead. "There isn't any need to. All of us walked into this with our eyes wide open."

"He's kidding himself and he knows it, but it gives him something to go on. As long as he can keep busy with all his puttering around, he'll be all right."

"He isn't going to repair the time unit, Chuck."

"I know he isn't. And he knows it, too. He hasn't got the tools or the materials. Back in the workshop, he might have a chance, but here he hasn't."

"It's rough on him."

"It's rough on all of us."

"Yes, but we didn't get a brainstorm that marooned two old friends in this tail end of nowhere. And we can't make him swallow it when we say that it's okay, we don't mind at all."

"That's a lot to swallow, Johnny."

"What's going to happen to us, Chuck?"

"We've got ourselves a place to live and there's lots to eat. Save our ammo for the big game—a lot of eating for each bullet—and trap the smaller animals."

"I'm wondering what will happen when the flour and all the other stuff is gone. We don't have too much of it because we always figured we could bring in more."

"We'll live on meat," said Hudson. "We got bison by the million. The plains Indians lived on them alone. And in the spring, we'll find roots and in the summer berries. And in the fall, we'll harvest a half-dozen kinds of nuts."

"Some day our ammo will be gone, no matter how careful we are with it."

"Bows and arrows. Slingshots. Spears."

"There's a lot of beasts here I wouldn't want to stand up to with nothing but a spear."

"We won't stand up to them. We'll duck when we can and

run when we can't duck. Without our guns, we're no lords of creation—not in this place. If we're going to live, we'll have to recognize that fact."

"And if one of us gets sick or breaks a leg or—"

"We'll do the best we can. Nobody lives forever."

But they were talking around the thing that really bothered them, Hudson told himself—each of them afraid to speak the thought aloud.

They'd live, all right, so far as food, shelter and clothing were concerned. And they'd live most of the time in plenty, for this was a fat and open-handed land and a man could make an easy living.

But the big problem—the one they were afraid to talk about—was their emptiness of purpose. To live, they had to find some meaning in a world without society.

A man cast away on a desert isle could always live for hope, but here there was no hope. A Robinson Crusoe was separated from his fellow-humans by, at the most, a few thousand miles. Here they were separated by a hundred and fifty thousand years.

Wes Adams was the lucky one so far. Even playing his thousand-to-one shot, he still held tightly to a purpose, feeble as it might be—the hope that he could repair the time machine.

We don't need to watch him now, thought Hudson. The time we'll have to watch is when he is forced to admit he can't fix the machine.

And both Hudson and Cooper had been kept sane enough, for there had been the cabin to be built and the winter's supply of wood to cut and the hunting to be done.

But then there would come a time when all the chores were finished and there was nothing left to do.

"You ready to go?" asked Cooper.

"Sure. All rested now," said Hudson.

They hoisted the pole to their shoulders and started off again.

Hudson had lain awake nights thinking of it and all the thoughts had been dead ends.

One could write a natural history of the Pleistocene, complete with photographs and sketches, and it would be a pointless thing to do, because no future scientist would ever have a chance to read it.

Or they might labor to build a memorial, a vast pyramid, perhaps, which would carry a message forward across fifteen hundred centuries, snatching with bare hands at a semblance of immortality. But if they did, they would be working against the sure and certain knowledge that it all would come to naught, for they knew in advance that no such pyramid existed in historic time.

Or they might set out to seek contemporary Man, hiking across four thousand miles of wilderness to Bering Strait and over into Asia. And having found contemporary Man cowering in his caves, they might be able to help him immeasurably along the road to his great inheritance. Except that they'd never make it and even if they did, contemporary Man undoubtedly would find some way to do them in and might eat them in the bargain.

They came out of the woods and there was the cabin, just a hundred yards away. It crouched against the hillside above the spring, with the sweep of grassland billowing beyond it to the slate-gray skyline. A trickle of smoke came up from the chimney and they saw the door was open.

"Wes oughtn't to leave it open that way," said Cooper. "No telling when a bear might decide to come visiting."

"Hey, Wes!" yelled Hudson.

But there was no sign of him.

Inside the cabin, a white sheet of paper lay on the table top. Hudson snatched it up and read it, with Cooper at his shoulder.

Dear guys—I don't want to get your hopes up again and have you disappointed. But I think I may have found the trouble. I'm going to try it out. If it doesn't work, I'll come back and burn this note and never say a word. But if you find the note, you'll know it worked and I'll be back to get you. Wes.

Hudson crumpled the note in his hand. "The crazy fool!"

"He's gone off his rocker," Cooper said. "He just thought . . ."

The same thought struck them both and they bolted for the door. At the corner of the cabin, they skidded to a halt and stood there, staring at the ridge above them.

The pyramid of rocks they'd built two months ago was gone!

XI

The crash brought Gen. Leslie Bowers (ret.) up out of bed—about two feet out of bed—old muscles tense, white mustache bristling.

Even at his age, the general was a man of action. He flipped the covers back, swung his feet out to the floor and grabbed the shotgun leaning against the wall.

Muttering, he blundered out of the bedroom, marched across the dining room and charged into the kitchen. There, beside the door, he snapped on the switch that turned on the floodlights. He practically took the door off its hinges getting to the stoop and he stood there, bare feet gripping the planks, nightshirt billowing in the wind, the shotgun poised and ready.

"What's going on out there?" he bellowed.

There was a tremendous pile of rocks resting where he'd parked his car. One crumpled fender and a drunken headlight peeped out of the rubble.

A man was clambering carefully down the jumbled stones, making a detour to dodge the battered fender.

The general pulled back the hammer of the gun and fought to control himself.

The man reached the bottom of the pile and turned around to face him. The general saw that he was hugging something tightly to his chest.

"Mister," the general told him, "your explanation better be a good one. That was a brand-new car. And this was the first time I was set for a night of sleep since my tooth quit aching."

The man just stood and looked at him.

"Who in thunder are you?" roared the general.

The man walked slowly forward. He stopped at the bottom of the stoop.

"My name is Wesley Adams," he said. "I'm—"

"Wesley Adams!" howled the general. "My God, man, where have you been all these years?"

"Well, I don't imagine you'll believe me, but the fact is . . ."

"We've been waiting for you. For twenty-five long years! Or, rather, I've been waiting for you. Those other idiots gave up. I've waited right here for you, Adams, for the last three years, ever since they called off the guard."

Adams gulped. "I'm sorry about the car. You see, it was this way . . ."

The general, he saw, was beaming at him fondly.

"I had faith in you," the general said.

He waved the shotgun by way of invitation. "Come on in. I have a call to make."

Adams stumbled up the stairs.

"Move!" the general ordered, shivering. "On the double! You want me to catch my death of cold out here?"

Inside, he fumbled for the lights and turned them on. He laid the shotgun across the kitchen table and picked up the telephone.

"Give me the White House at Washington," he said. "Yes, I said the White House . . . The President? Naturally he's the one I want to talk to . . . Yes, it's all right. He won't mind my calling him."

"Sir," said Adams tentatively.

The general looked up. "What is it, Adams? Go ahead and say it."

"Did you say *twenty-five* years?"

"That's what I said. What were you doing all that time?"

Adams grasped the table and hung on. "But it wasn't . . ."

"Yes," said the general to the operator. "Yes, I'll wait."

He held his hand over the receiver and looked inquiringly at Adams. "I imagine you'll want the same terms as before."

"Terms?"

"Sure. Recognition. Point Four Aid. Defense pact."

"I suppose so," Adams said.

"You got these saps across the barrel," the general told him happily. "You can get anything you want. You rate it, too, after what you've done and the bonehead treatment you got—but especially for not selling out."

XII

The night editor read the bulletin just off the teletype.

"Well, what do you know!" he said. "We just recognized Mastodonia."

He looked at the copy chief.

"Where the hell is Mastodonia?" he asked.

The copy chief shrugged. "Don't ask me. You're the brains in this joint."

"Well, let's get a map for the next edition," said the night editor.

XIII

Tabby, the saber-tooth, dabbed playfully at Cooper with his mighty paw.

Cooper kicked him in the ribs—an equally playful gesture.

Tabby snarled at him.

"Show your teeth at me, will you!" said Cooper. "Raised you from a kitten and that's the gratitude you show. Do it just once more and I'll belt you in the chops."

Tabby lay down blissfully and began to wash his face.

"Some day," warned Hudson, "that cat will miss a meal and that's the day you'll be it."

"Gentle as a dove," Cooper assured him. "Wouldn't hurt a fly."

"Well, one thing about it, nothing dares to bother us with that monstrosity around."

"Best watchdog there ever was. Got to have something to guard all this stuff we've got. When Wes gets back, we'll be millionaires. All those furs and ginseng and the ivory."

"*If* he gets back."

"He'll be back. Quit your worrying."

"But it's been five years," Hudson protested.

"He'll be back. Something happened, that's all. He's probably working on it right now. Could be that he messed up the time setting when he repaired the unit or it might have been knocked out of kilter when Buster hit the helicopter. That would take a while to fix. I don't worry that he won't come back. What I can't figure out is why did he go and leave us?"

"I've told you," Hudson said. "He was afraid it wouldn't work."

"There wasn't any need to be scared of that. We never would have laughed at him."

"No. Of course we wouldn't."

"Then what was he scared of?" Cooper asked.

"If the unit failed and we knew it failed, Wes was afraid we'd try to make him see how hopeless and insane it was. And he knew we'd probably convince him and then all his hope would be gone. And he wanted to hang onto that, Johnny. He wanted to hang onto his hope even when there wasn't any left."

"That doesn't matter now," said Cooper. "What counts is that he'll come back. I can feel it in my bones."

And here's another case, thought Hudson, of hope begging to be allowed to go on living.

God, he thought, I wish I could be that blind!

"Wes is working on it right now," said Cooper confidently.

XIV

He was. Not he alone, but a thousand others, working desperately, knowing that the time was short, working not alone for two men trapped in time, but for the peace they all had dreamed about—that the whole world had yearned for through the ages.

For to be of any use, it was imperative that they could zero in the time machines they meant to build as an artilleryman would zero in a battery of guns, that each time machine would take its occupants to the same instant of the past, that their operation would extend over the same period of time, to the exact second.

It was a problem of control and calibration—starting with a prototype that was calibrated, as its finest adjustment, for jumps of 50,000 years.

Project Mastodon was finally under way.

CLIFFORD D. SIMAK, during his fifty-five-year career, produced some of the most iconic science fiction stories ever written. Born in 1904 on a farm in southwestern Wisconsin, Simak got a job at a small-town newspaper in 1929 and eventually became news editor of the Minneapolis Star-Tribune, writing fiction in his spare time.

Simak was best known for the book City, a reaction to the horrors of World War II, and for his novel Way Station. In 1953 City was awarded the International Fantasy Award, and in following years, Simak won three Hugo Awards and a Nebula Award. In 1977 he became the third Grand Master of the Science Fiction and Fantasy Writers of America, and before his death in 1988, he was named one of three inaugural winners of the Horror Writers Association's Bram Stoker Award for Lifetime Achievement.

DAVID W. WIXON was a close friend of Clifford D. Simak's. As Simak's health declined, Wixon, already familiar with science fiction publishing, began more and more to handle such things as his friend's business correspondence and contract matters. Named literary executor of the estate after Simak's death, Wixon began a long-term project to secure the rights to all of Simak's stories and find a way to make them available to readers who, given the fifty-five-year span of Simak's writing career, might never have gotten the chance to enjoy all of his short fiction. Along the way, Wixon also read the author's surviving journals and rejected manuscripts, which made him uniquely able to provide Simak's readers with interesting and thought-provoking commentary that sheds new light on the work and thought of a great writer.

THE COMPLETE SHORT FICTION OF CLIFFORD D. SIMAK

FROM OPEN ROAD MEDIA

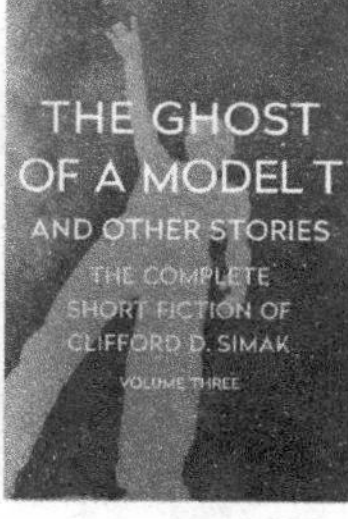

OPEN ROAD
INTEGRATED MEDIA

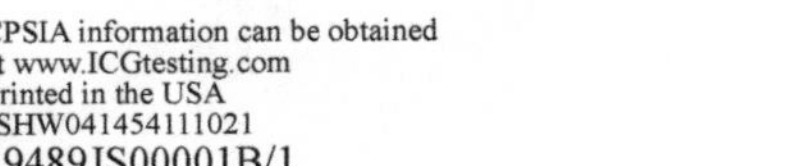

CPSIA information can be obtained
at www.ICGtesting.com
Printed in the USA
JSHW041454111021
19489JS00001B/1

9 781504 069052